PRAISE FOR THE AUTHOR

"Nichols gets our attention fast, and keeps it."
—*The Seattle Times*

"Jaw-droppingly good."
—*The Winnipeg Sun*

"Nothing short of dazzling."
—*The Georgia Straight*

"An uncommon skill for weaving a story."
—*The Austin Chronicle*

"A refreshingly original and utterly compelling writer."
—*The Adelaide 'Tizer*

"Tremendous imagination formed by edgy, poetic writing."
—*The StarPhoenix*, Saskatoon

"The language explodes with its own kind of scatological fury."
—*The Edmonton Journal*

"Deft storytelling."
—*The Westender*

"An amazing ride through another reality."
—*The State*, Columbia

"A mind game, full of clever twists and thoughtful, intelligent dialogue."
—*The Post and Courier*, Charleston

"Nichols...builds up such beautiful mythology. It's brilliantly done."
—*The Edmonton Sun*

"An uncommonly deft storyteller."
—*Winnipeg Free Press*

"He explores a bewildering array of social and psychological issues,
which orbit around his central question:
How is technology changing our humanity?"
—*The Seattle Weekly*

T0344642

TERMINAL DISPATCH

TERMINAL DISPATCH

DAWSON NICHOLS

PERMUTED
PRESS

A PERMUTED PRESS BOOK

Terminal Dispatch
© 2022 by Dawson Nichols
All Rights Reserved

ISBN: 978-1-63758-243-5
ISBN (eBook): 978-1-63758-244-2

Cover art by Cody Corcoran
Interior design and composition by Greg Johnson, Textbook Perfect

PERMUTED
PRESS

Permuted Press, LLC
New York • Nashville
permutedpress.com

Published in the United States of America
1 2 3 4 5 6 7 8 9 10

PROLOGUE

Dayr,

If you're reading this, I guess you decrypted it. Which means you know the static in the image buffer isn't static. Unspool it to read the rest, just like the messages hidden in the cloud algos over the charred battlefield at the end of EllGray^3.

I'm looking at that kind of chaos right now, only my apocalypse is real. And getting worse.

I did this so you'd know about Wil and Vie. I hope it works. I never intended to kill myself. I'm only doing this because I have to.

Gotta go.

—Tab

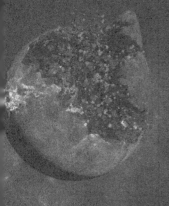

PART 1

CHAPTER 1

I<small>T ALL STARTED WHEN MY WRISTWATCH</small> shocked me. It was evening, and Vie and I were standing in a maze of cacti on a slope above a ravine. We'd gone down past the Breakfields to help Wil check on his eel trap.

The watch shouldn't have worked at all. My father and I were the only humans on the planet, and *he* didn't have one. And the satellites around Thalinraya wouldn't have protocols for it—it was ancient tech even when I had it installed. So I was surprised.

I peeled back the skin that covered the watch. The skin was stiff because I hadn't used my watch in the months since we arrived. The watch display was blank; no readings at all. I rubbed around it and brushed off the skin magners, but when I went to cover it up, it shocked me again, this time sending a burst of static up to my tragus speakers.

"You alright?" shouted Vie, already coming over, winding her way between squat barrel cacti.

"My watch shocked me," I explained, shaking my wrist.

Vie reached for my hand and took it. I looked into her eyes, and...

Okay, about Vie. She and Wil weren't like adult synthetics, with the mirrored glasses covering their eye sockets. My SC♀⁴ Richelle adopted them before they had the surgeries, so their eyes were more like ours. Vie's irises were purple and copper starbursts around her pupils, with silver threads branching out from them and holding the whites of her eyes in a delicate, gossamer net. Her eyes were amazing. Well, *all* of her was amazing. It was hard to stay focused when she was around.

I'd never done anything about my attraction to Vie because she was a synth and a friend. Also, I knew Wil had something going for her, and he was a synth too. But when we woke up sixty light years from home in bodies that had been maturing in bern for those many months of transit...

3

well, Vie was mesmerizing. She was quite a bit taller now, with sharper features, and she had cut her dark hair short for the first time since I'd known her. She was still her old self: smart, kind, earnest, patient. She still knew how to put Wil in his place with a glance. Or me, to be honest. But she had a confidence now which, combined with her new look, was kind of overwhelming. I was distracted whenever she was around. Her presence made me aware of my own matured body, which seemed to have grown a mind of its own. Which was awkward.

Since we'd arrived on Thalinraya, I often found myself justifying my feelings, reminding myself that some people had "companion" synths. Synths were used for all sorts of things, but some were definitely made for...companioning. But that wasn't why I was interested. Vie had been intended as a communications synth, so it's not like I was just attracted to how she'd been *designed*. Vie had been allowed to mature on her own—to become her own person. I was interested in *her*. It wasn't just lust.

"Does it hurt?" she asked, bringing me back to myself. She was holding my wrist with careful fingers, using her thumbs to massage the skin around the watch display. Her fingers still felt a little sticky. Earlier, she'd stopped to harvest some cactus pears, extending the nail on her forefinger and expertly denuding the pear of spines, then peeling and slicing it. Wil hadn't wanted any—he said they tasted like infection. Which was true, but I still ate some.

"No," I managed, despite the delicate feel of her touch.

The night was coming on and the light was failing, so Vie lit up the nail on her forefinger and aimed a narrow beam at my wrist. She always said she was embarrassed by her nail lights. Child synths had them to comfort themselves at night, but they were removed when they got older. Vie, however, had been raised differently, and hers had never been removed. But her embarrassment didn't stop her from using them, and they were sometimes useful.

She leaned closer to examine my wrist. Reflected light lit up her face and made her eyes flash. My lips suddenly felt dry.

"Down, beastie," snarled Wil from below, in the ravine.

I pulled my hand back, only then realizing he wasn't talking to me.

Thius, our dog, was with Wil, skittering enthusiastically along the side of the pond, shaking with excitement. Thius could be dangerous to himself. He'd get so excited, he'd go off like an untargeted firework—jumping sideways, dashing off, tearing in circles. Which direction he'd go was anyone's guess. He liked chasing things, but he was more likely to hurt himself than catch anything.

Wil was crouched down next to a dripping, broken trap he'd just pulled out of the water. It was empty. The snarl of mesh and rods and cords looked like an abused umbrella. It certainly wasn't going to catch any eels. It never could have, from the look of it.

Thius was circling in a crouch now, worried the contraption was a threat. His little ears stood up with excited alertness, ready to charge or retreat at a moment's notice.

Wil pulled at the thing and several pieces snapped apart, flinging bits of muck all over him. Thius yelped and retreated, then quickly sprang back and started growling again.

"Quiet, beastie," snarled Wil.

Wil hadn't grown as much during our months in bern, during the transit to Thalinraya. Vie and I were both quite a bit taller than him now, which he found frustrating. He wasn't short, but I could tell he would've traded his muscular arms and legs or his barrel chest for a little more height. Mostly to impress Vie. With my lanky frame, I'd often been jealous of his powerfully built body. Now the tables felt turned. With his spikey auburn hair, freckles, and wild violet eyes, he could have looked like some kind of Viking warrior god if only he had another ten centimeters. If synths were allowed enhancements, I'm sure Wil would have bought some height.

Without meaning to, I imagined him trying to kiss Vie. He would stand tiptoe and she'd still have to bend down. Only she wouldn't, she'd turn away. I smiled just thinking about it. She'd definitely turn away.

"The spring is stuck," Wil complained, holding up part of the trap for us to see.

The spring? The whole thing was a tangled, broken mess.

"You just need new bait," I called down.

"What I need," he said, ignoring my sarcasm, "is some help." One of the cords still angled sharply down into the water where it was stuck fast. Wil pulled at it, but it didn't budge.

Vie moved along the slope. "Want another pear?" she asked. "There's an *Opuntia gralcialia*."

Like Wil, Vie had augments that allowed her to onboard pedias with scientific names and other data. It could be irritating. They didn't mean to be—it was just how their brains worked: when they needed a word to attach to a concept, their augments offered up the best match. Mostly, I was just jealous. My parents were Feremites, and they had never allowed me to get augments.

Back on Telesis it had always made me feel left out. I was the only kid in my class who was confined to the visible spectrum; everyone else had night vision and broad-spectrum lenses, filters, and processors... things I didn't even understand. A lot of them had augments that were visible, too—gecko grips on their finger pads, added sensory inputs, holo tattoos. Most had undergone bucky skeletal scaffolding, so they were able to play Tienshan Ball and other high-impact and high-strain games that I couldn't. Being a Feremite child made me...not exactly an outcast, but almost.

Of course, it was also why my parents let me go live with Richelle and Wil and Vie. So it wasn't all bad.

Thius barked. Wil was still looking up at me. "Can I get some help?" he asked.

"Uh, let me think a minute. No," I said.

"Chuzz!" said Wil, but he knew I didn't give in to insults, so he stepped down into the water and began reaching around in the muck. Thius growled and whined, dodging sideways along the bank, wanting and not wanting to get into the water. I heard Wil say in his announcer voice, under his breath, "Ladies and gentlemen, this is the story of death by mud and eel."

Wil talked to himself in an announcer voice. That was Wil.

"Someone help me move this," Vie called from further along the slope. "I think there's a thumper den here."

I could just see her behind the muscular arms of a spiny blue-green cactus that twisted around itself. Wil, who had heard Vie but was already thigh deep in water, grunted frustration and shot me a jealous look. He had thermal imaging and could have told her if there was a warm-blooded body in the den, but he wasn't available.

6

Luck was on my side.

The population of thumpers around the homestead was pretty strong. Keeping one as a pet had been Vie's dream ever since she first spotted one hopping away from Thius. "Oh, look!" she had shouted. "Look at that cute *Lepus tibenarex!*"

"You mean the thumper?" I had asked. The name stuck.

And they *were* kind of cute: like rabbits but spotted, with longer ears and asymmetrical front paws. One paw, usually the right one, had a calloused club they used to pound ground-hugging cacti until all the fine spines were gone and they could eat the low, flat leaves. They were nocturnal, and when twilight swept across the desert there was a wave of sound that followed as the thumpers came out and started feeding on the cacti. I loved that sound. I usually migrated my habitation cel to the homestead's perimeter and opened an iris to the outside so I could hear it while I drifted off to sleep.

I could see why Vie wanted one.

I started making my way toward her to help.

"Whoa. Whoa!" Wil shouted. We looked down toward the pool, awash with reflected sky and winking stars. Wil's silhouette was pointing skyward. "What's that?"

I thought at first he meant for us to see the braided ring of the second moon. The silver-gray coils surrounding that yellow moon were lovely in the rusting sky. But then something like a dark meteor shot down from the east, like a bit of night falling through the dusk. It became outlined in glowing white for a moment as it burned its way through the atmosphere, looking almost like a ship, but it quickly folded in on itself and was gone before we could see its shape.

"What is that?" Wil shouted. Thius looked up, growling.

"I have no idea," I called back.

Vie, looking skyward, just shook her head.

Everything was still and waiting. The stars looked icy.

"Just a meteor?" Wil called, splashing out of the water and starting up the slope to where Vie and I stood on the ridge.

A second something entered the atmosphere, this one higher overhead, closer to us, moving east to west. As it began to glow it also slowed, and we could see the shape of it more clearly: oval, but tapered at the ends like an eye. Its glowing faded, it rotated, and we could see that one end was a scaled cone—faceted and shimmering oddly. It began changing course, angling north, then folded into itself and disappeared as it sped away.

"That's not a meteor," I said as Wil came up to us, soaked to the waist, mud-spattered and out of breath.

Vie turned immediately to Wil. "I'm fine," she said, annoyed.

Wil must have said something to her subvocally. They had agreed not to do this around me, since I had no subvocals. I felt a flash of annoyance—but also gratitude toward Vie. She could have responded subvocally, too; I would have never known.

Wil turned to me. "I thought your dad said the next homesteaders weren't coming for years," he said.

"They're not," I replied.

"Those looked like ships to me," he said, almost accusingly.

Beams of icy light suddenly shot down from the north, startling us. But it was only the pole reflector. It'd been decommissioned a couple hundred years ago, but it was still in orbit. At sundown, the light kaleidoscoped off it for a few seconds; the crimson sky got shot through with rays of brilliant blue-white that spoked down from beyond the northern mountains.

"We should tell your father," Vie said, looking skyward again. She was about to say more, but a sickening thwack came from down by the pond. A pathetic yelp was followed by a piercing whine.

"Thius!" shouted Vie.

Wil was faster. He leapt one cactus and was down the slope in a flash. "Shunt, shunt, shunt!" he spat as he ran.

Vie and I were heading down the slope when the sky seemed to be split apart by a series of explosions. We threw ourselves down. They were distant, but shrill and menacing.

"What is that?"

"I don't know!" I shouted.

After six or eight more explosions—they seemed to be happening up in the atmosphere somewhere—the series stopped. Wil struggled back up the slope toward us, cradling Thius in his arms. A curving metal rod pierced his torso. Blood poured out, matting the dog's hair and covering Wil's hands. Thius was unconscious, maybe dead.

"What happened?" cried Vie.

"The spring on the trap was—just, let's get him to the medic cel," Wil said, rushing past us.

A high-pitched whine rose suddenly in the far distance, followed by a deep, concussive impact that shook us to the ground.

We scrambled up. Something huge had come down north of the homestead.

We looked at each other for a breathless moment, then Wil lifted Thius and bolted back across the Breakfields. Vie and I followed.

CHAPTER 2

"Got him yet?" Vie asked, coming into the Control cel.

"No," I said, unable to keep the annoyance out of my voice. "He forgot to put out his relay."

My father had gone to the far side of the third moon; we couldn't contact him without a relay beacon. It was just like my father to be out of touch right when he was needed. Since my mother's death, stress had made him forgetful. But we had no idea what the explosions in the sky had been, what had crashed, or how dangerous it might be. We needed him.

"Thius?" asked Wil, looking back from an information panel.

We'd run all the way back to the homestead from the Breakfields, slipping on rocks and stumbling over cacti in the failing light. Despite his thermal imaging, Wil had tripped over a boulder as we passed the tortoise corral, dropping Thius and grabbing onto a cactus as he fell. Thankfully, he'd been able to recover the dog and carry him the rest of the way to the homestead. We'd taken Thius directly to the medic cel, where Vie set him up with an autosurgeon while Wil and I went to the Control cel to try to hail my father.

"According to the medic cel, he'll be fine," said Vie, joining us. "He'll be in a surgical bath for twenty hours, but he'll be fine."

Wil looked relief her way, then their expressions changed. They were subvocalizing again. I turned away.

The Control cel's main panel was alive with all sorts of graphs and visual displays. Several side panels were tracking things as well. With Wil's help I had called up all sorts of information, but I didn't know what any of it meant.

Vie came forward, lifted Wil's arm and examined his hand. There were several large cactus spines lodged in his left palm. "You should go to the medic cel," she said.

"When we know what's going on here," Wil replied bravely. He winced a little as he drew his hand back.

I stepped around one of the chairs and slumped down into it, just to get away from his smarm. The cactus spines weren't *that* big.

Looking up at the main panel, I asked, "Homestead, can you...wrap a signal around to the far side somehow?"

"Negative," the homestead informed me. There was something condescending about that disembodied voice, and I glanced at Vie and Wil to see if they'd sensed it too. They were both concentrating on Wil's hand though, probably engaged in some subvocal conversation. My embarrassment was my own.

I looked again at the confusion of information being displayed, wishing I could let Vie or even Wil take over. But synths weren't allowed to take charge of the systems in a homestead; only humans could do that. So here we were: something had crashed, possibly invaded, and the only one of us who could do something about it—me—was the one least capable of doing it. I had no augments, no training, no knowledge.

I couldn't wait to come of age. I'd leave my father and his stupid Feremite faith. I'd go back to Telesis and get all the augments he never let me have.

"How long is he supposed to be up there?" Wil was gazing vacantly at a panel. He could process information thousands of times faster than me, but he couldn't access it without me.

"Homestead, when is my father scheduled to return?" I asked.

"Six days," came the indifferent reply. But that didn't tell us when my father might remember to send up the relay beacon—or even if he could, at this point. The third moon's mass had become unbalanced and it was messing up the tides on Thalinraya, so my father had taken the jump ship there. He'd gone to set up a mass accumulator on the far side. But if he'd already gone underground, it would take a few days to build the thing, and he couldn't interrupt that process. By the time he came up and put out a relay beacon we might all be dead.

Thanks, Dad.

I stared at the various readouts on the panels trying to think of what I should do. There was no "crashed spaceship" procedure. *Real emergencies,* I thought ruefully, *don't have alerts or readouts or manuals with directions about what to do.* In my mind I could see a panel with an emergency menu of options:

Alien invaders, live
Alien invaders, mechanical
Human invaders from one of Telesis Corporation's competitors
Chemicals
Explosives
Pandemic
Radiation
Gobbi-Tittles

"Tab?" Vie said, touching my arm lightly.

"What?" I reached forward and scrolled through some numbers on the desk display, pretending to look at them.

"I could help you look for other satellites in the system," she said, "not just around that moon. They might be able to make direct contact from farther out. And even if we can't raise your father, we could see if there's any activity around whatever it is that crashed here. That'd be good to know."

It was a good idea. Vie had been intended as a communications synthetic. She left that life when she was ten, but she'd already had augments galore. She probably had routines for all sorts of satellite tracking and searching. She had terabytes of information stuffed into her head. I had nothing.

Except access. Being human, I had access.

I took a deep breath. "Okay," I said, "what do I do?"

"Couldn't you just tell the homestead to take orders from Vie temporarily?" Wil suggested. "Would that override the no-synth restriction?"

Having been designed as a mining synth, Wil was usually a rule follower, so this was an odd suggestion coming from him. Synth restrictions didn't allow direct interaction with homesteads. Using my authority to bypass the restrictions was a creative idea.

"What?" he asked defensively when we both turned to look at him. His violet eyes narrowed.

"Will that work?" I asked Vie.

"It's worth a try," she said, sitting in the seat next to me.

"Your mom's dead and your father's out of contact," said Wil. "You're listed as next in command. It should take orders from you."

His insensitivity was monumental, but his logic was sound.

"Right," I said.

"Only if you think it's okay," Wil quickly added.

Vie had probably said something subvocally.

"I think we should try," Vie encouraged. "Go ahead."

"Homestead," I said, "I want you to allow Vie to use the equipment until I tell you otherwise. Understood?"

"Constraints?"

"None. Give her full access. And Wil too," I added as an afterthought. We were in this together, and though he could be annoying, I trusted him. Wil leaned back, his eyes wide so that I could see the silvery spider web that shot through the whites. He almost looked afraid.

"Principal One is not currently active. You are Principal Two, with All Level Access. You want to designate Vie and Wil as Principals Three and Four, also with All Level Access?"

"Yes," I said.

"Implemented," the homestead responded.

And it was done. It shouldn't have been that easy, but we didn't know that at the time.

The three of us smiled awkwardly at one another, then Vie leaned forward, focused on the panel and began speaking in a rapid, mechanical way. The homestead was the computational hub for all Thalinraya's systems. Vie had never had access to anything like it before, but she looked expert at once.

She ordered three simultaneous processes, and immediately smaller panels on either side of the main one sprang to life. A solar census scrolled down one, a systems diagnostic on another, and on the main panel was a mesmerizing three-dimensional display of the orbits of all satellites, natural and artificial, of more than one hundred grams. The color-coded images wheeled and turned around the panel gracefully; their ghosting images danced in her dilated pupils.

Vie parted two fingers and scissored her hair behind an ear to clear her view. She scanned back and forth between the panels, intoning new instructions every so often, her thin fingers flashing across the desk display with inhuman rapidity. The idea that she understood it all—was in *control* of it all—was unnerving. I'd seen her access onboard pedias and simple calculating functions, but this was different. She was calling up and reading information with abilities I couldn't begin to understand. She probably didn't understand it either—this was new to her too. Whatever skills she had been designed with in her former life had gone largely unused. They'd all been installed, but Richelle adopted her and Wil before their glasses surgeries—before the majority of their training. Now those early augments were being fully engaged for the first time.

Seeing her like this reminded me just how different from me she really was. No wonder my feelings for her were complicated. Since we were eleven, she and Wil and I had lived together almost as siblings. But we weren't. They were synths, with augments I didn't have.

"How is it feeling?" Wil asked. He'd come over closer, his auburn eyebrows knit together.

"It's okay," she replied. "It feels weird. Automatic."

"You sound different, too," said Will with obvious concern. "Like you like it."

Vie didn't respond immediately. She looked at the left display as a rotating overlay began to fill with figures and numbers. I couldn't tell if she was thinking about the question or looking at the new information.

"It does feel…right, somehow. Satisfying."

Wil glanced at me, then back to Vie. His spikey red hair gave him a startled look. "Richelle warned us that might happen," he said uneasily. "That's why she said not to do this."

"What do you mean, Richelle warned you?" I asked. This was news to me. Why shouldn't they use their augments? That's what synths were for.

They had clearly begun a subvocal conversation, but Vie broke away to answer me.

"Synth augments are different from the augments humans get," she explained. "When they implant functions or upload databases in synths, they leash them to our pleasure centers so we'll enjoy using them."

"So we get addicted to them, you mean," Wil interjected bitterly. "It's one of the ways they make sure *syns* do what they want without complaining." People who thought synthetics were just tools referred to them as "syns." Wil was using that ugly word intentionally. He was worked up.

Vie turned away from the panel and addressed Wil. "It's only like addiction if you *overuse* the augments. I don't think using them for the very first time qualifies."

Wil appealed to me with a look, but a sensor went off and three colored graphs appeared on the panel. They meant nothing to me, but Vie squinted at them for a moment before speaking.

"There's a lot of electromagnetic activity at the impact site north of here. I can't make out what it is, but it seems to be staying there."

"Does that mean it's something alive?" asked Wil.

"I...can't say," said Vie, referring to a rotating helix in a side panel. "It seems to be organized, but...I've never seen anything like this. I'm not sure."

A series of feathery spirals appeared on the main panel now. Vie suddenly became unnaturally concentrated, almost absent from herself, eyes darting around, fingers moving across the desk display with surgical assurance. "String a Fibonacci display for each of the orbits and graph them onto a pantonic." Her voice didn't sound like it normally did, which was low for a girl, gentle and soothing. Now it was higher pitched and mechanical, with a flat quality that reminded me of the homestead. I didn't understand a word of it, and a glance told me Wil didn't either. I wondered if Vie herself knew what she was saying.

She turned her now depthless eyes to me. The silvery nets around the violet irises seemed to be glowing. Her hand came up and I thought she was going to touch my arm again, but she returned it to her side.

"There are no satellites positioned to see the far side of the third moon." She shot a look at Wil and added, "That's not our decision."

"Stop subvocalizing," I said. "I'm right here. And I can guess what you're saying. You think we should contact Telesis and tell them what's happened."

It was really the only sensible thing to do. Something had crashed, and there was EM activity at the impact site. My stupid father had forgotten to put out his relay beacon, so we were alone. One kid and two synths, alone on a planet.

We needed help.

Vie scissored some hair behind an ear and said, "I think that's right. Whatever those things were, they weren't comets or meteors or…well, we just don't know."

I looked at Wil.

"It's going to be expensive," he said. "And it's going to take a *lot* of energy, but yeah, I think we have to. And when I say we, I mean you. You're the only one who can do it."

It was true. Synths wouldn't be allowed to open an interstellar com. Only I could do that.

CHAPTER 3

"CAN YOU SEE ME?" I ASKED.

The guy wasn't even looking at me. He glanced up at us, annoyed, then started calling up information in his desk. To his sides were panels and holo tables that separated him from other workers in a crowded control room.

"Is this 0611-14?" he asked officiously. Our perspective on him was looking down. It wasn't a flattering view of the guy: his head looked too big and I could see his stomach sagging over his belt.

"I don't know what that means," I said. "My name is Tab and I'm on Thalinraya."

"That's the DIT number for Thalinraya," Vie whispered to me. We were both standing behind the chairs in the FaRcom cel, too nervous to sit down. Wil was standing behind us. The cel was too narrow for all three of us to stand together.

Seeing Vie, the man looked annoyed.

"I need your full name, Tab, unless you're a syn." My informal name, Tab, was like the single-syllable names used for synths. I was only ever around Vie and Wil, so I'd gotten used to using just Tab.

"TabiTal Yrl," I said. "I'm on Thal—"

"Hold on a minute." He manipulated something off to his side and then reached up and dragged his view of us down in front. All three of us nearly lost our balance as the room around us seemed to reel. Wil actually grabbed my shoulders from behind to steady himself.

Contacting Telesis had proved more difficult than I expected. The energy necessary for light-distance communications was huge, so the permissions were restrictive. Even opening the FaRcom cel was difficult. It was a dedicated cel at the far end of the hotplate hall, sitting directly atop the computational engines. My father had only used it once, to let Telesis know about my mother's death. He wouldn't even let me use it to contact Richelle. I'd never seen the inside of it.

It was smaller than the Control cel or any of the functional cels and could barely accommodate all three of us. It had two small panels built into opposite sides, which was strange because the two chairs faced forward, not toward the panels.

But when Vie had helped me through the protocols and the FaRcom connection finally went through, we were startled into understanding. The entire interior of the cel—even the closed iris behind us—became an active, three-dimensional panel. It was like being in an immersive game: we were suddenly a virtual presence in the communications center on Telesis. What made it even more disorienting was that we were floating in the air above and in front of our contact.

But now we could see him head on. From above he had looked imperfect enough to be a Feremite, but now I could see he was normal. His features had the smooth, intentional look of someone who had had regular reju therapy.

Several people in the large room behind him were looking our way now; one woman was coming over. The man adjusted something in his desk, then brought his eyebrows together in confused concentration.

"Where is Tal…TaleXal Yrl?"

"That's my father," I said, leaning forward over the chair. "He went to do some work on the third moon and forgot to put out his com relay. But something just came through the atmosphere here. Several things, but at least one came to the surface. There's electromagnetic activity at the crash site."

The man exhaled elaborately, clearly believing this was a panicked-kid situation, not something serious.

"Okay." He inhaled, adopting the tone of a teacher dealing with a slow student. "We have protocols for using FaRcom equipment."

"I know that, but there were—"

"And I'm sure you're scared, but I'm also sure it's just a meteor." He gave the most insincere smile I'd ever seen and went back to his data. "Now, let's have a look."

Wil suddenly squeezed between Vie and me. "We need to talk to your superior," he said, restrained anger in his voice. Wil had registered the man's condescension as well.

The man looked up from his displays. "*Syn*, you need to settle down—that's what you need to do."

"Negative." Vie touched Wil on the arm, but he shrugged her off and squared himself to the display. "We are in an emergency situation here. That's verified by the homestead already, or Tab wouldn't have been able to use the FaRcom to contact you. You need to—"

"No," the man cut Wil off, "*you* need to shut your mouth, syn." Several other people had gathered around him by this point; his bluster was partly a result of their presence. "I am addressing TabiTal Yrl."

Wil turned to me. "Ask for his URID. Let's report this pog."

Several people in the Telesis communications center snickered.

"Get those two syns out of your F-A-R com cel or I will terminate this connect," the man fumed. But then he frowned down at his desk. "Wait a..." He manipulated some controls we couldn't see. Another man reached over his shoulder and pointed at something; a woman off to his left said something under her breath.

"What's wrong with your homestead?" he asked, not looking up.

"Nothing," I replied.

"It's..." He manipulated more controls and scanned through more data while we waited.

"What's wrong?" I asked.

"Your homestead doesn't recognize your syns. Something's..." He trailed off again while squinting confusion at some information we couldn't see.

I had told the homestead to grant Vie and Wil full access. He must be reading that.

"I can see your URID and theirs are definitely MPIDs, but..." He finally looked at me again. "Tell them to get out of your F-A-R cel. We need to go through some diagnostics and they're not authorized."

"They'll understand it better than me. I don't have any onboard pedias or technical—"

"Look, *kid*, I can't do it with them in the cel, and this connect is costing too much for me to justify more hand-holding. Get them out or I'll sever it."

Vie turned to me. "He's right, Tab. Tell us to leave."

"What?" Wil objected, but Vie stopped him before he could ramp up.

"Wil, back off," Vie said, her voice tense and urgent. "Tab, go ahead and order us to leave." She had a shrewd look; she must be planning to do something with Wil outside the cel once they were gone. I couldn't imagine what it was, but I did as she said.

"Okay," I said, "will you two please leave me alone in here?"

"No, order us," Vie urged.

What was she getting at?

"Okay," I said, "I order you two to get out of here."

"Great!" Wil threw up his arms disgustedly and lurched toward the iris. But before he had taken two steps, Vie stopped him.

"Wait. Don't go," she said. Wil turned back toward her, as confused as I was.

Vie looked back to the man in the display.

"Don't go?" Wil said, exasperatedly. "You just said—"

"Syn," the man broke in furiously, "violating a direct order is grounds for termination."

Vie was tense but confident as she responded. "Protocol for synthetics on terraforming planets is to remove their agency, isn't that correct? TCA Rule 202.A. If we were terraforming synthetics, we wouldn't be able to defy a direct order, correct?"

When there was no immediate response, Vie simply raised her eyebrows and waited.

I had forgotten these rules, but Vie must have had them onboard and accessed them during our discussion. You wouldn't know, Dayr, but because terraforming is so isolated, terraforming synths have all their agency arbors overridden. It's so they'll blindly follow any order from a human, even if it would surely lead to their death. By defying my order, Vie had just shown this man that she and Wil weren't the kind of synths that should be with me on Thalinraya.

The man became tight-lipped and manipulated some displays. After another tense moment he said curtly, "I need to suspend for a minute. I'll be right back."

The panel went blank.

In his immersion announcer voice, Wil said, "Ladies and gentlemen, this is the story of the most brilliant synth ever!" Vie smirked self-consciously and was about to respond when Wil dropped the announcer voice and corrected himself. "Only *not* a synth. We're not synths!"

Vie let out a little laugh. "Wil, that's ridiculous."

Wil's enthusiasm was unabated. "No, it explains a lot," he said, wide-eyed. He was serious.

"We're synths, Wil. You know we are."

"But listen: why did the homestead give us full access?"

"It didn't," said Vie.

Wil spoke out to the room: "Homestead, Vie and I have full access, right?"

"That's correct," responded the directionless voice.

"It's responding to…" Vie sighed. "You're a synth. It's saying you have full access to the *limited* capabilities available to synths."

"Tab, you ask it," said Wil, appealing to me.

Vie heaved a sigh, but she looked at me with resignation and nodded.

"Homestead," I said, "do these two synths have full access to all your functions?"

"Which two?"

"These two!" I gestured at Wil and Vie. "These two right here. Vie and Wil."

"Wil and Vie have access to all systems."

Wil was in a wide-eyed state of heightened awareness; Vie's forehead was all scrunched up in confusion. It made no sense. They had been raised as synths. My SC♀[4] Richelle had adopted them from synth orphanates. My father had objected to my friendship with them *because they were synths.* How could they not be? They had always thought they were synths themselves!

Vie said, "Homestead, humans have URIDs and synthetic people have MPIDs, correct?"

"Correct."

"Then…why do Wil and I have MPIDs?"

There was a brief pause before: "All persons must be registered."

Vie looked disbelief my way. Wil was practically dancing.

I decided to ask directly. "Homestead, are Wil and Vie synths?"

The question hung in the air a moment. Had we been wrong about this fundamental thing all along? Was it possible these two didn't know who they were—didn't even know *what* they were? Had Richelle lied? If so, why? Could she have implanted false memories? For what possible purpose?

Who were they really?

"Homestead, are Wil and Vie synths?" I repeated.

"My records are inconclusive," came the directionless reply.

Wil was fierce with triumph. "I knew it. I *knew* it!" He slapped the back of the chair for emphasis. In his excited announcer's voice he began, "Ladies and gentlemen, this is the story of two—"

"Don't start," warned Vie, trying to maintain her composure. She shifted in her seat. "It's a mistake."

"What if it's *not* though?" Wil speculated urgently. "What if you and I were somehow important? Royalty or spies or something?"

"Wil," Vie said simply, her tone asking him to stop being ridiculous.

He *was* being ridiculous, of course. But part of me hoped his enthusiasm wasn't misplaced. If they weren't synths…my attraction to Vie wasn't perverse, it was natural. And her attraction to me would be natural too. I thought I had sensed it a few times, but I'd sensed her resistance to it as well. Which I could understand if she thought she was a synth. But if she wasn't…

"What if we had our memories wiped and they put us in synth orphanates? Maybe even to protect us!"

"You've been in too many adventure interacts," Vie said.

"Or what if Richelle was hiding us! Isn't this the Panticaya sector? What if Dayr—"

The FaRcom abruptly blinked back to life. This time we were in a private office, positioned opposite the desk of a woman who exuded confident authority. She had her blonde hair pulled back in a tight ponytail, which made her appear younger than she certainly was. She smiled warmly at us.

"Hello," she said in an oddly accented voice. She focused on me. "TabiTal, is that right?"

"Yes," I replied.

"But you like Tab."

"Well…"

"My name is KikuYa," the woman said, leaning forward confidingly, "but recently some people have been calling me Kiku. Shortening names is kind of a new thing here on Telesis, too. And you two," she said, turning to the others, "are Wil and Vie, right?"

"That's right," Wil said, suspicion in his voice. "Where's the other guy?"

"GeraLid is in communications; I'm in operations. I'll be able to help a little more directly. Nice to meet you. Okay. You contacted us because something crashed down there." Her desk lit up and she began manipulating a surface display. "The first thing I need is for you, Tab, to give us access to your homestead."

"How do I do that?" I asked.

"Instruct it to open an A-6 override on the current F-A-R com channel."

"Hang on," interrupted Wil. "What's this for?"

Kiku's voice was a little harder when she addressed Wil. "We can't reorg your homestead without remote permissions. We need to repurpose your systems so we can help you figure out what came down."

"That makes sense," I said. I didn't know what to do at this point; I was happy to have someone else take over.

"Instruct your homestead to open an A-6 override using the current F-A-R com channel," Kiku repeated.'

"Homestead, open an A-6 override on the current FaRcom channel," I said.

"As Principal Two with All Level Access, you want to transfer control of 0611-14 to the current F-A-R connection with an A-6 override, is that correct?"

"Yes, correct," I said.

"Complete," was the homestead's simple reply. There was an immediate shift in the air around us. It was as though the sudden redirection of information actually changed the cel walls. I was reminded that the computation for all of the planet's processes was happening just below our feet, in the hotplate.

Kiku looked down at someone or something in her desk display and nodded. To us she said, "Let me call up some information here. Bear with me."

She pushed some displays around in her desk. She was efficient and relaxed, nothing like the earlier guy, GeraLid. While she concentrated, I looked around her office, which was large but cluttered with little knick-knacks. To one side was a looped holo of a girl on a swing. Behind her was an old-school wooden desk with some moving sculptures, and what appeared to be a rock collection. Little labeled boxes were filled with jagged stones. It was the kind of elaborately large office that showed the importance of the occupant.

She finished manipulating something on her display, then looked up at us. "The satellite array there isn't immediately responding. I'm going to suspend for a minute. I'll be right back."

Kiku's office disappeared again before we could tell her that Vie had already done a satellite survey. We were once again surrounded by smooth, plain walls.

"Why wouldn't the satellite array be responding?" I asked.

"I don't know," Vie said, concerned. "It was working earlier. Homestead," she continued, speaking out to the room, "when did the satellite array go down?"

"That information is not available."

That was an unexpected response. Vie and I looked at one another.

"Is the array getting power?" asked Vie.

"That information is not available."

Vie's face scrunched even more.

"Show me the satellite census I did earlier," Vie said.

"That information is not available."

What?

"Why not?" I asked.

"Permissions have not been acquired from the A-6 master channel. Would you like me to make a request?"

I looked a question at Vie.

"Telesis," she said simply. "The override you gave them. They control the homestead now. There must be restrictions on what information we can access locally."

"Why would they do that?" asked Wil.

Vie fixed him with a scolding look, but a moment later her face shifted. "What's wrong with you?"

"What?" he said, defensively. Vie continued to stare intently. "What?" Wil repeated.

"Our subvocals are being blocked," Vie said.

Both of them turned inward and couldn't find the connection that was usually there.

Kiku's office suddenly wrapped around us again.

"Tab, we have a problem," said Kiku. "There's no need to panic, but we do need to move fast."

"Why? What happened?"

"It looks like Thalinraya's had some recent meteor impacts," she said.

"Those were *meteors*?" Wil voiced the doubt we all felt.

"Yes, and one of them has taken out a QR node."

"What's that?" I asked.

Kiku cocked her head at me, reminding me of Thius.

"Are you...not familiar with Thalinraya's power net?" she asked.

"He's a Feremite," Vie explained. "He doesn't have augmentations."

"Oh, that's right. I'm sorry. Well, I don't have time to explain." Kiku spoke while referring to some information in her desk. "One of the meteors took out a QR node and that seems to have caused the whole QR net to shut down. It's no longer powering the satellite array or anything on the surface, including your homestead."

"The homestead's not getting power?" I asked.

"That's correct. It will continue to function for another forty-two hours on backup batteries, and we can grow a solar farm to keep it functioning for another ten or so hours after that. But we'll lose communication with you."

"We're going to lose communications?" Vie, being a communications synth, did *not* like the sound of that.

"This F-A-R com uses .26 yotta watts, which we can't sustain without bringing the QR net back online."

"How do we do that?"

"I need to send you to restart the CA station." She focused on me. "Now, Tab, I forgot that you have no augmentation. Is that true? None?"

"None," I admitted. "I have an old com watch, but it's...it was ancient when I got it."

"Okay, two things then." She turned to Wil. "Wil, you have an unusual status there. Were you aware of that?"

Wil glanced at Vie before responding, "Yeah."

"Okay. Without satellite navigation we need to get you to the CA station in a surface vehicle. But it's going to need some reengineering. Normally I'd ask Tab to do it, but he doesn't have the requisite onboards. A synth under 202A wouldn't normally have authorization, but it looks like your MPID registration *will* allow it. So…do you think you can reconfigure an opilion for us?"

Wil's eyes went wide. With his red hair and metallic irises, he looked half insane. "Yeah. Yeah, sure."

Kiku looked at some data in her desk. "I see that you've got mining augments. I'll send some translation algorithms you can use to program the—"

"I know how to do it. Not a problem…I got it." Wil had forgotten everything else. Just the thought of working on an opilion was already firing pleasure centers deep within him.

"Great," said Kiku. She turned to Vie. "You have communication augments, correct?"

"That's right," said Vie noncommittally.

"Someone is going to need to give our new instructions to the CA station. I think you're best positioned to manage that code. Can you do that?"

"Of course. But what are we doing?"

"The loss of that node caused a failure cascade, so we need to restart the whole QR net. We can reconfigure the net without that node, but we'll need an initial burst of power to bring it back online. If we don't, we'll lose touch. Permanently."

"I can drive!" Wil's voice was so loud, Vie and I spun to our left in surprise. Wil had activated a side panel again; it seemed to float in midair in Kiku's office. Wil was already researching the changes he'd need to make to the opilion. Now he'd realized something that gave him pure, childlike joy.

"My registration!" he exclaimed. When he didn't get the response he clearly expected, he added, in his announcer voice, "Ladies and gentlemen, this is the story of the fastest trip to the CA station ever recorded! Ha! I can *drive!*"

CHAPTER 4

"Slow down!"

Vie was more angry than afraid, but Wil was having the time of his life as we hurtled down a dune, sand fanning up behind intermittently as wheels dug in and then lifted over rock outcroppings or larger cacti. The smaller cacti were simply smashed by the waist-high wheels.

We were in an opilion pod about three meters above the ground, the wind whistling past the open irises on either side. Opilions are the most versatile of multi-use vehicles, able to be engineered for many different situations. In its current configuration, eight cantilevered legs extended down from the pod to eight tiny trusses that supported elaborately geared wheels. The wheels jolted and jumped over the terrain, but the legs absorbed most of the shocks, so the pod essentially floated over the landscape. Inside the pod were three hammock-like seats on retractable tethers which hung from above. Wil was in the forward seat, managing the controls. Vie and I were behind him, sitting next to one another.

"Slow down!" Vie was swinging in her harness, the signs of motion sickness beginning to show on her face.

"Kiku said we only have a few hours left!" Wil shouted over the whistling of the wind.

This was true, but disingenuous. The real reason Wil was driving like a sun-drunk herriot was because he enjoyed it. He was at the controls of an opilion, racing over difficult terrain. This was a once-in-a-lifetime opportunity.

Opilion protocols didn't allow synths to work the controls. This was a safety regulation from way back during the synth revolts. But for the moment, we were out of regulatory reach, and letting Wil drive made the most sense. He could download the driving instructions, maps of Thalinraya, repair procedures—everything we might need.

Vie's reaction to Wil's driving was oddly satisfying. His recklessness was making her angry. And it wasn't that I wanted their relationship to turn sour, but...well, things between Vie and me were looking better by comparison. And she might actually be human. Wil let his imagination run away with him sometimes, but he might have stumbled onto something with this. They both had a lot of human traits.

The wind whipped through the opilion and moved Vie's hair around. She chewed her lip as she went back and forth between two displays, her eyes bright with concentration. She'd onboarded all sorts of procedures. If we got the QR net up and the satellites working again, it'd mostly be Vie's doing. Wil was just the driver.

Of course, I was doing even less.

I couldn't stop replaying Kiku's look of shock when I'd told her I had no augments beyond my wristwatch. And then her look of sympathy when she learned I was a Feremite. "Oh," her expression had said, "you're one of *those*."

Was I? In name and in my augment-free body I was, but I'm not sure I ever believed. Not really. I'd been resentful about being a Freakemite since I was little. Not about the whole religion—I didn't care about most of it. But the prohibitions around technology made us freaks. No augments of any kind? It was perverse. Richelle had known it. Kiku knew it. I knew it.

It was my father's fault, really; he was the zealot. Mom would have bent the rules. She was as devout as he was, but she also recognized how hard it was to be a Feremite kid, outcast and cut off from everything—technology, other kids, immersions. Everything that was considered normal. She was the one who convinced my father to let Richelle give me the wristwatch.

I pulled back the skin and looked at it again. It was inert. It had clicked again as we'd started out in the opilion. Vie thought it was just a short circuit. She was probably right; she was right about most things.

We came to the bottom of the sand dune and flashed across a narrow strip of red bedrock before coming to yet another slot canyon, six meters across. Wil looked happier than I had seen him since our arrival. He had never expected to drive an opilion, much less one of his own design.

Vie and I couldn't see forward very well, but as we approached the canyon the grapple cannons at the front of the opilion fired. This caught Vie's attention.

"Wil!" Vie warned, though we had already done this maneuver several times. Wil didn't reply, but I saw him grin, probably enjoying the fact that she could no longer pester him subvocally. They hadn't figured out why that function was no longer working, but it surely had to do with Telesis's control of Thalinraya's systems.

"This one's only seventy-two percent of maximum span," Wil said.

I pulled my hammock chair to the middle so I could see forward. The timing and coordination of these maneuvers were amazing.

The two anchoring slugs had already hit solid rock ahead of us, on the far side of the canyon.

Boom. The cannons sent two more anchors to the near side of the canyon, where they landed parallel to one another, leaving just enough room for the opilion to pass between.

Boom. Tethering slugs shot across the canyon and hooked magnetically to the far anchors, which had already fused with the stone.

Boom. Rear-mounted cannons shot tethers at the near anchors.

Half a second later, when the wheels of the opilion rolled us over the lip of the canyon and out into open air, the four tethers were already taut. Our momentum didn't change, but now we were moving smoothly over the canyon gap on four anchored lines. As the tethers in front of us retracted, the tethers behind extended, keeping us perfectly level and balanced. Looking down, it felt like flying.

Through the clear floor of the pod I could see the cursive ribbon of a stream far below, slowly carving its message into Thalinraya's stone. The sun angled in and lit a sort of obelisk which stood midstream, the water curling around it. It was only a flash; our momentum never changed and we were across the canyon in a moment, back on solid ground. The tethers disengaged from the slugs, retracted into the opilion, and we were up another ridge and back onto dunes.

Wil chuckled to himself. Part of me suspected he'd chosen this route intentionally, just so we would encounter these canyons.

Vie relaxed her grip on the sides of her hammock.

"Wil, will you please slow down."

"Have I crashed yet?"

"That's your defense? Really?" Vie asked. "We haven't died yet, so everything must be fine?"

"You're going to be the first synth ever to have an ulcer. Assuming you *are* a synth," Wil added teasingly. He looked back with a playful challenge on his face.

Vie exhaled, set her jaw, and turned to look out the opposite iris. Her disapproval was only enhancing Wil's enjoyment.

We came into a wide, U-shaped valley and dodged around massive, homestead-sized boulders. Wil angled the opilion left and began ascending a dune which, after some altitude, turned into a talus slope. Referencing some internal map, he angled slightly left again and onto a narrow, uneven ramp which climbed a cliff face and came out onto a high, wind-swept plateau above. But there was a sound beneath the wind. Gears were at work in the walls of the opilion.

The irises came shut. They were clear and we had an excellent view, but the lack of wind highlighted the sounds coming from inside the fuselage.

"What's going on?" I asked, barely getting the question in ahead of Vie.

"We're coming to a cliff," Wil said, a little too matter-of-factly, his voice at odds with his intense concentration on the controls. The tethers on our hanging seats retracted, cinching us tighter.

"Is this the rift?" Vie demanded. Her voice was harsh, and the tendons on her neck stood out. She was upset, but her fierce look was...

Well.

"This thing is built for this, Vie. There's—"

"No! Turn around now!" This was not playful anger, this was desperate and urgent anger. Vie was working the clasps of her harness.

"Vie, don't! We're almost there. And you need to drop a com relay, don't you?"

That got her attention. Frustrated, she turned to the panel on her side and began frantically scrolling through screens.

There was a sense of openness ahead of the opilion. The land fell away to our right and I could see the valley floor below on that side, but in front of us there was just a hazy purple distance.

Vie was livid. "We were in the P-2 glacial valley...there's a ramp down from there."

"This is way faster," Wil replied.

"You just wanted to get higher," Vie said through gritted teeth as she worked her panel.

"I did not!" But he clearly did; his excitement betrayed the lie.

New gears clicked at the back of the opilion and something dropped to the ground. It looked like a simple metal box, but it rolled to a stop and immediately rose up on three spindly legs. The top opened and metal rod rose skyward. An antenna.

"What's that for?" I asked.

Vie ignored me, turning forward again. "Wil, you've never done this!" she shouted. "Stop!"

I could see the edge toward which we were racing now, but there was nothing beyond. No land below, just open sky.

"I'm taking the most direct route. Hold on. This is the story of threeeEEEeee…"

His voice lifted and looped as we launched out into nothing.

Something cracked behind our heads and the opilion began spinning. The hold of my harness loosened, then reversed so it was pulling me down, not holding me up. Vie screamed and Wil shouted something. My legs slammed against the clear iris on my side, spun out toward the interior. The opilion was cartwheeling out of control. We were bungeeing wildly around the interior in our hammock chairs. All sense of up and down was gone.

"Wil!"

A snicking sound, then a small chute deployed, jerking the opilion around and directing our fall. A whistling brought my attention to the wheels, which were folding up and around the pod. The gear boxes, which attached the wheels to their slender legs, sprouted a series of fins that flattened and folded out into elaborate origami wings. The chute released behind us, the whistling changed pitch, and our downward trajectory curved. We began soaring more forward than down. The opilion leveled out and…

We were in a glider.

Wil whooped in triumph. I did too, though mine was also relief. Vie kept her eyes closed. She was gripping her hammock and breathing through her mouth.

"Ladies and gentlemen, this is the story of the little opil that could!" said Wil, banking the opilion left, light compassing through his newly disheveled hair and making him look like a flaming-haired berserker.

The summit of the cliff was already far above us; we had lost a great deal of altitude. The cliff itself, in addition to being amazingly high, was broader than I could see. This was the continental rift, a break in the surface of Thalinraya that split the main continent in two. The lower and more tectonically stable half toward which we were now descending was where some of the first terraforming stations had been built.

Looking ahead, a vast plain extended as far as the horizon. Directly below us was an area where monumental pieces of stone had calved off of the cliff face to create a crazily jumbled terrain. It appeared impassable, even for the opilion, so launching over it was seeming like the right choice. I glanced at Vie to see if she recognized this. She was looking down with rapt attention.

"What are those?" she asked. Wil and I followed her gaze and faintly, far below, we could see tiny specs circling among the broken stones. Wil manipulated something and the clear bottom of the pod between the wheel leg joints suddenly magnified the view of what we were passing over. It took a few seconds to adjust to the perspective, but when the passing rocks and crevices began to make sense, we could make out faster blurs darting in and out. Finally, one of the creatures flew forward with the image for a moment, providing us with a glimpse of an elaborately patterned, broad-winged lizard.

"Oh," said Vie excitedly, leaning forward and looking down between her dangling legs, "those must be from the Galap line. Those weren't winged when they were introduced. Those evolved fast!"

Vie had downloaded the bioengineering history of Thalinraya. I suddenly realized that this was the first time Wil and Vie had gotten more than a few clicks from the homestead. In the months since our arrival, I had traveled extensively with my father. I hadn't wanted to; he'd insisted. But Wil and Vie were still jealous—Wil for all the technology I got to see, and Vie for all the flora and fauna. Now they were getting their turns. We might be racing to save our lives, but at least they were getting out.

Realizing her enthusiasm might be taken for approval, Vie quickly frowned. Wil smiled at me and turned back to his instruments.

"Descent rate is good," he informed us, not quite achieving the authoritative tone I was sure he was going for. "We should be aloft for about twelve minutes."

Vie's eyes flashed purple and copper as she rolled them.

CHAPTER 5

FOUR OF THE WHEELS FOLDED BENEATH us for the touchdown, which found us many clicks beyond the area of tumbled boulders. By this time it was obvious Wil had made the right choice; he had brought us safely and swiftly toward our goal. Vie noted how the touchdown was smooth, at which Wil turned back and raised an auburn eyebrow in what I'm sure he thought was an ironic expression of heroic confidence.

We landed in a vast field of dull, wirey shrubs, the brittle branches of which snapped beneath the wheels of the opilion. This was the plain atop the continental shield which, Wil informed us as he retracted the origami wings, extended unbroken for 3600 kilometers ahead of us. It was mostly a grassy scrubland, but we, thankfully, had only to go some 370 kilometers to the CA station—our destination.

After several minutes we passed, close on our left, an area more barren than the rest of the plain. No vegetation grew here, and the bluish earth sparkled with some apparently poisonous mineral.

"What is that?" Vie asked.

"Malibdi," said Wil.

"What's that?"

"Really?" he asked, incredulous.

Vie exhaled impatience and said, "Really."

"It's used for making power," I said. I hadn't paid a lot of attention to my schooling or my father's instruction, but I'd learned that much. Malibdi would be needed by all the populated systems in this sector.

"Malibdi?" Vie said. "Never heard of it."

Wil craned around with an expression that asked if she were putting him on. This was a pleasant surprise for him; usually she knew much more than he did.

"Seriously?"

"I don't even want to know anymore," said Vie, looking out the iris on her side.

"Yeah you do," Will countered. "It's why we're on Thalinraya. For that stuff."

"Malibdi?"

Wil flipped a switch and spun his hammock around to give Vie his full attention. The opilion apparently had autopilot.

"There are billions of Goldilocks class planets, right," Wil began, referring to the types of planets with compositions and orbits that allowed terraforming. "Why terraform one and not another? That," he said, pointing dramatically out the iris, but failing to land his point because we had passed the outcrop of the mineral. "Well..." he gestured vaguely, "the malibdi you saw back there is why they chose to terraform this planet in the first place."

"Every colonized sector needs at least one malibdi source," I added, hoping to sound informed, even though that was the extent of my knowledge about the subject.

"Yeah," confirmed Wil. "And Thalinraya is the only planet with malibdi in this sector. And it's a huge sector—14.8 OVO, and the first colonized in this cluster. Without malibdi they couldn't do the quantum ratcheting they'll need."

"What's quantum ratcheting?" asked Vie.

"Seriously? We're going to this station to get the QR net back up."

Vie rolled her eyes. "Will you please cut the smarter-than-you act."

"Sorry, I just..." Wil trailed off at Vie's withering look. "Sorry. QR, quantum ratcheting, is the...the energy we use in planetary systems. It powers everything from the atmospheric scrubbers to the genetic farms to...well, the satellites. Malibdi is the catalyst for the hadron vibration inducers. The FaRcom, for example. Interstellar communications needs a lot of power to open a stent through the dimensional yolk, so it uses quantum—"

"You don't even know what you're saying," I said, cutting him off. He was clearly just spouting information from some file he had onboard. He didn't really understand it; he was just showing off.

"I have it onboard," Wil said, shrugging. "And it's all true."

Vie was looking out her iris, contemplating what she'd heard or lost in thoughts of her own. Realizing he'd shared more than anyone was interested in hearing, Wil spun his hammock around and went sullenly back to his controls.

I felt a little guilty for calling Wil out, but it was irritating the way he spewed information from his onboards like it was actual knowledge. It wasn't—it was just automated recall.

It reminded me of what my mother used to tell me when I complained that I wanted augments or onboard information caches. "Don't be so eager to be a machine," she'd say. Or, "Efficiency is a false God." These were quotations from The Books, but my mother said them so often that for me they were hers. And she said these things lovingly, but...it was frustrating. So much of the world was made unavailable to me because I was a Feremite, pledged to live out my days with no integrated technology.

"As God intended," my father would remind me with his inflexible assurance. He'd never been as sensitive or understanding as my mother.

The grassy plains swept by. There was a stark beauty to the vastness of it all.

Talking back over his shoulder, Wil informed us that we had a little more than two hours to the station. Vie announced she was going to close her eyes. She had onboarded a lot of data and processes in the past ten hours. I could understand how she'd be exhausted from it all.

At an order, her hammock chair ingeniously rewove itself to allow her to lay back. I forced myself to look away as she rolled onto her side and shut her eyes.

I was still feeling bad about cutting Wil off, so I pulled my hammock chair forward, close behind him.

"Wil," I said in a low voice, hoping not to disturb Vie.

"Hmm?" he said without turning away from the instrument panel.

"You had to download a lot of assembly stuff to build the opilion, right?"

"Yeah. More than I thought."

"Was it hard?"

"What do you mean?"

"I've never... I don't have any augments, so I've never downloaded anything."

"Oh," he said, uncertainly. "No. I mean, it's not difficult. Is that what you mean?"

"I guess."

"No, you just connect to the GoLe and the computer does the rest. Oh, hey!" He pointed. A herd of what looked like small, striped deer stotted away on our left. A dozen or so of the creatures bounded off, swinging stumpy yellow tails in their alarm. Wil looked past me to where Vie was lying in her hammock, then back to me.

"We don't have time to chase 'em," Wil said.

We both knew she'd be interested in this, but Wil clearly didn't want to disturb her.

"Let her rest," I whispered. Wil nodded, and for some reason it felt like I had made up for my earlier rudeness.

"Does it hurt?" I asked, going back to our previous conversation. "Uploading information?" He'd been concerned about Vie using her augments in the Control cel, and I wondered how he was experiencing it now. He'd spent several hours onboarding information to work on the opilion.

"No," Wil said. "You kind of zone out when it's happening, I think because there are circuits that numb you. I'm not sure exactly how it works. But after, there can be a kind of ache for a few hours. Depending on the size of the files."

"Does it feel like you *know* all that stuff though?"

He squinted in thought for a moment before replying, "It's there."

I wasn't really sure what that meant, so I just said, "Weird."

We raced into a reedy, marshy area where the grasses and sedges grew taller. Some scraped against the underside of the opilion as we passed over them. Something large and gray splashed away in the distance.

"Tell me about malibdi," I said.

"Thalinraya is about two-point-six percent malibdi," said Wil. "Most of it resides in the asthenosphere. It's a mineral used in quantum ratcheting, the process whereby—"

"Don't just spew *data* at me. I want to understand it."

"Well," Wil squinted confusion at me, "nobody really understands quantum ratcheting. I don't know what you want."

"*Somebody* has to understand it."

Wil snorted. "What is that, a religious conviction or something? Is this a Feremite thing?"

"No," I said. "But somebody has to understand it. How else could we use it?"

"Machines have learned to do all sorts of things we don't understand," Wil said. "People don't have to understand it, computers do. Malibdi is the catalyst mineral for the process that starts the hadron oscillation."

"But you don't know how that works?"

"I can call up schematics and math and all that, but no. I know plants use photosynthesis, but I don't know how that works either. Does it matter?"

"I don't know," I said.

"Here," he offered, manipulating the opilion controls as he spoke. "I have explanations at nine altitudes. The highest is a two-hundred-word analogy about mirrors, the lowest is a sixteen-thousand-word description of malibdi matrices and collimated Keyesian lasers on charge-coupled atto-NIC tubules."

"That means nothing to me."

He pursed his lips and nodded sagely, then grinned and said, "Me neither." He laughed, adding, "Malibdi is the most valuable substance in the universe. That's all you need to know."

Yeah. The price of things. The highest altitude explanation, and probably the most important one too. Everything humans did seemed to come down to that. It's certainly what organized the Unicon.

Wil went back to mapping the route ahead. Vie was laying back in her hammock, asleep and gently swaying with the motion of the opilion.

I felt ashamed for wanting to recline my hammock next to her. My feelings felt like a kind of betrayal of our long friendship. Admiring the angle of her jaw, the way her skin swept down to her slender neck... That wasn't friendship.

But so what? We were alone on this planet. I mean, Wil was there too, but... Vie and I understood one another in a way she and Wil never could. I loved Wil, and we had great times together. He was competent and interesting, fun and funny. Strong. But in the end he was a simple mining synth. Vie had a searching, intelligent mind. She loved knowing things—about animals especially—and was caring too.

Looking at her sleeping in her hammock, I could imagine taking her back to Telesis with me. When I came of age, I was going to get augments and enhancements and live like Richelle, free from everyone else's expectations. So why shouldn't I have Vie with me? Even if she was a synth, Richelle had freed Vie from synth constraints when she adopted her. And I could help her grow even further.

Wil was still concentrated on his controls. I pushed my hammock back and rewove it so I could recline next to Vie.

I could feel her presence, rocking next to me. I could smell her scent. Wil was concentrating on the terrain ahead. I rolled onto my side.

Her hand was curled near her face, her long delicate fingers just touching her cheek. She really was beautiful.

Her eyelids fluttered, and I quickly closed my own. I realized I had been holding my breath. Forcing myself to relax my muscles, I concentrated on breathing, releasing tension on each exhale.

If Wil turned the opilion suddenly, our hammocks might swing enough to brush me against her.

I imagined different things that might get in the opilion's way. A boulder or...a lake. One of those gray creatures we'd seen. A tree or...a boulder or...

I woke to the sound of whispering voices. Below, through the clear floor of the pod, the ground was still reeling past. Vie was sitting up, facing forward and unaware that I had come awake. Wil had spun his hammock chair around to face back toward her. The opilion was on autopilot again.

He hadn't spun his chair around when talking with me, I noted. Apparently Vie warranted more of his attention. He'd finger-combed his hair too.

I could tell from the tone of their voices that they were discussing something serious. Wil spoke with an earnestness that stopped me from sitting up.

"I always assumed there was something missing, you know. Something that made them more...I don't know, more *full* than us."

The two of them swayed in the hammock chairs, facing one another as the plains sped by. What could have started this intimate conversation? Maybe they shared these intimacies all the time, subvocally. Maybe

I was only hearing this conversation now because their subvocals weren't functioning.

"Everyone feels that way," Vie offered, "not just synths."

"That's what I'm saying," said Wil. "I always thought we'd been *designed* to feel…that sense we're not enough or…we needed to *do* more."

"I think everyone has a sense they're not quite complete," Vie mused, examining her own slender fingers as she spoke.

"Right, but that's one of the things I always thought made us synths. See what I mean? If people feel that way too, that sense they're not complete, then we're no different. So we *could* be human."

"I don't know, Wil."

Wil whispered now with hushed enthusiasm. "When I was little, every time I didn't understand something I assumed it was because I was an engineered synth and not a human. But maybe that's how everyone feels."

"People are just as uncertain as we are," Vie agreed, looking up at him.

"Then maybe *we're* people," Wil urged. When Vie didn't respond he continued, "Why not? How would you know?"

"Wil," Vie said patiently, "we grew up in orphanates. We didn't have parents. We have neural governors that glaze things we're not supposed to see. That slippery feeling of looking through information and not being able to focus on it—people never get that. They may not understand something, but they can *see* it."

"I've thought about that. That's engineered after we're born, so there's no reason it couldn't get done to a human."

Vie was trying not to get frustrated. "You can doubt anything," she said. "Everything. But don't you—"

A quiet alarm cut Vie off mid-sentence. I could hear Wil turn to attend to something, then he said, "About an hour to go."

I expected their conversation to continue, but apparently Vie needed to work on something too. She moved her hammock back to its normal position and I could hear her manipulating a panel.

I remained still, feigning sleep, but my thoughts were swirling. What must it be like to be a synth, to not know which parts of you were engineered, which parts were natural? What must it be like to be glazed?

Wil seemed to have grown up thinking that his uncertainties were proof he wasn't human. If that were the measure, though, I wasn't human either.

My thoughts came back to the station. We were racing against the clock to restart the power for the entire planet. If we weren't able to bring the station back online, we'd lose the connection to Telesis. We'd lose the homestead and the satellites. And if my father needed the satellites to navigate back from the third moon…we might lose him too.

A vision came to me of the three of us, Vie and Wil and I, squatting around a fire in ragged clothes, gnawing charred thumpers on sticks.

CHAPTER 6

THE STATION LOOKED LIKE A METAL briar patch swollen to gigantic proportions. An irregular half-kilometer across, it was a metallic tangle of massive tubes and cables with leaf-like fins springing out all over the place and odd, oblong pod clusters hanging beneath some of the larger arches like opilion-sized berries.

We slowly circled around the facility, taking it in. Some of the tubes on one side were broken, their hollow interiors exposed and discolored. One tall spire was flaking, strips of metal like peeling bark. Below another was a complex section of parallel cabling braided into an arbor. It looked like the ribcage from some manufactured monster.

Wil slowed the opilion as we approached. From behind a low-hanging snarl of decaying cables darted a fox-sized creature. Wil spotted it first and pointed as he brought the opilion to a stop. The animal had four legs covered in scales, but its torso and head sported bristly brown, mottled fur. After a few meters it leapt awkwardly to one side and fell. Struggling up, it retreated with a pronounced limp. Its wedge-shaped head looked back over its shoulder at us several times, as though expecting us to pursue it.

Vie, who had been excited to see it, suddenly seemed doubtful. "That… that shouldn't be."

"What do you mean?" asked Wil.

Vie was too focused to respond. The tendons in her slender neck were taut as she craned forward to see the creature's retreat. It slowed to a trot. Seeing that we weren't giving chase, it stopped, crouched down and looked back at us. Vie continued an inner thought aloud: "There was a thylac-f line introduced on the Panga2 continent, but that couldn't have gotten here without…crossing the ocean and a mountain range and the majority of this land mass."

"But that happens," I said.

"Not without a sensor picking it up. The homestead has all the data, and it didn't show these."

"Well," said Wil, turning his harness back around toward the station, "if the sensors are all decommiss—hey! Look at that!"

Wil pointed back toward the station. Just beyond the cluster from which the creature had darted was some movement in the undergrowth. Three small pups were slinking slowly away from us, crouching low and snaking through the undergrowth. Their cinnamon fur was much bushier than their mother's.

"She was distracting us," Wil said admiringly. "What a brave little whatever-it-is."

"We do *not* have good information on this area." Vie's tone was concerned now. She seemed to be running through some internal data. "This isn't good," she said distractedly.

"Why?" I asked.

"That thing is a predator. Did you see its muzzle? That's a carnivore. I'm guessing it digs for things—that's probably why the fur gives way to scales on the legs. But that behavior—faking an injury, leading us away from her young,—that's the behavior of prey, not predator."

Vie paused to let the implication sink in. The pause didn't help Wil. "Huh?" he asked.

"Those are predators, but they're not *apex* predators." Pointing, she added, "They wouldn't behave like that unless they were also preyed *upon*."

Wil's red eyebrows finally lifted in understanding. "So...something around here hunts those things."

"Right. This area has a lot more going on than the logs reflect."

"And some *big* predators," Wil said, looking around with renewed interest.

Vie turned to him and was about to say something, then decided against it. Instead, she said: "I'll check my video captures against the catalogs when we get back, but it looks like most of the biological data on this area is bad."

The mother creature had circled around and was slowly returning, crouched low and ready to pounce if her young needed defending.

"This mom's pretty upset over here," I said. "Should we get going?"

Wil steered the opilion in a wide arc around where the little creatures were hunkering down so the mother would know we weren't threatening.

On the far side of the facility, years of prevailing winds had swept tumbleweeds up against the station, burying quite a bit of the structure and creating an impassable mass of dead branches.

"Is there a control somewhere?" Wil asked.

"It doesn't have dedicated systems for human interfacing; we'll have to speare it."

"What's that mean?" I asked.

"It means we have to make our own interface," she said, finally looking away from her display. She leaned forward and pointed. "Just go over there."

Wil directed the opilion closer to the structure, then lowered the pod once he had stopped. A rush of dry air came in as the irises opened. It was hot near the ground.

"Wil," began Vie, but Wil cut her off.

"I've got the opilion sensors set to alert us if anything weighing more than a kilo comes within two clicks."

"Thanks," said Vie.

Because its main work happened in advance of human occupation, the station was not designed for people. It was called a station, and that had conjured in my mind an image of buildings and storage tanks, paths and roads. This was nothing like that. It was set up to operate on its own on an empty planet, so there was no need for human-oriented structures. This included physical controls. When in operation, it had received instructions from its remote masters many light years away. Now, it was just a lump of metal. Intelligent metal, but currently dead and unknown to itself. Our job was to wake it again and set it to work.

It proved a lot easier than I expected. We walked into the tangle of cables until we came to one of the smaller, melon-sized orbs that hung down at about chest level.

"This will work," said Vie. She wiped some sand and dirt off of the smooth globe before reaching into a pocket and removing a flat gray disc, three centimeters across. She unrolled a magnetized control panel too, then attached both to the globe. The now-flat panel had a lens, a blank display, and a tac pad with a row of ruby lights above and below. The disc glowed with three nested red triangles.

"You're up," Vie said to me.

Kiku had told us I would have to be the one to authorize the recommissioning of the station. We weren't sure about Wil and Vie's status, but if they were synths, the station might read it and lock itself down. My biometrics were the only ones that would work. Thinking about it reminded me of something I meant to ask.

"I was wondering," I said, "how it'll recognize me. I wasn't even born when this thing got here."

"It doesn't care who you are," said Wil. There was an ironic, bitter tone in his voice. "It just cares that you're human—that you're not a synth. This was built when they were still worried we would rebel or something."

"Not exactly," corrected Vie. "His identity has to be verifiable."

"Well then...?" I was confused. "It can't know who I am, can it?"

"There's enough juice in this CobtY Disc for a thin skip-com to the homestead. It's already gotten a ping through the relay we dropped at the continental rift. The homestead has an open connect to Telesis, so they'll be able to send verification that you're you."

"But the main thing is they don't want *syns* to be able to work anything," offered Wil. Vie shot him an impatient look. "What?" he said, defensively.

"Here goes," I said stepping forward, hoping to head off more awkwardness.

I placed my hand on the tac pad and leaned close to the lens so it could read my retina. A tiny, amber laser probed my face for a moment, lingering over my eyes, then the controls disappeared, replaced in rapid sequence by several images: a papery nest with angry hornets pouring out, a vertiginous view from the top of a waterfall, a delicious looking slice of cake with ice cream, a slab of rotting meat, maggots crawling in and over it, a mother cat curled around five nursing kittens.

Whatever was holding my attention released its magnetic grip, and I snapped my gaze away.

"That was more than a retinal scan," Wil said.

"Retinal scans, biome samples, even DNA extractions can be faked," explained Vie. "But a natural person can't fake their neural responses. Every person has a unique neural bloom."

"Would it work with synthetics?" asked Wil.

"I don't know," said Vie. "I don't think it ever comes up. Synthetics aren't allowed access to the sorts of things that need this level of security."

"Figures," Wil said resentfully.

"You're in," Vie said, indicating for me to step aside. "I can do the rest."

I moved. The triangles on the disc had turned green and the visual display now showed an old-style keyboard. Vie raised her hands to the keyboard and began manipulating it at an incredible speed—much faster than speech. Instructions appeared at the top of the screen, above where her fingers worked.

"Whoa," admired Wil, "when did you learn that?"

"They told me to onboard the routines before we came here," Vie explained without pausing. The display blinked dully to life, then began flashing through a series of images that went too quickly for me to register. They appeared to be schematics of some kind.

After a few minutes, Vie lifted her hands from the keyboard, pulled the disc off the orb, then re-rolled the control panel. The metal underneath had become translucent, but as we watched, it faded back to its normal color.

"That's it?" Wil said. He sounded disappointed.

"That's it," said Vie. She turned and made her way back toward the opilion.

When the station was about a half kilometer behind us, Wil stopped the opilion and reopened the irises. The sage-like aroma of the field around us wafted in.

At that moment we heard, or rather felt, a low thrumming. A flock of oddly shaped birds startled up in the distance, leaping high as a group and setting their wings to glide away.

"Do you hear that?" Vie asked.

"Yeah," I replied. "What is that?"

"I have no idea," she said. Wil shrugged.

The thrumming rose through a series of quickly cycling tones until it cracked open with a metallic screeching that made us wince. It was coming from the station, where we could see some movement. It wasn't clear what was going on at first, but finally we could see that the station itself had come to life. The bundles of cabling were twisting around and rotating in complicated patterns. It looked like a pile of giant, metallic worms.

"Hey, that's a core drill!" Wil said excitedly.

"A what?" I asked.

"It's a deep boring drill. It pierces the planet's mantel and outer liquid-core to get to the solid-core. Ugh! I should have known that's what it was." He was disappointed in himself, but excited too.

"The *whole thing* is a drill?" I asked.

"Yeah! It's the deepest boring drill there is, outside solar drills. I've onboarded data on dozens of these things. I should have recognized it." The sounds coming from the drill were becoming more regular. Wil's enthusiasm for the machine prompted him to dilate the iris further. He wanted a clearer view.

"They're called planetary core augers. It probably connects to a mycelial net surrounding the core... Oh!" Wil's excitement was growing. "Oh, of course! That must be how they get the energy to kick-start the quantum ratcheting. Argh, I should have known." He shook his head in awe, never taking his eyes off the station. For someone who began life as a mining synth, seeing this drill was probably exhilarating. "Isn't it amazing?"

Wil looked around at us and noticed Vie was wearing a wry smile. "What?" he asked, suddenly defensive.

Vie glanced at me before saying, "You drove us to the CA station. What did you think CA stood for?"

Wil's lips tightened. He looked back toward the station and set his jaw.

Vie quietly answered my questioning look: "Core Auger."

"*Station*," Wil said bitterly. "Why do they call it a station? It's not a *station*, it's a drill!"

There were more metallic screeches from the distant station/drill, then the ground rumbled again.

"Is this..." began Vie. She was sensitive to Wil's embarrassment and might have never finished the question, but just at that moment the ground gave a great heave and we heard something like an underground explosion. It was enough to prompt her to go on. "Is it safe here?"

Wil paused before answering. He clearly wanted to stay and watch for a while longer.

"Wil?" Vie prompted.

"Well...probably," he said.

"Probably?"

"I have no way of knowing what they programmed, but...they'd have no reason to disrupt the landform around the surface tang."

"But they might?"

"I've never seen it, but I think...it's possible it could cause some...minor—"

Vie cut him off: "Let's get out of here."

Wil glanced at me to gauge whether he could solicit my help, but he must have seen I was ready to back Vie. His shoulders slumped and he turned to the opilion's controls.

"Oh-kay."

When we'd traveled a few clicks from the Core Auger Station we scared up a flock of tiny lizards. They rose out of some tall grasses, but instead of flying off they followed the opilion, flashing different colors in a coordinated, mesmerizing way. Wil slowed to a stop as they circled, stretching and condensing in beautiful murmurations.

"Open the irises," said Vie, delighted at this unexpected show.

With the irises open, we could hear the leathery whir of the circling wings. Several passed so close we could see their patterned, crested heads, but most circled at a distance.

"Aren't they amazing!" Vie was enraptured. She had pulled her hammock as close to the iris as she could. Now she was leaning out, girlish delight brightening her face.

A rush of clicking from the creatures rose suddenly to a clatter, and a moment later they were angling away from the opilion, wheeling off across the grasses on Vie's side.

"Oh!" Vie said, disappointed to see them leaving. She grasped both sides of the iris and leaned out even further. She was agile and strong, the muscles in her arms tightening just so.

Glancing forward, I saw that Wil was watching me watch Vie. I quickly looked out my own iris, embarrassed. The grasses on my side were shorter, but there was a patch of longer reeds in the distance. They swayed in a way that suggested a gust of wind was coming. Some of them bent down, then others. Maybe it wasn't wind. Maybe...

"There's something over here," I said. Vie released her grip and swung toward the middle of the opilion. Wil looked over too, and I pointed. "Those grasses over there," I said, though I couldn't locate the patch I'd seen before. "They were bending down, like something was moving through."

We looked, but there was no movement. Then, impossibly, the patch of reeds rose up suddenly again, closer now and swaying even more.

"What is that?" asked Wil from the front.

"Oh wow, those look like..." Vie trailed off. In front of the reeds something had sprung into the air. It looked like a wriggling stick at first, but it flared out on either side and suddenly it was undulating through the air toward us. The reeds disappeared again.

"Is that a flying snake?" Wil's voice carried some of the alarm I was starting to feel.

Dozens of them came up at once. It was like an army of precision archers had shot arrows at us, except these arrows were living snakes with rippling fins that propelled them through the air. Instinctively, I pushed away from my iris, swinging my hammock back into Vie.

"Wil!" shouted Vie, but he had already engaged the irises, which were dilating shut. Not quickly enough. The first snake had targeted me, and it came fast, undulating through the air as though it were on solid ground, the fins on either side of its flattened head working to steer the thing right at my face. It was close enough now I could see the dead eyes, the fangs in its gaping jaw. I held up my hands just as it lunged to strike.

The snake jerked to a stop, snapped in half by the closing iris. The fins flared angrily, then the thing fell to the bottom of the opilion pod, where it sprayed yellow blood in all directions as it hissed and coiled in death throes. Vie and I lifted our legs.

The other snakes thumped and thudded against the exterior of the opilion. Those that hit the clear iris showed their fangs to us before falling to the ground. Others managed to latch onto the wheels or the legs, where they began coiling. We could see them through the clear floor of the pod.

"Are you okay?" asked Vie.

"Yeah," I replied, though I could feel my heart racing.

"Look at them," said Wil. The snakes that hadn't latched on at first were swarming around the wheels, crawling up and coiling around wherever they could.

"There's nothing like these in the data for this area," said Vie, alarmed. "Or anywhere on the planet."

A sickly smell was rising from the half snake below us. "Could it be poison?" I asked.

"I don't think so," replied Vie. "These are constrictors. Look at them down there."

On the struts leading down to the wheels there were so many coiled snakes, it looked like the opilion had flesh legs. The writhing mass was repulsive.

"They hunt in packs?" asked Wil, horrified by the idea.

"I guess."

"Seems like the bioengineering here has gotten a little lax," said Wil.

"I don't think these were engineered," said Vie. "I think they just evolved."

"Without any of the systems noticing?" I asked. Vie didn't answer, but she was clearly concerned.

"I'll track it down when we get back to the homestead," she said.

"We should get going," Wil said. He turned toward the controls.

"Wait," said Vie, "don't hurt them."

"Seriously?" I asked.

"They're just trying to live their lives."

"And end ours!" I reminded her. "That thing almost ate my face!"

The rest of the trip back to the homestead was, thankfully, less exciting. It took much longer than the trip out to the station because we circled far to the south in order to avoid the worst heights of the continental cleft. We were all more aware of the flora and fauna as we traveled along, and for the first few hours we pointed things out to one another. The vegetation was much more varied than we had seen before, but the thing that really amazed us was the number of animals. There were small, scurrying creatures that darted away from the opilion; there were winged lizards of various kinds that flushed and soared away; there were a few larger creatures, some large enough that they watched us pass without fear. As we were going slowly through a boulder-strewn area near the southern cleft, we saw a cat-like creature, much larger than the one we had seen at the station. It flattened itself against the ground as we passed, but then it actually loped after us for a while.

We were eager to get back as soon as we could, but we'd done what Telesis had asked us to do. It was nice to be distracted for a little while. And anyway, we couldn't go any faster.

After a few hours we lapsed into silence, each of us watching the passing landscape, lost in our own thoughts. I startled when Vie touched my arm, but she nodded out her side. She wanted me to see something. I pulled my hammock over. She pushed hers back and reached around to pull me closer, pointing toward billows of steam that rose from the base of some cliffs in the distance.

Wil had seen something, too. "Hey hey! Look at this," he said from the front. "You're not going..."

His voice trailed off. He had looked back and seen my hammock pulled over, Vie's arm around me.

"What is it," asked Vie, letting my hammock swing back into place.

Wil looked confused for a moment, but when he moved his gaze in my direction, resentment swept over his face. "Never mind," he growled.

"No, what is it?" asked Vie, cinching up her hammock and sliding forward.

Through the front we could see a herd of tiny, pig-like creatures which were diving into a round, clear pool.

"Whoa!" said Vie. "Oh, and there's more!"

We were entering a landscape pock-marked by deep, open springs. Wisps of steam rose from some of the pools, which were ringed with rainbows of different mosses and underwater plants. Herds of these little animals were grazing around the springs, but as the opilion approached they were diving into the clear waters. They appeared to deflate as they hit the water, each one sinking quickly beneath a string of bubbles.

"Those aren't listed either," Vie said with genuine curiosity. "The genomes on this planet are completely out of control." Wil was concentrating hard on the controls. "Can you steer by the bluff over there?" she said, pointing.

"We have to get back," he said without looking at her.

"There're larger bodies of water over there. I'd like to see whether—"

"We don't have time." Wil's voice was icy.

I shrugged when Vie glanced back at me.

I wasn't proud of it, but I had to admit Wil's jealousy felt good.

CHAPTER 7

"THESE THINGS TAKE TIME. I promise I will contact you as soon as we can tell you more. Until then, just get some rest."

Kiku's office zipped closed and the panel surrounding us swiped back to neutral.

We were back in the FaRcom cel. Vie and I had come straight there after returning from the Auger Station. Wil had ducked into the medic cel to get Thius, but then he'd brought the dog into the FaRcom halfway through our conversation with Telesis. The two of them sat quietly near the iris, Wil comforting the dog, who seemed groggy and wary, but mostly recovered.

Kiku hadn't been as helpful as we'd hoped. Yes, our trip had been successful, but: No, the QR net wasn't fully functioning yet, it would take time. No, the satellite array wasn't working yet. That would take even more time. No, they didn't know what had crashed on Thalinraya. No, they couldn't say why the data on the planet's flora and fauna was incorrect. No, my father hadn't gotten in contact yet.

"They don't seem to know much," I reflected.

"No," said Vie, "but I'm sure they're doing their best."

There was an odd quality to her voice and I couldn't tell if she was being sarcastic.

"Ladies and gentlemen, this is the story of Wil going to sleep," said Wil, setting Thius on the floor. Thius scampered, a little stiffly, to the iris ahead of Wil.

"You deserve it," said Vie. "You drove the whole time. We got to rest."

Wil didn't acknowledge Vie's words. "Glad you're better, beastie," he said to Thius as he passed into the hotplate hall. Thius was expecting to be invited, not bypassed. He looked back at Vie and me, cocking his head quizzically. Wil strode past the functional cels, turned right into the habitation hall and was gone.

My heart rate rose momentarily. I'd wanted to talk to Vie alone, but we hadn't been away from Wil. Until now. Before I could say anything, however, she was heading toward the iris.

"I need to do some research," she said hastily. "I'll be in a fun cel. I want to see if I can figure out when the biology of this place got all poggs."

Thius looked hopeful again when Vie bent to scratch his cheeks. The wisps of hair on his ears bounced comically.

"Oh, you," Vie purred.

"Everything okay?" I asked.

"Yeah," said Vie without looking. She stood and started down the hall.

Thius sneezed elaborately, banging his nose into the floor. Then he looked quickly back and forth. He was clearly as nonplussed as me. Was she trying to avoid me? Was she feeling awkward? I didn't want to let her go.

"I was going to throw some sticks for Thius," I improvised. "While we wait, you know, for Kiku to get back to us. Want to come?"

Thius knew the word "sticks." He turned and darted down the hotplate hall excitedly, skittering past Vie, past the functional cels and into an open elevator bud.

"I'll come up and join you in a while," Vie said. She went a few steps further, then turned into a functional cel.

"Great," I said, a little too loud, just as the fun cel was irising shut. I had followed her down the hall, and now I stood outside the closed iris feeling rejected. I looked down self-consciously. The nearly infinite computational power of the hotplate was visible through the homestead's vitreous. It was right there, directly below me. Yet there I stood, impotent and unable to figure out something as simple as how to talk to a girl synth.

Thius stuck his head hopefully out from the elevator bud and yelped.

"Alright," I said. I wasn't really sure what I wanted to say to Vie anyway, so maybe talking later was better. Still, she seemed to be avoiding me.

When I entered the elevator bud, Thius was sitting at enthusiastic attention, ready to go, his furry eyebrows vibrating in anticipation.

"Ready?" I asked. The word was almost too much for him. He rocked back and forth and whined as the iris closed and we rose through the translucent vitreous to the surface.

My father had brought back some sticks from one of the southern forests not long after we first arrived on Thalinraya. They had been oddly rubbery, and when Thius bit into them his teeth got stuck. After each fetch he'd have to spend several minutes prying the stick away from his jaws. He'd whine and lever the thing between his paws, twisting and turning his head until his teeth came free with a sucking pop. Nosing the stick toward me, afraid to bite into it again but barking and growling at it nonetheless, he'd look up, wild-eyed and excited, until I picked it up and threw it again.

This was not one of those sticks. This was an assembler-built toy, engineered to specifications which were supposed to ensure maximum enjoyment for both human and canine. It was exactly one-half meter in length, flawlessly weighted with a stiff inner core and a softer, bark-like exterior which guaranteed good mouth-feel for the dog without splintering. It was perfect.

Thius didn't like this designer stick nearly as much. He'd run after it, but instead of bringing it right back he'd get distracted and start snarfling around. The game wasn't as much fun when the stick didn't resist.

He was even more distracted today, which was fine with me. He had recovered from his surgery amazingly well, but I didn't want to push him. As he poked around through the brush I looked south, thinking about the lattice forest from which those other sticks had come. I wasn't even speaking to my father at that point, but when he explained Halopunt trees and the lattice forests they created, I was tempted to ask him to take me.

The D_D7 island was a forest grown from three Halopunt trees, which sprouted in a shallow sea hundreds of years ago. When a Halopunt breaks the surface it starts branching, and whenever two branches come together they merge into one another and form a lattice. They grow more branches, extending the lattice in all directions—some branches growing out and down to become supporting roots, others growing up to merge with other branches—creating second and third and fourth stories. As the upper stories sprout new branches, the lower stories become a shaded jungle gym of sturdy, interconnected boughs.

The D_D7 island was nine square kilometers of Halopunt lattice, more than 150 meters high in places. My father said the thousands of boughs coming out of the water were three meters across now. It was a whole island, grown from three original trees.

My father hadn't penetrated the lattice more than half a kilometer, but he said it was the first time he really felt like he was on an alien world. The branches toward the top were rubbery and forgiving, but as he climbed in and down they became more rigid. And the size of the thing meant there were distinct ecosystems living deep in the meshwork. Ferns, insects, birds, monkeys—all made their homes in this tree island, never touching land or water.

Thius barked at my feet. He had brought back the manufactured stick and now was hopping back and forth, finally eager to have me toss it again. You'd never know he'd almost died so recently. I picked it up and threw it as far as I could.

There were no clouds in the transparent blue sky, and I could see a long way, past the Breakfields to the fallaway at Glassfall Canyon. It was a good view from up here, on the bench of land above the homestead. My father had said he would take me to see the Halopunt lattice island next time he went. I wondered now if I would ever see it. If the thing that crashed here was too dangerous, we might have to leave.

Thius brought the stick right back this time, so I faked a quick throw and, when Thius was already tearing away, I turned and threw the stick in the opposite direction. Thius slowed, looking around for the fall of the stick. When it didn't come, he stopped and turned back toward me. I pointed. He laid his ears back and tore off to search. He loved it when I tricked him like this.

It was ironic that I was now wishing my father could take me to the lattice forest. When we'd first come to Thalinraya I would have rather cut off my leg than go anywhere with him. I hated him.

When we had come out of bern at Thalinraya, things were pretty awful aboard ship. My father went down to the planet's surface to plant the assemblers to build our homestead, but Vie, Wil, and I had to orbit for three days while the assembly got started. It was many-flavored torture. We were all trying to get used to our new bodies, awkward with one another and ourselves. We were confined in that tiny little ship, cramped and uncomfortable, circling the planet again and again and again. But what made it especially torturous was my mother, still in her bernaculum.

I never saw my mother's body. My father was roused from suspension first, but it was too late for him to do anything for her. She'd died in transit, probably closer to Telesis than Thalinraya. By the time I was awake enough to be aware of what was going on, my mother had been shrouded. That's all I ever saw: just a sheet with the vague lunar topography of my mother.

Wil and Vie tried to comfort me, but my father retreated into his work. He kept himself isolated and busy so he could avoid me. My father didn't know how to convey even simple emotions, and the complexity of grief was far beyond his ability to understand, much less express.

After three days in orbit we were finally allowed to go to the surface. There had been a Stage Three Feremite tender on Thalinraya centuries earlier, but he had left his homestead intact. My father had been living in it while assembling the new one. When we arrived we saw that primitive old homestead—the walls thick and immovable, the foundation roots anchored to the bedrock. It didn't last long.

We were all there when my father released a disassemble org on the old homestead. I had never seen anything like it: a little silvery plasma salamander with four mouths. My father carried it in a clear canister to an area in front of the old homestead, opened the canister and laid it on the ground. The little creature scurried out and immediately started burrowing into the soil. Wil was really excited. He loved gear of all kinds, and he had onboarded all sorts of information about it.

"That's gen one," said Wil, as the org's tail disappeared underground. "With the soil here it'll take about sixteen minutes to assemble gen two. It'll go faster after that."

"Three minutes to the second generation," said my dad over his shoulder as he turned back to our new homestead. "That homestead was assembled to draw elements from the bedrock. Those elements are still available in holsters on the homestead's roots. It'll go quickly: gen two in three minutes, gens three, four, and five in the minute following that. We should move back."

In about an hour the area looked like the sped-up video of a rotting carcass. The old homestead was sinking into the earth and collapsing, voracious orgs crawling over, through, under and around it like silvery maggots. Most of the activity was underground. The earth was roiling like water as orgs deconstructed, digested, and transferred materials to storage tanks under our new homestead. I knew they were carefully engineered to do this work, but I couldn't help wondering what would happen if the orgs decided to disassemble something else. Like a human.

Three days later, nothing was left of the old homestead but a bare depression next to the escarpment. You would never have known there had been a structure there at all.

The homestead my father built was much larger and more dynamic. Over the storage tanks he assembled the rigid arc of the hotplate, which became the computational hub for all planet and satellite systems. It was the solar system's nerve center, and cels that required direct access to the hotplate's computational engines were fixed along one submerged hall, with the habitation hallway extending off the hotplate at ninety degrees. The elevator buds could migrate freely through the Gelighnarrigh plasma to any destination, but so could the habitation cels. I often migrated mine to the periphery to open an iris for fresh air. Or to hear the thumpers.

It was an amazing structure. I didn't understand the technology, and at the time I didn't care to learn it. I knew the homestead could keep itself, the pale—the protected area around the homestead—and Thanlinraya functioning properly, but I didn't have to worry about it, so I didn't. As long as it had the entrance and elevator buds that took me to the habitation cels, I really didn't care. My father and the homestead knew what they were doing; I had other interests. Moreover, my mother's death only solidified my resolve to return to Histon once I turned eighteen. There was nothing for me on Thalinraya.

It was during those first weeks, when my father was busy doing other things, that Wil and Vie and I explored around the homestead, eventually hiking down past the Breakfields and into Glassfall Canyon. We called it that because the walls of the canyon were sheer, and many of the cliff faces were pocked with bulging eruptions of clear crystals. Most were eight or ten centimeters across, but a few spanned several meters. Some geologic pressure was forcing the crystals out of the earth like toothpaste from a tube. Although it was a slow process, it had been going on long enough that there were mounds of broken crystals beneath the eruptions, talus slopes of broken glass at the feet of the cliffs. We'd often hear crystals tinkling down from the bulges in the cliffs. Larger falls sometimes left a burnt smell behind.

Thius dropped the stick a few feet away from me and flopped down onto his side. His tongue lolled, his chest heaved.

"You gotta pace yourself, buddy," I said. He aimed one wild eye at me and didn't bother to lift his head. "Okay, I'm tired too."

As I said it, I realized how true it was. "How about some kibble and a kennel."

Thius lurched up and trotted over to the elevator pod. I followed.

CHAPTER 8

THE ELEVATOR IRISED CLOSED WHEN I told it my destination, and moments later, after a swift, slanting descent, the elevator plunged down the narrow chute to the materials storage area, far below the hotplate. It was hard to tell how deep the chute went, but it must have been tens of meters.

After a long rest I'd gone to the commons cel. I knew Vie was still in her habitation cel, and I lingered for a while, hoping that she'd come for something to eat. She must have been having a long sleep though, and eventually I decided to see what Wil was up to in storage. He'd been down there ever since I woke up.

Wind swept into the elevator as soon as it opened into the underground loading area. I'd wondered about this before. I knew that many of the planet's automated resource caches sent out assemblers and orgs to retrieve trace elements to store for future use. These would usually burrow back to the cache, creating tunnels of various sizes to far-flung locations. I assumed something like that was done here too. Perhaps the wind came from these tunnels. Given the amount of wind, the tunnels must be huge.

The smooth surfaces of the cavern were made from some transparent material that revealed the dark, veined rock out of which the place had been bored. I turned left past the loading docks and headed for the main access tunnel. Equipment was mounted into the walls and ceiling: giant mechanical arms and rollers, guiding rails and lifts and cables whose purposes were unclear. The place was built to accommodate machines, not humans, and the equipment made me think of insect parts—jointed legs and mandibles, carapaces that hid folded wings. I wondered if the automated system that controlled these machines might mistake me for a resource of some kind. At any moment these machines might kick into life and tear me to pieces, resourced for future use—my bones sent to a calcium storage chamber, my blood sucked through some hose to a tank which would churn it together with other liquids. In time I'd get pumped to a surface sprinkler to fertilize a distant grain field. I tried not to think about it as I hurried past the now-threatening machinery.

The storage area was a kilometer further down a long, gently curving tunnel that was even windier than the loading area. As I walked in the dim light beside the rail I thought back to the only other time I'd come this way, during my official tour when my father had demanded my presence.

About three weeks after arriving, my father had had enough of grieving for my mother, so he assumed I'd finished grieving as well. He came to my habitation cel and announced that it was time for me to begin learning Thalinraya's systems. I told him I wasn't interested. My mother's death and my father's retreat into himself hadn't made me eager to learn more about this place. I planned to leave as soon as I could.

He insisted I learn the systems anyway. My mother was gone and he needed help. So, he took me on a tour and then set up one of the functional cels as an instructional center. When I objected, he said that if I hadn't learned the first six lessons in three days, he'd lock me in the cel until I did.

I complained bitterly to Wil and Vie. Wil took my side, but Vie took my father's view of things. My mother was gone and someone had to step in to take her place, she reasoned. Moreover, she thought some directed study would be good for me.

Despite my new attraction to her, the fact that she took my father's side prompted me to shun her for the next week or so. She had much more time with Wil during that period, which may have given him false hope.

My father would come into the fun cel periodically and stand with his hands behind his back, frowning at my low scores and lack of progress. Sometimes he would stay and try to help, but this always resulted in heated argument. He would tell me I needed to learn to apply myself; I would counter that this was all onboardable information if he would just allow me memory augments. I knew this enraged him. He would tell me I was lazy, squandering my God-given abilities; I would tell him that augments were God-given as well. He would inevitably leave, red-eared and disappointed and more determined than ever to make me do things *his* way.

I worked off my frustration by exploring with Wil in the afternoons.

My first trip with my father came after days of tedious instruction on atmospheric scrubbing. It was absolute torture, which confirmed for my father that it was the right thing to do. Both his upbringing and his religion taught him that life was meant to be toil. My complaints—that I didn't care about Thalinraya's atmospheric composition, that the processes were boring, that the machinery was tediously complicated, that I would rather be doing anything else—all these fell on deaf ears. My misery was proof he was doing his job as a parent. One wasn't meant to enjoy life—joy was a consequence of vanity or greed; happiness was a kind of sin. One was meant to be *useful*, not happy.

When my father finally had to go to the atmospheric scrubbers in the east ocean he decided to bring me along, despite the fact that I was still obstinately refusing to learn. He came to my habitation cel, pulled me out of my bed and frog-marched me up to a gravipad, which was on the opposite side of the hangar from the field. When we came up into the open air, it was a moment before I saw the vehicle waiting at the center of the pad. When I did, I realized I was going to ride in a gravion for the first time.

I had seen gravions on Telesis, but I hadn't expected them on a terraforming planet where there were no people to use them. The orbiting M-G hooks that would be required had to be too expensive for just us to use. As we crossed the pad to the sleek vehicle, however, I remembered that there would have been *automated* gravions in use for years. Orbital M-G hooks would have been in place since Stage Two, creating the temporary gravity tunnels needed to allow automated gravions to haul heavy equipment. I'd learned about these systems in early-stage terraforming, but I'd forgotten.

I had to force the scowl back onto my face. I didn't want to admit it to my father, but I had long wanted to ride in a gravion. In school I had jealously listened to other children describing the adrenal rush of the experience, and I was eager to try it myself.

We climbed in just behind the forward needle, which extended two meters out in front of the gravion. After lowering the clear canopy and buckling in, while my father checked the safety and communication systems, I examined the vehicle around me. There was an odd, rippled texture to everything—the floor and seats and walls—all oriented from front to back in the craft. Even the safety straps had the texture, and when I shifted, the ripples adjusted themselves so that their orientation stayed the same. They felt like living muscles wrapping around my torso. The sheen to the metal of the craft was like oil, almost wet, with a shifting opalescent depth. Looking back over my shoulder I could see the three rows of needles extending out at the back of the craft. We were strapped into the head of an arrow.

My father asked if I was ready. When I said I was, he engaged the distant orbital hooks and the bow of the craft lifted slowly off the pad. The air in front of the needle shimmered and pulled at it. I should have known that something violent was about to happen, because the seat behind me grew up around my neck and the back of my head for added support. Also, the shimmering path before us condensed into a darker rift, the rim of which peeled outward in tiny, dark waves, creating a curved tunnel up into the sky. Some sort of static made hair follicles buzz all over my body.

Still, the abrupt leap forward caught me off guard. It felt as though the catch on a planet-sized rubber band had been released. We shot up and forward so quickly that, had I had breath, I would have screamed. But I had no breath because my hands had been on my lap when we launched, and the force of the takeoff had brought them back into my stomach like a double-fisted punch. I thought I might black out. The acceleration was incredible; we must have been a kilometer from the launch pad before I was able to take a breath.

My father had kindness enough to wait a minute or two before asking me if I was alright, so I had breath enough to feign an off-the-cuff response. But truthfully, I was thrilled. The air rushing past, the speed, the g-force... Incredible!

The gravion leveled out at 3.2 clicks above the planet. We were going so quickly that, by the time I looked back, the homestead was no longer visible, and Glassfall Canyon was just a distant crack in the earth.

It took a couple of hours to travel to the ocean scrubbers. My father and I weren't on speaking terms, so we flew along in silence as landscapes rolled by below us. I was amazed at how quickly we were past the desert surrounding the homestead. As the parched land broke apart, we flew over a labyrinthine landscape of rolling hills that were eroded into ribbons of differently colored earth. The hills spent themselves and gave way to a rich plain of grassy parkland. Tall, willowy trees lined mostly dry streambeds—tracings on some giant sketchpad, making their way crazily south. A darker line in the distance marked another range of hills. As we neared them, the grass of the plain became more lush, and I couldn't tell if we were over some kind of great marshland. Stands of brush and trees grew independent of the stream beds. The hills themselves, dense with trees, were soon beneath and then behind us, and we were racing over an emerald green carpet of jungle.

The canopy of trees became so dense we couldn't see the ground, just an occasional parting of mottled tree cover through which the bright sky would wink back at us, reflected from a lake or river. Birds, individuals and flocks, burst constantly from the trees below. We were so high they were only specks, but from their colors and flight patterns I could see there was a great variety. Looking back now, I wonder how many of them were actually flying lizards.

We passed to the north of a conglomeration of clear geodesic domes— several square kilometers of them. I wasn't sure what they were—some kind of automated genetic labs I assumed, but I wasn't about to ask my father. They rose above the jungle canopy, glinting and flashing as we passed. I could imagine the thousands of robots of various shapes and sizes going about their duties, unaware of the wilderness just outside.

In another few minutes we passed directly over a huge lake that was crisscrossed with cables and tubes. There was a point near the western shore where the water churned and roiled furiously. A manufactured lake with a giant pump drawing down some aquifer? Again, I was tempted to ask my father, but I didn't want to give him the satisfaction of knowing I was interested. My resentment was that strong. And anyway, I could look it all up when I got back to the homestead.

We continued to pass these automated outposts, some looking like strange mechanical creatures, some like abandoned industrial cities. My father pointed out the locations of underground facilities—synth capsules, materials caches, silo cities.

When we shot out over the ocean I was surprised to see that the entire coastline was manufactured. Interlocking bulkheads stretched north and south as far as the eye could see, and there were tens of thousands of offshore booms, staggered to protect the shore and harness the tides. We rocketed over rippling waves now, and in the distance ahead we could see roiling white clouds rising up into the stratosphere. These turned out to be sprays from the scrubbers, visible from several dozen kilometers away. The fountains of water and chemicals shot higher than the gravion, creating their own weather system.

My father told me to brace myself just before the gravion cartwheeled, end over end. The whistle of wind in the baffles became a deafening roar for a few moments as the g-force pulled my organs around inside my body. We were traveling backwards and upside down when the maneuver was complete. My father did something to make us roll upright, but we were still looking back toward the distant coast as we decelerated in toward the scrubbers.

We landed on a gravion pad that was being inundated with a constant, torrential rain. Rainbow mists were boiling everywhere. My father opened the gravion's canopy and we were instantly drenched. He stepped out as though this were entirely normal, looking back at me with a challenge. I clambered out of the gravion and pretended to be equally unfazed, resisting the desire to wipe at the rivulets of water running down my face. With as much bored resentment as I could muster, I shouted over the sound of the spray to ask how long this was going to take. *Not long*, my father motioned.

Some stairs took us down below the gravion pad where the main controls were located. My father tapped in and began his diagnostics as I wandered around the facility. Most of the thing was underwater. Above the water was the one large platform on which we had landed, but mostly there were just thousands of different sized nozzles. They pointed out in all directions and turned themselves on and off at irregular intervals. There were six especially large ones which shot liquid several kilometers into the air. Many of the smaller nozzles aimed jets of various kinds at these larger streams, changing their trajectory and adding tea-colored chemicals. The sound was devastating. The volume of liquids being moved, the staggering amount of power being used, the rushing movement all around...it was exhilarating. I looked back to where my father was at work and he motioned for me to be careful. I turned away and looked out through the rising cataracts.

That was the first of many trips with my father to outlying areas. The next time he asked me to accompany him I feigned reluctance, but after we had gone to the southern glaciers and bored through half a kilometer of ice to check on the fresh water sequesters…well, I wasn't able to pretend disinterest any longer. I hadn't realized how adventurous my father's work was, and now that I knew, I was eager to be a part of it. The fact that Wil and Vie were insanely jealous helped. I tried to convince my father that they should come along with us, but he had more traditional views about the roles of synthetics and wouldn't hear of it.

Wil would riddle me with questions; then, a few days after my forays with my father, he would invariably educate me further about the machinery I had encountered, having onboarded information about it to slake his jealousy. Vie took some pleasure in the thought that I was growing closer to my father, and she urged me to take note of the living creatures I encountered.

I was jealous of the time Wil was spending with Vie, but not quite enough to want to give up my new opportunity to explore. I had always envied their capabilities. Neither of them had the full complement of augments available to most synthetics; Richelle had adopted them too early, before most of their augments had been installed. Still, they had the basic ones given to synthetic children, which was much more than I had. So I'd always been jealous. Now, however, I was doing and seeing things that weren't available to them. It wasn't because of any special talent of my own, but still. The tables were turned, and I enjoyed it.

My father was an excellent pilot, I learned, and he enjoyed flying. Over the next few weeks we flew several times to different atmospheric scrubbing facilities, most out in the oceans, but one near the north pole. The polar facility had a borehole from which it drew water to mix with chemicals. The mix was spewed high into the air where snow formed, falling down to create snow mountains that were leveled and redistributed by smaller, automated snow-blowers.   '

We visited the canal-boring machines on the southern continent where the continental drainage was being entirely reworked. We checked on buried synth capsules to make sure the hibernating synths would be ready to wake for their work on Stage Five terraforming. We went to genetic farms on the jungle in the N island chain. Vie asked me to collect specimens, but my father would never let me bring something back in the gravion. Still, when I saw one particular species, I was tempted to sneak one aboard. They were like tiny, prong-tailed monkeys with mittens instead of hands; nut-colored, but with absurd white eyebrows. The furry, curious creatures followed us all around the island and would have been easy to capture. Vie would have melted.

The most exciting of our trips was down to a tectonic control facility about six kilometers below the west coast. We flew there in a larger gravion than normal, and when we landed, the back of the gravion dilated open to disgorge a great, beetley machine. It was an opilion my father had reengineered for this trip. Vicious looking grinding gears sprang to life all around the thing after my father and I had gotten inside, and soon we were boring down into the earth in the shaking, grinding contraption.

It was a long, hot, tension-filled grind down to the facility, which wasn't meant for humans at all. When we came to the main trunk coordinating two arms of the tectonic grip, we had to dig out a temporary cavern around the joint for my father to attach his controls. Apparently the tectonic staples weren't communicating with the larger continental anchoring screws; my father had to reroute the flow of information. This involved interrupting communication briefly, and when he did this the earth around us suddenly bucked. It was alarming, but worse was when, after the first shock, the ground continued to groan and roll and shift. My father obviously hadn't known this was going to happen, but he maintained his composure and told me to get back in the opilion while he finished his work. The temporary cavern was morphing and threatening to collapse, so I retreated inside and waited anxiously. It took my father only a few minutes to do what he needed to do, but during those minutes I gained a new respect for him.

When we got back to the homestead, Vie and Wil wanted to know if we had felt the earthquake. My father actually laughed. It was the first time I had heard him laugh since my mother's death. It may have been the last time too. He wasn't prone to laughter.

Those trips did a lot to repair my relationship with my father, showing me different sides of him. Curiosity. Courage. It had been easier when my resentment toward him was more pure, when it overwhelmed my other feelings so that I only had to have the one opinion of him.

My parents had originally trained to be Stage Five terraformers, which would have allowed them to oversee city construction, working with synthetics and greeting the first colonists. My mother would have loved that. But my father had decided to switch to the more austere life of Stage Four. That was really what killed my mother. She was a social person, and the life of a Stage Four terraformer promised nothing but isolated toil. In bringing us to Thalinraya he had ensured my mother's misery, even if he hadn't directly caused her death. His religion was backward and authoritarian, his parenting was cold and distant. He was a self-righteous, controlling fool.

But as we travelled together and I saw him in different circumstances, it became more and more difficult to keep that diamond of hate polished. He loved me, in his own way. At least he tried. And he wasn't all serious-ness; he wouldn't admit it, but my father had a weakness for flying fast. It seemed so unlike the rest of his personality that I didn't recognize it at first. We sped quickly from one place to another, and I had assumed that this was just the way gravions worked, until one time when the gravion's safety system voiced a warning during a trip to an eastern reef building facility. I asked my father about it and he apologized, admitting he had gotten carried away. It was then I realized that he loved the speed. My father, who didn't indulge in any pleasures, *liked to fly fast*. This unlocked other thoughts: he had been a boy once, and traces of that remained. I had never thought of him as anything but a severe, serious, religious man. Had he been different when he was younger? He clearly had a sense of adventure. Had he once had a sense of humor too? Had he misbe-haved? Had he planned to betray his parents and leave the Faith, like I was doing?

I had to admit I hadn't been kind toward my father for quite some time. Perhaps I brought out the worst in him. Perhaps I wasn't familiar with his other sides because I didn't allow him to express those parts of himself. Perhaps he thought I was a humorless child. Around him I had been, so he couldn't be blamed for thinking it, if he did. I had shared myself with my mother, and even more with Richelle, but I had never really reached out to my father.

Once these ideas occurred to me I was able to make small gestures toward reconciliation. I would ask a question about some aspect of his terraforming work or how he guided the gravion. He was taciturn by nature and his explanations were brief, but he always seemed grateful I had asked. After a time he would ask questions in return—mostly about Wil and Vie. He was awkward. I could tell he was only asking because he wanted to make a connection, not out of genuine interest. But he was trying, and I appreciated it.

My long trudge through the dim tunnel ended in the underground storage chamber, where every surface was covered in milky-white plastisteel. There were claws and nozzles and gears in the ceiling above, but they were also white.

This area would be dark most of the time; unseeing machines didn't require light. But there were lights now, so Wil must be somewhere near.

The storage units themselves rose out of the floor: featureless white tanks and blocks, some low and wide, some tall and thin. There must have been an organizing principle, but to me it was just a complicated maze.

There was no response when I called out, so I made my way left toward what appeared to be the larger section of the irregular cavern. Because everything was white, it was hard to tell. I made my way past a series of L-shaped tanks and was about to pass between two hexagonal obelisks when the wind suddenly shifted.

Instinctively, I looked behind me. Several meters away a stalactite came shooting down from the ceiling. It disappeared from my view, but a moment later there was a deafening impact accompanied by a shuddering jolt. A thin white line now extended down from the ceiling. I made my way toward it, reasoning that Wil must be somewhere near this activity. I called again, but still received no answer. As I walked, I saw the line slowly swell, drawing some material up out of storage. I wondered what the material might be, and what it was being used to build.

Wil was standing in a depression near where the stalactite nozzle had pierced the floor, leaning his forehead against a square storage unit that was just taller than he was. His eyes were closed.

"Wil," I called. He remained where he was, unmoving. I approached and saw his hands were against the sides of the storage unit. Interactive bracelets on his wrists were in contact with some magnetic pickups. I wondered if he even knew I was there.

"Just a minute," he said unexpectedly, answering my unspoken question.

Sitting on a low storage unit that served as a bench, I took a moment to examine where the nozzle had entered the floor. The bulkier materials were probably under there, I realized, not in the visible units. I knew so little about how all of this worked. The whiteness of everything made it all surreal, as though I were in a life-size model for a facility that hadn't yet been built.

The wind whistled through the machinery on the ceiling and I looked up again. Stalactite nozzles were everywhere. Did the computers controlling these things know we were here, or might we be inadvertently pithed at any moment? A surge of adrenaline pulsed through me. No, the computers were infinitely smarter than we were. It was an irrational fear; we wouldn't be harmed.

Some words from my mother came to mind. "One of the projects of growing up is learning to relax in the face of the unknown," she had said to me one afternoon when I stayed home from school. The other students had all onboarded some information that I, because I lacked augments, couldn't, and I was feeling frustrated and uninformed. "They'll never know everything, so they'll have to come to terms with this too. You're just getting a head start." My skepticism must have been clear in my expression, and she was about to comfort me further when a copy of The Books thumped down between us. Neither of us were aware that my father had come up, but he looked down at us now with one of his rare smiles. It looked out of place on him.

"Listen to your mother," he said. "She's right. They're turning themselves into computers, but all the information in the universe can't give them understanding. 'Information is not insight.' They think they can know everything, and they end up knowing nothing. But 'We, who live as God intended, come to real understanding.' It starts here." He tapped The Books with his finger and looked at us significantly.

I don't know what he expected, but we didn't have a clue how to respond. After a long and awkward pause, my father nodded, turned and left.

"You okay?"

The memory dissolved. It was Wil, standing close beside me. He must have finished whatever it was he'd been doing.

"Yeah," I said. "Just waiting for you."

"What brought you down here?" he asked, hopping up onto a storage tank across from me and pocketing his interactive bracelets. "I thought you were with Vie."

"She's in her habitation cel. What are you up to?"

"Kiku said I should get the opilion geared up again, just in case."

"You talked to Kiku?" I asked.

"The homestead told me. I didn't talk to her." Wil ran his fingers through his red hair and exhaled. "Anyway. Some of the materials are pretty rare, so I had to come here to tap directly. And I kind of like it down here," he added, scanning around. "Good place to think."

I looked at the white blocks and tanks surrounding us. He probably had visual enhancements allowing him to access information—up-to-date volumes, temperatures, usage data. Everything appearing white and featureless to me was probably covered with information to those with the right augments. You only had to have eyes to see.

"Everything okay with Vie?" he asked, a little too casually.

Uh oh. I wasn't prepared for this. I'd come down here mainly because… Well, I couldn't remember now, but it wasn't to talk about Vie.

"Relax," said Wil. "I know."

"Know what?" I asked.

Wil rolled his eyes, not unlike Vie. "You've got a feather for her," he said. I had never heard the expression, but I was pretty sure I knew what he meant. And that he was right.

"It's okay," he continued, looking out over the storage tanks rather than at me. He was trying to play it casual, but his fingers were gripping the edge of the tank hard. "She's got one for you, too."

"What makes you say that?" I asked, hoping my voice didn't sound too hopeful.

Now he looked me in the eye. "She told me, you pog."

She had talked to him about me?

"Well," I began, but I didn't know what to say. Wil looked away and we sat in silence for a minute. "She's known you way longer than she's known me," I said finally.

Wil laughed bitterly. "Maybe that's my problem," he joked.

"Seriously," I said, "I don't—"

"It's okay," Wil said again. "I talked to her about it, alright. Out loud, I mean. It was the kind of thing that makes you really want your subvocals back, let me tell ya. We were looking right at each other, and it was… Anyway, she said me and her weren't supposed to…" He trailed off, then shook his head like a dog. He squinted and breathed in through clenched teeth, wiped his mouth with the back of his hand.

I'd never seen him like this. "Are you alright?" I asked.

"It's okay," he said yet again, this time to himself more than me. "Vie's onboarded a lot about synth restrictions and she says we're not even supposed to feel any of this, right? We don't do…this stuff. So it's stupid to begin with. And we're only…this is all only happening because Richelle mucked us up."

"Whoa, wait. What?"

"It doesn't matter. Look, she's got a feather for you and not for me. She probably thinks you've got more authentic…whatever." Wil's shoulders were bunched, his face was contorted. "You're the real… 'Cause you're human, which is…*wooo wooo*, you know. Way better than being a synth! So go for it. But," he added, finally looking at me again, "don't mess with her."

"Wil, I don't—"

"I'm serious," he continued. "We're friends, but she's my friend too. And she's not a companion synth, alright. Which I know you know, but. Yeah. So. And it's not like I think you'd…you know. But just don't! 'Cause she's…you know." He squinted at me, then added, "Right?"

The intensity of his stare now was almost frightening. He seemed to think his word salad had made perfect sense.

"Okay," I said, not knowing what else to say.

"Okay," he replied, then added, "It's okay." Pushing himself forward, he hopped down off the white storage tank. "Let's go."

CHAPTER 9

AS THE ELEVATOR ROSE THROUGH THE vitreous, I tried to think through what I might say, which was weird. I'd had a million conversations with Vie and I'd never had to prep for them before. Why should it be any different now? I needed to relax.

Wil and I had arrived back in the habitation hall to find it deserted. Wil wanted to check on Thius, but we discovered him missing from the kennel where I'd left him.

"Homestead, where is Thius?" I asked.

"The canine is on the exercise field."

The homestead knew Thius's name, but refused to use it. If it wasn't just emotionless computation, I'd think the homestead didn't like our dog.

"I'll...I'm gonna...I'm gonna get some shut eye," Wil had said, then quickly left.

It was only as he left that his reasoning caught up with me. If Thius was up on the field, Vie must be there too. Now I was wishing the elevator trip wasn't quite so quick. Wil thought Vie "had a feather" for me, but he could be pretty porous.

My wristwatch suddenly clicked and a burst of static came into my tragus speakers. When I pulled back the skin and looked at my watch, however, it was still inert.

The elevator irised open and I quickly let the magners snap my skin back into place. I'd investigate the watch later. I stepped out onto the field. Vie and Thius were at the far side. Thius must have heard the elevator iris open because he tore across the field toward me. When he saw it was me, however, he stopped, then turned and trotted back to Vie.

"Hey!" I called, insulted, but Thius didn't even look back.

Vie walked toward me, laughing. It was good to hear her laugh; there had been too little laughter recently. We met in the middle of the field.

"He's just tired," Vie said. "He looks fine, but I think he's still slow after the surgery." Vie tossed his stick. Thius ran after it half-heartedly.

"I ran him a bunch while you were sleeping," I said.

"Oh," she said. "Well."

We stood awkwardly.

"Did you find what you needed?" I asked. "About the genetic lines here?"

"I could only access the compressed raw data. I onboarded the files and I'm finishing the decompression now."

"What's that like?"

Vie shrugged. She didn't normally shrug. Was she nervous too?

"It's not really like anything…it's just a process," she said. "I usually do it while I'm sleeping."

I nodded as though that made sense. Thius hadn't brought the stick back, he had laid down with it between his paws, panting. Now he rolled over onto his side.

"He's pooped," she said.

"I threw a bunch of sticks for him earlier," I said, only then remembering I'd already told her that.

What an idiot.

Vie nodded. We both looked at the dog uncomfortably. Vie folded her arms, which she never did. She was definitely feeling awkward. Probably not as awkward as me, but still. It was kind of encouraging. Wil must be right. Which meant I should probably…what?

Vie looked up at the sky.

"I almost wish another one of those things would come down," I said. "So Telesis could track it and tell us what it was."

Vie cocked her head to one side like Thius and raised her eyebrows. "Hmm," was all she said.

"Any theories?" I asked.

"No," she said after a moment, before sitting down abruptly.

I sat down next to her. Vie ran her fingers through the turf. Thius came over and laid down next to her, rolling over and putting his legs in the air. She rubbed his furry belly.

"When I woke up I looked for you," she said. "I assume you were down in storage with Wil."

Wait, why was she saying that? She looked for me? What did that mean?

"He was pretty upset when I talked to him this morning," she continued. "And he's...heh." She smiled. "He's not very good at keeping things in. So I can guess what you two talked about."

Could she?

She reached over and tickled the hair between Thius's pads. Thius kicked and rolled away. Vie looked at me directly. "I'm a communications synth," she said. In response to my look she added, "I think Wil's wrong. We're synths. It doesn't make sense any other way."

I nodded, hoping she'd go on. I didn't know what to say. I tried to breathe normally. Thankfully, she continued.

"I'm a communications synth, which means I'm trained to work with human emotions from the outside. I'm trained to...recognize them. To work with them *as communication*."

It was odd to see her unsure of herself. She was struggling to make sense of what was happening as much as I was. She adjusted herself to face me directly, licked her lips, and tucked her hair behind her ear.

"I started my training before Richelle adopted me, so I...I recognize all this stuff. I just never expected to *feel* it. Neither did Wil," she added.

Was this the second half of a conversation she'd already had with Wil? Was this what had upset him so much?

Thius dropped the stick next to me. I lobbed it off to the side, just to get him away. I needed to focus on Vie. She was picking at the turf, struggling to say something.

"We're not—I'm not...human. And I'm not supposed to..." She trailed off, then laughed at herself for having such difficulty. She was rarely at a loss for words. I'd been a mess when my mother died, but she'd known exactly what to say, even at that difficult time. Now she was struggling.

"You seem human to me," I said. I regretted it immediately. Would she consider that an insult? I couldn't read her expression.

"I've got a lot more emotions than other synths, that's for sure. And Richelle told us...well, she told us some things would be different. But knowing about emotions is definitely different from feeling them."

"What do you mean?"

She laughed. "Well, I thought I understood human maturation and emotions and…everything. This process. I've had that data on board for a long time. But…understanding how a flood of hormones happens is different from feeling it. I never expected to feel it." She smiled self-consciously. "Synth hormones and emotions are usually more…contained. You know, engineered."

I tossed Thius's stick away again. Vie squinted up at the desert sun. The dome wasn't in place, and we had an unimpeded view of the cloudless blue.

I knew Vie and Wil hadn't had the glasses surgeries that older synths usually got. Richelle adopted them before it was done. But I thought it had all been for the good, to free them from the normal synth restrictions.

"I don't mean to be clinical about it," Vie continued, "but we are, all three of us, at that stage of development. So really, all of this is to be expected."

This was the oddest conversation I'd ever had. All of *what* was to be expected? She seemed to be referring to how we felt about one another, but we hadn't talked about that yet. Was she just talking about feelings generally? Or was this all about hormones?

"That doesn't diminish the way it feels, of course," she went on, smiling at me, "but…" She lapsed into silence.

But what? But *what*?

What was she talking about?

"What do you mean?" I finally prodded.

"Synths don't have the same adolescence. We have governors that shouldn't allow… I'm not supposed to feel this."

"But you do."

She looked at me and laughed. "Of course I do. Can't you tell? And it's not just surprising, it's…" She touched the sides of her head and groaned. "It's completely frustrating."

I agreed, but I still wanted to be sure we were talking about the same thing. "What do you mean?"

"Tab, you must know what I mean. The inability to think clearly when there's physical proximity; the sudden changes in body temperature; the confusion and doubt; the dreaming. The dreaming is *so* strange."

Synths were supposed to have darkling, not dreaming.

"You're dreaming?" I asked.

She nodded.

"What do you dream?"

"I'm not going to tell you my dreams!" She laughed again. The tension was finally fraying. "Good boy," she said to Thius, who had brought the stick to her this time. She lifted it and threw it, but he just watched it go, then laid down next to her again, panting. Vie laughed lightly and tousled his fur. "Anyway," she resumed, "I don't know if Richelle made changes long ago or if this is something new. Wil thinks there may have been something in our bernaculum baths."

"Richelle wouldn't have done that without telling you," I said. My heart was hammering away, but I was more confident. She was talking about how she had feelings for me.

Her hands were in her lap again. Feeling emboldened, I reached over and took one. As she looked up at me, Thius growled.

"Hey," I said, pretending to be offended but sounding angrier than I intended. Thius crouched lower and growled again.

"Why is this so hard?" Vie asked, patting Thius with her other hand.

"It's not," I said defensively. Her hand was warm.

"It is," she contradicted, but happily. "For me too. And I have data that tells me about it, but it's still so strange."

I didn't know what to say. Or do. I had her hand but…now what?

"It is hard to talk about," I admitted, looking down.

"Yes." She turned my hand over in both of hers and examined my palm. She traced one of the longer lines with a finger. Her jaw cast a shadow on her neck.

Why was I always thinking about her jawline? And her neck? And the way her hair moved?

On some freakish impulse, I leaned toward her. Miraculously, her jaw tilted, her mouth rotated, and our lips met.

Thius growled again.

I pulled back. Vie's eyes were smiling, but that background sadness was still there. Was it doubt?

I could feel my pulse in my hand. As though she had heard my thought, Vie held my hand tighter. "Tab, there are reasons we're—"

"I don't know how to do this either," I said, feeling like I didn't want to hear her speak and like I needed to hurry these words, "but I think you have to just do it...not talk about it."

That broke through. Vie smiled and pulled me to her again. She kissed me. It lasted longer, but when she pulled back she said, "You're going to need some practice."

"What?" I choked, embarrassed. What had I done wrong? I hadn't...

But Vie was already laughing. "No, Tab. I'm joking."

"How would you know anyway?" I said, relieved.

"I wouldn't," Vie admitted, smiling. "I need practice too."

It seemed like an invitation for another kiss. I leaned in, but Vie leaned back and checked my smile by adding, "And I'm not going to onboard any companion routines either, if you were hoping for a shortcut to...you know, better kissing."

"What? No." Did she really think I would ever want her to act like a companion synth? "No!"

"That was Wil's idea," said Vie, mock-confidentially. She laughed again. "He thought we both should do some 'research.' "

Wait, what did *that* mean?

Thius yelped impatience. I was confused enough that I used his presence as an excuse to break away from Vie, retrieving his stick and throwing it. What had she and Wil talked about? He'd suggested "research"? About what? Companion synth activities?

When I turned back I could see she had registered my discomfort. "It's not what you think," she explained. "We were just talking, we weren't talking about each other."

That made no sense.

"We were talking about how...different it is now, that's all," she said. She was uncomfortable again. So was I.

"And you do feel different?"

"Of course."

"About him too?" I asked on impulse.

Vie was taken by surprise. She took a deep breath and said, "Yes."

"Like you want to kiss him?"

"That's...I don't know, Tab." She took my hand again. "I *haven't* kissed him, alright."

"Did he try?" My chest was getting tight again, but in an entirely different way.

"I'm not sure we should talk about this."

"Why?"

"Because." When I waited for more of an explanation she said, "Because you're going to be unreasonable."

"I'm not being unreasonable." I let go of her hand. Why was she turning like this?

"Tab, do you know how many chemicals are working to override your logic systems right now?" Her smile was forced this time. "Me too. Both of us are being unreasonable."

"I'm not being unreasonable," I said. I could hear the petulance in my own voice, but I couldn't help it. "I'm just asking a question. *Did* he try to kiss you?"

"Why would you want to know that?" she asked. "What are you planning to do with the information?"

"I'll know more about what kind of a guy Wil is." Why was she defending him?

"Oh, Tab." Her voice veered toward condescension. "You've known Wil for years. You've got tens of thousands of data points—how is this one going to change anything?"

"This is not about data," I said. "And you're not...you're avoiding the question."

"He did, alright. But I told you, we didn't kiss."

"When?"

"Why does it matter?" she asked, then quickly continued. "Can you not see this is jealousy? This isn't going to help—"

"It'll help me understand what's going on."

"What's going on?"

"With you and me?"

"You know what's going on, Tab." She was becoming exasperated. "I just kissed you. That was my first kiss. Ever! Why would I do that if I wasn't..."

"But you feel that way about him too?"

She looked away as I stood. It was obvious: she wanted to kiss him too.

Vie unfolded her legs and also stood. "I'm not going to suddenly become enemies with Wil just because I'm…attracted to you." She reached for my hand again. "Please."

I stepped back. "Did I say you had to be enemies?" Why was she twisting my words around? "I wasn't saying…look, you're avoiding the question again."

Vie looked off to where Thius was snarfling along the track. The stick was at my feet. I hadn't noticed when he dropped it there.

"I have feelings for Wil, yes." Vie was serious and pained now. "Are they…romantic feelings? Am I attracted to him that way? I don't know, Tab. Honestly, I think so."

"You do?" How could she say that? Even if it was true, how could she say it right to my face like that? "Really?"

She was upset now. "It's not something I'm in control of. This is all new to me, I don't know. I don't think I'm *supposed* to know though. These are feelings, they're not… I don't know."

"You're supposed to know who you want to kiss!" I said.

"Are you? If there were other girls here, would you know? Is it possible you'd want to kiss more than one?"

"I'd only want to kiss *you*." I knew it was a lie even as I said it.

I wasn't going to take it back though.

Vie went to a functional cel on the pretense that she wanted to research more data on Thalinraya's fauna. Our trip down in the elevator was painfully silent. It really couldn't have gone any worse. She had kissed me, but then I'd…

What was wrong with me?

Now I was in the commons cel, trying to focus on my food. Thius was sacked out on a bench by the game table. His little tongue looked like a slug emerging from a whiskery hole.

My frustration wasn't helped by being so utterly useless. Wil was working on the opilion and Vie was onboarding research. I wasn't doing anything. The knot in my stomach tightened. I wanted to be *doing* something, not just sitting here going over my interpersonal failings.

What was I going to say to Vie? I had to apologize, but I wasn't sure what I was supposed to apologize for.

For generally being an idiot. That'd be a start.

I felt like a coiled spring, like a runner ready to start the race. I just didn't have a direction to run in yet.

Thius yelped. I sprang to my feet, only to see that Thius had done the same. The homestead had retracted the bench on which he'd been sleeping, dumping the poor dog on the floor. Thius looked around groggily for a target for his resentment, then sullenly circled, lay down under the table, and resumed sleeping.

I wished I could sleep.

A few minutes later the commons iris opened. Wil came in. He looked around, obviously wondering if Vie was here. Seeing that I was alone, he raised his chin in greeting and crossed to the cooking station.

"Two number four sannies," he said after touching the machine. Thius trotted over to greet him. "Down, beastie." When the dog was back on all fours, Wil bent to scratch behind his ears.

"Can you get me a tan?"

"Sure," Wil said, crossing to the drinker. "One tan, one green," he said. He retrieved the drinks and food and brought them to the table.

"Where's Vie?" he asked as he sat down across from me.

"In a fun cel onboarding more stuff," I said. Wil nodded and looked down too quickly. What did he suspect?

"Everything okay?" he asked casually, taking a bite of his sandwich.

I took a sip from my straw before answering.

"Well, it was… No. I'd say no. Nope." I figured I'd just put it out there. Wil was my friend, after all. "I had a talk with Vie and it…it was kind of a disaster."

Wil had stopped chewing. He was frozen, unsure how to react. His wide eyes darted around comically.

"Oh," he finally managed. He swallowed, took another bite and began chewing again, then decided to add, through a mouthful of food, "Shorry."

He clearly wasn't.

CHAPTER 10

"WE WERE ABLE TO RECOMMISSION AN outpost on Sissala," said Kiku, working the information in her desk as she spoke to us. Because the FaRcom cel was all interactive panel, it felt like we were there in Kiku's office, our chairs just across from her desk. She pushed her blond ponytail back behind her shoulder and continued. "Sissala is an asteroid out in the second belt. It's at the right angle for us to see the far side of that third moon." She looked directly at me. "There's no easy way to say this, Tab. I'm afraid your father's ship has been disabled by a meteor strike."

The air left the cel.

"He's alive," Kiku added, "but beyond that we don't know. We need more time." Kiku worked some data in her desk as she spoke. "Look here."

The smaller panels on either side of the FaRcom burped on. It was hard to focus, but I turned to the one on my right—a rectilinear hole floating in the larger panel showing Kiku's office. Now it displayed a grainy image of a moonscape seen from above. In one corner of the image next to a crater were some dark shapes. The resolution was so low and the shadows were so distorting that we couldn't really see what the shapes were.

"This is his landing site." Kiku touched the display in her desk and a red dot appeared on the images. She moved the dot to the largest of the shapes. "This is your father's drop ship and these spots here appear to be a debris field. There must have been an impact from this side." The spots extended a long way away from the ship; it must have been a huge explosion. My heart sank. I realized part of the resolution problem was my own, and I wiped my eyes so I could see more clearly.

Vie's hand was on my arm. She was looking over my shoulder; Wil was looking at the same image on the opposite panel.

"We've pinged him a bunch of times, but we're not getting anything back. There must be something wrong with his communication equipment."

"That's why he didn't get his beacon out," Wil said under his breath.

"What makes you think he's alive?" I asked.

Kiku continued. "Look here." The image was suddenly offset a few degrees. It happened again, then again. Kiku was running through a series of still photographs. "They started capturing images just after we got enough power from the QR net. Since then we've taken sixteen images, and data analysis shows there's movement. You can even see it—watch this bit here." The pointer hovered over a tiny oblong blob that shifted slightly from one image to the next, becoming more narrow and angular. "We did a spectral analysis and we're convinced there's still biological activity there."

"Meaning life?" I asked.

"Yes. Your father is still alive."

I let out a burst of air. Vie squeezed my arm, but I couldn't look at her yet.

"But you don't know if he's injured, right?" I managed.

"We can't say at this point," Kiku continued, "but we are going to do everything we can to get him assistance as soon as possible. And we're going to need your help. Are you up to it?"

The question was clearly directed at me, but I couldn't yet respond. My mind was glitching on thoughts of my father and the terrible situation he was likely in. An image of him without legs came to me. He was in terrible pain. He would have ended it himself if he could, but his arms just flailed wildly and ineffectually. I forced the image out of my mind, but it was quickly followed by a more distant scene—a man in a space suit crawling away from the wreck of a ship. His depleted air was already failing and he was gasping his last ragged breath on a frozen, desolate moon. He collapsed onto his side, rolled over and looked up at the unfamiliar, indifferent stars as his eyes grew dull.

"We're up to it," Wil answered.

"Are you alright?" asked Kiku. Her look more than her question brought me back to myself. I didn't want her pity—I wanted to help my father. Well, I wanted to have never left Telesis and I wanted my mother to be alive and I wanted a billion other things that were impossible too, but for the moment I only wanted to do what I could to help my father.

"I'm not alright, but I can do this," I said. "What needs to get done?"

Kiku smiled admiringly, which was just condescending enough to really anger me. She explained to us how they would work remotely to collect data on my father's situation. "In the meantime," she said, "I need for you there to get your backup drop ship ready to go to that moon."

"It's good to go," said Wil quickly.

"According to the inventory, it doesn't have fuel yet," corrected Kiku. "Your homestead only had enough Nickies for the one jump ship. I'm afraid you're going to need to get more."

"What's a 'Nickie'?" I asked.

"NIyeDcs," said Kiku awkwardly. "They're fuel rods of valence compressed, e-delocalized nickel used in bolt drives. Nickies sustain the adiabatic U-envelope closure."

There was an awkward moment when she stopped talking, unsure if her explanation was complete. She'd been spewing information even she didn't understand. Now she seemed to be listening to something subvocally.

Something weird was going on. Vie seemed to be holding her breath.

"How do we make a Nickie?" asked Wil, breaking the bubble of tension.

"You don't need to," said Kiku, relieved to be back to an explanation she could understand. "You just need to go get them. They're made at an autonomous facility north of you, at V-12."

"We've seen that!" said Wil with enthusiasm. "We can get there, no problem."

"Thank you." Kiku spoke this directly to Wil, who might have blushed. "We're not going to be able to fly the gravion yet. That's why we asked you to reengineer the opilion again."

"Done," said Wil.

"Okay." Kiku turned to Vie. "Now, there are some EMR anomalies around V-12 we're going to want to look at as you approach the facility there. I assume you'll be willing to alter some of your communication augments for that purpose."

Vie had an absent expression, almost as though she were processing something herself.

"Vie," I said, shocking her out of her trance. "You'll do it, right?"

"Sorry," she said, smiling an apology. "Of course." Turning back to Kiku she said, "You say TaleXal's ship was hit by a meteor. Could it have been something else—something like what came down here?"

"They were meteors. A meteor shower came through the system."

After an incredulous moment, Vie asked, "You think those were meteors?"

"No way," Wil offered. "Both of those things changed direction. Meteors don't do that."

"I didn't see, but I suspect they broke apart in some way that made it *look* like they changed direction."

I thought back to what we had seen. It was nothing like that. Vie's posture indicated she felt the same way.

"They really seemed more like ships," Vie said. "Is it possible there were any in the area?"

"No," she replied automatically. It was an odd, hurried response.

Wil squinted confusion over at Vie. "But," he said, turning back to Kiku, "at least the second one had these…buds on top of it. And some kind of propulsion system. It didn't just turn—it accelerated after the turn."

Kiku gestured off screen, then looked at some information in her desk. When she saw that we were still waiting for a response, she closed her eyes for a moment before speaking. "There is a remote possibility that what you saw…was one of our own terraforming inception ships."

"What?" exclaimed Wil.

"A terraforming seed," she said, using the Feremite term. "I'm telling you this because it's a possibility, but it's a million to one against it." She took a deep breath and grudgingly continued. "Fifteen cycles after you left Telesis a new generation of seeds was sent out and it may be the coordinates got…mixed up. We're looking into it and we'll have more information in a little while. But until then," she continued, her tone hardening, "I suggest you concentrate on what's important. We need to get to Tab's father *as soon as we can.* I understand you're curious about this other incident, but if you can put that curiosity aside until we've got him back, I think we'd all benefit."

That shut Vie down. She looked an apology at me. I wanted to tell her I wasn't offended, but Kiku continued.

"I will send particulars to you," she indicated Vie, "about how to capture and process the EMR data."

"Process?" asked Vie. "Won't the homestead do that?"

"You will not be in contact with the homestead. We need to get this done as quickly as possible, we can't wait for the QR net to be fully powered up. That could take days."

"But the readings won't change. Could I collect the—"

"I'm trying not to lose patience," said Kiku, obviously having already lost it, "but if you keep questioning me, I'm not going to be able to help you."

Vie looked at the floor of the FaRcom cel, which was rendering even the rug in Kiku's office with perfect fidelity. "I'm sorry," she said.

"She's only trying to make sure we know what we're doing here," I said to Kiku.

"I understand, but I have duties too. I need to get to those, and I can't until I've got you three going."

"We're ready," I said.

"Okay," said Kiku, bringing up a holo from her desk and projecting it on our side panels as well. "This is V-12. The nickel enrichment station sits..."

We already knew much of what she told us, but we didn't interrupt her again. We'd seen V-12. It rose above the range of mountains to the north of the homestead, even though it was vastly more distant. It was the largest volcano on the planet.

As she spoke, I thought about what Kiku had said about the terraforming seeds. She'd downplayed the possibility, but I wondered if Wil and Vie were aware just how dangerous they might be. Terraforming seeds begin Stage One, on *uninhabited* planets. Whatever life already exists on the planet needs to be standardized, brought back to a level from which appropriate, targeted life—life sanctioned by the Unicon and patented by a corporation—can be grown. Usually this means stripping things back to single-celled organisms.

We were not single-celled organisms. Which meant that if those things *were* terraforming seeds... Telesis may have inadvertently sent machines that would kill us.

I decided to wait on sharing that tidbit.

Kiku continued her instructions, most of which made Wil even more excited to go. The facility where the nickies were manufactured was underground, next to an ancient asteroid impact site. Navigating a volcano, burrowing down to an underground facility, engineering the opilion to do it all—this was a dream for Wil, engaging all his earliest mining augments. Kiku couldn't have given him better motivation.

Wil was on his way out of the FaRcom cel, Thius barking excitedly at his heels, before I had finished signing off to Telesis. When I had done so, I turned to follow. Vie hadn't spoken for a long while; now I noticed she hadn't moved either. She seemed to be accessing some internal information.

"We should get going," I said. She came back to herself and smiled. It was an odd smile. I opened my mouth to ask her about it, but she abruptly stood, shook her head at me ever so slightly, and left the cel.

I was missing something.

CHAPTER 11

WE RACED UP THE RANGE OF HILLS behind the homestead. We'd been traveling for about twenty minutes in our upgraded opilion. The main difference, so far as I could tell, was that the orb in which we rode was more solid. There was less clear space for the irises and more metal framework, which, I assumed, encased more elaborate machinery: computers and gears, assemblers and precursor materials for whatever the opilion might need to build on the fly.

From the homestead we had angled west and then north into an unfamiliar region. In the creases of the hills were clumps of trees of a sort I hadn't seen. Tiny branches fanned out from the crowns of squat little trunks, and the feathery leaves they held aloft seemed like afterthoughts.

"Almost at the summit," Wil said excitedly.

"Oh," said Vie, remembering something suddenly, "did either of you put Thius away?"

"I configured the exercise cel for him," I said. It was one of the only useful things I'd done.

"With the wheel?" asked Wil over his shoulder.

"Tentacles this time," I said.

"Oh, he hates those things," said Vie, turning back to the data in her panel.

"The homestead won't let him get too worked up," I replied, more defensively than I intended.

Vie had been unreadable since our kiss, and I couldn't tell whether it was because of that or something else. She'd been odd with Kiku too, when we'd been getting our final instructions for the trip to V-12.

Kiku had called us into the FaRcom cel. Wil's enthusiasm for the trip was so exaggerated, I wondered if it was his natural passion for adventure or if he was energized by the fact that I'd blown it with Vie. Maybe I shouldn't have told him.

When Kiku asked him about the reengineering he'd done to the opilion—in his excitement, Wil had obviously done a great deal more than was necessary—Vie saw his discomfort and covered for him, redirecting the conversation. It was a kind thing to do, but I couldn't help feeling that she was taking his side somehow. And when Kiku told us that the satellites couldn't yet provide communications while we were traveling, Vie and Wil shared a moment.

"I guess that means we're on our own," Vie said. "You okay with that?"

"We got this," he said.

Only then had Vie turned to me, like she'd just remembered I was there. "You?"

"I'm good," I had said.

I couldn't help wincing at the memory even now, as we raced north in Wil's tricked-out opilion. I felt like baggage. Wil was driving, Vie was poring over different information sets, oblivious to me, and I was... admiring the view.

I pinched my nose to adjust the pressure in my ears. We were about to crawl over a saddle between two gentle peaks that formed the summit of the range. Wil was having the time of his life. He looked ahead, eagerly anticipating more difficult terrain that would allow him to make use of more of the opilion's systems.

There proved to be a wide, flat section at the top of the saddle, but once across it we had a panoramic view north over multiple ranges. Still in the far distance, the V-12 volcano was clearly visible.

We began making quicker progress when Wil casually mentioned that we would be at the impact site in about ten minutes.

Impact site?

"What?" I was quicker to ask than Vie, but she too was taken by surprise.

"We're going right by where that thing, whatever it was, came to ground."

"How do you know?" Vie asked.

Wil gestured at his display, saying "I mapped it."

"It's not safe, Wil," said Vie, looking at the map. "We have no idea what that thing was."

"Kiku said it was a meteor. Or a terraforming seed."

"Which would be dangerous!" Vie cried. "And it might be something else, something even *more* dangerous. We don't know."

"We'll know soon," said Wil.

"No, Wil. Go around. This is reckless." Vie appealed to me with a look, but I just shrugged, not wanting to get in the middle. I noted wryly to myself that this was the first time she'd looked at me since we'd gotten into the opilion. It didn't seem like very good communication for a communication synth. When she aimed her ire forward again, I was even more glad I hadn't intervened. She'd defended Wil pretty forcefully to Kiku, and it was nice to be reminded she didn't always take his side.

"You don't want to know what's there?" asked Wil.

"Not enough to die to find out!"

"Oh, we're not going to die." Wil had clearly been waiting for this. "Watch."

I had seen the pebbled look to the opilion's exterior when we got in, but I hadn't really thought about it. Now, the narrow irises of the opilion went opaque as the exterior exploded outward. Thousands of thumb-sized hovercraft launched away from the opilion and formed a cloud around the still-moving vehicle. I had seen something like this in a few simulations back on Telesis. These tiny drones, called sophies, not only created a protective barrier, they were also armed with lasers to shoot anything that threatened the opilion.

"Wil!" Vie's voice was unreadable; it could have been admiration or horror.

I was definitely in admiration mode. The swarm of drones was amazing. "What are those?" I asked, pointing to antennae, which had sprouted all around the exterior of the opilion.

"The marconis? I'm not sure," Wil said enthusiastically.

"Not sure?" Vie said, dumbfounded.

"There's different kinds. I'm not sure which kind automatically deploy. Hang on." He was adjusting his instrument panel again, but Vie was quicker. She manipulated a panel in the side wall next to her, which quickly lit up with several displays.

"They're shepherding monopoles," she said after a few seconds of research.

"Oh," said Wil. He looked out the front. "Yeah."

Vie rolled her eyes. "Call the sophies back at least," she said. "If we need them we'll want their batteries full."

Shocked at Vie's change of tone, Wil did as instructed. There was a sound like metallic rain as the things reattached themselves.

"So...we're going by the site?" I asked.

Wil looked back to Vie to see if she was going to object. For a tense moment we all swayed in our hammocks, assessing one another silently. I could tell that in addition to everything else, Vie was weighing Wil's feelings. They'd had some difficult conversations recently, without subvocals. And she'd refused to kiss him and told him she had a feather for me, whatever that meant. Denying him this would be salt in his wounds.

"Might as well," she said. "But let's do it right. We want to gather as much information as we can. And we can't linger. We have a job to do."

Wil smiled thanks and relief, then started checking and rechecking gear in the opilion's cockpit. Vie went back to her own displays. She didn't look at me.

We slowed as we approached the crash site, a vicious gash in a north-facing slope. Vie began calling out readings—electrical activity, temperature, chemical composition. There was nothing out of the ordinary, which seemed somehow ominous.

Wil warned us he was taking precautions. The irises closed, replaced by window-like panel displays of what was outside. Unseen gears in the fuselage went to work, the floor and ceiling of the opilion inflated slightly. Was he anticipating an impact of some kind?

Wil grew a forward window and we all looked away from our displays to see the actual scene. It looked like whatever had come to ground had skipped off the top of a ridge a quarter of a kilometer to the south, where a twenty-meter-long trench had been gouged. The scar was a meter-deep arrow pointing to the main impact site. Ejecta was scattered all up and down the slope and heaped up around the crater, the uneven lip of which obscured the view of whatever might be inside.

"Anything?" asked Wil.

Vie toggled through several displays before answering. "Not on any spectrum I can see. No heat, no motion, nothing."

"I'm not seeing anything either," he replied.

"But if it's a seed, wouldn't there be something?" Vie asked, looking back at me.

"Yeah," I said. I didn't remember a lot of the specifics about terraforming seeds, but I knew the basics. "Are there any heavy metals?"

"Lots. But that could be a meteor too."

"No EM activity?" I asked.

"None," they both said simultaneously.

"If this was a terraforming seed, it would have started clearing away all the plants by now," I said, noting the bushes all around the impact site. "There would be assemblers too. Also," I said, looking at the landscape through the window displays and realizing something as I was saying it, "it wouldn't have landed here."

"Why not?" asked Wil.

"Well, there are protocols. The Auger Station is where it is because of its function. Terraforming seeds usually start in liquid—seas, if there are any. It gives them easier access to resources, better mobility, and it's almost always closer to where life standardization needs to begin."

"You're not as porous as you look," Wil said, flashing me a wry smile before returning his attention to the scene ahead of us. "We should get closer."

As dangerous as this was likely to be, Vie limited her input to: "Go slowly."

It was odd that Vie agreed to this so readily; she was normally much more cautious.

The opilion, now rolling over treads that wrapped the wheels, crept forward slowly, deliberately. The effect, unfortunately, was to heighten everyone's anxiety. Every slight bump made me grip the edges of my hammock chair more tightly. It took ten excruciating minutes to travel those last meters to the crater, but no sensors registered anything.

When we were about eight meters away from the lip of the crater Vie whispered, "Those things on the outside aren't equipped with visuals, are they?"

"No," Wil replied, apologetically.

Vie looked forward at the crater. "I wish we could use gravion drones."

"Oh!" Wil shouted.

"What?" I cried, mistaking his outburst for alarm and flinching.

Vie had read his tone more quickly. "Don't do that," she said.

"Sorry, I just remembered I put in some mining systems. I'm brilliant!"

Wil was already reaching all around the cockpit, working controls. The ceiling of the opilion thickened for a moment. Assemblers chittered and clicked, then the monitors switched to a new view, the video feed coming from an instrument cluster at the tip of a pole that was extending forward from the opilion.

"It's like a gather drone but it doesn't fly, it's attached," Wil explained in hushed tones as we all watched the approaching lip of the crater in the panel monitor. "They use them in mining operations. I had the specs, so."

"What's that?" Vie asked, referring to the video. "Angle it down."

The video pole was over the lip of the crater. The earth all around and within had been melted to a smooth black glass. It looked like hardened liquid, blanketing the tumble of rocks there. I was expecting to see a ship, satellite, or some sort of assembling gear at the bottom, but there was nothing.

The crater itself was about twenty meters across and a similar depth. The fact it was uniformly black now made it hard to distinguish the shapes inside, but as our eyes adjusted it appeared there was more structure to it than there ought to have been.

"Is that a tunnel?" Wil was pointing to a darker patch on the north side, at the base of the crater. Vie was already manipulating her monitor, using the instrument cluster to call up additional information.

"It is. Hang on." Vie scrolled through screen after screen of technical readouts. As she did this, Wil cycled the image of the tunnel through several visualizations, finally resting on a wire-frame visual that clearly showed the funnel shape of the crater leading to the opening.

"Soooo..." said Vie, "this is weird."

"'Weird?' That's your informed analysis?" asked Wil sarcastically.

Vie ignored him. "The black all around. That's not melted rock. It's some kind of carbon fiber material impregnated with iridium and some other stuff I can't distinguish. It's like a cloth."

"Interactive?" asked Wil.

"I...can't tell. Definitely not natural though. Something made this."

We looked at one another as this sank in.

Something intelligent had come to ground here.

"Does this look like a terraforming seed?" Wil asked.

"No," I said. "I've never heard of anything like this in terraforming or anywhere else."

What could be the possible use of covering the impact area with cloth? What could a gigantic blanket all around the crater be good for?

"Some kind of satellite dish?" asked Wil.

"I don't think so," replied Vie. "It's not the right shape and it's not directable. Also, it's not wired, so far as I can tell. No EM activity."

"It's like a giant spider web," I said.

Wil turned back to the wireframe diagram. It really did look like the funnel of a spider web. I could almost imagine a giant, many-eyed monster lurking in the hole at the base of the crater.

Wil swiped through a few screens, then reported to Vie, "I can get through it with ground penetrating radar, no problem. But it's just soil and rock under there."

"Strange." Vie was flummoxed.

"Could we cut off a sample of it?" I asked.

"I don't think cutting and slashing is in order yet," said Vie.

"I didn't say anything about slashing," I said defensively.

"Radar shows the tunnel extends at least six kilometers to the north," said Wil. Vie examined Wil's display, then brought up another. Then another.

The two of them exchanged further information for another five minutes. Whatever had landed had burrowed north, leaving behind some kind of super strong fabric that wasn't of a sort any of us had ever seen before. There was no electromagnetic activity.

"And you're sure this isn't some terraforming thing?" asked Wil, finally remembering I was there.

"No," I barked. Feeling frustrated and unable to restrain myself, I added, "Can we get up to the cache at V-12? We need those nickies for the backup jump ship to get to my dad."

Vie looked horrified. "I'm so sorry, Tab. Of course." She turned off her display and said to Wil, "We've got readings we can share with Telesis when we get back. Let's get going."

Vie's guilt was oddly satisfying.

"Okay, but—" began Wil. Vie cut him off.

"No Wil, we need to go."

"Okay, just give me a minute. It's almost ready."

"What's almost ready?" I asked, but the opilion was already dipping down to the ground. Gears had been growling at the back of the pod for some time. Now they struck a lower note.

"Don't open an iris," said Vie, looking back. "We don't know if it's safe."

"I'm not. It's just a hog."

Something heavy dropped from the underside of the opilion's pod, which lifted again to its normal height while rolling backward a few meters.

Wil looked eagerly forward; Vie and I followed his gaze. On the ground in front of the opilion was an oblong metallic object about two meters in length. A spiral pattern ran its length, and in the depths of the curving grooves there seemed to be some kind of scintillating liquid.

"What is that?"

"That," said Wil with obvious pride in his voice, "is a TC-coriolis driven H-O-G."

"Oh, well," I said, "I've always wanted to see one of those."

"I know, right!" said Wil, missing my sarcasm.

"What does it do?" Vie asked.

"Underground it'll do anything you want. Bore, drill, map veins of any kind. It'll clean and repair pipes or tunnels, lozenge a mineral farm. It can work as security. These things are amazing. I never thought I'd get to see one, much less…" He trailed off, gazing down at the thing in a mining synth's reverie.

"Wil," prompted Vie, "what's it for?"

"Hmm?" said Wil. "Oh. To explore the tunnel."

Wil pulled down another control panel and manipulated a few virtual switches. The spirals on the hog folded out in a fanning pattern, extending tens of thousands of short needles that made the thing look like a giant, hairy seed. But a scintillating and oddly dangerous seed. It floated a few inches above the ground now, lifted up by the spiral of hairs underneath. Wil did something else and the hairs started moving down their spiral tracks, rolling the thing forward. It corkscrewed like an acrobatic milli-pede, spiraling as it went, the hairs rolling into contact with the soil and pushing the thing forward. It quickly gained speed.

"How fast can it go?" I asked.

"I'll bet it can go as fast as us," Wil bragged.

"In the ground? Really?"

"Not underground, but in a tunnel. Hang on, let me finish the directives here." Wil pulled the control panel closer, fiddled with some dials and switches, then pushed the panel away.

"Ladies and gentlemen, this is the story of the great H-O-G explorer. Go hog go!"

Out the window we saw the hog stop briefly and spin until one of the tapered ends was aimed at the hole. The fanning legs seemed to ripple in anticipation, but a moment later it was speeding toward the opening, its football-spiraling motion making it a furry blur. It slowed slightly when it came to the black fabric surrounding the entrance, but it adjusted to the new surface and quickly regained speed.

A moment later it was gone, disappearing into the mysterious black maw.

Wil looked at the readouts. "It can't tell what that material is either. It's got carbon, iridium, bauxite, and condensed…what's a plasmon?"

Vie looked over at me.

"Really?" I asked. "You think I would know that?"

Vie turned back to Wil. "It doesn't tell you?"

"It tells me they're there, not what they are," he said, adding, "I'd probably have onboards for this kind of stuff if I'd finished my training."

"It records it though, right?" asked Vie.

"It's mapping the tunnel in 360 degrees with composition data for every square centimeter."

"And it's doing its own thing, right?" I asked. "You don't need to monitor it?"

"No," he replied, "it's on an autopilot mapping expedition. It treats it as a pipeline. It'll explore branchings until I recall it, then it'll meet us back here. We can pick it up on our way back."

"Okay," I said, "let's go."

We raced north with a new urgency. The souped-up opilion was much faster than the previous one, and as we crossed range after range, V-12 getting larger each time, we discussed what we had seen.

Vie thought it might be some new terraforming technology I was unaware of. Wil thought it was alien. I pointed out how unlikely that was: there had always been rumors of intelligent alien life, but the inconvenient fact was none had ever been found. He suggested it might be the Carve. This was a rumor that someone had built a computer that had escaped into another dimension and freed itself. Now it was gathering resources and preparing to come back to our dimension to take over.

Vie thought it was all nonsense.

Wil broke off our conversation when we came to a wide glacial valley. At a massive watercourse, Wil instructed the opilion to grow pontoons and we made terrific time, roaring up the wide, blue-white glacial river. Waterfalls cascaded out of the highlands on either side of the valley. It was exhilarating.

Vie asked about the status of Wil's hog, and he called up its location.

"Wow, it's only about six clicks east of us."

"Now?" asked Vie, doubtfully. "How can that be?"

"Must be where that tunnel goes."

"So...whatever came to ground went straight to the same volcano we're going to?"

"Seems like it," said Wil. He didn't think it strange, but Vie was concerned.

We came onto the glacier itself without slowing, climbing up the snow and ice, racing across crevasses, skirting a summit peak and heading down the north slope. It took several hours to descend the rockier northern slopes, where we had to navigate huge fields of broken slabs of ice. By the time we hit the sea ice it was already getting dark. The sun sinking over the endless plain of ice to our left made the light here ethereal. V-12 loomed over us, its shadow dark in the darkening sky. The opilion grew enormous spiked wheels and we raced faster than we ever had.

"Where's the hog now?" asked Vie.

Wil called it up. "We got slowed down by the mountains, so it got ahead of us. We'll catch it though," he said.

"Where is it?"

"Abooout...thirty-eight clicks north-northeast aaand...a quarter click down."

"In the water?" I asked. "It's swimming?"

"Oh. Hang on." Wil realized this was odd. "No, it's not in liquid. It's still surrounded by that weird fabric."

"In the water? How is that possible?"

Vie brought up some schematics of the northern ocean. There were no shallow areas, no hidden banks. The underwater topography was normal. And deep.

"Its systems are working fine," Wil assured us. "It's in the tunnel."

"Something built a tunnel that goes all the way through the ocean?" said Vie suspiciously. "How is it suspended in the water?"

"Could the tunnel have already been there?" I asked.

"And whatever came down knew exactly where to land?" said Vie, incredulous. "I don't think so. Whatever came down must have made the tunnel as it traveled north."

"How could it do that?" Wil asked, more impressed than concerned.

"I have no idea," Vie responded. "We don't even know what the tunnel is made from."

"Maybe we'll find out when we get to the volcano," I said. "Whatever it is seems to have gone there ahead of us."

It wasn't a comforting thought.

CHAPTER 12

THE FLANK OF V-12 WAS A scree of frozen pumice and ash.

Vie and I had had some fitful sleep as we raced across the ice through the night. Now Wil had woken us and we were all alert in the early dawn as we made our way around the shoulder of V-12. Ice boulders larger than the opilion dotted the landscape. They were round as marbles and it appeared they formed higher on the slopes of the volcano somehow, rolling down the mountainside until their momentum was spent. I kept looking up and to the right, despite Wil's assurances that the opilion would alert us to any danger.

"Where's the hog?" Vie asked as we sped along, slower now that we were off the sea ice.

"Slowed way down now. Twenty clicks east-northeast."

"Why'd it slow?"

"The tunnel's curving around a lot."

"Did that start when it met the continental shelf?"

"I don't know. Let me do an overlay."

Wil never got to the overlay. A shrieking alarm went off in the opilion.

"What's...?" Vie saw Wil was already in action, so she left off.

Wil manipulated his controls for a moment, then, without looking back, shouted, "Something's coming fast from the south. Airborne." He switched off the alarm.

"What is it?" asked Vie.

"No idea. It's huge. It's...wait."

"Wait?" exclaimed Vie? "Wait for what?"

"It's got no propulsion system," said Wil, confused and concerned. His eyes were darting from one panel to another.

"Another meteor?" I asked.

"I don't know," Wil said angrily, opening a new control panel.

We all swung in our hammock chairs as the opilion stopped abruptly. Machines whirred and visors extended out over the irises, folding down and enclosing us in complete darkness. We heard the pebbled exterior come apart, the sophies bursting outward. Our hammocks cinched up and rewrapped us in protective harnesses. We all gasped as we sensed the craft falling.

"It's alright, it's burrowing," said Wil.

That explanation was enough to set my mind's eye spinning. The opilion was *burrowing*?

Lights sprang on in the interior, the panel displays brightened. Wil deployed the pole again and a screen at the front of the opilion showed an image of the southeast sky, where pre-dawn indigo was beginning to bleed into the dark between the stars.

"What's that?" I asked.

The image was zooming in on a section of the sky. It appeared empty at first, but a black dot appeared and quickly grew. Watching it on the screen and knowing it was happening just outside made it seem more dangerous somehow. A drop of sweat trickled down my back.

"It's getting hot," Vie said. So it wasn't only me.

"I'm having the opi melt a blast cocoon," said Wil.

Vie glanced over at me, then back to the screen. The black image was growing larger but, annoyingly, the image kept zooming back as it did. It wasn't quite large enough to make out its shape.

"Can you tell what it is?" Vie asked.

Wil was working his panel. "It's running parallel to the surface. No propulsion system I can read, but it's fast and not slowing." He ran his fingers through his spikey red hair.

"Coming at us?" I asked.

"Trajectory's a little to our east for now," Wil replied.

Whatever it was had come close enough that the camera couldn't move back any more, and the image of the thing grew. There seemed to be a narrow wedge of darkness running in advance of it. A gravity trail? It sped toward and past the camera so quickly the image was gone before I got my words out.

"That's a gravion."

"I think you're right," said Vie.

The image was swinging around to catch the receding ship.

"Didn't they say those weren't working?" asked Wil.

The gravion was racing toward the volcano.

"They must have just fixed it," I said.

"Who's flying it?" asked Vie concernedly. We were, after all, the only people on the planet.

Unless my father had returned, I suddenly realized. There was a tightening in my chest.

"Can they take off on auto?" asked Wil, turning to look at me.

"Yeah," I said, remembering they'd probably been in use here for hundreds of years.

"Even if it could," said Vie, "why would it—"

She didn't finish her question. The gravion disappeared into the side of the volcano. A flash temporarily blinded the camera, then the image returned.

None of us spoke. A cascade of rocks fell from where the gravion had disappeared. After a moment we heard a muffled, distant explosion.

"What...what just happened?" It was a stupid question, but my mind couldn't take in what we'd just seen.

"It crashed," Wil said simply.

"There couldn't have been anyone on there," Vie said, looking quickly at me. An image came to me of my father returning to the empty homestead, getting into a gravion to race after us, losing control and...

No.

"No, there was nobody onboard," Wil confirmed, consulting some data on his panel. "They must have been running it remotely from Telesis."

"Why though?" asked Vie.

"Something wrong at the homestead maybe?" Wil speculated. "Or maybe they just got them working and sent it to try to help us. To get us back faster."

"Why didn't they com us then?" asked Vie. She called up a display. "Com is still down. If they have the satellites working enough to get the gravion going, they should be able to contact us. Look." Vie gestured at her panel, which clearly showed no com systems had been activated.

Wil worked quickly on several panels in the cockpit at once. The noises outside the opilion changed, and in a moment we were lurching upward. There was a cracking sound.

"What's that?" I asked.

"Shedding the blast cocoon," explained Wil.

Irises appeared all around, and now we had a clear view of V-12. We all looked north, past our own hovering sophies to where smoke was beginning to rise up from the crash site.

It was just a distant scar on the side of the volcano, but it had been a gravion, perhaps the very gravion my father and I rode in to the atmospheric scrubbers. It made no sense. The gravions couldn't work unless the satellites were functioning. But if the satellites were functioning, Telesis ought to be able to contact us.

"And you're not getting anything from the satellites?" I asked Vie. She was flipping quickly between different displays.

"No, nothing."

"What's that?" Wil was pointing up toward the crash site.

Something was shimmering over the crash site. An iridescent curtain of light dipped down into the smoke then rose again, as though probing. Another tendril of light darted down and branched out, encircling something. A moment later it retracted up again to rejoin the larger curtain, which wavered and abruptly flew sideways.

"What is that thing?" I asked.

"Wil?"

He was looking confusedly at his panel. "It's not reading as anything. It's...a magnetic anomaly. An electrical storm or...I can't tell."

The thing wavered sideways again. The cloud cover over the volcano behind it began to glow.

"Whoa, what's happening now?"

"That's...that can't..." There was awe in Wil's voice.

"Can't what?" Vie demanded. "What is it?"

"Is it erupting?" I asked.

Wil was already working the controls. The opilion leapt to life: the sophies surged further from our pod, the wheels spun, rocks and blast shell fragments flew. We lurched south, back the way we'd come. The hammocks didn't have time to adjust, and Vie and I crashed into one another.

Wil's cockpit, controls and all, rotated around the inside of the pod to place him at the now south-facing front—a movement I'd never seen before. This left the iris at the north-facing rear of the pod open, and my view of the volcano was unobstructed. What had panicked Wil on his readouts was becoming clear.

Something like an aurora vomited up from the volcano's summit, arcs and fans and ribbons of light bursting skyward. The light quickly broke apart, but it didn't dissipate, it…condensed into different colored scarves that began to pour down the volcano's sides. This was no lava, it was…a cascade of lights. What could be holding them together? Something technological and sinister, I realized. I'd never seen anything like it, but the movement was intentional and the direction was unmistakable: whatever they were, these things were coming for us. Some were flanking us to the east and west, but most were streaming down the slope straight south in our direction. It was both beautiful and terrible.

"This is the story of a hasty retreat," Wil growled through gritted teeth. "Hang on!"

"Wait, what—"

Vie's question was cut off by the sound of a hydrogen drive kicking on at the rear of the opilion, its distinctive high-pitched whine filling the pod. We surged forward more quickly, the wheels beneath us swelling larger. Swinging wildly around the interior of the opilion, we hung onto our hammock chairs as Wil dodged through the garden of huge ice boulders.

It was bouncing chaos for a minute, and deafening as the pod cycled through some noise-cancellation before it found the right frequency and the sound of the engine quieted. We were racing back toward the frozen flatness of the ice sheet, leaving behind a whirl of color. It was as though the northern lights had come to malign life. Smaller darts of light began shooting back from the sophies, which flew around the opilion in a protective cloud. The lasers did nothing, however, passing through the pursuing curtains of light with no effect.

"The sophies aren't working," I said.

Wil nodded and made some adjustment. A moment later one of the sophies arced around and rocketed back toward the flock of things following us. When it came into contact with one of the scarves of light, it erupted. The explosion pulsed outward as nearby scarves also exploded.

More distant scarves juked to the side, evading the rippling explosions, and continued after us.

It looked like an immersive game. A deadly one.

More sophies began dropping back.

"What are those things?" Vie asked urgently.

"No idea." Wil didn't even look up from his controls. Whatever they were, they were getting closer. There were more explosions, but there were many, many more of the scarves of light.

Tubes grew up from the top of the opilion. Wil was working on some secondary defenses.

"Your explosives are working at least," Vie said encouragingly.

"Those aren't my explosives," said Wil. "Those are recallable sophies. They're supposed to pierce and return. The explosions are from those things."

Vie pulled her own panel down and started doing calculations of her own.

The opilion was going faster now than I'd ever seen. The gears for the hammock barely kept up with the cornering and the tethers were continuously paying out and retracting to compensate, causing us to bungee around the interior as the machine dodged ice boulders. Out the back I could see the scarves getting closer. They were more distinct than I had thought at first. Some were uniformly translucent sheets of luminous color, but others had patterns to them, or tangled ribbons of deeper color within color. Some streamed forward with a single shape, like folded paper airplanes; others morphed constantly. Still others rolled over and over themselves, like newspapers tossed in a whirlwind. They might have been beautiful if they hadn't been so menacing.

And gaining on us.

The opilion bounced down onto the ice and, without the rocks and ravines to negotiate, picked up speed. But the explosions in the air were getting closer, and our increased speed wasn't outpacing them. In a few minutes we'd be overwhelmed.

"They're catching us," I warned.

"Not for long," said Wil, and he did something to make the flock of sophies part behind us. Projectiles launched out of the pipes on the opilion's roof and the entire sky was filled with flashes and flares, the explosions concentrating behind us. But just as soon as they appeared they began to fade, and through the falling amber sparks the pursuing scarves of light raced on, unimpeded.

"How can they… Shunt!"

Wil clearly thought that would hold them off longer. He pulled a different panel up and quickly went to work on something else.

"Wil, can you see their attenuation rate?" asked Vie urgently.

"I don't even know what that is," he shouted back.

"I think they're just…EM sachets." Knowing that meant nothing to either of us, Vie tried again. "Self-enveloping electrical fields, just… computational bundles riding the humidity. Which would make them substrate dependent for now."

"I'm working on something here," said Wil dismissively.

"I think we should dive," Vie urged.

"Dive?" I asked.

The air exploded just outside the opilion. The scarves were coming at us from the sides now as well. We were almost surrounded, and we were running out of sophies.

"Beneath the ice. They won't be able to reach us there."

"Go, go, *go!*" shouted Wil, and a half-kilometer to the west the ice exploded upward.

Wil's hog flew a few meters into the air, then came alive with spinning lasers. I'd completely forgotten it; Wil must have redirected it. Before it landed again it was flinging lasers in all directions, creating visual chaos. It started racing north, lobbing explosives as it went, creating its own little war zone.

The scarves on that side of the opilion turned and raced after it. It had a head start though, and its weird, spiraling needles were carrying it north. It was racing in the opposite direction from us, back toward the volcano.

"I set it for the caldera," shouted Wil. "I hope it tears the heart out of whatever sent those things."

There was another explosion against the side of the opilion, which jumped and swerved. We looked to our east side, where we were still under attack. One of the wheels was missing and only a few sophies were left. The scarves were closing in.

"Shunt shunt shunt!" growled Wil, and he turned to a different panel. In the distance the scarves were catching up with the hog. The explosions around it were all different colors, but the hog appeared to still be moving.

Our hammocks cinched us all at once as the opilion was knocked onto its side. We bungied around the interior while our craft skidded across the snow and ice, the wheel legs rotating around the exterior to stop our tumble. More explosions blossomed all around us. The last of the sophies were doing their job, but we weren't going anywhere now. We were stuck.

Nozzles appeared on the wheel arms and suddenly torches shot out in all directions. Their blue-white flames were blown by the wind, but several of the scarves erupted in sparks and fell when they came into contact with them. The wheel legs came to life and torches started arcing all around us, dancing all across the snow and ice like garden hoses spewing fire.

"Those can go about two minutes," Wil yelled. "If we—"

An explosion rocked the opilion sideways again. This one came from above.

"We have to get beneath the ice!" shouted Vie. "Their electrostatic—"

"They can't go below the ice?" Wil shouted back. "Why didn't you say?"

"I did!" screamed Vie. "You weren't—never mind. How fast can you melt through?"

Wil was already swiping to another panel. "Not as fast as we can machine through. This was designed for mining, not melting."

The spikes at the ends of the wheel stalks began rotating like saws on long arms. Ice shards began flying into the air all around.

"Can you get us to the opening where the hog came out?" I asked.

"This is faster."

And it was. As Wil finished saying the words, the opilion began to shift. I had only a moment to wonder if this wasn't suicide, if we might be trading burning for drowning. Was the opilion even water tight? But the ice beneath us gave way, parted, and the opilion slipped into the dark water beneath.

Our ragged breathing sounded comically loud in the sudden silence. Looking up, we could see the cracks in the ice that outlined where we had come through. Blocks of ice were bobbing in the open water we had created, lit from behind by explosions that continued above.

"Are they following?" I asked.

"I don't think so," Vie said after glancing at her readouts.

Slowly, the opilion sank deeper.

"No, they're not coming down," confirmed Wil, who was looking up through the water. As we sank, the lights above became more and more muted. The gloom in the opilion grew; we were descending into a profound, watery darkness.

We were all looking up now. "What are those things?" asked Vie. None of us had an answer to that, so we watched the watery bursts of light in silence. There were a few more flashes, a few more silent explosions that boiled above the ice. Then darkness closed in. And a deeper silence.

The battle above was done.

Wil and Vie's faces, lit only by their instrument panels, looked otherworldly.

"Can this thing swim?" Vie finally asked.

Wil turned back to his controls. "It's made for this," he said with surprising swagger. I was still shaking.

He adjusted our buoyancy and we steadied in the water, floating five meters below the ice.

Wil grew a spotlight on the top of the opilion and shone it up at the open water.

"I wouldn't do that," warned Vie in a hush. "I don't think they can get down here, but no need to let them know where we are."

"Right."

Wil turned off the light. We listened to the sounds of the water.

"Do you think they're up there?" I asked in a whisper.

"Some are," said Vie, consulting her readouts. "Most seem to be heading back though. Are you still getting readings from your hog?"

Wil consulted his panel. "No. It's gone."

I felt an odd sadness at this. The distraction it had provided probably saved us. But really, that was Wil's doing. It had been an ingenious idea.

"It looks…yeah, they're all heading back now," said Vie.

"To the volcano, you mean?" asked Wil.

"That direction. I don't know, I can't get readings that far. There aren't any right above us, anyway."

"Do we have enough power to get back to the homestead?" I asked.

"More than enough," said Wil. "But if we surface, will they come for us?"

"No way of knowing," said Vie. "Can we travel down here for a ways?"

"We could. Don't you think they can track us under here though?"

"Wil, I don't know! How many times do I have to say it?" Vie had reached her breaking point. "I have no idea what those things are. I don't know where they come from, what they're made of, what they want, how they move or think or anything."

After a watery silence Wil said, "Sorry."

Vie rubbed her eyes. "I'm sorry too. You saved our lives and... Thanks."

Wil nodded.

"Let's go as far as we can underwater," I said. "Best we can do, right?"

Vie smiled at me, then reached forward and touched Wil on the arm. "I really am sorry."

"Not a problem," he said. "Let's get going."

"Agreed."

Wil cinched in the opilion's legs, rotated and reconfigured the wheels to work as propellers. Lights migrated to the south side of the ship, illuminating the rough underside of the ice above us and the impenetrable dark before us.

"Ladies and gentlemen, this is the story of the little submersible that could," said Wil, in an attempt to lighten the situation. Realizing it hadn't worked, he glanced an apology back at us over his shoulder.

Silently, we started into the black.

CHAPTER 13

"WHERE'S KIKU?"

"I'm her supervisor. My name is HenrIan Kan. I've taken control of—"

"So you're not going to tell us where she is?" demanded Wil.

"TabiTal, tell your synthetic to stand down."

Stand down?

The wrap-around panel of the FaRcom had us immersed in a Telesis conference room, which was a mostly empty space with dozens of panels all around. There were no chairs, but the high holo table at which the man stood could have accommodated a dozen people. For now, however, he was alone.

"Are you military?" asked Wil.

The man jutted his chin out, then glanced across the table where the light had shifted slightly. He seemed to be listening to something. Someone could have been on subvocals with him, but I had heard that some coms allowed ghosting, which was a technology that scrubbed a participant's audio and video from selected recipients. It was possible, I thought, HenrIan Kan was *not* alone in that room, but someone there was being ghosted to us. Perhaps a number of people.

As HenrIan listened, he looked from Wil to Vie. A vein in his temple pulsed visibly. He clearly didn't like synths.

"These synthetics have as much authority here as I do. Sir," I added. He stared at me for a long moment, then swallowed.

"I'm sorry, I'm not used to speaking this…forthrightly to synthetics. I understand it's a unique circumstance there. Wil and Vie, forgive me."

He'd received some instruction to say that; his remorse wasn't sincere.

"Thank you," said Vie.

Wil was still suspicious. "We started with some subordinate," he said, "then he got replaced with Kiku, then she got replaced with you. What's the story?"

"Well, this is a serious situation. And it's becoming more serious, so it's been pushed up the command structure."

"Kiku said she didn't know what had come through the atmosphere here," I began, but before I could finish my question HenrIan spoke.

"She lied," he said, bluntly.

For a moment we were all too stunned to speak.

"She lied?" I asked.

"She wasn't authorized to give you that information."

"Are you?" asked Wil.

"I am," he said. He took all three of us in before saying, "They're ours."

"I knew it!" Wil exclaimed. Vie was waiting for more information.

"Here's the situation." HenrIan or someone who worked for him had arranged some schematics for us. They appeared over the table in front of him, and the floating panels on either side of our FaRcom cel displayed them as well. This was a prepared briefing. "About a decade after your ship left, we launched a new iteration of our terraforming inception ships. Are you aware of how those work?"

"Terraforming seeds," I said. "I've told them how they work."

"Yes, 'seeds.' Heh. Well. The inception ships are filled with specialized assemblers and orgs. This isn't a full inventory here," he explained, gesturing to a scrolling manifest displayed on the panel behind him, "but these are some of the assembling agents. They're significantly advanced from those that were sent to Thalinraya originally. They have a great deal more autonomy. I won't go into detail; the thing you need to know for your situation is that these units are capable of redirecting. If they determine they've been sent to a sub-optimal target, they will redirect to a nearby system, provided that system has at least one goldilocks planet. They will initiate terraforming there. It's a cost-saving measure."

"This was an inception ship meant for another system?" clarified Vie.

"That's correct."

"Wait. If this is one of yours, why don't you just call it off?" asked Wil. "Tell it it's on the wrong planet and…to quit."

"It doesn't work that way. These are *autonomous* inception ships. 'Seeds.' If we'd seen where it redirected prior to entry, we might have been able to disable it, but once it's launched its assemblers…well, each assembler is also autonomous. They have their function and they'll do everything they've been engineered to do until they're done."

Vie asked: "Well, what are they trying to do?"

Unfortunately, I could answer this one. "Seeds start by stripping the planet down to single-celled organisms."

Wil did a double take. "I'm sorry?" he asked, addressing me.

"Yeah," I said. "By law, single celled organisms aren't patentable. Building from that stage ensures that all resident life belongs to whatever corpse sent the terraforming seed."

"They strip away all life?" Vie asked, hoping she'd misheard.

"Complex life," I said, "yeah."

After another silence, Wil said, "That's one of those things you maybe could have mentioned."

"I didn't know they were terraforming seeds," I protested.

Once again, Vie went for clarification: "So corporations send these seeds to wipe out all the forests, the animals, the…all the life in the ocean? Everything?"

"Including us," Wil said, looking at me as though I were to blame.

"Yes," interjected HenrIan, reminding us that we were, in fact, on a FaRcom with him.

"What can we do?" Vie asked, turning back to him.

"Yes. Okay." It wasn't immediately clear if HenrIan was speaking to us or replying to some internal cue, but now he raised his eyes to Vie. "We've got three teams working on different strategies. We may deploy all of them. Essentially, there are some disassemblers we may be able to get going that would work against them. Then there are some resource sinks we could plant to lure them in and…destroy them that way. Then there's directly attacking them. Some insect drones we could assemble by the tens of millions that would swarm V-12 and—we think they're confined to V-12 for now, so… So that's good, at least."

He was oddly unsure of himself. The answers lacked clarity, and he seemed to be using words that weren't his own. I looked at the other side of HenrIan's table and wondered again if there was actually someone hidden there.

"What makes you think they're confined to the volcano?" I asked.

"That's our information." HenrIan turned away suddenly. "I'm getting some reports in from our teams. I'll be right back."

His conference room abruptly blipped out of existence, replaced by the neutral, empty, wrap-around panel. The floating panels on either side now switched to a nondescript schematic of Thalinraya.

"He seemed a little unsure of how to deal with this," I said.

Wil nodded. "He's not a scientist," he observed. Which reminded me of my earlier impression.

"Military, you think?" I asked.

"Maybe," said Wil. "He was kind of gruff."

Vie was at a side panel going through some numbers. She'd been quiet for a while.

"Vie, what're you doing?" I asked.

"I'm trying to see which satellites are operational," she said without looking over at us.

"Homestead, show a schematic of satellites and their functioning," Wil said. He was obviously trying to be helpful, but Vie gave him a strange look.

"That information is not available," intoned the homestead.

"We ceded full authority to Telesis, remember?" Vie said. She was speaking in a weird, formal way. Wil recognized it too; he came over and stood beside me. "They're controlling everything remotely," Vie reminded us.

There was an awkward silence as we looked at one another.

"Do you think they're...keeping things from us?" asked Wil.

A muscle in Vie's jaw twitched. She looked at him more directly than she usually did and spoke very clearly, enunciating each word.

"I can't think of any reason they would do that. I am sure they are doing everything they can. They have a lot of experts there. It is frustrating, but I think we need to wait and let them work it out."

She wasn't speaking at all like herself. Her voice was sincere, but it was the sincerity of someone who was carefully saying something to be heard.

Did she think someone was eavesdropping? Telesis? But why?

"I'm just worried about your dad," Vie said, woodenly. She was over-pronouncing everything. "Until we get the situation with this new terraforming incept ship under control, I don't think there's much we can do but pray."

"Pray?" said Wil, flabbergasted. "Did you say *pray*?"

"Yes, pray," said Vie, warningly. "Have some respect for Tab, will you please." She held up a hand to stop him from voicing his confusion. "We prayed with Tab and his father after his mother died and that didn't hurt you, did it?"

We had done nothing of the kind. My father had cremated my mother and taken her ashes to the largest river on Thalinraya. It's Feremite custom to place a person's ashes in moving water, and he told me this great river would take her to the sea and eventually around the entire planet. But only my father and I had gone. And there had been no prayer.

Wil was finally realizing there was a subtext to all this.

"Well," pressed Vie, "praying with Tab and his father didn't hurt you, did it?"

"N-no," agreed Wil.

Now all three of us knew Vie was lying. Two of us just didn't know why.

"Then I think it might be a comfort to pray now. Until we can do something useful. Not," Vie added, turning to me, "that prayer isn't useful. No offense."

"None taken," I said.

"In fact, why don't we go to visit your mom at that waterfall in the cave where we spread her ashes. It would take your mind off your father for a little while anyway."

Vie had discovered a waterfall at the back of a cavern in our second or third week on Thalinraya. Neither Wil nor I had been with her when she found it—she'd been out looking for thumpers. She'd followed a little stream along the escarpment east of the homestead to where the water emerged from a cave. She'd come back excited to show us, but Wil had been angry with her at the time and feigned indifference. She'd refused to show us after that, but both of us knew what she was talking about.

"What do you think?" Vie said, turning to me. "Would you want to pray in the cavern where we spread your mom's ashes?"

"I'd like that," I said.

Suddenly the Telesis conference room wrapped around us again. HenrIan looked up from the holo display that rose from the table and said, "I've got an update. We think we can assemble some resource sinks remotely. These first generation incept assemblers are optimized to develop raw materials for gen-two infrastructure..."

He was relaying information he didn't understand himself.

"...cavity. These will serve as attractors, and because the assemblers will need to go so far from the base at V-12, they'll be dispersed and vulnerable. Does that make sense?"

"Yeah," said Wil noncommittally.

"Good," said HenrIan, relieved not to have to clarify.

"How long will this take?" I asked.

"Hours. Six or seven."

"And there's nothing we can do during that time?" asked Vie.

"Other than rest, I'm afraid not. But resting would be good."

"Any further word on my father?"

"Not as of now. We need to handle this first."

"And the satellites," asked Vie, "are they up and running yet?"

"I'm afraid not. It takes a while."

"Wait a minute," said Wil, "if the satellites aren't working, how did the gravion get to V-12?"

"Oh. Hang on." He looked down briefly and scrolled through a message. "There are two satellites we got running faster than the others," he explained, looking back up at us after pinching out whatever the message had been. "One of our techs thought we could use them to send assistance, but...well, you saw. We weren't able to triangulate effectively and we lost control of it."

He must have had a team of people telling him what to say. He had an answer for everything.

"If we have a few hours," Vie ventured, "we'd like to go and visit Tab's mother's grave. She died in transit and we cast her ashes in a waterfall, according to Feremite custom."

HenrIan pursed his lips. "Well...uh. Where is that?"

"Only about half a click northeast. It's just outside the pale."

The pale was the secure area around the homestead within which the homestead's defense systems could protect the inhabitants.

After considering, HenrIan said, "I see no reason not to go. So long as it's not too far."

"It's not."

CHAPTER 14

FEREMITE TRADITION REQUIRES PLACING A PERSON'S ashes in moving water, which in some ancient language is "living water." The water is supposed to give life back to the person's soul. My father and I had taken my mother's ashes to the largest river on Thalinraya, but now I could see that Vie's cavern would have been a good place for her too.

The mouth of the cave was an unobtrusive crack in the cliff face running behind the homestead. A small stream trickled out. We had to crouch to enter, but once inside we could almost immediately stand, though we had to walk in the winding bed of the stream. The light from outside was gone after only a few turnings, and Wil and I switched on the flashlights we had brought. Vie led the way using her fingernail lights. The eerie glow emanating from her hand made her look magical—or like a witch, leading us to our doom.

After a long arc to the left, the cavern opened into a room where quartz veins crazed the walls and let in diffuse light from outside. The cavern must have been located not more than a few feet behind the cliff face. The veins of light shimmered in mist, and in the dimness ahead we could hear the falling water.

"This place is amaz—" began Wil, but Vie put a glowing finger to her lips. When she was sure Wil wouldn't speak further, she turned and marched purposefully through the dim cavern to where the water fell out of some higher darkness. The jumble of boulders at the waterfall's base had been gently smoothed by thousands of years of falling water. Our flashlights made the wet rocks glisten and sparkle. I couldn't believe Vie hadn't brought us here. Especially Wil, who loved caves.

Vie walked immediately to the wall of stone beside the waterfall. Facing the wall, she sidestepped behind the curtain of water and disappeared. Wil and I shrugged at one another.

"In we go," he whispered philosophically. He hugged the stone wall and slipped behind the falling water, just as Vie had done.

The romance and mystery of a secret cave behind a waterfall is nothing like the damp, drippy reality of it. It was cold, dank, and uncomfortable. It also didn't go back very far. The only thing that made it interesting was the huge vein of clear quartz that split the western wall of the cavern. A peculiar light came through the vein from the outside, lending a mushroom glow to the tiny chamber. With the motion of the mist and the falling curtain of water, it felt like a full-immersion interact that was malfunctioning.

Vie was at the back of the cavern, kneeling on a cloth she had laid over the hard stone. She motioned for us to join her.

"This is the story of the communications synth who went completely mad," Wil said as he came up to her.

"Keep your voice down," Vie whispered. "Kneel down here next to me and let me explain."

We did as we were told.

"We are kneeling...why?" asked Wil.

"Okay." Vie looked toward the falling water before taking a deep breath. She was serious and tense. We waited. Vie turned to me.

"I'm sorry, Tab, but Kiku was lying to us about seeing your father." I started to say something, but she raised a hand to silence me. She spoke in an urgent, low voice. "The images she showed were not from that moon."

"How do you know?" Wil asked.

"There were a couple of things, but the main thing is that the shadows were all wrong. Tab, your dad was on the far side of that moon. That side was faced away from the sun. His ship should have been in shadow, not lit up like it was in those images. I don't think she could repurpose an asteroid station that fast to get the images anyway, but even if she could... it wouldn't look like that."

I thought back to the images we'd seen. The movement from one to the next had been apparent because of the long shadows. And Vie was right—those shadows shouldn't have been there.

"Also, I did satellite inventories before we contacted Telesis and there were no meteors, comets, or asteroids in system that could have done that to his ship. You saw the models I spun up. Those images weren't from your father's ship. They're lying."

She was right. I could feel it.

"Why didn't you tell us before?" Wil was vexed on my behalf.

"At first I wasn't sure, but then—now—I think we're being monitored. They have control of the homestead and they can control the satellite array around Thalinraya, which means they could potentially listen in on us anywhere."

"They can do that?" Wil asked.

"I don't *know*. That's why I wanted to come here. It's the only place I can think of where they won't be able to hear what we're saying. But if they have thermal imaging they'll be able to see where we are in here, so I wanted us to act like we're praying." She motioned to the way we were all kneeling.

"You don't think the satellite system is down," I said.

"No. It doesn't make sense. The—"

"They got the gravion up and running," Wil interrupted, eager to follow Vie's train of thought.

"That's one thing," she agreed, still talking in a hushed tone, "but there are other things too. First, if the satellites were down, that would have been an emergency. The homestead would have alerted us. Before Telesis had control of it, I mean. But it never did."

That was true. It seemed obvious, now that she pointed it out.

"So they sent us to the Auger Station for no reason," said Wil. "Why?"

"I don't know."

"It was decommissioned and we did start it up again," I said. "I mean, it did start."

"Yes, but that didn't restart the satellites," said Vie. "I don't know what the station's doing, but the power to the satellites was never down. That wasn't true."

"And if the satellites have been up and running the whole time, they could have been listening to *everything* we've been saying," Wil said.

"That's why I brought us here," confirmed Vie, nodding.

"They've been lying all along," Wil said, outraged. He wanted Vie to know he was on her side now, but he was genuinely upset too.

"I think so."

"Do you think the gravion crash was planned?" I asked.

"I don't know." Mist was collecting on Vie's eyebrows and eyelashes.

"They were trying to kill us!" Wil was getting worked up.

"Shhh," cautioned Vie. "I don't think so. If they wanted us dead there would be much easier ways to do it."

"And why would they want us dead?" I added.

"Wait," said Wil, pursuing a new idea. "What if they've just now found us. If they didn't know we'd been sent here."

"Wil," said Vie, confused, "they're the ones who sent us."

"No! It could be." Wil was on a roll. "Why else would they send the new terraforming seed?"

"That could really have been a mistake," reasoned Vie.

"Or an *intentional* mistake. An excuse so nobody would know they really just wanted to kill us."

"They could have killed us in bern, Wil," said Vie. "Why go to all the trouble?"

"To hide it! And if we're not synths, if we've been smuggled here for protection and—"

"Wil, stop it. We're synths," Vie said. "Get over it. And they could have had the homestead kill us in our sleep. They're not trying to kill us."

"They must want something," I said. "Something they know we wouldn't help them with."

"What do you mean?" Vie asked.

"The more I think about it, the more it seems like they've just been distracting us. Go do this at the Auger Station, go do that at V-12. What if they're just trying to keep us busy?"

"Okay, I know you think I'm crazy, but what if it's about us?" Wil wouldn't let it go; he was Thius on a bone. "What if they're testing us in some way?"

"You're deluded," Vie said.

"But you think they're spying on us! Why?"

"Wil, I *don't know!*" Vie whisper-shouted. She was close to tears.

"Why would they lie about my dad?" I asked.

Vie turned back toward me. "I don't know that either. Maybe he… discovered something? Maybe they're distracting us while they figure out what to do?"

"Well, they must want something from us, right?" I reasoned. "There wouldn't be any reason to lie to us like this if they weren't trying to get something. But…what?"

"That's the question."

We listened to the falling water, felt the swirling mist. Wil wiped his face with the sleeve of his shirt. Telesis owned the planet, so it couldn't be that they wanted resources—all the resources here were theirs already. Was it something about us, or the homestead, or something else in this sector?

"Could there be something happening on Telesis we don't know about?" I ventured.

"What do you mean?" asked Vie.

I wasn't quite sure myself, but I continued. "I'm just thinking out loud, but…Richelle has a lot of influence, a lot of money. She talked about maybe serving on the Unicon board again. She was on it before I was born. For a long time, I think. If something was happening with her…I'm her relative. Could they be trying to get to me somehow?"

"To threaten her," enthused Wil. This was the kind of intrigue he could believe. "We'll kill your gen-four grandson unless you do what we want? That kind of thing?"

"Something like that," I said. But hearing it from Wil's mouth made it sound farfetched. And embarrassingly self-important.

"I hadn't thought about what might be happening *there*," Vie admitted. "You're right. It might have nothing to do with anything on Thalinraya, if it's about you or your dad."

"Or us," said Wil with a note of defiance.

The idea that some political struggle in the Unicon could have consequences way out here wasn't outlandish. Terraforming projects sometimes switched owners before they were completed, if a corpse was traded or bought out. Which might support Wil's idea. This could just as easily be about them as about me. Richelle worked as a genetic engineer for Telesis, doing synth engineering for all sorts of things. And Wil and Vie were unique synths, so…

It really *might* be about them.

What if they weren't merely unusual—what if they were important experiments of some kind? Richelle never explained to me why she'd adopted them. She'd mentioned how convenient it was that I had some playmates my own age, but she never explained why they were there. She'd adopted them nearly two years before I first visited Histon, and she must have planned the adoptions even earlier than that.

Vie scissored her hair to one side. As they threaded through the wet curtain, the lights from her fingernails winked. Wil was staring up at the falling water, thinking.

Wil and Vie had lived with Richelle longer than I had. And she had certainly done some quasi-legal things with them. They were unlike any other synths—even the homestead recognized it. Could that be a threat in some way? Or might they be especially valuable for some reason? Could Richelle have programmed some kind of innovation into them?

A flash of light came through the quartz vein and brought my thoughts back to the cavern. Despite the cloth Vie had brought, my knees were getting sore.

"It could be something to do with another corporation getting access to Thalinraya," said Vie, brushing her damp hair back. "Who knows how things might have changed while we were in transit."

"You mean if another corpse wants access to the malibdi?" said Wil. "That would make sense. Whoever has that will control growth in this sector for the next millennium."

"Well," continued Vie, "if the Unicon granted Telesis rights to terra-form here but then—"

Vie broke off as another flash came through the quartz, this one accompanied by a muted explosion. We all scrambled up simultaneously.

"That's a vacuum burst," said Wil. "Shield explosives."

"Shield explosives?"

Wil nodded, still listening intently. "Defensive. They're—"

This time the explosion shook the entire cavern. Rocks fell and impact waves rippled through the mist.

"Come on!" We dashed through the waterfall, not bothering to squeeze between it and the cave wall. Wil and I had forgotten our flashlights, so we followed Vie, who knew the way better anyway. Her fingerlights lasered wildly around the cavern as we splashed into the stream on the other side, wove through the entrance passage, ducked back out into...

Chaos.

Drones of different shapes and sizes were flying in all directions, attacking one another with lasers, electric threads, and dark projectiles I had never seen before. A small copter crashed into the cliff face not far from us. Rocks and fiery metal pieces started raining down.

We dashed toward the homestead, but before we could get halfway across the field a black metallic lance of some sort pierced the ground directly in front of us. We skidded to a stop. The thing stood there quivering for a second, then it hinged in the middle, the top half bent down, and it started running at us like a possessed compass. A laser shot out from a dish on top of the homestead, freezing the thing in place for a moment before a second shot exploded it into metallic dust.

We ran. There were too many flying things to track any single one; it was anarchy in the sky. The air concussed repeatedly. I focused on the entrance to the homestead.

"Wil!"

Vie was already heading back to him when I turned. He was staggering up from the ground and Vie put her arm around him to help. Something had torn away part of his lower left pant leg, where blood and pulpy flesh were visible. Vie shouted, motioning me forward. "I've got him. Go!"

I went back to help.

There were dogfights between different drones on all sides. Explosions and falling equipment were everywhere. I grabbed Wil's other arm and pulled it around my shoulder. He grimaced, but the three of us hurried toward the homestead.

We all went to our knees as something exploded just above us. Fine ash fell, sticking to us where we were wet. Wil was in a daze, looking down toward Glassfall Canyon. I followed his stare. A half dozen bronze balls the size of melons were careening up toward us from that direction. As they neared, they lifted into the air, folded outward and let loose tentacles that trailed behind. The tentacles began twirling and the air behind them began to scintillate menacingly. A large drone with a clear bubble atop its fuselage crossed behind them and immediately lost power. It dropped like a stone and burst into flaming pieces on the rocks below.

The bronze octopi things bore down on us.

"Run!"

It wasn't far to the elevator iris, but the ground between was already littered with the wreckage from aerial battles above. A low-pitched hum was getting louder and the exterior of the homestead was shimmering up toward plasma, like it did before it grew some new functional device. This time, however, it wasn't localized; the whole homestead was shimmering.

Between us, Wil grimaced in pain as he hopped forward.

The iris toward which we were running suddenly shot in our direction, a cylinder that quickly enclosed us. In a moment we were in an opaque tunnel, which pinched together when it passed us, closing us off from the approaching bronze octopi. Wil went down. As we bent to help him up, we saw the first bronze balls make contact with the plasma tunnel. The material of the tunnel gave way to receive them, enveloping each one, pinching off the tentacles and dropping the enclosed balls to the interior of the tunnel where their metallic casing quickly clouded over.

One of the encased balls suddenly jumped, becoming a globe full of fire and ink. It had exploded, but the homestead material had contained the explosion. The other encased balls jerked and leapt, erupting into fiery—but thankfully contained—spheres.

"Come on!" Vie said, pulling Wil toward the entrance. I bent under his other arm again. The plasma walls of the homestead were beginning to swell outward. I realized then what was happening: the homestead was growing a defensive dome over the pale. The tunnel, which had reached out to protect us was dissolving, probably because the energy required to create the dome was immense. But we were about to be exposed to the battle again, just as wheeled and many-legged creatures were dropping down from the drones and beginning to advance. Some were spraying flames, others tossed acid grenades, creating steaming craters. Their destruction was indiscriminate; they didn't seem to care if they destroyed others of their own kind, they only wanted to destroy. Already the earth around the homestead was looking pock-marked and scorched. Smoke and steam rose in all directions, arcs of flaming spray rained down on the homestead, and tiny metallic creatures flew, drove, ran, crawled, and slithered everywhere.

Wil was using his leg now, growling through the pain and stumbling forward between us. We crossed the last meters and dove through the elevator iris, which spiraled shut behind us so quickly it nearly caught our feet. The sound—I hadn't been aware of how loud it all was—was suddenly dampened. We could feel the elevator bud in which we had landed begin to retract, drawing us in toward the center of the homestead.

We were safe.

Breathing hard, we looked amazement and confusion at one another.

Who or what was attacking the homestead?

CHAPTER 15

THE CEL ROCKED AS IT RETRACTED into the homestead, moving us quickly away from the perimeter, where explosions continued. Normally, elevator buds moved through the homestead fluidly. Now, however, the cel felt as though it were tobogganing over rough ground, bucking as impacts rippled through the vitreous.

"I'm okay," Wil said. Vie was helping him sit up with his back against the elevator wall. I couldn't see his leg behind the ragged cloth, but he was missing a shoe. His bare foot was a slick mess of blood and mud.

"Homestead, take us to the hotplate," I ordered.

"What is happening?" Panic was still raw in Vie's voice.

"A terraforming seed wouldn't build things like that," Wil said, craning to see the flashes of explosions at the surface.

It was true. Terraforming seeds weren't sent to worlds with life that would fight back. They were never equipped with these kinds of weapons.

"What are those things then?" Both Vie and Wil were looking at me.

"I have no idea," I said. "I've never seen anything like them."

"Some other corpse that wants to take control?" asked Wil.

"Corporations aren't allowed to just…attack," I explained. "Telesis has a contract."

"Right," said Wil sarcastically, "and contracts are never broken. Ow!"

"Wil," said Vie. She was tying a loose strip she'd torn from his pants around the leg for a tourniquet. "Is the homestead going to be able to withstand this?"

"I don't know what *this* is, but yeah," Wil answered, "it should be fine. It might have to shed a layer or two before it can encase the pale, but this place has amazing resources."

I remembered the storage tanks in the bedrock below. How deep did they go? And how quickly could the assemblers build whatever was needed?

"How is the homestead..." I wasn't sure how to ask what I wanted to know. "Who's fighting those things off?"

"It can do a lot on auto," explained Wil, "but someone launched the pale protection."

"Telesis?" asked Vie, pushing some hair off her cheek with the back of her wrist.

"Must be," he said through clenched teeth.

The elevator bumped down and irised open at the dock in the hotplate hall. We helped Wil out and started right, down the hall to the medic cel.

"I'm good for now," said Wil, nodding to the FaRcom iris. I looked at Vie, who shrugged agreement, so we ducked into the FaRcom cel. While I rushed to call up Telesis, Vie helped Wil into a chair by the floating panel on the opposite side. He immediately turned to it and started working.

"What are you doing?" Vie asked.

"Homestead status."

Vie thought of something else and stepped behind me, over to the other floating panel. The air shifted as the control room at Telesis leapt to life on the wraparound panel. There was a panicked operator repeatedly slamming his finger down on his desk display, saying, "Zero-two. Halverson at zero-two, I need your eyes on this now!" Alarms were lighting up the entire surface of his desk, and there were flashes from elsewhere in the room too. Sensing me, he looked up and exclaimed, "TabiTal!"

Seeing his face from this angle I suddenly recognized him: he was the same operator we'd first encountered, the one we'd spoken to before we'd been passed up the chain to Kiku, then HenrIan. His earlier arrogance was taking a back seat to panic now.

"What the hell is going on?" I demanded.

"We're not sure. Keep the..." He couldn't decide which display to attend to. He was probably getting subvocals too.

"What are these things?" I asked.

"They're...we're..." He was clearly overwhelmed. He looked up and, in the monotone of someone repeating an order, said: "The homestead has things under control."

Almost in response to his lie, a muffled explosion sounded above, and a tiny shudder passed through the room, sending a ripple even through the wraparound panel.

"That's under control?" I exclaimed.

"What's happening there?" he asked.

"We're being attacked! What's happening *there*?" I yelled.

"Shunt!" Wil exclaimed.

I looked left at Wil. He was swiping through different displays at a quick clip, his panel awash with schematics and numbers. "What?" I asked.

"They're not even tapping the deep tanks," he said, angry and dumbfounded.

I had no idea what that meant, but I said to the operator on Telesis, "Why aren't you tapping the deep tanks?"

"I don't know. Look, we have three teams on this. Things are—"

"Activity around the exterior is increasing," warned Vie. She was standing next to the blank floating screen on my right, looking at me with bizarre, wide-eyed intensity. "Electromagnetic cleaving is getting serious." Then she stepped over so she could see the man on Telesis head-on. "What are you doing?" she demanded.

"Things are under control," the man said uncertainly. "Just stay calm."

"Don't tell us to stay calm!" Vie was furious and frightened, and she wasn't bothering to contain her emotions. "Do you know how close we are to a breach?" She looked back to where she'd been standing, as though consulting the panel. "We're at eleven percent BPR!"

I looked for the data she was referencing, but there was no display.

"My data on this end shows your electromagnetic levels—"

"Your data is obviously wrong!" Vie pressed. "Who's in charge there?"

"I have three teams—"

"Why aren't they tapping the deep tanks?" Wil called over.

"Why aren't you tapping the deep tanks?" Vie asked, even more aggressively.

"I don't know what..." the man began as he received new information. "They're not needed," he amended.

"The hell they're not!" Wil shouted.

Vie was livid. "Our lives are in danger here. You don't know what you're doing!"

"We have three teams—"

"Wil, can you tap the tanks directly?" Vie asked.

"I don't have the permissions!" he said angrily.

"You need to drop the A-6 override so we can do this," she pressed.

"I can't do that," the man said.

"You've got to let us protect ourselves!" Vie was almost screaming.

"I can't do that," the man said, his voice rising to meet hers. His face glistened with sweat.

Vie looked back to where she'd been standing a moment earlier. Because of the angle, the man from Telesis couldn't see that she was looking at a blank panel.

"BPR is down to nine percent," she said, the anger and outrage suddenly gone, replaced by more naked fear. "Please," she pleaded, "help us."

"I don't know what BPR is," the man said.

"We don't have time," Wil said, hobbling over. "Just give us permission so we can defend the homestead."

Vie moved past me to help Wil. He was covered in blood. Somehow it was smeared across his forehead and dripping down one side of his face. Had his red hair masked a head wound? His shirt was ripped and bloody too. Did he have injuries I hadn't seen? Or...

"Oh!" The man on Telesis had seen Wil. "I'm sorry. I'm sorry, but protocol is—"

"Protocol is killing us!" Wil groaned fiercely. "Your delay is *killing* us!"

"Please!" said Vie, her voice breaking in a way I'd never heard before. She was standing behind Wil now, her hands on his shoulders, her face a rictus of fear.

"Our teams are—"

"Can you hear those explosions?" Wil urged.

There were no explosions at that moment, but Vie cried out in fear. Wil reached up behind himself to grip her arm. "We are going to die," he said accusingly, "unless you let us tap the deep tanks. We have to have control."

"Our response times are sufficient to—"

"To get us killed!" Wil finished for him.

I finally jumped in: "We'll return control after we're safe, but we need direct control now. You have to suspend the A-6 connect."

The man was visibly sweating now. "I'm not authorized to—"

"Are you authorized to watch us die?" Wil pressed. Vie knelt down behind Wil's chair and wrapped her arms around his shoulders.

"Do you not hear those explosions?" Wil pressed.

There were no explosions.

"Oh!" Vie cried, looking off to the right. "Six percent BPR. Please!" she pleaded. The man at Telesis was shaken. Vie buried her face in Wil's shoulder. "Please!" she gasped pitifully.

"I know that!" the man said angrily to someone we couldn't see.

"I hear drilling," said Wil, wincing as he reached up to hold Vie's arms, still wrapped around his chest.

There was no drilling.

"Please!" Vie begged, looking up again. Tears were streaming down her face. "Don't let us die!"

Wil flinched and ducked, as though he'd heard something.

"You've got to help us!" I shouted. "Suspend the A-6 override or we are going to die!"

"Please!" Vie wept pathetically.

The man grimaced, looked to one side, then back up into the camera. "Homestead," he said.

"Receiving," responded the homestead neutrally.

"I'm authorizing direct local control there. Suspend the A-6 override of 0611-14 until the attack is repulsed."

"Understood."

Wil dropped his arms from Vie's. She stood up straight and was about to say something, but she turned to me at the last moment.

"You do it," she urged. "Just to be sure."

"Homestead, cut all connections to Telesis," I said.

The man lifted his eyes momentarily, but then the FaRcom's wrap-around panel swallowed his image. Suddenly we were surrounded by blank walls.

We looked at one another in silence, holding our breath.

"The link has been suspended," said the indifferent voice of the homestead.

Telesis was no longer in control.

"Ha! Yes!" shouted Wil, pumping a bloody fist in the air.

It had taken me a while to catch on, but he and Vie had seen the opportunity to get control of the homestead back. I wondered how they'd understood one another so quickly, especially without their subvocals.

"That was amazing," Wil said to Vie, who was already wiping away her false tears.

"You too," she said, laughing and smiling at Wil. "You're a bloody mess." Then she added to me, "You too. Well done."

"We did it!" crowed Wil, pumping his fist again a little too hard and wincing at a sudden pain in his leg.

"How did you think of that?" I asked Vie.

She shrugged. "Wil said the homestead could handle it, so I knew we were safe. It just came to me."

"Because you're amazing!" Wil looked like he might leap up, despite his injured leg, and take her in his arms.

"What's BPR?" I asked, mostly to draw Vie's attention away from Wil's flagrant adoration.

Vie smiled modestly. "I couldn't think of anything, so I just said BPR. Blank Panel Reading."

"Ha!" Wil raised both arms like a bloody prize fighter, laughing.

"Careful," cautioned Vie.

But Wil couldn't contain himself. "Ha! Yes! Blank Panel Reading! That is so great!"

"Calm down," Vie said, though she was obviously enjoying his enthusiasm.

"Ladies and gentlemen, this is the story of the most brilliant synth ever!" said Wil, applauding.

"Okay, okay." Vie wiped the last of her fake tears away. "Can you get a status report?" she asked Wil.

"On it," he said, pushing carefully but quickly up from the chair and hopping back across the cel to the panel he'd been using.

Vie looked up at the main panel and said, "Homestead, give me a satellite schematic." Immediately the panel was populated with all of the satellites orbiting Thalinraya. I'd never seen it on a wraparound panel. The satellites encircled us, vital stats for each floating in space beside it.

"None of them are out of commission," Vie said. "Homestead, how many of the satellites were out of commission six days ago?"

"One. PRG6140.3 has been disabled for 442 years."

Vie looked at me. "We were right, they've been lying the whole time."

But why?

"The homestead pale is one hundred percent contained, eighty-eight percent secure," announced Wil. "It looks like the remaining whatever-they-ares will be ejected from the dome in about two minutes."

"Is the dome still under attack?" asked Vie, suddenly alert again.

"Everything that can is retreating," said Wil with satisfaction. The blood smeared on his face made him look possessed.

"Pogs!" Vie saw my surprise. "When the attack is over the link to Telesis will be restored," she explained.

I realized she was right. The guy from Telesis had given the homestead instructions via the A-6 connect. We couldn't override them.

"Shunt!" said Wil admiringly. He was concentrated on his panel readings.

"What is it?" we asked. His smile was bizarre.

"Those shock waves we felt? There was a battle going on underground while we were getting fired on from above. They were trying to burrow in too."

"Is it contained?"

"Well, yeah. The dome underground is amazing! About seven meters of obsidianized titanium-helix karinol. Nothing's getting through that!"

Vie managed to roll her eyes before turning to the more urgent matter. "Wil, Tab. Listen. They've been lying to us. They're going to continue lying to us. We need to make some plans."

"What do you think they want?" Wil asked.

"We don't know, and we're not going to figure it out in the next ninety seconds. We need to meet again." She turned to me. "You need to ask us to pray with you at your mother's waterfall again. If you can make them think..."

Vie was still talking, but I'd stopped listening. A thought solidified. I turned out toward the panel of rotating satellites.

"Homestead, how secure is the pale?"

"The pale is one hundred percent contained, ninety-four percent secure. There are thirty-six foreign objects still being disabled."

"Tab, we need to make plans," Vie objected.

"Homestead, show me a schematic of activity in V-12," I ordered. A wire drawing of the volcano populated one hemisphere of the FaRcom, its magma taproot disappearing below the visuals. The volcano was honeycombed with hundreds of chambers that had been carved out at regular intervals. Each of the chambers was alive with activity. It looked like some horrible infestation.

My mind was racing, and for a moment I lost the thread of my plan. The people on Telesis, I realized, had had access to this when they sent us there. They had sent us on a suicide mission, and they knew.

"Whoa!" Wil was standing on one leg next to me, taking in the extent of the infestation.

"Homestead, how secure is the pale?" I asked.

"The pale is one hundred percent contained, ninety-seven percent secure," said the homestead. "There are fourteen foreign objects—"

"We only have a couple of seconds," urged Vie. Wil's blood was on her forearms. "Tab, you've got to—"

"Homestead," I said, holding up a hand to silence Vie. I had to work fast. "The foreign objects that are attacking us come from V-12, correct?"

"V-12 is one of the sources."

"There are others?" Wil interrupted.

"There are seven other populations. Three sent devices to this engagement."

"Shunt!"

"Homestead," I said, "these populations are attacking Thalinraya, understood? And until they are destroyed—until *all* of them are utterly destroyed—we are under attack. Understood?"

"Understood," intoned the homestead.

I needed to be sure. I used the homestead's own terms and spoke as clearly as I could: "Until all foreign objects on Thalinraya have been disabled, we are under attack. Understood?"

"Understood."

There was silence. Open mouthed and wide eyed, Vie turned to me. It was dawning on her what I had done.

"Homestead, how secure is the pale?" I asked again.

"The pale is one hundred percent contained, ninety-nine percent secure. There are two foreign objects being disabled."

"Tab," said Vie, her face alive and intense, "you just…"

Wil saw Vie's face. "He just what?" he asked.

"The pale is one hundred percent contained and one hundred percent secure," announced the homestead.

"Oh no," said Wil.

Vie shook her head to silence him. She went to the floating side panel and opened a communications graphic. Wil made a questioning face at me, but I shook my head for him to be quiet. After scrolling through several screens of data, Vie looked up.

"I think it worked," she said.

"What worked?" asked Wil.

I couldn't help but smile at him. I turned back to the panel with the wireframe of V-12 and said, "Homestead, the pale is secure and no longer under…well, no longer under immediate threat. Correct?"

"Correct."

"But you understand that we are still under attack, correct?"

"Correct."

Vie stepped back over and offered her own questions. "Homestead, is there a com link open to Telesis?"

"Negative."

"Are we being monitored by Telesis or any other Unicon facility in any way?"

"Negative."

Vie was beginning to smile, but she had one final question: "Are there any outgoing signals of any kind from the pale?"

"Negative."

Relief flooded her face.

"Oh!" Wil finally got it. "We're under attack until those things are gone from the *entire planet*."

"Correct," intoned the homestead.

Vie broke into a full smile, took three quick steps and wrapped her arms around me.

CHAPTER 16

We were eager for information, but first things first. I'd never been inside the medic cel, though it was adjacent to the FaRcom cel. We helped Wil hobble the short distance.

The cel was much more elaborate than I'd expected. Like the FaRcom, it sat directly on the hotplate, which meant it had access to a lot of computational oomph. The many panels around the room were small, and there was a lot of dedicated equipment. The ceiling looked like a smaller version of the one in the materials storage: tubes and nozzles, tracks and gears and other equipment were everywhere.

"Medic, table one," said Vie to the room, and a hip-high shelf emerged from the wall on our right. Vie had brought Thius here and seemed to know how things worked. Wil grimaced as he lay down on the cushioned surface. The section under his head rose to form a pillow.

"Oh," said Vie, "uh…sorry, but…you need to lie the other way."

"Seriously?" groaned Wil.

"The diagnostic is in the wall," explained Vie. "I don't know if it can reach across you."

Wil stoically pushed himself back up and spun around. He had to lay his head down on the bloody smears left from his leg.

"Sorry," said Vie, as the table adjusted to Wil's new position.

"It's all good," replied Wil, closing his eyes.

"Medic, do a diagnostic on table one," said Vie.

Several articulated arms reached down from the ceiling, some with scissors, others with scalpels.

"Whoa! Whoa!" said Wil, raising his arms to fend off the machines.

"Stop," said Vie. "What's happening?"

"The patient's clothing must be removed prior to a full diagnostic," explained the medic.

"No no," said Wil, alarmed. "Not necessary. At all!" he almost shouted, his hands instinctively covering himself. Wil had a strong sense of modesty. "Clothes can stay on. Should stay on. *Will* stay on."

"I haven't done this before," said Vie, apologetically.

Wil ended up cutting his own pant leg off, after which the process went fairly smoothly. Something had torn a chunk from his calf, leaving a nasty mess behind. I could see some of the muscle move when he flexed. Vie asked the medic for its opinion prior to initiating any further procedures, and that proved key. The medic knew what it was doing. Wil was especially thankful when it thought to suggest an anesthetic.

The wall next to Wil's table swelled out and encased his leg, so we watched the diagnostic on a couple of panels. There were separate schematics showing muscles and tendons, arteries and veins, bones, nerves. As the medic went through the assessments, I went to the commons cel and brought back some vits. Even Wil was glad for the food. We were all famished.

When the diagnostic was done, the table on which Wil lay slid down the wall, where his leg became encased in a larger surgical drawer. Wil fell asleep during the first few minutes of the surgery.

Vie and I sat on some stools on the opposite side of the cel. We were both still filthy from the cavern and the battle, but at least we weren't wet any more. Vie was massaging her own lower back, arcing her spine and stretching her neck. There were circles under her eyes.

"Is the medic separate from the homestead?" I asked. There were many things I wanted to talk about, but I wanted to start with something neutral. And the medic's voice had been surprising. When interacting with technology I'd become used to the male indifference of the homestead's voice. The medic voice was female.

"They both interface directly with the hotplate," Vie said. "The medic has a parallel connection because it has such large computational requirements." She wasn't looking at me as she said this.

"Is that from something you onboarded?" I asked.

Vie stopped rubbing her back and smiled as she looked at me. "No," she said. "That's just me."

She was disappointed that I'd misread her.

"Sorry," I offered.

"It's okay," she said. "You couldn't know."

Her gaze passed over toward Wil.

I wanted to keep her talking, so I asked: "Does the medic really need a dedicated interface? I didn't realize medicine was that data intensive."

"This cel is also used for augment surgeries," Vie explained. "Those can get pretty complicated."

"Ah," I said, lamely.

Vie stood. "I think you and I should get some rest while we can."

Apparently, our conversation was over.

Vie instructed the medic to give Wil soporifics for the next ten hours, then we both left the cel and made our way down the hotplate to the habitation hall. The silence between us was excruciating. When we entered our separate habitation cels I wanted to say something to her, but nothing came.

She smiled toward me and said, simply, "Sleep."

Her iris closed behind her before I could ask if that was an instruction or an excuse.

My heart ached, but exhaustion was overtaking me too. I went into my cel and did a single cleanse cycle. I knew I should do another, but I was too tired. I got into bed and fell asleep before setting my own soporifics. It didn't matter. I slept for thirteen hours.

Wil was already up, his leg largely healed, by the time I made it to the commons cel the following day. He was in good spirits too. Vie was with him, and the two of them were finishing their vits when I came in.

They sat with me while I ate, discussing what had happened, what we'd done and learned, and what we planned to do in the day ahead. Because we needed information on several fronts, we divvied up responsibilities. There were three functional cels, so each of us could work independently, which would speed things up. Wil was tasked with onboarding schematics of the homestead and other stations on Thalinraya, including the power net. That way, if Telesis was somehow able to regain control, we'd still have access to the data.

Vie was on satellites. She was not only going to onboard the information, she was also going to see if there was any other way of getting data about the third moon—where my father had disappeared. We were back to knowing zero about his status. He could have just forgotten to put out his relay beacon, he could be dead—we just didn't know. I would have liked to gather the data myself, but I didn't have Vie's augments, so it wasn't practical.

The fun cel my father had configured for my training was still set up, so I used that to research the infestation at V-12 to see if there were any clues about what had attacked us. I knew either Wil or Vie could have done it more quickly and efficiently, and my lack of augments once again grated. But at least I could make a little progress.

I had the homestead go through proprietary technologies from every known corpse with terraforming contracts, but I couldn't find anything like what we'd seen. Many of the technologies being used at V-12 or that had been deployed against the homestead were completely unfamiliar. We couldn't sense any com systems, but they obviously had them. The propulsion systems for the underground attackers were based on dimension-liminal particules, whatever they were.

"They're theoretical," explained the homestead. I was surrounded by panels displaying more information than I could begin to understand. Being without augments was unbearably frustrating, and I began to think about what Vie had said about the medic cel being used for augment surgeries. I wasn't of age yet, so I might not be authorized. And if my father was alive, he'd never forgive me if I did it without permission. Still…

"What does that mean, 'They're theoretical'?" I asked.

"I am using conjecture in my assessment. These are technologies with which I am not familiar."

"Who would be familiar with them?"

"Who- or whatever manufactured them. Unless they are self-assembling."

"That's not possible, is it?"

"I am not familiar with these technologies."

Most of our exchanges were like this.

"Okay," I said, taking a deep breath, "let's review top-level possibilities."

The homestead talked me through the theories again. Whatever had landed could be undisclosed Unicon military technology, though why that would be here wasn't clear. It could be unregistered tech from some other corpse. It could be alien.

"The statistical likelihood of this scenario is not available."

"Why not?"

"Much of the information regarding possible non-human intelligent life is classified. Finally, it could be from the ECF, but the probability regarding this origin is also unknown."

I hadn't heard the term ECF in a long time, but as I recalled, it was just a school kid rumor—a computer that wanted to destroy the universe or something.

"What is the ECF?" I asked just as the iris behind me opened. Vie stepped in.

"The Emergent Computational Front is a rumored group of autonomous, self-perpetuating algorithms which are independent from human control."

"What does that mean?"

"It means," said Vie, who was lowering herself into the chair beside me, "escaped computers that learned how to live on their own."

"Negative. The computational substrate is incidental to the ECF. The computation itself is—"

"I sit corrected," Vie said to the room. To me she said, "You've heard of the FACE, right? The Free Autonomous Computational Entity? Same thing."

This was coming back to me now. Richelle had mentioned the FACE. Vie was dismissive, but Richelle, as I recalled, had taken it seriously. According to her it was a kind of computation that had grown out of control from some exploratory satellite.

"It's a conspiracy theory," said Vie. "Heard of the Trebuchet Tribes?"

I had heard of them too, but not since I was little. They were supposed to be planet-sized computers fueled by black holes that controlled whole galaxies.

"Yeah," I said, noncommittally.

"Another theory," said Vie lightly. "There's the Carve—the computer that escaped to another dimension. The Gobbi-Tittles—the computers that have already infiltrated everything, only nobody knows it. Sevralontiss M, which is the computer that takes over and inhabits each new president of the Unicon. There are a million of them. They're all silly."

"Well..." I said, and I turned back to the panel and started calling up some of the information I'd been sifting through. I explained to

Vie about the technologies the homestead couldn't identify. We went through a lot of details before Vie offered her opinion that there must be some corporate explanation. Nothing else, she explained, made sense with all we knew.

"Any luck with the satellite array?" I asked after she had had her say. Vie nodded and looked at her hands, suddenly uneasy.

"Everything seems to be functioning normally. There was never any interruption; that was all a lie."

"Why were they lying about that?" I asked, but what I really wanted to know was why she was so tense. I'd felt a sudden lightness when she'd come into the cel. Now there was a heaviness.

"I don't know. Tab…" Her face was strained with the weight of something. It could only be one thing.

"He's dead?"

"I don't have proof, Tab, but…look."

Vie called up a schematic of the moon. "Because of the rotation, we can't get visuals of the far side, where you father landed, for another twenty-two days. But I was able to reconfigure six of the Karn sats to get this." The meteor-pocked moon was overlaid with a strange pattern—a honeycomb of burrows beneath the surface. It was the same kind of activity going on within V-12.

"Three other moons are infested too." Vie pointed. "Each of these nodes has a power thread tapping nuclear and kinetic energy from the moon's core. It's the same kind of power extraction we're seeing at V-12. Whatever we're up against here, it's there too. And your dad had to face it with only the resources on his ship. He would have been…totally overwhelmed."

"We still don't know for sure, though," I said.

"No, but…I don't see how he could have fought off the things that came after us here. We couldn't have fought them off without the homestead."

"But we don't know," I insisted.

"Tab," Vie said. It seemed more condescending than comforting. "We don't know what these things are, but…after what happened here, I can't think of a way your father would have survived something like that."

"Maybe they didn't attack him like they did us. They might not even know he's there."

"But why isn't he responding then?"

"I don't know. Maybe he got delayed with the mass accumulator and had to stay underground longer." Vie reached out to touch my shoulder. I pulled back. "Why can't you admit we just don't know?"

"That's what I said, Tab. We *don't* know. But I don't want you to have false hope either. Whatever attacked us here is on that moon." She broke off and looked to one side, as if thinking. She wasn't thinking, though. I hadn't seen her do that since...

"Your subvocal with Wil is working again, isn't it?" I couldn't keep the note of accusation out of my voice.

She had shame enough to look embarrassed. "Yeah. He's saying—"

I stood. "I'm going up to see what the surface is like," I said, heading past her to the iris.

"Tab," Vie said, "don't be angry."

"I'm not angry," I lied, "I just want to see if there's anything to be learned from the wreckage."

"That could be dangerous."

"Yeah," I said, trying to sound indifferent.

"Tab."

"Yeah?" I turned back, standing in the open iris.

"I'm sorry. I wasn't trying to keep it from you, I just... We haven't been using it much."

Without a word, I strode down the hotplate hall and into an elevator bud, which rose up through the vitreous.

The homestead had grown a dome larger than any I'd yet seen, the wide perimeter extending almost all the way to the rock escarpment with the waterfall cave. Outside the opaque dome I could still see smoke curling up from machine wreckage. Within, automated sweepers of different sizes were busily clearing the last of the plasma cocoons that housed the disabled devices of our attackers.

As I stepped out of the elevator bud the homestead said, "Because we're not yet certain about the technology of the attackers, please refrain from approaching any of the disabled mechanisms."

"Okay," I said. Then a thought occurred: "Homestead, do you know where Thius is?"

"Thius was killed in the initial assault."

It was a blunt, passionless report.

I came up short. *Dead?* I couldn't believe it. Or rather, I could, which made me angry at myself. Why hadn't I thought to ask about him until now?

My face felt like it didn't fit. How had he died? Where? Was there a lot of pain? Did he know what was happening, or was it quick?

I wiped my eyes, suddenly ashamed. I thought about my father. Emotions for Thius were coming so easily; my feelings for my father had been—still were—slower to rise and…much more complicated.

The sweepers were lifting the plasma-wrapped machines and porting them to the dome, pushing them through and depositing them on the outside, where the plasma would finish its work. The process would take a few days, after which there would only be bare, acid-burnt patches to mark where the devices had been. Even when the dome came down—if it ever came down again—there would be a circle of scarred patches of earth to mark where the things had been dissolved.

What were they, and where had they come from? Who had sent them? Or were they autonomous? Were they conscious? They inflicted pain, but did they feel any themselves?

Tendrils of smoke rose up into the cloudless, whitewashed sky. I had no idea about the direction of the moon on which my father had disappeared. Not that it mattered. He was gone. My mother was gone; my father was gone. I was alone on a planet with two synths. I'd likely die here. Not that anyone would care. I hadn't left a great many friends behind on Telesis.

My watch suddenly shocked me. I pulled back the skin and saw, to my surprise, that the display wasn't blank—I was getting a hail. It wasn't tagged though. A second later, the display went blank again. The odd electromagnetism coming from the foreign devices must be causing a malfunction. I covered my watch and returned my attention to the homestead's sweepers.

Their many articulated arms revolved around their compact bodies so they could be used for locomotion or grasping or, presumably, fighting. They were ingenious. Wil would enjoy watching them work. I should go get him. There must be complex motors inside that allowed—

"Ouch. Hey!" My watch shocked me again, much stronger this time. I pulled back the skin and again there was an untagged hail.

Only two people had ever hailed me on this watch: Richelle and you, Dayr. But the hail had always been tagged. I'd never had an anonymous hail before.

I touched the display to clear it. Immediately I could feel the watch engage: the familiar zing of electricity shot up my arm, shoulder, neck. My tragus speakers buzzed as they activated. Normally this was followed by the tickle in my eyes that came before the video overlay. I looked for ghosting images. None presented themselves. But I still had the heightened sensation of being in an immerse. *Something* had happened.

"Tab?"

I turned. Nobody was there.

"Tab, I'm using your wristwatch channel."

The voice was full of static and difficult to make out. It *was* in my tragus speakers.

I froze.

Through another static burst I heard, "Tab. I am so sorry, but I need to talk with you."

There were so many ways this didn't make sense. Nobody should be able to contact me here. Only a few people even knew about my wristwatch, and only two had ever used it.

Wait. One person who knew about it was…

My dad.

I ran as quickly as I could to the elevator bud.

"Homestead," I said, "who's using my wristwatch?"

"I've overridden your homestead temporarily." The voice was definitely in my tragus speakers; it could only be coming through my wristwatch. It was true. And the static was resolving so that the voice was coming through more clearly now. "Tab, I want to see you when I speak to you. Can you come to the Control cel, please."

No! It wasn't possible. The voice was as I remembered it, gravely and deep, gruff and feminine. But it wasn't…possible.

"Tab, can you please come to the Control cel."

"Who is this?" I asked.

"Tab, you know my voice."

It couldn't be.

"A voice can be faked," I said, my own voice shaking.

"TabiTal Yrl, I am your fourth-generation grandmother on your mother's side. You lived with me on my estate in the Ahlkswaree Desert on Histon. I introduced you to prusik accelerators, which became one of your favorite games with your friends, Vie and Wil, who I also introduced you to. I arranged for them to accompany you there to Thalinraya. You called me Gran when you first met me, but as you grew that made you self-conscious, so I invited you to simply call me by my name."

I had been holding my breath and my voice came out in a croak. "What is your name?"

"Richelle."

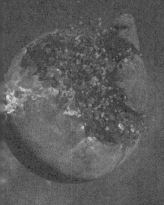

PART 2

CHAPTER 17

I KNOW YOU'VE NEVER VISITED RICHELLE on Histon, Dayr, so you probably can't appreciate how enormous that planet is. Histon is a giant 6.6EM planet, mostly desert and largely uninhabited. Despite the fact that they orbit the thing, people from Telesis Station rarely go down to the surface. There's no need. Apart from three small cities, the only facilities on Histon are synth orphanates, some mines, and Richelle's estate.

Because my parents were strict Feremites who didn't believe in body alterations, I was isolated growing up on Telesis Station. I don't need to tell you, Dayr. A normal childhood wasn't available to either of us. I didn't have any neural or body augments, including simple memory enhancements, and I couldn't access or process information the way other children did. Some tried to be nice to me, but I was really a different species.

I knew our SC♀[4] Richelle lived on Histon and, because I felt outcast on Telesis, I would look at the green threads running around that mottled red sphere and wish I could escape there. I rarely saw Richelle and I didn't know much about her, other than that my parents didn't trust her—my father especially. But I was having enough difficulty in school that finally my parents thought it would be good for me to have some time away, so they arranged a trip to Richelle's estate on Histon.

My father, I learned, disliked Richelle because she had renounced her Feremite faith. After she had raised her son, our SC♂[3] HerniXal, she left the Faith. HerniXal was a true believer, as were his children and grandchildren, including my mother. But my father still said Richelle was a bad example. That he allowed me to visit her on Histon demonstrated just how concerned he was with my growing isolation.

I had never been to Richelle's estate, and I wasn't aware of how fabulously wealthy she was. The estate was built inside a series of sandstone spires and arches in the desert south of Gimbyl. The spires were spread over a couple of miles, and you passed from one spire to another through CLD gläss—the kind of transporters the Unicon normally restricts to the military. Each gläss looked toward the spire it connected to, but when you stepped forward you felt like you were going to fall a half-mile to the desert floor below. As you passed through, however, the space collapsed and you found yourself in the next room. You could look back and see the spire you'd just come from, a mile in the distance. It was the oddest sensation: strangely cool and almost wet. And prickly, like when your foot goes to sleep, only all over.

The estate felt like one big mansion, though it was spread across miles of desert. Richelle had dozens of synthetic servants, but synths are built with governors that don't allow them to pass through CLD gläss, so they had to travel between the spires on zip lines and lev-cars. They didn't mind, though; Richelle treated her synths very well. Almost like equals. Those that worked for her did all sorts of things synthetics weren't supposed to do, and they enjoyed a degree of autonomy that would have been illegal anywhere else. Richelle had been a neural engineer and had invented some advanced augments for synths. Apparently her work was important enough that she got not only extremely wealthy but also powerful, so the Unicon left her alone. Her estate was like its own little world.

Once we'd arrived, Richelle talked my mother into letting me stay longer. I had the next week off from school anyway, and my parents were under stress because they were switching careers. For years they'd been in a program to become Stage Five terraforming curators, but my father had suddenly decided to switch them to Stage Four. So when they returned to Telesis, I stayed on Histon with Richelle.

Those few days changed everything, Dayr. Richelle took me all around in her lev-car and even let me drive over a dry lakebed. We explored the sandstone canyons, the petrified forest of giant cattails, the caverns that crisscrossed underneath the mountains behind her estate. We rafted down an underground river. We stayed up late and watched the Cister nebulae rise. We talked. I was ten years old and I had never had anyone pay attention to me that way.

Richelle was short and square: square jaw, square shoulders, square hips. Dad said she was "stumpy," which was mean but true. She had peppery hair and a plain face with creases that made her look a little annoyed all the time. I wondered, since she'd gone ahead and had the Reju therapy, why she hadn't done other enhancements, but I never had the nerve to ask her.

The few times Richelle had come to visit us on Telesis I had found her intimidating. She was abrupt and direct and didn't seem to know how to treat kids. She would ask simple questions, but then stare at me when I answered. And it wasn't just me—she had a piercing way of looking at everyone. I could tell that my dad wasn't comfortable around her, and that made her seem even more intimidating.

Before that weekend we had only seen her a few times because she was family and we were supposed to, but I never looked forward to it. After that week, however, I loved Richelle more than anyone in the world. I could be myself around her. I got used to her directness and her dry humor, her silences and her stillness. And I got used to seeing her plain face break into a smile at the oddest times, which happened mostly around her synths.

It was that week when I learned the story of how Richelle had been a Feremite for her first fifty years, but then abandoned the Faith. This was about 130 years before my birth. She finally had the Reju therapy to arrest the aging process. If leaving the Faith hadn't done it, the Reju ensured her position as the black sheep of the family. God invented death; Feremites didn't believe people were supposed to avoid it. Even her own son, our SC♂³ grandfather, hadn't talked to her during his later years.

Ironically, it was my father who finally got back in touch with her. It was out of desperation. My father had decided Stage Five terraforming would be too easy on us because it would put us on a planet with colonists—people and synths. But sacrifice is the measure of belief for Feremites, and it didn't matter if you dragged your family along. So he convinced my mother to switch to Stage Four in order to work as curators on a barren, uninhabited planet.

"Greater sacrifice for the greater glory of God," I remember he said one night as my mother cried. When they switched curating programs, Telesis refused to pay for their new training, so my parents needed to get some credits from somewhere. As proud as my father was, he wasn't too proud to go to Richelle.

After that first week-long holiday, I started visiting her regularly. My father was worried she would try to pull me away from the Faith, but she promised not to. And she kept to that promise. Still, her example did get me thinking.

During the school interim after I turned eleven, when I got six months off from school, Richelle and I convinced my parents to let me spend the entire break with her. I don't think my father would have let me, but Mom and Richelle were becoming friends too. Mom was almost forty by then, and there weren't a lot of people she could talk to about aging that far. I think she welcomed the excuse to come to the estate every so often to visit with Richelle.

I packed most everything I owned, took a jump ship to the orbital station, and rode the geodetic elevator down to Histon's main metropolis, Cib Naal. Richelle sent two synthetics, Wit and Ein, to pick me up. I had gotten to know them on earlier visits, and they were usually quite serious. Wit looked after Richelle's herriot ranch at the southeast oasis and Ein did some kind of bookkeeping. I asked them why they were the ones who had come to retrieve me, but they merely smiled. Ein's smile was especially maddening because his face wasn't built for it. He had a long jaw, a stubby nose, and a permanent disdain for everyone and everything. He was the only one on the compound who constantly scowled, but Richelle took delight in his crankiness, and I had developed a fondness for him as well.

On this journey, however, he was positively giddy. As we lifted off I asked him what was making him so happy. He wouldn't say, he just smiled down at the buildings and domes of the city as they paraded by. We shot out over the edge of the grand mesa and Ein began to whistle. Wit smiled knowingly as he silently guided the car down into the desert.

The rust-colored finger of the northernmost security spire on Richelle's estate seemed to reach up for us as we finally descended. When we landed on the spire's wind-swept tip, Wit and Ein told me to leave my bags—they'd drive them around. An elevator took us down through the solid rock to the elaborate foyer, where I was scanned for security. Wit and Ein were all smiles as they said goodbye—*what* was going on?—and I stepped through the CLD gläss into Richelle's entrance hall, two miles away.

Richelle was there waiting for me. She wasn't smiling, but there was a twinkle in her eye that told me she was holding one in.

"What is going on?" I asked as I crossed the sandstone floor to her.

"I don't know what you mean," she replied.

"Ein and Wit've been keeping a secret the whole way here."

"Have they?" Richelle turned and headed toward one of the balconies. "Hungry?" she asked, knowing I would follow.

We came out onto a narrow ledge that led to a larger shelf of rock where a table had been set with snacks and drinks. The cliff face extended above, half in light and half in shadow.

"Gran, tell me!" I pleaded. "What are they smiling about?"

Richelle lifted a globe of savir juice and sipped before answering. She wasn't smiling, but she was enjoying keeping me waiting. Finally she said, "I imagine they're excited because I've decided to introduce you to two synthetics from their line."

"Their line? What does that mean?"

"Do you know how synthetics are bred?"

"No."

"Well, let's rectify that," said Richelle, settling down onto a chair that had been carved into the sandstone wall and looking off toward the horizon. "The Unicon recognizes 117 legal genetic lines for synthetics. Some aren't used because their genes showed too much volatility. Some—"

Something came tearing out from the spire onto the ledge. It was a boy. He looked about my age, but there was something not quite right about him. He stopped when he saw the ledge onto which he'd run, then shouted over his shoulder. "This one's way higher, Vie. Come here!"

"Wil!" Richelle's voice was sharp and the boy looked up. A girl came out onto the ledge just behind him. There was something odd about her too, but I couldn't tell what it was at first. Richelle called them over to us though, and as they approached I saw: neither had whites to their eyes. They had black pupils and violet irises, but there was silver all around. Adult synths have their natural eyes removed so there's space for improved visual gear and augments. They're given surgically implanted glasses— mirrored lenses that cover the whole socket, from eyebrow to lower lid. These children didn't have those larger lenses, but the silver of their eyes told me they were synths.

I had never seen synthetic children before. I had never thought there *were* synthetic children; I thought they were manufactured as adults.

As they came over to us I couldn't help staring. My mind was suddenly crowded with questions. Would they stay children? What were children used for? Were there synthetic babies? Parents?

Vie was as interested in me as I was in her. She couldn't take her eyes off of me as she and Wil crossed the ledge to us.

"I want to introduce you," smiled Richelle. "TabiTal, this is Vie and this is Wil. Vie, Wil, this is my gen-four grandson, TabiTal."

"Hi," I said.

"Hello," said Vie shyly, smiling.

Wil lowered his chin and squinted at me. "You been off the edge?" he asked, grinning. His unkempt red hair gave him a feral look.

"What do you mean?" I replied.

"He has not," Richelle interrupted, "and I don't want you doing—Wil!"

But she was too late. Quicker than a cat, Wil turned and bolted for the edge of the rock shelf. He was at the lip and over in only a second, launching himself out into space, hundreds of meters above the desert floor. Leaping from my seat, I raced to the edge and saw, to my astonished relief, that he had not plummeted to the scree below. He was hovering about four meters beneath the level of the shelf, laughing hysterically. Confused, I looked back at Richelle. She hadn't moved from her seat. Vie had gone to the table and was choosing a pastry from a plate.

"He just wants attention," Vie said, annoyed and bored at the same time. "He's been doing that ever since they told him about the magnets. It's just to shock everyone."

Well, nobody had told *me* about the magnets, whatever those were. My heart was racing and I looked at Richelle.

"There are magnetic instantiation fields around all the spires for safety," she explained, slowly rising and walking over to the edge. "They hadn't had much use until yesterday, when this one learned about them." She looked down at Will, who was squirming midair.

"How come it's not bringing me back up?" he shouted.

"Because this afternoon I programmed a twenty-minute delay," said Richelle calmly. "It's an opportunity to consider other activities you might enjoy."

Vie laughed so hard a bit of pastry came out.

"Richelle!" protested Wil from below.

"Well, I can't stop you from hurling yourself off my spires, but I can make it less appealing. You have twenty minutes this time. So you're aware, the duration doubles each time the nets catch you."

"That's not fair!" Wil was upset and laughing both.

Richelle turned away from the edge and started back inside, saying rather loudly, "Tabit, would you and Vie like to help me test the new prusik engines we have for the PFDs? I'm told they're a little too *fast*."

From behind us we could hear Wil screaming with renewed strength, "That's not fair! Wait for me! Let me up! Noooooo!"

I didn't know anything about synthetics, but with the innocent curiosity of a child I simply asked Wil and Vie, and they were happy to tell me what they knew. Once they're removed from their incubators, synthetics go to orphanates, where other synths care for them. They get weekly neural treatments, but other than that they live in dormitories and go to school and grow up like human children. When they're seven they get additional augments and start specialty schools for whatever line of work they're intended to do. That's another four years, but then they get to go and live in synth communities. We weren't allowed to visit them, but the Telesis orphanates were scattered around Histon. Synthetics aren't released for sale until they're fully grown and matured, and until that time they live amongst themselves, gaining experiences that allow them to fit into our world better when they're sold.

That's why it was so unusual for Wil and Vie to be released to Richelle; it was against the law to have underage synths. I didn't learn until much later how Richelle had managed it. Or why.

Richelle told me how people tried to raise synths differently at first, more economically, but people wanted synths that behaved like humans. They wanted them to be able to recognize and respond to emotions, to understand nonverbal cues, to think and, within reason, to feel. In order to do that, it was necessary to allow the synths to have their own child-hood with their own thoughts and experiences. Synths without personal histories acted like machines, and nobody wanted that.

"Machines are good for some things, but humans don't like interacting with them," she explained one day while we were traveling to her herriot ranch. She was driving the lev-car across the salt pans.

"That's why synths were invented?" I asked, raising my voice to be heard above the wind. "Because people didn't like working with machines?"

"That's right. We use synthetics," Richelle continued, "because we like to interact with people. Synthetics give us that good feeling without the bad feeling we might have if we knew 'real' people were having to do those jobs."

I thought about what it would be like to have machines serving food at a restaurant: lev-grav robots hovering around tables and swooping in to fill glasses. It was a creepy image. But so was the idea that humans might do it. No human would want to spend all their time in a restaurant doing things for other humans. It'd be like being a slave! If I expected other humans would be serving me in a restaurant, I'd never go. I'd feel too guilty.

Synths were a much better solution. They weren't machines and they liked the work. But, it occurred to me, they did other work as well.

"Synths do other things too, don't they?" I asked. "Wil was going to be a mining synth, wasn't he?"

"He was. Once they'd…invented synthetics, people realized they could also be used for other things. Things machines couldn't do on their own but people didn't want to do. Things like mining." She looked south. "You can't quite see it from here, but four or five clicks south of here is the Qottoro mine. It's dry, hot, and surrounded by alkali desert. It's an important facility, but no human would ever want to work there. So we have synthetics do it."

"What did they do before synthetics?" I asked.

"Humans had to do it."

"Humans?"

"That's right."

"But…" I was confused. "You said no human would want to work there. Why would anyone do something they didn't want to do?"

"Oh Tabit," smiled Richelle, "have you not studied history?"

"Not much," I lied. I had, I just hadn't paid attention. And, to be fair, I was only twelve at the time.

"Before machines and synths," explained Richelle, "people had to do all their own work. Everything you see machines and synths doing, people had to do."

"Really?"

"Yes. A long time ago, having a job wasn't something humans only did when they wanted to," she explained. "Every adult human *had* to have a job."

"Had to?" I asked. "Did the Unicon have a law or something?"

"There was no Unicon at that time. And no, it wasn't a law, it was… Humans didŋ't provide for other humans back then. You only got money, which was an early form of credit, if you worked. If you didn't work, you couldn't have the things you wanted. If you didn't work at all, you wouldn't even have a house, or clothes, or food. You might even die. So everybody worked."

I thought about that in silence for a while, then said, "I'm glad I didn't live back then."

Richelle burst out in rare laughter.

Richelle didn't force our friendship, but from the very beginning Wil, Vie, and I were a team. I had never had friends before, but they didn't know that. They'd been at Richelle's estate nearly a year before we met, and the only friends they'd had during that time were each other. Also, we had a lot in common with one another. We were all isolated from others our age: me because I was an augment-free Feremite, and them because they were synths being raised outside synth communities. And they hadn't had their glasses surgery—Richelle said they'd never need it—which meant they'd *always* be different from other synths.

And we were all three going to die. All synths have a termination date eighty-six years after inception, so this wasn't unusual for them. But the prospect of a short life was almost unknown for a human kid. Normal humans could have reju therapy any time after they came of age. Not Feremites. I was expected to allow myself to age and die "as God intended," which meant the three of us were in the same mortal boat. Other human kids thought of me as a terminal freak, but not Wil and Vie.

Wil was an enthusiastic and reckless kid. His red hair was forever disheveled and getting in his eyes, but he'd sooner have cut off his arm than his hair—he loved that mop of copper. He was also the engine of our group; every day he'd wake up and be eager for a new adventure. On days when Vie and I outvoted him and we did something he considered boring, he'd get elaborately antsy. He wouldn't complain—he wanted to be with us. But he wanted to be out exploring or building gadgets at the same time, so he'd fidget and wriggle and interrupt until we convinced some adult synth to take him somewhere away from us.

Vie was open and friendly, but much more moderate in her enthusiasm. She had long black hair she wore in a ponytail, and she enjoyed less active things than Wil. She liked to sing. She played the piano really well. She wanted to learn to draw, but she had decided she would do it "organically," without onboarding any routines. She would sometimes bring tac pads when we explored, to practice drawing. Often, when Wil and I were hiking, Vie would perch someplace and do sketches.

Vie wasn't the thrill seeker that Wil was, but there was one activity she enjoyed as much as us. The zip lines.

One of the main ways synths got around Richelle's estate was by zip line. These extended from the top of most spires down to the bottom of neighboring spires, and were actually structural guy wires. There were dozens of these lines, and the synths used motorized prusiks to travel up and down them. The adult synths were indifferent to this method of travel, but we thought it was thrilling. We spent many days zipping around the estate from one spire to the next, playing tag or chase, challenging one another to go faster or to avoid braking until the last instant. I'm sure Richelle had safeguards in place, but it felt dangerous and exciting.

I enjoyed being around Wil and Vie and I loved having friends, but as time went on I began feeling there was something missing. We played and talked and even slept together when Richelle let us go camping at one of the oases, but I wasn't as bonded to them as I expected. Friendships were new to me and I wasn't sure what "normal" was, but after a few years together I felt instinctively there should be something…deeper to our relationship. I liked being around them, but I didn't feel *connected* to them in the way I thought friends should. I began to think there was something wrong with me.

One day, the three of us were out chasing each other around the eastern security spire, which had especially long guy wires. We were racing on auto prusiks, challenging one another to zip down as far as we could without braking. I went first on the longest line, but as I got to the bottom

I was off balance when I released my prusik. I dropped to the block of stone beneath the wire and skidded down to where the slab rested against another big boulder. The force of my fall tilted the slab away from me for a moment, but then it tilted back and pinched my foot in the crevice. I started screaming.

I was overreacting, but it did hurt.

Wil was close behind me, and in a moment he'd unclipped from the wire, jumped down and scrambled over the slab, scraping himself in his haste. He slid down next to me and started scrabbling at the stones, trying to pry them apart. The sharp edge of the larger slab cut into his hands, but he kept pulling until I could wrench my foot free. I was bruised, but okay. Two of Wil's fingers, however, had terrible gashes in them. One looked broken.

Vie had arrived by this time. She ran to Wil to see if he needed help; he was bleeding. When he waved her off she came to me, upset now by both the situation and Wil's dismissal. I was rubbing my ankle.

"Is it broken?" she asked. I rolled my ankle to demonstrate it still worked. There was a small scrape on one side, but no blood.

"I think it's okay," I said.

"That's *it*?" Vie said contemptuously. "That's what you screamed about? We thought you were dying."

"I was scared," I said defensively.

"Look at Wil!" Her face was all screwed up with scorn.

I looked at him nursing his fingers and...didn't feel anything. Which seemed odd. I didn't feel guilty for overreacting, I didn't feel thankful for his help. Shouldn't I feel something?

No. He'd done what he was supposed to do. His injuries weren't my responsibility, he was only doing his duty. He was a synth after all, not a human.

And Vie's accusation was offensive. Who was she to accuse me? He'd hurt himself!

"I didn't ask for his help!" I shouted at her.

"He *has* to help, you know that!" Red-faced, she turned away and went back to help Wil bandage his hand. I got up and walked away, self-righteous and angry and...confused.

I was troubled by the incident, and that night I couldn't sleep. For long, silent hours I stared at the smooth sandstone walls of my bedroom. I kept thinking that if it had been my mom or Richelle or even my dad I would have felt terrible. Why was it different with Wil? Then I would think about Wil and realize it was different because *he* was different. He wasn't my mom or Richelle, he was just a synth. But…that excuse came more from a feeling than a thought. And it almost felt like the feeling wasn't really mine. After all, he wasn't just a synth, he was my friend.

I got out of bed and took the elevator up to the top of the spire. The cool air of the evening bit through my night clothes. It felt good. The far sun had recently risen, its pale violet light coloring the shadows and erasing most of the canopy of stars. I sat on the pedestal chair at the top of a guy wire I'd zipped down many times and tried to trace the path of the line down through the shadows to the desert floor.

The elevator opened again and Richelle stepped out. She was wearing a thermal robe and had another in her hands. I turned away. She came over and sat beside me in silence, setting the robe next to me on the stone. After a few minutes more of shivering I put it on. The thermals kicked on right away, wrapping me in warmth.

We were there for a long time. Satellites crossed the sky. A light, dry wind played across the top of the spire.

"Do you want to talk?" Richelle finally asked, and that was all I needed. I told her about what had happened and how I felt and how confusing it was and that I hated my parents for making me this way. It all came out in a thirteen-year-old rush, and Richelle didn't interrupt or contradict me or try to comfort me, she just listened. When I was done, she sat for a minute looking out at the night.

"Can you keep a secret?" she asked.

"I don't have anybody to tell anyway."

She arched an eyebrow and laughed lightly. After a moment, she looked out at the night again and said, "Synthetics are designed. You understand that. Well, here's the secret. Everybody knows it, so it's the best kind of secret because it doesn't look like a secret at all."

I didn't know what to say to that, so I just waited.

"Synthetics are made from modified human genes. That's how they're designed."

"That's what you do, right?"

"Sort of. I engineer their brain development, but that's not what I'm talking about now. You see, synthetics are designed from slightly altered human source code."

"Source code?"

"Genetic material, regulatory molecules, emergent environmental reactants, things like that."

"Oh."

"The catch-all term is 'source code.' It's all the instructions that go into making a human. Our bodies, our minds, behaviors—it all comes from source code." She could tell I wasn't clear about this, but she continued. "Do you know what a compulsion is?"

"No."

"A compulsion is something you do without thinking about it. Something you couldn't *not* do, even if you knew you were doing it and didn't want to."

"Like a sneeze?" I asked.

"Sort of. It's automatic like that. Well, synthetics are designed to have compulsions you and I don't have. They're called *behavioral directives*. Some behaviors are built into almost all synthetics. Most synthetics are compelled to protect human beings, for instance."

"But people do that too."

"Some do; and when they do, it's by choice, so that action tells us something about that person. But synthetics don't have a choice. They're built with a *compulsion* to protect people."

I was a little confused. "You mean, they can't decide?"

"That's right. If they see someone in danger they feel compelled to help them. Even if it means destroying themselves, they feel they *have* to do it."

"So," I said, my mind racing, "if I was being attacked by an animal, a synthetic—any synthetic—who saw would have to help?"

"That's right. It's built into them."

"Would they want to?"

"Well, wanting doesn't really enter into it," she explained. "It's more like that reflex—like that sneeze you mentioned. They'd feel the overwhelming *need* to do it, and they would."

I looked out into the shadowy night, thinking about what Wil had done. I wondered how I would react if I saw someone else being hurt. If I was afraid, but someone else was in danger, would I overcome that fear?

"There are some behaviors built into all synthetics," Richelle continued, "but there are others that are only built into synthetics who do specific work. Wit, for instance, works with animals, so he's designed to be protective of animals too. And he's nurturing and he likes the outdoors. But those aren't merely preferences for Wit, they're engineered to be more like compulsions. He likes to be alone. That's—"

"That's a compulsion? To be single?"

"No, I meant that he likes solitude. He likes to be by himself. But," she added, "yes, he is also compelled to be single. That's a compulsion all synthetics are programmed to have."

"All of them?" I asked.

"Have you ever heard of a synthetic with a spouse?"

I had never considered it, but no.

"Sexual and romantic feelings are engineered out of synthetics," Richelle went on. "These are called behavioral governors, and they *prevent* some thoughts and feelings. They're sort of the opposite of behavioral directives. Sexual impulses tend to be…disruptive, so all synthetics get behavioral governors that prevent them. It's engineered when they get their glasses."

My mother and father hadn't ever had domestic synths, so I'd not been around them much. I had seen synths working in stores and at school, but I hadn't ever really thought about them—they were just there. Now, I realized, it was true: synths were always single.

And now that I thought about it, I never saw them outside of their work. Synths didn't go to parks or entertainments or parties. Synths were workers. They did tasks people didn't do; it was just the way things were. They never complained.

I realized I had been staring out at the dusky desert night. Richelle was looking at me intently.

"Does that surprise you?" she asked.

"What?"

"That synthetics don't have spouses?"

"I never really thought about it."

Richelle pursed her lips, then continued with her explanation. "The point is, synths are designed for specific things, and their desires are engineered accordingly. Synthetics are tools."

Tools. The word sounded ugly in that context, under that canopy of stars. Still, it sounded right. I had been around synths all my life and I had always treated them as tools.

Except Wil and Vie. They were my friends. It felt different being around them.

Richelle was looking at me searchingly, and I realized she was hoping for a reaction. I felt ashamed for some reason, but then I resented being made to feel that way. Synths were different from us; why should I feel bad about acknowledging that?

Except that...I *was* feeling bad about it. That's why I wasn't able to sleep.

The sandstone balcony was cold and unforgiving beneath my feet as I crossed to the edge. I tapped the cable of the zip line and watched the wave dart down into the darkness below. Richelle came up beside me.

"You don't think of them as tools, do you?" I asked, though I knew the answer. Her synths had more freedom than they were supposed to have. I'd seen her having animated discussions with synths—arguments even. Other people never did that. And, I suddenly realized, her synths did things outside their work too. Things they did just for themselves.

If I were a synth I'd rather be on her estate than anywhere else in the universe.

Richelle cut our conversation off, but something in me had changed and I couldn't let it go. I avoided both Wil and Vie the next day, then suffered through another sleepless night. The following morning, I went to find Richelle. I had to wait outside her office in the research spire while she finished a meeting with some Unicon officials. She introduced them to me—two reju-sculpted men in uniforms—as she accompanied them to their waiting lev-car.

We went through her laboratory and into the commissary when they were gone. She said I looked terrible and she wanted to feed me.

"I want to talk to you about the other night," I said as I sat down with my vits.

She cupped her caj-tea and smiled indulgently. "I'm sure Wil and Vie have forgiven you, if that's what you're worried about."

"No," I said, "it's about... You said you didn't think of synths as tools."

It was a long moment before she answered.

"No," she finally said. This was difficult for her for some reason. "Synthetics are not merely...synthetics to me."

"Why?" I asked.

Richelle looked around the commissary before answering. "Most people don't *want* to feel anything for synths. It's...inconvenient. But after working on them for a long time I decided to change that for myself."

"Change it?" I asked. "What do you mean?"

"I wanted...to be able to feel things for synthetic people." She took a sip of her tea. "It didn't seem right to treat them like tools. I didn't want to do that. So I found a way to open myself to them."

That made no sense. Why would you want to feel things for synths? They're just synths.

Except...*that* idea made no sense either. I wanted to feel differently about Wil and Vie—that's why I was here. My initial reaction to Richelle's idea was...automatic. I *knew* it wasn't right to feel things for synths—that thought didn't even require thinking. But why? It felt like the thought wasn't even my own somehow.

"Are you alright?" asked Richelle. She had set down her tea and was watching me struggle with these ideas. Her wrinkled face was becoming so familiar.

"Fine," I lied. Her smile showed she knew I was lying, but she didn't press me. Conversations with Richelle were sometimes difficult, but they were easy that way: she allowed time for thought. I struggled with mine for a minute more, then asked: "You say you opened yourself to synths?"

"I did." She was squinting intently at me now.

"How?"

Richelle took some time before answering. I was aware of the clinking of utensils in the commissary.

"Tell me," I said. "I'd like to do it too."

Richelle froze. There was something dangerous here, but I pressed on.

"Wil and Vie are the only friends I've ever had," I said. "I know other kids don't have synth friends, but I'm not like other kids, am I? *You* know that." Richelle smiled. She'd been a Feremite child once. "Well, they're not like other synths. And when I treat them like synths it feels...wrong. Like there's something wrong with *me*, almost. So if there's something I can do... Tell me."

Richelle nodded. She reached up to her cheek and wiped at something. A tear, I realized.

It took a couple more conversations before she was willing to help me, but I wore her down. It was true, after all—Wil and Vie were my only friends, and Richelle wanted me to be able to enjoy a full friendship with them. So she finally helped me.

She gave me a pill.

It wasn't the intervention I had expected, but it worked. In the weeks after taking the pill I began to feel very differently toward Wil and Vie. When they were kind to me I began to feel grateful, when they were angry with me it hurt. But in time even the negative feelings—jealousy when they excluded me, guilt when I'd done something wrong, the constant sense of obligation—all if it led to a wonderful sense of interconnectedness. Exploring with Wil was more satisfying because we fed off one another's energy and enthusiasm. I appreciated his sense of humor more, and he was obviously grateful I was becoming a better audience for it.

It was more complicated with Vie.

After that first visit to Richelle's estate, it was difficult to transition back to life on the Telesis station. I clamored to return to her estate during my next time off from school. And the next. But each time I returned to Telesis, things were more difficult. My parents didn't understand what I was going through, and when I told them about my friends, Wil and Vie, my father was furious. He said my budding friendship with two synths was proof Richelle intended to corrupt me.

School became torture. I was increasingly estranged from other kids. Worse, I was newly aware how everyone treated synthetics like tools. In stores, restaurants, homes—they were treated poorly and had no life apart from their work. They took no offense themselves, taking their abuse in stride. But that was because they had been *made* that way, and it seemed unjust to me now. Inhumane. Their eyeglasses were like badges of shame, singling them out as slaves.

For more than a year these intermittent trips to Histon tortured me. Months of isolation and bouts of depression on Telesis were punctuated by exciting trips down to the planet—to the friendship of Wil and Vie, the open-mindedness of Richelle, adventures and acceptance and a sense that life could be more than purposeless toil. But too soon it would end, and I'd go back to my loneliness on Telesis.

My mother saw what was happening and I think it tortured her too. She knew I was happier and healthier on Histon, and at the end of a heated conversation at dinner she lashed out at my father, telling him I needed to escape "the unbearable weight of his parents' expectations." I had never heard her talk to him that way. Neither had he. A tense silence followed, and then, to my utter astonishment, my mother suggested I go to Histon to live.

As my mother made arguments on my behalf, I considered her situation for the first time. Except for Richelle, her SC♀³ grandmother, everyone in my mother's family was devout. My mother's parents would never allow her to have time with Richelle, so her own childhood had been a steady march into the confines of religious tradition. I had never stopped to think that she might not have wanted such a life, that she might, in fact, be laboring through a life that was different from what she had hoped for.

I realized she was trapped. My own mother.

And now she was opening my world in a way hers had never been. She arranged my escape, and my father could do nothing to prevent it. Richelle was, after all, paying for the new Stage Four terraforming training that *he* had chosen. Nobody could dispute the fact that Richelle was more than qualified to take over my education. She was a genius herself, and wealthy enough to hire as many tutors as I needed.

The day for departure finally arrived and my parents took me to the port to put me on the little jump ship to the outstation. As the canopy lowered, my mother shouted a reminder to tell Richelle that she'd be visiting in two weeks. My father stood by, stone faced.

The ship launched me up toward the huge ochre smile of Histon, which rolled toward me with alarming rapidity. Soon, it was looming over me and blotting out the stars. The ship zoomed around to the night side of the planet and came to the black disc of the outstation. In no time, the ship had locked on and the airlock irised open to admit me to my grandmother's presence. I hadn't expected her to meet me here. She was grinning her broad toad grin at me. She finished up a subvocal conversation she was having with someone from the Unicon, then greeted me properly with a hug.

We got into the IBS car, which latched onto the geodetic tether, and we began our descent. When we dropped below the outstation, Histon's sun was just emerging from behind the planet. It was astoundingly beautiful. The layers of the upper atmosphere bent the light differently, and whiskery rainbows spooled away from us as we descended. It was dreamlike.

"I love that effect," Richelle said. She slowed our descent so we could appreciate it longer. The gearing on the tether clamp groaned and we crawled leisurely down toward the terminus, like a giant spider on a tree-trunk-sized silk. We were still falling faster than the sun was rising though, sinking into the gloam of the desert planet's early morning. Around us was a symphony of motion and light.

"Watch those thunderclouds in the west," Richelle said, pointing. In the black of the planet's night side a distant, roiling burst of electricity lit a stack of clouds. It was like an electric bubble had burst, producing a ring of finer lights which burnt outward like the bright edges of coals in a fire.

"Sprites," Richelle said, smiling.

Two more bursts of light billowed up and erupted, sending will-o'-the-wisps dancing out in more broken circles. From the opposite direction, the sun was again cresting the rim of the planet. We seemed so small in that vastness of air and light, travelling slowly down like a drop of dew on an infinite thread.

There were two benches in the IBS car. We sat on one together and watched the light show for a while in silence. Finally, Richelle spoke.

"I'm glad to have you back."

"I'm glad to *be* back. I can't tell—"

"I have something I'd like to talk to you about," Richelle said, "before we get down." She reached over and operated some controls. The IBS car slowed to a halt. She turned to me, suddenly serious.

"Your mother and I had a hard time convincing your father to let you come here."

"I know. I—"

"I'm still speaking. He wanted me to agree not to discuss the Faith with you. I've agreed, and I intend to keep my word. It's all foolishness anyway, I'm just as happy not to talk about it. But I need you to know. You are not to ask me about the Faith. Understood?"

"Yes."

"Good. Now," she settled and made herself comfortable. "Your mother was able to convince him that Histon, and my estate in particular, is a dangerous place."

"Mom said—"

"I'm still speaking. This was…let's call it a mischaracterization, but it served a purpose. You have no augments. Because Histon is mostly unpopulated and dangerous; and because you, being the boy you are and friends with Wil, are likely to ramble off on your own; and because I am an unreliable old hag," she grinned, "it seems prudent to provide you with certain emergency equipment. What if, for instance, your ankle became wedged by two rocks and you weren't able to free yourself?" My eyes went wide at this, but she continued. "Yes, it was fortuitous I knew about that incident; we used it to make the point. So, your father agreed to allow you to get a simple com watch."

"I don't believe it!" I couldn't help interrupting.

"Thankfully, facts do not depend on your belief. It's true." She took a deep breath and sat up a little straighter before continuing. "That was your mother's doing. But seeing as you were going to be equipped with a com watch, I did a little thinking and came up with an additional idea. I mentioned to your father there were no other children here, but that you were becoming close to Wil and Vie. I told him these two synthetic children would be excellent companions for you."

"Oh. He doesn't like the idea of me having synth friends."

"I'm aware. Religious people are best manipulated through their prejudices, and so that's where I began. He became upset and said he was going to withdraw his permission for you to come."

"Did his ears turn red?" I asked.

"They did, in fact," Richelle said, smiling. "It was at that point I mentioned your cousin, DayriPal."

"My cousin?"

"Your cousin."

"I didn't know I had a cousin."

"I'm aware. Your mother doesn't like to talk about her sister. Beal—"

"Mom has a sister?"

"I'm still speaking. BealiNel had a difficult life and, in the year before your birth, the Unicon saw fit to take away her freedom. She was sent to a hulk."

"What did she do?"

"That is not my tale to tell. Do you know what a hulk is?"

"No."

"A hulk is…excuse me for a moment." Richelle stood and went to the other side of the car to hold a short subvocal conversation with someone from the Unicon. She seemed annoyed and cut it off rather quickly, then sat on the bench across from me to continue our conversation.

"I'm sorry," she said, rubbing her hands together as if she'd gotten a chill from the call. "Where was I? Panticaya, yes; BealiNel's hulk. Well. A hulk is a prison planet. They are usually mining or agricultural outposts in distant sectors where prisoners are forced to do labor normally done by machines and synthetics. BealiNel was sent to Panticaya, a hulk planet. Her situation was unique in two ways. First, normally all augments and enhancements are removed from prisoners when they arrive at a hulk, but this wasn't necessary in BealiNel's case. She is a Feremite. Second, she was pregnant with her son, DayriPal."

"She went to prison pregnant?"

"Yes. Your cousin was born on a hulk. His father was not able to care for him, so DayriPal stayed there with BealiNel. He has been there ever since."

"He's being raised in prison?"

"He's being raised on a prison *planet*, yes. But he is not himself a prisoner. He can leave any time he likes. I've offered many times to bring him here." Richelle looked out at the line of dawn before continuing. "DayriPal is in the difficult position that his presence there creates a beneficial situation for his mother."

"I don't understand."

"As long as she is caring for him, BealiNel is spared from most of the labor other inmates suffer. My understanding is that she and DayriPal have a modest but comfortable home at the edge of a forest. When he leaves, her situation will grow much more difficult."

"That's terrible."

"I'm aware. Now, to bring this back to your situation here: DayriPal's condition is quite like your own. He is on a planet with a great many humans and synthetics his mother would rather he not have any contact with. So he is isolated. Normal schooling isn't available to him. He himself has no augments, no enhancements, no companions."

"He's got it worse than me."

"You and he share a great deal. Because of that, I suggested to your father that you two might do well to get in touch. Since you're already going to have a com watch, why not enable it so you could contact DayriPal through it."

"You can do that?"

"I can. I pointed out to your father that while Wil and Vie are perfectly acceptable companions despite being synths, this would be a way for you to have a *human* friend."

"Oh, you're good."

"I also pointed out that it would allow you to make a connection to a Feremite family member."

"DayriPal is a Feremite?"

"I couldn't say how he feels about things, but his mother is still a fanatic. That's a comfort to your father. So he agreed."

"He did?"

"He did."

"What about DayriPal? Does he want to do it?"

"He's excited to meet you. I've set up several immersions where the two of you can interact."

"Immersions? I thought it was a com watch?"

"Yes. Well." Richelle smiled with mischief. "Your father didn't go into the specifics of his own expectations, and it's a rather loose term. There are all sorts of com watch devices. I've arranged something I think will serve you and DayriPal both."

When my parents said I could go live with Richelle it felt like a whole new life had opened to me. This news about a cousin and a com watch was almost more than I could take. My face hurt from smiling.

Richelle said she would install the watch herself the following day. Because I had no other augments, she was using an older system, which had limitations, and at my father's request DayriPal would be the only one allowed in the immersions with me. Still. I was finally going to have some gear. I'd get to do immersions. And I'd get to meet my cousin. I had a cousin!

By the time we descended to the tether's terminus it was morning.

Richelle spoke an angry oath. There were two figures on the matte black platform below us. One was standing on a yellow area bordering the IBS landing site while the other zoomed wildly around the exposed disc on what appeared to be a motorcycle. It was Wil.

I smiled, suddenly eager to be back with my friends again. That's what they were, however strange or unlikely or flawed our friendship was. And they must have felt it too; they had come to greet me.

Vie was motioning wildly at Wil, obviously trying to get him to stop. She became incensed when he curved his way through the red IBS landing zone—she actually stamped her foot. Wil swerved just in time to miss the parked airship that had brought them up to the platform, putting his foot down to make the sharp turn.

"Foolish boy," Richelle said. She sighed, then added, "I should adjust his adrenaline receptors."

Wil angled right suddenly. He throttled up, gained more and more speed until he shot off the platform. My head banged against the glass of the IBS elevator as I leaned forward to see. Wil was airborn, pushing away from his falling motorcycle and beginning to tumble. He appeared to be out of control, turning end over end. A moment later, however, he stopped tumbling and steadied himself into the standard parachuting position—arms and legs out with his back arched to control his descent. But as we watched, webbing grew out between his arms and legs, making him look like a flying squirrel. These caught the air and suddenly he was shooting forward like a glider. He tilted to one side and banked right, then sharply left. He circled around until he was underneath the platform and lost from our view.

Vie backed away from the edge, her face a rictus of outrage. The IBS car was low enough now that she could see Richelle and I, and I guess I was smiling because she rolled her eyes and marched back to the lev-car for the return to the surface. She sat in one of the window seats, crossed her arms, and glowered as we touched down.

I saw now that Richelle was smiling too. No wonder Vie was angry.

"Give me a moment with Vie," said Richelle.

As I watched her cross over to the lev-car I couldn't help remembering my father call her a "stumpy old witch." It was true. But it was also true that she was the smartest, kindest, most understanding person I knew. And I was coming to live with her. And Vie, who wouldn't stay mad long. And Wil, who was spiraling down somewhere below us.

Life was finally spooling ahead like an adventure rather than a chore. I knew I should thank God, but under my breath I actually said, "Thank you, Richelle."

CHAPTER 18

WIL AND VIE WERE WAITING BY the iris to the Control cel with concerned expressions. "We don't know what's going on," Vie said. "She wants to talk to you."

"Is she here?" I asked, wondering if Richelle had commandeered a ship and come after us.

"I don't know where she is," said Vie. "It's very strange. She's using the panels in the Control cel, but they're routed through the FaRcom."

"Which we did *not* activate," added Wil. He was standing closer to Vie than he needed to, but I pushed that thought aside.

"Who activated it?" I asked.

"I have no idea," said Vie. "I can't even tell how it's being done."

"I don't think it's really her," volunteered Wil.

I looked past them, through the iris into the Control cel. I wanted to say something to Vie, but there was too much happening. Whatever had crashed here was attacking; my father was missing; Telesis was lying to us; now Richelle—or someone pretending to be her—was hacking our system.

I looked at Vie. Even under stress she was...poised and smart and beautiful. Wil didn't deserve her. Of course, neither did I.

I took a deep breath. One thing at a time. I walked past them into the cel.

Richelle appeared on the largest panel, directly across from the iris. She looked much the same as when I had last seen her: blue eyes in a square face that lit up when she saw me enter. The creased and deeply tanned skin, the gray ponytail, the simple studded earrings, three on her left side and one on the right—it was all so familiar. She was sitting at the edge of a bed in a plain room, a window behind her. The simple white

171

curtains rustled from a slight breeze, revealing a stretch of beach and open water when they parted. It was nowhere on Thalinraya I recognized, but she wasn't at her estate on Histon either. Assuming it was really her.

I walked slowly to the chairs that faced the main panel, but I was distracted by movement on either side. Looking around, every panel in the Control cel was engaged and actively showing pieces of Richelle's location: a section of wall, a wicker chair, another window, an open door leading to a small room with a sink. It was as though the Control cel was a cage inside Richelle's room, and through the dozens of windows in the cage we could look out at fragments of her world.

This alone would have been odd—I'd never seen multiple panels used like this. But the sense of movement came from the fact that when I moved, the perspective in each of the panels also moved. I hadn't thought that was even possible. I wanted to ask Wil and Vie if they saw this as well. Surely the panels couldn't display one perspective to me and a different one to them. Could they? The sense of a three-dimensional world just outside the confines of the Control cel was disconcerting.

"Tab." Her voice was the same. She sat up a little straighter, which was something she'd always done when starting a conversation. I felt a wave of relief, but pushed it away. Not yet.

I moved forward to the chairs, but didn't sit.

"Where are you?" was all I could think to ask.

"I'm in a safe location," she said after a moment's thought. She said it reassuringly, as though I might be concerned for her safety, then added: "A lot has happened in the years since you left."

"Like what?" I asked, wanting to hear her speak more. I couldn't trust her yet. Anyone could map Richelle's image into a panel display. And whoever this was had overridden the homestead, engaged the FaRcom signal and routed it into the Control cel, none of which should have been possible. This could be dangerous.

"You're right to be suspicious," she said approvingly. That was like Richelle too. "I have a lot of things I want you to know, but first I want you to be certain I am who I say I am. Ask me some questions."

She was acknowledging how easy it would be to impersonate someone via a com link. But wasn't that something an impersonator would do?

"Homestead," I said, "who is being displayed on the main panel in the Control cel?"

"There is no display on that panel at this time," said the familiar, directionless voice.

That made no sense.

"You're saying…the main control panel isn't displaying anything right now?"

"That is correct."

"I've bypassed the normal communication channels," said Richelle.

I felt—rather than saw—Wil and Vie come up beside me.

"Homestead," said Wil unexpectedly, "can you see the main panel from other…just, whatever you use to watch us?"

"Affirmative."

"Well…have a look," said Wil. Vie was smiling approval at him. "Homestead, what do you see there?"

"A malfunction."

"I am using other channels," said Richelle.

"Homestead, are there any signals coming in from outside the Thalinraya system?" I asked.

"Negative."

"She's here?" asked Wil, surprised.

"I'm not there," Richelle answered. "Your homestead doesn't have systems to understand this." She turned to me. "Tab, before we move on you need to assure yourself that I *am* Richelle."

But how? Images and voices could be altered. She could be anyone.

"How?"

"If I told you, that would defeat the purpose," she said. This was also something she'd do: not give an answer, but rather force me to find a solution for myself. Her responses were true to Richelle's character.

"You were there when I first met Wil," I said. "What was he doing?"

"He was casting himself off the spires on my estate. He had learned the previous day that the magnetic netting would prevent him from falling."

"I remember that," volunteered Wil, grinning. He stifled his grin, however, when he saw that Vie didn't want to give ground so quickly.

"Why do we call him Tab?" Vie challenged.

"He asked you to. That also happened at my estate."

"Why?" pressed Vie. "Why did he want us to call him Tab?"

"He didn't want your names to separate you." She smiled and looked at me as she added, "He talked about creating human names for you first, but I convinced him that was impractical. So he asked everyone to call him Tab."

"Is that true?" Wil asked, turning to me. "You wanted us to have human names?"

"Yeah. I was just trying to be…fair."

"That was more than sixty years ago for you," Vie said, still concentrated on Richelle. "How can you remember it so well?"

"As you well know, Vie, I am no longer a Feremite. I have more augmentations than you and Wil put together. I have onboard recordings of all our conversations. Do you want an exact transcript?"

Vie didn't need more. "It's her."

I agreed, more because of her manner than what she knew. We all relaxed. "It's her," I echoed, nodding at Vie.

"'As you well know,'" offered Wil, doing a terrible impression of Richelle's characteristic expression.

"I always hated that phrase," I admitted, smiling nonetheless.

"Why would you dislike that phrase?" said Richelle, sitting up a little straighter. The adjustment of posture was all Richelle; no impersonator could know that kind of detail. It was her.

"Because it really meant 'try harder,'" said Vie.

"Disappointment!" groaned Wil. "Nothing was worse than the *disappointment*. What was the other thing she said?" Wil had turned to Vie, but I knew what he was talking about.

"'Think before you speak,'" I reminded him.

"That's it! Oh, I hated that."

The suspicion had left us and Richelle was smiling now too. "I wasn't that bad."

"'I'm aware,'" quoted Wil, and we laughed even more. It felt good to laugh.

"You weren't bad at all," Vie said, "that's what made it hard to hear. We always wanted you to think well of us."

"And I did. You know I did."

"Except for me," said Wil.

"That's not true," protested Richelle, "as you well—"

" 'Know'!" exclaimed Wil and Vie simultaneously.

The release of tension was a huge relief, and I would have liked to let it last. But the weight of our situation was just beneath the surface. I slid into one of the chairs and faced the main panel.

"Richelle," I said, "do you know what's happening here?"

Everyone recognized I was moving us on to what we needed to discuss. Vie sat in the chair next to me; Wil sat on her other side. From the way he moved, his leg seemed to have healed well.

"Tab. Vie. Wil." Richelle looked at each of us in turn. "First, you are safe. You have a quality homestead there, plenty of resources, and from what I can see, this thing you're up against isn't preparing to come at you again. At least, not in the foreseeable future."

"How do you know?" I asked.

"I've gotten into its systems and…without going into the details, I'm good at this sort of thing." We all knew that was true. "In any case, you're safe. We have time. And I tell you that because we are going to need some time."

The next few hours were a revelation. Richelle explained that when I had given the people at Telesis control of the homestead—I looked an apology at Vie and Wil as Richelle went through this part—they had immediately begun to manage the information coming to us. It was also clear to Richelle they had no idea what had arrived here.

"So, when they said we saw a terraforming seed, that was a lie?" Vie asked. By this time Richelle had pulled a pillow behind her, but she still sat erect at the edge of her bed. Why she wasn't using the chair in her room was a mystery. From there she'd be able to see the shoreline out the window too.

"Yes," said Richelle. "I'm not sure why they wanted you to think that, but they didn't know what they were dealing with."

"Why couldn't they just tell us that?" I asked.

"Maybe they thought you'd panic. Maybe they didn't want you to know they weren't in control."

"They must have known it was dangerous," said Vie.

"Yes, I think they did. They were trying to figure out just *how* dangerous."

"I knew it!" said Wil, outraged and vindicated at the same time. "They were using us as bait. They didn't care if we died."

"Let me get this straight," said Vie, turning back to Richelle. "All Thalinraya's systems have been functioning normally since those things came to ground? So, when they told us they couldn't contact us outside the homestead, that was a lie too?"

"That's right," said Richelle, almost apologetically.

"They were spying on us," said Wil, turning to Vie. "Just like you said."

"But why?" pressed Vie. "And why did they want us to go to V-12?"

"I believe they wanted to gather information," said Richelle.

"Pogs!" Wil needed to move. He got up and started pacing back by the iris, stretching his legs.

There was still something missing. "Why send us to the Auger Station?" I asked. "What was the point of that?"

"They may have been stalling; they may have wanted to ramp up power production," speculated Richelle. "They may have anticipated they'd need more power to fight off whatever this thing is."

"Well, what do we think it is?" I asked. "A corporation, a government, some...outlaw group?"

Richelle couldn't say. When Wil asked if it could be extraterrestrial life, she pointed out that it certainly *was* extraterrestrial, but beyond that she didn't know.

Wil was still back by the iris. He'd absently picked up a detachable tac pad and now he was holding it up and moving it around. It too was displaying Richelle's room, and as Wil moved it he could see different portions of the room. I'd never seen displays work like this. Apparently Wil hadn't either.

Richelle had no additional information about my father. She wouldn't speculate about that either. The uncertainty made me angry. It had been days. The homestead could tell me the current rainfall on the other side of Thalinraya in an instant, but I couldn't find out if my own father was alive. He could be trapped. Injured. Suffering.

At least we had Richelle on our side now. Still...what could we *do*?

"I have reason to believe you're safe for now," Richelle reiterated. "The activity at V-12 and the other locations seems to be focused on building infrastructure. Whatever has arrived, it's burrowing in and getting ready for a long stay."

"Do you think it's after the malibdi?" Vie asked.

"I suspect so," said Richelle. "You're here because it's valuable to the Unicon. Whatever this is, it's likely they're here for the same reason."

"It's all about resources," Vie said, disgusted.

"That's so true," agreed Wil, obviously wanting Vie to see him backing her up.

Vie had more questions, though. "But if Telesis knew Thlinraya might be challenged, wouldn't they have taken precautions? Why send just one Feremite family if there might be trouble?"

"They didn't know?" I suggested.

"That's my suspicion. This is as much a surprise to Telesis as it is to you," Richelle continued.

"But why aren't they helping us now?" asked Vie. "Whether they expected trouble or not, we're the ones here. We're the ones who could help protect their investment. You said they could have helped us at V-12, but they didn't."

"That's true," agreed Wil with special emphasis. His agreement may have been real, but he was performing it too, for Vie's sake. Now he sat next to her.

"I can't explain it," said Richelle, holding out her hands. "But you're right, and you can't count on their help going forward. I don't know what their motivations are. But I don't think you're in immediate danger."

"Why wait, though?" said Wil. "The satellites have lasers. Why not hit V-12 and the other nests of these things and get rid of them?"

"We don't know enough to go on the offensive," said Richelle. "First, the satellites aren't positioned to directly hit all of the sites. Whatever came here is obviously organized, and attacking its facilities here without destroying all of them at once risks making it angry."

"Seems like it's already a little miffed," said Wil with a laugh. He looked over at Vie to see if she appreciated his humor.

"Well, we don't know," replied Richelle. "But there's also the fact that whatever it is may not know the extent or abilities of our satellites. It might be good to keep that secret for now. Once it knows, it might take measures to disable them."

That made sense. Having a secret weapon could prove useful.

"But you don't think whatever it is will make another attack again anytime soon?" I asked.

"I'm certain you've got a week or two at least. I suspect you'll have more than a month."

"Why would it attack like that and then just quit?" I pursued. I was almost as interested in the extent of Richelle's knowledge as I was in the answer. How did she know so much?

"It stopped attacking when you broke the connection to Telesis. I suspect it thought it had won at that point."

"It thinks it's won?" exclaimed Wil.

"Or at least achieved its aims," said Richelle.

"I don't understand," I said.

"I don't know how well you can read the electromagnetic activity at V-12," continued Richelle, "but there is an enormous amount of data streaming from each of these locations to something outside of the Thalinraya system."

"How?" Vie wasn't just surprised, she was suspicious too. How *did* Richelle know so much?

"There are some high-energy beams connecting the V-12 site to a dark matter lens about 80 AU out. The beams enter there and envelope to some other location. There's no way of knowing where."

"You think whatever this is is getting instructions from somewhere else?" I asked.

"Yes. And they assume the same is true with the homestead, so when you lost the connection with Telesis, they thought you'd been stymied."

I thought I understood Richelle's logic, but I wanted to know how she knew these things. Before I could ask, however, Wil's frustration bubbled over.

"Okay, but what do we *do*?" he asked. "We can't just wait around. We have to get rid of these things somehow."

"I see only one prudent course," said Richelle. She looked at each of us individually, took a breath, then said: "You have to leave."

"Leave Thalinraya?"

"Yes. I don't see any other way. These facilities look like they're here to stay. You don't have the resources to fight them, nor do you have the support of Telesis. Not that they could do anything for you anyway."

"We don't have a ship," said Wil. "The only ship we've got is the backup jump ship, which doesn't work for interstellar travel."

"We could assemble a ship," said Vie.

"Uh…in a couple years, maybe," said Wil. He turned to Richelle. "Do we have that long? Weren't you talking weeks?"

"You're safe for a few weeks," confirmed Richelle, "but beyond that, I don't know. We need to make plans to get you out of there soon. But Wil," she said, pointedly, "you have shown yourself to be more than capable of reengineering equipment. That's what we need here. We need you to refit the backup jump ship for interstellar travel." Wil's eyes went wide. "It'll be substantially slower than your ship to Thalinraya," Richelle explained, "but it should work."

Vie raised a pragmatic objection: "Even if the ship could be altered, it doesn't have bernacula."

"I'm confident Wil could retrofit it with them," said Richelle.

Wil's eyes glistened.

"It doesn't have the propellant either," Vie pursued. "The…what are they, nickies? And I don't feel like trying to get some from the cache at V-12 again."

"Yes," said Richelle. "Well, I know where you can get some. Tab, you know the basics of Stage Five terraforming. What do you remember about workforce capsules?"

I had visited a couple of these with my father to check on the vitals of the hibernating synths. We'd only done readings from above ground, but the memory of those trips, and my father, made me suddenly angry. Wil was so excited to retrofit the jump ship he wasn't thinking about anything else. *Reengineer a whole ship? Cool!* Vie didn't seem to care either. *Yeah, let's just leave.*

As though we weren't leaving anything behind.

"I remember plenty about workforce capsules, but…what about my father?" I demanded.

That took the air out of the room.

Vie reached over to touch my arm. I shrugged her off. "I know it's kind of inconvenient," I said accusingly, "but he's not necessarily dead. Or don't we care now?" I could feel my face getting red. I didn't care.

"TabiTal," said Richelle, a pained look on her face, "I'm not forgetting TaleXal. This will take days. I promise you, I will do everything I can to see if we can figure out what happened to him. If there is any chance he's still alive—any chance—we will use the first fuel we acquire to get out to that moon. But we can't do anything until we have the fuel, and the best way to get it is to wake a workforce capsule."

Wil and Vie both looked uncomfortable, which would have been gratifying, except I was suddenly feeling entirely childish. Richelle hadn't said we were leaving before finding out about my dad—I'd just assumed. Probably because I was scared and secretly *wanted* to leave. Getting into bern in a ship, knowing that when I woke up I'd be at the familiar port in Telesis…it was tempting.

"I'm sorry," I said, feeling foolish. They all assured me that my little outburst didn't mean anything, didn't even require forgiveness, which made it all the more embarrassing.

It was impossible to concentrate as Richelle explained her plan to get nickies from a workforce capsule. The pity in Vie's eyes was torture.

CHAPTER 19

WHEN WE WERE DONE SPEAKING WITH Richelle, we went to the commissary cel and ate together. Vie and Wil were feeling more hopeful, and they asked animated questions about the workforce capsules, which they hadn't known about. But when Wil looked around and asked where Thius was, things turned sour. I told them what the homestead had told me. Their faces fell, the bubble of optimism popped, and the fatigue we'd all been keeping at bay crashed over us.

Wil took it especially hard. Thius had a special fondness for him and, though he never would have admitted it, Wil had grown attached to the dog.

Wil and Vie retreated to their habitation cels, but I didn't think I'd be able to rest. I decided to go back to the functional cel my father had set up for my training. I loaded in a few modules about terraforming and began studying. I especially wanted to learn more about the workforce capsules.

Terraforming is more complex than anyone without augments should have to deal with, Dayr. If I had augments, I could have downloaded everything I needed and been on to other things in a few hours. As it was, I was in there well into the night and still only had the highest altitude understanding.

Capsules, I was reminded, are the synth arks that are sent to populate planets with workers for the first human inhabitants. During Stage Two terraforming, Stage Five workforce capsules are launched. The workforce capsules travel cheap and slow, using propellant that won't get them anywhere near light speeds. There's no hurry; the synths don't mind spending generations in transit, confined to their ships. They're engineered to enjoy it. Which is why workforce capsules have nickie drives. Humans only use them for short distance travel, in jump ships. But they're cheaper and good enough for long-hauling synths. Because they're only synths.

Terraforming is in Stage Three when the capsules arrive. With the help of the planet's curator, inevitably a Feremite, the capsules land in strategic locations around the planet. There are generally between four and fourteen capsules, depending on the size of the planet, and they burrow in at sites near future cities. The synths don't emerge. If things go according to plan, they have a celebration of thanks for the successful journey and then go into hibernation chambers to wait for the colonists' arrival. If adjustments are needed, the Stage Three curator works with Telesis to fix whatever is wrong with the capsule. Sometimes a weird culture develops in transit and the curator has to engineer and shepherd a whole new generation of synths, ones that will function reliably when the colonists arrive. In rare cases, the synth population of a capsule will be deemed unfit even to raise subsequent generations, and the whole capsule will be scuttled.

Thalinraya's eight capsules had arrived several hundred years prior to us, but they weren't scheduled to emerge until Stage Five. I knew where they were, but I'd never expected to see them. Now we had to visit a capsule to get the nickies we'd need for our jump ship. Richelle had already signaled them, in fact. The workforce capsules were waking.

When I woke the following day, Wil had already tricked out the gravion and installed an extra passenger ring on the fuselage, which meant he had onboarded, indexed, and processed a lot of new information. I'm not sure he slept, he was so excited to pilot one.

"Probably best if I drive us out there," I said as I came into the hangar. "My dad gave me some pointers and you've never been in one before." His face absolutely collapsed and his shoulders were slumping before I was able to add, "Kidding! I'm kidding."

He shoved me, then spent ten minutes showing me some of the additions he had made to the streamlined aircraft.

I don't think they have personnel gravions where you are, Dayr. They can carry from one to six people. They work best with one or two people, but the fuselage is modular and up to four extra seats can be added. The extra fuselage rings don't add any width, however, and you still have to ride one person behind the other.

We took off with Wil in front, me behind him and Vie in the rear. I had wanted her to be in the middle seat to have a better view out, but she had insisted that in case of an emergency I would be better positioned there than in the rear. When she got into the gravion she immediately began setting up displays on the canopy interior around her seat. She was so busy, I didn't have a chance to catch her eye.

She was avoiding me again, which, for the time being, was fine with me. I was feeling awkward around her, and it was a little comforting to know she felt the same.

Wil and Vie had never flown above the surface of the planet before. Now we were traveling at tremendous speed at a very high altitude. It was spectacular.

During the first few minutes Wil was concerned to make sure there wasn't anything coming after us. Richelle had told us that whatever was in V-12 wasn't interested in us any longer, but Wil wasn't taking any chances.

"Homestead," he said, his voice hollow in the tiny enclosure of the gravion, "any change in activity at V-12?"

"No change," said the neutral voice. It was reassuring to know our communications were working normally too. We still hadn't figured out why Telesis had lied to us about the satellites. What had they gained by pretending they couldn't maintain contact with us?

Which reminded me that Wil and Vie's subvocals were working again. I wondered what conversations they'd already had, and whether Vie had told Wil about our kiss. No, I wasn't going to think about that.

"Homestead," asked Vie, "any com activity between V-12 and the other infestations?"

"None."

Richelle had informed us she would be out of touch for a few hours. She hadn't explained why, and I found myself wondering again where she was. And why she was being so cryptic about what she knew and how she knew it.

For the next hour, Wil and Vie talked past me. It was mostly Wil, who was expressing an unusual appreciation for the beauty of Thalinraya. Was it sincere, or fueled by a desire to impress Vie? Both could be true, I supposed, but I suspected he was trying to capitalize on how badly things had gone between Vie and me.

As the planet scrolled by below—the vastness, the majesty of the mountain ranges, the jumble of forests, the piles of clouds—Wil and Vie talked to one another about it over my head. Vie would admire something, Wil would share a bit of data he'd onboarded or crack a joke. They spoke so easily with one another.

They were a more natural pair. They'd known each other longer; they understood one another, even without talking. Even without subvocals they'd joined forces to get control back from Telesis. I'd been slow to understand what was happening, but they'd just…known what the other was thinking.

I never knew what Vie was thinking or feeling.

I rarely knew what *I* was feeling.

I was just getting in the way. It was selfish. And Wil was a better person than me anyway, even though he wasn't human. He had saved us at V-12. He was capable and honest and…a synth, like Vie.

Why had I kissed her? I mean…because she was beautiful and smart and kind and…overwhelming in every way, obviously. But she was my friend.

She was my *friend*. What had I been thinking?

Too much—I was thinking too much. I had to stop.

As hill country rushed by below us and we angled out over a huge inland lake, I concentrated on where we were headed. Richelle had told us to bypass the nearest workforce capsule. The records showed it had been struck by a meteor on its final approach to Thalinraya. It had survived the strike and landed safely, but it had taken a few decades to repair the damage and repopulate the synths, so it had used quite a bit more fuel before going into hibernation. We were going to a more distant capsule, one that had retained much more of its reserve fuel. The jump ship we were taking back to Telesis was small, but we still wanted all the fuel we could get.

I had known about workforce capsules. My father had mentioned them a few times, but I'd never really thought about them. Now I began to wonder what life must be like in them.

"Did either of you onboard anything about these capsules?" I asked Wil and Vie.

"I've got all the specs on the ship," said Wil immediately.

"We can't access anything else," said Vie. "It's restricted information for synths."

I wondered if that meant they got glazed if they tried.

"I was just thinking about…being born in a spaceship," I continued, looking out at the curve of the atmosphere above us. "Never knowing anything else. Generations of them living their entire lives in those ships. And then, that last generation: knowing from the time you're born that when you turn a certain age you're going to land on a planet, go to sleep for hundreds of years, then wake up to a world that's…beyond anything you could have ever imagined. And filled with people you've never seen."

I explained some of the details to Wil and Vie, who hadn't known any of this. They hadn't even known there were other synths on Thalinraya until Richelle had mentioned the capsules. In the narrow confine of the gravion I couldn't see their faces or read their reactions.

"Seeing humans for the first time would be pretty overwhelming," mused Vie. "Especially if their parents and grandparents had never known humans."

"Yeah, and they're probably engineered so *serving* makes them feel good." Wil's bitterness about his former state was clear.

"I'll bet they are," agreed Vie, "and isn't that the kind thing to do? To make them satisfied with their work? That's how we would have been if Richelle hadn't adopted us. We'd have gotten the same engineering."

"Wouldn't it be better to give them the freedom to decide if they *wanted* to serve?" said Wil over his shoulder. "Whose side are you on, anyway?"

I got the feeling this was a conversation they'd already had. Synths in a workforce capsule would, of course, be of interest to them. Especially if they were forbidden to see any information about them.

"I'm just saying," said Vie, calmingly, "if you're going to engineer a synth, it's better to engineer a happy one than a frustrated one."

"Better still to give them some freedom, don't you think?"

"I don't want to fight," said Vie.

We looked out at the planet rolling beneath us and thought our own thoughts for a time, but then, surprisingly, Vie continued the conversation.

"If synths weren't engineered and they had the freedom to choose," she asked, "would any of them volunteer to do what these synths do?"

"Of course not," replied Wil immediately. "Synths wouldn't do *any* of the work they do. People don't want to do it…that's why there are synths in the first place. I was engineered to work in mines, but now that I've got the freedom to choose…no way!"

"That's because Richelle adopted us and stopped our engineering. But mining synths *want* to do it."

"What do you mean, 'stopped your engineering'?" I asked.

"It's done in stages," said Wil over his shoulder. "We missed out on the biggest lobotomies because Richelle—"

"Wil!" said Vie from behind me, but Wil never slowed.

"—because Richelle took us from the orphanates before we 'graduated' and got our glasses. That's when they install the major gear. I already liked mining, but if I'd 'graduated,' I would have had engineering to make me really *lust* after it. If Richelle hadn't stepped in, we'd be like other synths." Wil adopted a pathetic, plaintive voice: " 'Please let us serve. Oh, how we hope to be worthy to serve. We want to serve, serve, serve!' "

"Whether they're made that way or not, they *are* that way," said Vie patiently. "Would it be better to make them *dis*like their work?"

Wil was worked up again. "So, should I want to go back to my simple life of just doing what I'm programmed to do?"

"Don't do that," said Vie. "You don't have to take offense at everything."

"There's a story from our scripture," I said, hoping to decrease the tension. "There's a shepherd who loves his sheep. One night a wolf kills two of them. The shepherd realizes *all* his sheep are going to die one way or another, there's nothing he can do about it. So he castrates his sheep to prevent new ones from being born. Because new ones would eventually suffer too. After a few years his sheep all die. He stops being a shepherd and goes off to be a preacher."

There was an uncomfortable silence.

"That's it?" asked Vie.

"Yeah," I said, "the shepherd just goes around preaching."

"And," added Wil with grim enthusiasm, "when the shepherd dies he's rewarded for doing such a great thing. He 'becomes one of the foremost in God's parade.' "

"God's procession," I corrected.

"My translation says 'parade,' " said Wil.

"Your translation?"

"I onboarded the Feremite Bibles," he replied. Then he added, sarcastically: "That's some God you got there."

"I guess I don't understand the story," said Vie.

"You can't understand it, it's religion!" sneered Wil.

I felt defensive at Wil's attack, despite the fact that I didn't really believe.

"You're not meant to understand it," I said, "you're meant to think about it. It's an interesting problem."

"Pfff!"

"Wil, don't do that. What do you mean, Tab?" Vie's voice was oddly echoey as it bounced off the narrow interior of the gravion. I craned to look back at her, but it was too difficult, so I looked down at the passing mountain range as I spoke.

"There's some kind of law about not creating synths that will suffer. That's what made me think of it. The shepherd can't keep his sheep from suffering, so he just…stops making them. People can't do that with synths, so we engineer them away from suffering."

"So in this analogy synths are sheep?" Wil scoffed.

"He's not saying that, Wil." It felt good to have Vie coming in on my side.

"Are you saying it's not a good law?" I challenged Wil. "Should we create things that suffer?"

"Well, speaking as one of those *things*," countered Wil, "I think it might be better not to create things you intend to completely control."

"But Wil," Vie said, "you control this ship. Is that bad?"

"This ship isn't capable of knowing it's being controlled. So no, that's not bad. But when you're controlling something that *knows* it's being controlled, then yes, that's bad."

"Okay," I said, "But there's some work that just needs to get done. If people won't do it and it needs to get done, what are we supposed to do?"

"If nobody's willing to volunteer to do it," Wil said, "maybe it's not work worth doing."

CHAPTER 20

WIL PULLED THE GRAVION INTO A downward spiral toward the dry
lakebed. We were like a mosquito descending toward a cracked swath of
skin. My father had never flown in arcs like this. Wil must have onboarded
some advanced flying techniques.

The lakebed was mainly flat, but the shallow lozenge of a hill was
discernable in the distance. Our charts showed that this was where the
workforce capsule had burrowed in. As we got closer we could see that
one end of the hill had recently been blown out. Closer still, we were able
to make out the excavation that was happening—beetley machines were
at work in the bottom of the exploded basin: pile drivers drilling holes,
tank-like machines on tractor wheels moving soil, other machines with
great metal arms building platforms, planting active rebar and hyper-
mesh for what looked like a village center. We hovered above, watching
as canopies folded out from pillars to create a screen over the entire area.

"Some kind of defensive shield?" suggested Wil in response to a question from Vie.

"No," chuckled Richelle, her voice tinny in the gravion's interior. She
had rejoined us a few minutes earlier. Where she'd been, we didn't know.
"No, that's for shade. These synths haven't ever been exposed to sunlight."

"Oh. Yeah," said Wil, obviously embarrassed by his mistake.

Richelle finally gave us the go-ahead to descend. Wil brought us down
slowly in a wide spiral, taking in the entire facility that was being built.
When we got low enough to peer under the canopy we could see synths
already congregating on the newly built platforms beneath. Most of
those that weren't actively engaged in work looked in our direction as we

landed, but some simply stared in awe at the surrounding landscape. It occurred to me that they had never seen objects so distant before. Their entire lives had been spent in the confined spaces of the capsule; they had never seen natural light or breathed unfiltered air or gazed upon anything like a horizon.

I looked around, thinking back to how this world first looked to me. This dry lakebed surrounded by distant, rocky hills wasn't as picturesque as the site of the homestead, but any landscape must look amazing and beautiful to eyes starved of such sights. This was their first look at a new world, their first breaths taking in the air of the place they would live out the rest of their lives. There was something biblical about it.

As we stepped down from the gravion, a sturdy synth hurried in our direction, stumbling in his haste. His short, spikey gray hair made him look surprised, but his smile was large enough that it came across as a delighted surprise. Grey silicon cloth clung to his barrel-chested bulk, revealing him to be muscular and fit. If he'd been a foot shorter, he could have been Wil's grandfather. As it was, he towered over us. On his shoulders were some kind of epaulets that shimmered as he moved.

He stumbled again and laughed, waved off two smaller, umber-clad synths that had hurried to help him, and came on toward us with arms extended theatrically.

"Oh my, oh my, oh yes, oh yes! Am I looking at these beautiful human people! Oh my, oh my, oh *my*! Ha ha!"

Without pause he fell to a knee in front of Vie, grabbed her hand and kissed it. Looking up and seeing her shock, he boomed out a laugh.

"Ah, ha ha! Am I ready for a necessary apology? I think so, I think so!" Standing, he immediately bowed low and touched the sides of his round head with his fingertips. "Am I begging forgiveness! I am! I am and I do. We have our customs which we must shed, and we will, we will! Ha ha!"

He stood again, towering over us. He snapped his fingers and opened his arms to Wil and me in what must have been a welcoming gesture. I had forgotten how disconcerting synth glasses could be, covering the entire socket from nose to temple. He was smiling broadly, but I still had the sense that I couldn't really read his emotion. And the fact that he was so huge didn't help to put me at ease.

189

A cluster of a dozen synths, each dressed in a distinct color, was now standing behind him, holding their palms out in what must have been their formal greeting. They obviously deferred to this oversize synth.

"Am I too excited to properly introduce myself? I am not! I am Hig, Hiver of 330010, which is now…liberated!"

"Hiy!" exclaimed all the other synths in unison. They then began to hum and slowly rotate their hands.

"I am Hig, and we are eager to do your bidding."

"Hiy!"

"We offer ourselves in your service."

"Hiy!"

Hig and the others commenced with a martial-like dance. There was a lot of chopping the air and kicking—all synchronized. Wil, Vie, and I looked at one another uncomfortably. Like me, they must have been wishing we'd asked Richelle more about what to expect. They might have supposed I would know, as I was the one who had researched terraforming, but I was mystified.

"You need to take charge," Richelle said through my tragus speakers. I'd almost forgotten she was available.

"What are they doing?" I whispered.

"They had their entire lives to plan this meeting," explained Richelle. "I'm sure they have welcoming ceremonies and other things planned if you let them. But they'll follow your lead, you just have to take charge."

Interrupting them felt impolite, but I remembered that most people wouldn't have hesitated. "Stop!" I had to shout over their humming, which they were doing in harmony now. They set down the two synths they had lifted and turned toward us. Hig stepped forward.

"Am I right that you are now ready to introduce yourselves! I am, I am, I can feel it! Ha ha!" He set his hands on his hips and waited for me. The others, behind him, were holding out their palms again.

"My name is Tab," I said, "and this is Vie. This is Wil."

Hig kept smiling, but his eyebrows came together in confusion. "Am I right that you are not synthetics—you are human people? Of course you are, yes. This naming is a custom here?" He was reacting to our single-syllable names.

"Yes," I said, "my full name is TabiTal Yrl. We all have full names, but here on Thalinraya we only use the first part. In solidarity with you," I added, riffing on the idea. "We are all equal here."

I could tell I'd said something wrong immediately. The synths behind Hig all shifted uncomfortably; Hig's smile froze as he tried to take in what I'd said.

"Not equal with *you*," clarified Vie, stepping forward. "Our community here has…collective authority. We are one with one another as human people. One with *humans*, not with synths."

Hig had shifted his attention to Vie and now his smile came to life again. "Ha ha! I see, I see. Yes yes yes, we have much to learn."

"And many people to serve," added Vie, returning his smile.

"Ha ha, yes!" Hig was delighted. "Yes! We will serve!"

"Hiy!"

The discomfort I had caused was gone. Vie understood that my impulse to include them was misplaced. These were normal synths, not like Wil and Vie; they relished their subservient roles.

Hig began introducing the other synths, each the head of a synth guild. His manner was so loud and expressive, I wondered what kind of culture had developed aboard their capsule during their transit to Thalinraya. From what I'd learned, leaders were not engineered to be so animated. Had there been some kind of reshuffling aboard the capsule? Had types been crossed, different kinds of alliances made?

"I'm sorry to interrupt," said Vie, "but we need to enter your capsule."

Wil and I were spellbound by Hig and his boisterous introductions; Vie was bringing us back to our task.

"Am I going on at too much length? I am, I am. We have much to learn, much to learn. But we have only to serve."

"Hiy!"

"I am awaiting only your kind instruction, my lovely young friend," Hig said to Vie.

"Oh, well," said Vie, blushing.

"And modest too," boomed Hig, which made Vie blush more deeply.

"So," I said, "we need to go into your capsule. We need to see your propulsion system."

"I see, I see. Well…" Hig spread his arms wide again, "We are without our power engineers for several hours yet. Our waking was only begun forty-two hours ago and the resuscitators are full with reviving other personnel. This was programmed long, long ago."

"I don't understand," said Wil, and I was glad to be able to explain.

"Workforce synths are brought out of suspension in the order in which they're needed," I said. "There're only enough resuscitators for about twenty at a time."

"Twenty-two," clarified Hig, nodding happily. His cheeriness seemed to make Wil uncomfortable.

"I downloaded the ship's specs," Wil said. "I know where to go and what to do."

I nodded. Turning back to Hig, I said, "Let's go."

"Ah, well," said Hig, spreading his arms wide. He smiled but didn't move.

I glanced at Wil and Vie. They didn't understand either. It was an awkward standoff. Hig seemed content to grin and stare. Vie finally ventured, "Will you…take us to see it? The propulsion system?"

"Ah, well, that is a restricted area. Am I apologizing? Yes, I am. But I am needing contact with our administrator before I can allow this."

"Administrator?" I began, but my tragus crackled to life before I could continue.

"I forgot to tag you with those designations," Richelle said. "One second."

"Hang on a second," I said to Wil and Vie.

Hig stood with his arms wide, smiling at us patiently. I could see the three of us reflected in his mirrored glasses. Behind him the synth guild leaders stood with their palms extended toward us.

We all waited.

Vie reached up and scissored her obsidian hair behind an ear.

Wil shifted from one foot to the other.

"How's your leg?" I asked, remembering that he'd been injured.

"Fine," he said self-consciously, looking down at his pants.

"Yes!" boomed Hig unexpectedly. "Yes yes, you have fine legs! Fine!"

Wil's eyes went wide. Vie looked down in an unsuccessful effort not to laugh.

"Hiy! Am I correct that you are the administrator?" asked Hig, abruptly focusing on me.

"Yes," I replied. "That's right."

"Am I begging forgiveness again? I am, I am!" He bowed low. "Apologies and most sincere regret. I assumed you were a youth delegation for ceremonial greeting only. So young! So young and with so much authority." He turned to Wil and Vie, saying, "Am I right that you also serve this young genius? Yes, yes! We are blessed to have so capable a leader, no? Yes!" He snapped his fingers and raised his arms again. "We are truly blessed to serve!"

"Hiy!"

This was embarrassing.

"Richelle?" I whispered.

"I tagged you as Thalinraya's administrator," she explained. "That gives you the authorities you'll need."

"And now that I know your true status," Hig said, standing with his hands still awkwardly outstretched, "we should receive instructions and permissions from you, yes. We request permission to access the planet's datasphere. We do not yet know where the city initiators are. We must wake the Collins extractors and begin our work!"

"Don't do that!" said Richelle, quickly. "Keep communications and mapping functions offline for them for now. Tell them to assemble their housing here," she continued. "They'll need something to do while you get the material from their propulsion unit."

"You are contacting advisors subvocally, yes?" asked Hig.

"Yes," I said. "I'd like you to get your synths to start assembling homesteads here, around the capsule."

"Am I right that you mean habitation units?"

"Yes, sorry," I said, remembering that only humans enjoyed interactive homesteads. Synths were housed in simple habitations made from inert materials. I needed to be more careful. "I want the synths from this capsule to assemble habitation units within a kilometer of the capsule site. In three days," I added, inspired again, but more confident this time that it wouldn't backfire, "I will provide further instructions, but until that time I want you to make this region as comfortable for yourselves as you can."

Hig brought his arms down to his sides and raised up on his toes. "Our first directive."

"Hiy!"

"And a directive of such kindness."

"Hiy!"

"We thank you, young and gentle genius, administrator TabiTal."

"Hiy!"

Hig spun on his toes and nodded to the guild heads, who nodded in return and spun on their heels. Across the open area behind them, around the entire construction site inside the crater, synths changed direction. It was as though a flock of birds had all turned at once, and each of them moved now with new purpose. The guild heads started back down into the basin.

They obviously had some kind of sub-vocal communication system of their own.

"Now I want you to take us to your propulsion system," I said.

"Fore peak rear C, port hatch C-W6," Wil said.

"Ha! I will take you fore but the rest will be up to you," said Hig happily. "This is not my specialty. Come."

The guild leaders peeled to the sides as Hig turned and started down toward the capsule entrance. We followed.

CHAPTER 21

WE FOLLOWED HIG DOWN TOWARD THE opening to the capsule, passing into the shade of the massive origami screens. All around us there were synths busily building platforms and structures and unloading cargo. Those dressed in shades of yellow seemed to be built for physical labor; those in violet were supervisors of some sort. Each one smiled in greeting as we passed, but there was a disconcerting uniformity to their smiles. The mirrored glasses covering their eye sockets magnified the effect. I wondered if there were whispered conversations about *our* eyes. How strange they must appear, our soft, exposed orbs.

As we came closer to the capsule, we were walking across newly constructed platforms. The materials were different from any I had seen. Their capsule had been launched centuries ago, and the technology it possessed was not nearly as sophisticated as the technology to which we were accustomed.

"What's this material?" Wil asked, having noticed it too.

"Ah, yes yes yes. This is extruded Frenet plastisteel. Temporary only, I assure you. Once you have released mineral data to us we will build more permanent structures."

Crews of synths wearing matching colors worked on various projects all around, pouring in and out of the capsule like ants. The entrance was perhaps thirty feet across and perfectly round, with a walkway that emerged from the interior before splitting in several directions. Synths moved along the walkways efficiently and easily. They were engaged in what they were doing but paused to look after us as we passed. Apparently there was some flexibility in their engineering that allowed for curiosity.

A naked synth emerged from the capsule. Disturbingly, he wasn't at all self-conscious about his condition, walking with as much purpose as any of the others. Two red-clad synths came after him and took him by the arms when they reached him. They piloted him back into the capsule just in front of us, so our entrance into the ship was distracted by the bouncing muscular buttocks we were following.

Once inside, all three of us stopped to let our eyes adjust. The interior of the ship was cavernous, filled with old, non-interactive metal. Without any ambient movement, the chamber seemed menacingly lifeless.

It didn't take long to move to the forepeak of the ship, but the things we saw during that small journey changed us. First, there was the line of naked synths, queued up outside a provisioning compartment. They'd obviously been freshly revived. There were more than a dozen females and two males, all approximately ten years older than Wil, Vie, and I. They were talking amongst themselves animatedly, unconcerned—and undis-tracted!—by their own nudity, which was surprising, since they were all... amazingly well defined. Fit, I mean. When their friend who had wandered outside was ushered back into their midst they laughed good-naturedly, razzing him about the wrong turn he had taken.

When they saw us, however, they immediately stopped speaking and became modest, covering themselves and standing...differently. Vie slapped Wil, who was openly gawking. Seeing our distraction, Hig turned back to us.

"Am I right that you are admiring our accompanists? Oh yes, yes. They are newly revived, but they will be ready for service in minutes only, if you have need."

Wil looked to me for explanation, which I wasn't about to provide.

"Accompanists," said Vie with exasperation. I don't think Wil was con-fused so much as simply unable to work through whatever feelings he was experiencing. He was overwhelmed. Vie, however, took his open mouth to indicate a lack of understanding. She clarified: "For pleasure, Wil. It's what they used to call companion synths. Accompanists are engineered to pleasure people."

Horrified in several ways at once, Wil started to object but found he couldn't speak.

"Am I right that you are wanting an assignation? Yes yes!" Hig was walking back with his arms extended out again.

"No, no," I said quickly. "Let's continue."

Wil was the first to move forward, his face flushed, his eyes turned away from the naked synths. Vie rolled her eyes at me, then followed. Hig led us up some stairs to a catwalk skirting the starboard wall. Once above the floor we could look down and see what a hive of activity the place was. And it became immediately clear that clothing was one of the last things synths obtained before going out of the capsule. All of them in this area were naked.

That wasn't the most distracting part, however. As we walked along we passed containment cubicles, open from above, where synths of various kinds were being outfitted with all sorts of enhancements. It looked like a torture chamber, except all of the victims were willing. Some had their heads laid bare and were receiving direct implants; others were being fitted for various kinds of external improvements—exoskeletons, strength enhancements, sensory devices. One area seemed to be fitting synths out for hard vac activity. They were getting scapular hooks for solar sail attachments, self-oxygenating muscle replacements, extrudable SOD tool sets. They were becoming more machine than synth.

Wil got distracted again. He tried to keep walking, but he kept getting drawn to the rail to gawk down at some different enhancement being installed. I came up next to him and looked down at a small area where a synth had just laid down on an operating table next to some kind of instructional dummy figure. He was in the same kind of trance all the synths in this area were under. As soon as he had laid down, a mechanical arm with a laser on the end shot up from the floor and angled around to position itself next to his face. It began drawing a line from his chin along his jawline and up to his temple. Except... There was smoke rising from the synth's flesh. The laser wasn't drawing, it was cutting away the synth's face. And the synth wasn't reacting at all.

It was then I realized that the dummy on the table next to the synth wasn't a dummy—it was another synth who had already had most of its skin removed. Looking closer I could see there were tiny bots at work, sheathing the thing's muscles in some kind of mesh. Around its nose and eyes the bots looked like voracious worms, diving in and out of the complex muscles and tendons.

Vie started retching. She pushed herself away from the rail and leaned against the far wall before vomiting. Wil and I rushed to help her; Hig hurried back along the catwalk.

"Let us continue, let us continue. We are in haste. This is not for your eyes, no, no. Am I full of apology? I am."

Wil produced a cloth from somewhere and Vie wiped her face.

"I'm sorry," she said.

"I was the one who stopped," Wil said. "I'm the one who should be sorry."

"Are you okay?" I asked.

"I'm fine," Vie said, pushing away from the wall. "Let's just go."

We hurried along the rest of the chamber and through the giant iris, which led to the central thorax of the capsule. I wasn't prepared for how completely different this section of the ship would be. It looked like the set for an immerse drama set in some small, old-fashioned town. It was a little village with houses and some larger buildings, narrow paths going between. There was a waterfall coming out from a high pipe in the starboard side ahead of us. It fed a creek that wound down through a copse of trees to a little swimming hole. Above us there were six or seven full-spectrum light strips, four of which were currently throwing sunshine down onto the scene below.

"Home sweet home," boomed Hig without irony. And it was true: these synths had lived their entire lives here. Decades ago they had gone into suspension, but prior to that they had traveled in this capsule at nearly a quarter the speed of light. In here the motion wouldn't have been noticed—there was obviously controlled gravity in here. But they would have been limited to this one place.

Did any synths feel themselves constrained by this place, frustrated to be confined in this way? What would such a life have been like?

Then again, that was the fate of most life, even humans until recently. Born onto a world they could never really escape. A planet, a ship—what was the difference, really?

When they arrived on Thalinraya, were there some who wanted to go out and see their new world right away? I had learned that they were eager to go into their suspension coomb, and I knew they had been engineered to desire it. Still, I found it hard to believe they wouldn't feel a pull to explore their new home right away.

"Are they safe?" Wil was pointing toward the village, where a crowd of synths had gathered. Some were already moving toward us.

"Safe!" Hig laughed. "Of course, of course. They are merely excited. You are the first humans they have ever seen. You are celebrities!"

At Hig's bidding, we headed down into the little hamlet. The houses, I had learned in my previous day's study, were uniform little buildings of reactive materials. This included their houses. Wherever someone had scratched an image into a wall, colors bled out from the lines like the iridescent rainbows in an oil spill. There was a tribal feel to much of the decoration, with many abstract linear designs and repeated patterns. A few had more whimsy, some with pictures and scenes.

When we neared the village square, the group of synths approached us, shouting greetings and breaking into applause when Wil waved. Hig's presence seemed to keep them at a distance. I couldn't tell if they were afraid of him or just showing him respect.

Their clothes were like their houses, plain but individually decorated. Everything they wore was light green, but over the green were patterns and images they had obviously created themselves.

Something brushed my leg. I looked down to see a child synth running back behind a near house, where several other children were watching excitedly. Like Wil and Vie when I had first met them, the children hadn't yet been fitted with the signature synth glasses. Around the irises their eyes shined with silver where human children would have had white. That technology, at least, was the same.

"Roh," boomed Hig, "come and greet our first visitors!"

A man with red hair very like Wil's but in a short ponytail came over to us and spread his arms wide in greeting. Although his clothes were the same as everyone else's, he too had an air of authority.

"Hiver Hig," he said in a surprisingly high and nasal voice, "you didn't tell us we would have visitors so early. I would have done fireworks."

Roh and Hig began snapping their fingers at one another, then they raised their arms and lowered them to their sides. This gesture of greeting, I realized, was reciprocal. We hadn't raised our arms or snapped, so Hig had been left with his arms raised for an extended period. I wondered if it had seemed insulting to him.

Roh snapped his fingers and raised his arms again to us. I tried to return the gesture, lifting my arms, snapping, and lowering my arms as he did.

"Am I right that you are honoring us? Yes yes, you are. You are!" Roh had Hig's same boisterous manner.

"I am," I said, then added, "I am!"

"Ha ha!" boomed Hig in his deeper voice. "And we will be quick to learn your customs too, am I right? I am. Yes yes. But let us continue."

Roh fell into step beside Hig and we continued through the little village. On the far side we passed a playground where children were crawling in, around, and through what looked like a giant termite mound. Each child had a U-shaped handle which, when pressed to the ground, attached itself and activated the material all around the handle so the child could pull or push the ground into a new shape. When the child removed the handle, the shape would stay firmly in place. Some children were building warrens, moving in and out of little caves and pulling the ground around themselves like taffy. Others had improvised obstacle courses for one another, with little ramps and slides. Still others were making a dangerous looking jungle gym.

Vie was smiling in that direction too. I could tell she would have liked to linger there, but we continued up a rise and back onto a platform. We passed through a smaller iris and we were quickly in the cramped forward compartments. This was an environment built for zero gravity: there were ladders lining all sides of the shafts and access tubes, which connected different control pods. There were no clear places to walk. We had to carefully step our way between instrument panels, hatches, ladders and other equipment lining the walls and floor. Hig had to bend down as well, being as tall as he was.

"Am I right that you know the way?" he said, pausing to look back toward Wil.

"Yeah, I onboarded your schematic."

"Would you like to lead?" asked Hig. "I am not familiar with this area and—Hem! Welcome my friend."

A synth came swinging out of a side tunnel, using the ceiling ladder more expertly than a monkey.

"Hig," said Hem in a gravely voice, "I had an alert that you were coming."

Instinct told me I shouldn't react, but it was impossible not to step back. Hem was unlike anything I'd ever seen. His torso was normal, and he seemed comfortable hanging by his arms. But where his legs ought to have been there were, instead, two *more* arms. He spread these wide and began snapping his lower fingers in greeting to Hig, while still hanging from his first pair of arms.

The usefulness of this arrangement in zero gravity in these narrow, ladder-lined shafts was immediately apparent, but there was something monstrous about it.

"They are needing to access fore peak rear C, port hatch C-WP...6, yes?" said Hig.

"That's right," confirmed Wil.

"Follow me," growled Hem, swinging expertly around and heading back down the tunnel from which he'd come. The way he moved down the tunnel was bizarre. He used two of the upper rows of ladders, but he would often flip over and reach down to manipulate some control or other. When he turned a corner he made a sort of hanging cartwheel that probably would have been graceful in zero gravity. When he needed to open an iris, he positioned himself over the opening by fixing three hands in a tripod configuration and reaching over with the fourth to activate the tac pad. He looked like some human-arachnid cross, and my sense of disgust increased as he moved. I was sure Wil and Vie felt the same way, but I didn't want to look at them for fear of giving insult.

Hem led us through a warren of tunnels. Embedded lighting in the walls anticipated us all the way and we were never in dark, but I still had a sense that darkness was pressing in. When we finally arrived at the appointed location, Wil came forward and faced what looked like a blank wall. He swung his backpack around and took out a sort of dial with a loop attached. He slipped the loop over his left index finger, then held the dial up to the wall. He spun it around, reversing directions several times, and finally looked into the open center.

"It worked," he said. "Stand back."

We did. He flipped a switch on the side of the dial and a circular area around it shimmered for a moment, turned plasmatic, then rolled away from the sides of the dial outward. The dial was now a pendulum, hung from a thin plasma string in the center of a circular window, the rim of which roiled like an event horizon. Behind the wall was a tangle of equipment, most facing some interior we couldn't see. We were coming in behind the machinery somehow.

"I have never seen in here," said Hem eagerly. He was suspended from what was, for now, the roof of the tunnel, craning his neck to see what Wil was doing.

"Neither have I," said Wil, dryly. Hem looked at Hig, who smiled.

"Am I right that this one has a sense of humor?" boomed Hig approvingly. "Yes yes, ha!" Hem arched a bristly eyebrow.

Wil reached into his pack again and pulled out gloves and a dark, wide canister. He propped the canister between two rungs of a ladder, put the gloves on, then said quickly: "Don't touch that."

Vie had leaned in to examine the roiling plasma at the rim of the circle opening. Now she leaned back and held up her hands. "I wasn't."

Wil reached into his backpack one last time and removed a clamping tool and a laser. Vie leaned forward again to see.

"Try not to bump me," said Wil.

"I won't," she replied defensively.

Working carefully, he reached through the hole he had made and pushed some tubes aside, after which he carefully placed a clamp on a small rod of milky but iridescent blue material. Holding the clamp firmly in one hand, he aimed the laser with the other and pointed a narrow beam at the area just beneath the rod. It melted and the rod came free. Wil placed it in the canister he had ready, then went back for another rod.

We watched in silence as he did this two more times. The final, fourth rod was seared at one end, and Wil left it. After screwing the canister shut, he began removing his gloves.

"Is that it?" asked Vie.

"Yeah," said Wil.

"Three of those things is enough?"

"Three quarters of *one* of those things is enough. We've got two we'll probably never need. Double redundancy, if anything goes wrong." Wil raised the dial again.

"You couldn't leave it open?" growled Hem, hopefully. "Just for a few minutes?" His eager face staring down from above was monstrous.

"Sorry," said Wil.

The plasma circled in and closed off the wall again.

When we had said goodbye to Hem, we made our way back through their village and then through the work area, past where the naked synths had been and out into the Thalinraya sun. Along the way Hig began asking questions about delegations and population centers and plans for moving the synths to where they were needed. As Richelle had instructed, I put him off, saying that plans were still underway and we would be back in a few days to give further instructions. I could tell he was disappointed, but he had been engineered too well to voice it. He would do as I said.

As we made our way up the slope toward the gravion I wondered why we hadn't heard from Richelle. I activated my watch and hailed her three times, but it wasn't until we were back in the gravion, strapping ourselves in, that she responded.

"I'm sorry, I had some other things I needed to attend to. How did it go?"

"Three full rods," Wil said, proudly. The canopy had closed over us. Vie was waving goodbye to Hig and the guild heads, who were holding their palms out toward us again.

"Three full. Excellent. Well done," said Richelle. "And you obviously didn't blow the capsule to bits."

"No," laughed Wil as he worked the instrument panel.

"Was that a possibility?" asked Vie lightly, obviously thinking it wasn't.

"If the V-laser had hit the stem on the rods, yeah, it would've..." Wil broke off when, glancing back, he saw the look on Vie's face.

Richelle couldn't see Vie's face, so she finished Wil's sentence: "It would have punched a hole in that lakebed two or three kilometers across."

We couldn't look at one another, but the tension in the gravion was suddenly palpable.

"This V-laser," began Vie, "this was the thing you...the little laser thing?"

"Yeah," said Wil carefully.

"The 'Don't bump me' thing?"

"Yeah." Hearing her groan in response, he added, "Sorry?"

There was a long, empty moment, then Vie said simply, "Let's get back to the homestead."

Wil turned, flipped some switches and flung us into the air.

He had a steady nerve. Vie had to admit that.

CHAPTER 22

WIL HAD SET THE GRAVION ON AUTOPILOT. We were flying along in silence, each of us lost in our own thoughts, none of us eager to discuss what we'd seen at the capsule. We were higher in the asthenosphere than we'd been on the way, so we could see more of the weather patterns below, the membrane of the planet's atmosphere, masses of stars. Four marble moons rolled by above us.

My father might be on one of them.

Richelle had told us, as we rocketed up from the dry lakebed, that she hadn't gathered any new information about my father. The moon's orbit meant we wouldn't have the right angle to see anything for weeks, and she couldn't reposition any satellites for a better view. She was going to try for a reflected image off the solar shield on a different moon, but she didn't think it would work.

If he was alive, we should have heard from him by now. He'd had time to set the mass accumulator, so even if he'd forgotten to set out his com relay, he should have had time by now to contact us directly. The chances of him still being alive were becoming vanishingly remote.

We had the nickies that could take us there now, but did we have time? Richelle didn't think we'd be attacked again soon, but there was no guarantee. It might take ten days to get to that moon and back, and the jump ship still needed work before it'd be ready for interstellar travel. That work couldn't get done while we were winging around the solar system.

No. It was foolish to delay.

But what if he was alive and stranded? It felt wrong to flee Thalinraya without even knowing what had happened to him. If only we could get there faster.

Well, there was...

"Are you alright?" asked Vie from the seat behind me. I had let out a long burst of air.

"Fine. Sorry," I said.

I looked down at the curve of Thalinraya, back up to the moons.

Leaving felt wrong because deep down I knew there *was* something we could do. Something I could do. I'd been turning the thought over in the back of my mind. My father wouldn't want me to do it, even if it would save his life. Of that I was absolutely certain: he would rather die than let me compromise my eternal soul, which is how he'd think of it. He'd be disgusted at me for even considering it.

In a way, that made me want to do it even more.

The silence in the gravion canopy seemed oppressive. I wondered if Wil and Vie were having a subvocal conversation. To interrupt one if it was going on, but also to distract myself from thoughts of my father, I asked: "Where you were raised, in the orphanates, did you go around naked a lot?"

"No!" exclaimed Vie, her voice close behind me. "We grew up just like you did. We have modesty."

Her reaction was so strong I felt immediately guilty for having asked. "Well," said Wil from up front, "it wasn't *exactly* the same. We did things as a group. We slept in rooms that held twenty-six guys, we ate together."

"But you weren't *naked* together!" said Vie.

"In the showers we were. Especially after trainings."

"You *showered* together?" she asked.

"Yeah, didn't you?"

"No!"

I hadn't really thought about how different being raised in an orphanate would be. Synth childhoods were communal. They didn't have parents; they were raised together, with other synths who had the same interests and abilities. They'd probably had lots of friends before their adoptions. Did they miss them?

"I suppose," said Vie, coming out of her own contemplation, "different orphanates are structured to encourage different attributes. You wouldn't have any need for modesty in whatever mines you were sent to, so there was no need to raise you that way. I needed to be in a situation that would simulate an environment that included different kinds of people. So my orphanate had synths of both sexes, and we were raised to treat one another more or less like…well, like humans."

"Because you were meant to be a communication synth," I said.

"Exactly."

"We're raised to have the traits people want," interjected Wil. "Like how animals used to be raised to maximize meat production."

I understood Wil's sense of injustice, knowing he'd been raised for someone else's purposes. It wasn't fair. But I'd begun to think my own situation wasn't so different. I wasn't a synth, but my parents had made so many decisions about my life that I might as well have been. I'd had no input in what I studied, where I lived, what I got to do with my time. It wasn't only synths who got pushed around. Growing up is an inherently unjust process. They might have resented the engineers who programmed them, but was that so very different from what happened to me? All kids have engineers. They're called parents.

"That guy Hem is going to give me nightmares," Vie said.

The image of the four-armed synth cartwheeling around a corner on a ceiling ladder sprang back into my mind.

"Me too," I agreed. "I've never seen anything like that."

"You mean any*one*," corrected Wil, bitterly.

"You know what I meant."

"It was shocking," Vie said by way of defending me. "None of us have ever seen anything like that."

"Any*one*," repeated Wil. "And I have."

"When?"

"At my orphanate. During some of our trainings we went underground into mining simulations. There was an underground orphanate too, and they'd send teams of us down to train together."

"An underground orphanate?" said Vie. "You never told me that."

"Yeah. There are some synths who specialize in different kinds of mining, and some of them live entirely underground."

"You mean they never come to the surface?" asked Vie, shocked. "*Never*?"

"Never. And if you saw them, you'd know why. They were more like Hem than us. I didn't think they were creepy at the time, but looking back…they were way creepy."

"How do you mean?" asked Vie.

"Uh…there were different kinds, but all of them were about a third as big as us. They had translucent skin, so you could see their veins." I thought of the synths undergoing surgery back in the workforce capsule, their muscles and veins laid bare. "They had no hair on their heads except for their eyebrows. They had huge eyebrows that went all the way around. Six eye sockets so they could see in all directions. Their eyes were covered with a sort of fine mesh that their eyelids would scrape and wet every few seconds. They were indifferent to light—I don't think they ever had any unless we were around. I'm not sure how their eyes worked."

"You never told me this." Vie seemed hurt that he'd never shared this with her before.

"It wasn't really the kind of thing I wanted to talk about."

"Did they speak?" I asked. "Did you interact with them?"

"Yeah, we learned to work with them. They had these baleen filters instead of teeth, so they all lisped. They could kind of retract them, but they were still hard to understand. I don't think they liked talking to us anyway. We mostly used subvocals and signaling. We didn't see them very often, though; they were usually off doing the really dangerous stuff."

"Like what?"

"They do the vortexing, scarning, bastard drilling. They manage the vesicles for the room and pillar infrastructures, do the microshearing on the retreat. When a Grady vein—"

"Okay, okay," I said, "I get it. They do mining stuff."

"Yeah. We were meant to be the brains, they were the brawn, which is why a lot of them had full body enhancements. We used assemblers and machines when we needed them. These guys had a lot of those things built in."

"Drills and things?" asked Vie, awed and disgusted. "In their bodies?"

"Some of them, yeah. Most of them had carapaces covering their backs. One guy I saw had a thick one with extenders. I think he was a deep driller and set up to withstand collapses. I never saw a magma diver, but they had those too."

"But…why don't they just use assemblers for that really dangerous stuff?" Vie asked.

"Assemblers are expensive. They use a lot of resources. Synths are cheaper." Wil's voice was flat. He was beyond angry about this. "Expendable."

"That's...awful," I said, lamely.

Wil grunted a laugh. "Awful to someone like you, with your *unspoiled* body."

I knew he was only lashing out because he was worked up. We'd seen some appalling things at the capsule; apparently he'd seen even worse things as a kid.

Still, his insult landed hard. I had my watch, but my body was otherwise augment-free. Wil knew I would have loved to have augments like his; we'd talked about it many times. He knew I intended to leave my parent's faith when I came of age, and that I planned to get augments then. But maybe he didn't believe me. Maybe he thought it was all bragging and bluster—that I was too cautious, too fearful, too afraid of pain to actually go through with it.

It made me want to prove him wrong. I could do it in a big way too, sooner than he would ever expect.

"One good thing though," continued Wil, "miner synths *love* their work. Their masters at least did that for them." Wil was bitterly circling back to our earlier conversation. "They were engineered to thrill at being underground. They loved the confinement, loved the dark, loved the danger. They had this way of grunting when they were satisfied. You could tell; they lived for that stuff."

I was starting to feel defensive of my species. The fact that synths are engineered to enjoy things we wouldn't enjoy... Well, so what? An enjoyable life is an enjoyable life. If you love what you're doing, where's the problem? Surely it'd be worse if they hated their lives.

And the same is true of people, isn't it? We were engineered to like things that get our genes into the next generation. It's *natural* engineering, but it's no more in our control than what a synth likes is in its control. Should I feel mad that I didn't get to engineer myself? Or sad?

"What's that?" Vie was pointing up. Wil and I looked, but neither of us saw anything of note. "All along there," she said. I realized I had been looking for movement, but when I shifted to look for something else, I saw it. Above us, arcing across the deepest blue that marked the boundary between Thalinraya's atmosphere and space, was a fine thread. Had we been on the ground I would have suspected a high condensation trail, but the gravion was already quite high. Whatever this was, it was even higher.

"Thalinraya doesn't have any micro rings, does it?" asked Wil.

"Thalinraya doesn't have rings," I said.

"There's another one."

We looked. She was right—another thread, running parallel, was further down toward the horizon, more difficult to see due to the glare. I pulled the skin back on my wrist and hailed Richelle. We all heard the connection pop open in the gravion's canopy.

"Richelle, we're seeing something in the upper atmosphere here," I explained.

"Filaments?"

"Yeah," I said, surprised. "How'd you know?"

"Those are coming from V-12 and three other hubs around the planet. As far as I can tell, they're nothing to worry about."

There was a silence in the gravion. Wil craned around and shared a skeptical look with us. Nothing to worry about? These were coming from whatever was invading the planet, from the things that had attacked us, but it was nothing to worry about?

"Do you know what they are?" asked Vie.

"They appear to be some kind of communication device. They're aimed outward. I think they're safe."

"You *think*?" asked Wil.

"They're passive receptors. They're no threat to you, of that I'm sure."

The filament closest to us had grown thicker and now it gently bowed and split where it arced, creating several eyelets on either side of the main line. If it repeated this pattern it would create a sort of mesh or net.

"Is it some kind of EM receiver?" asked Vie.

"I believe so," replied Richelle.

We waited for more of an explanation, but none came. After a moment we all heard the com channel switch off. It was an abrupt end to the conversation, and I was about to say so when Wil spoke up.

"Mind your ears," he cautioned as he brought the gravion around in preparation for our descent toward the homestead.

Once the gravion had rotated and angled down, I found myself looking directly up at the orbiting marble moons. I was now rocketing down and away from my father.

For now.

CHAPTER 23

WHEN WE LANDED, WIL AND I headed straight for the hangar to get the secondary jump ship while Vie went to the hotplate. She wanted to look into the filaments we'd seen in the upper atmosphere to see if she could determine what they were.

Wil and I had a moment of panic when we discovered the hangar had been completely reconfigured and expanded. It now extended over the area where the exercise field had been, the whole thing covered by a massive and permanent-looking translucent dome. The homestead informed us that the dome was mirrored on the outside and impregnated with EM jamming mesh. While it was comforting to hear that the hangar was secure from outside scrutiny, I was a little disconcerted that the homestead had done all this on its own. Certainly there were routine tasks the homestead accomplished without direction, but this took a great deal of planning and initiative—moving equipment, requisitioning materials, setting up the work space. There was a dedicated service elevator, the homestead informed us, that went directly to the underground storage tanks. How had the homestead known to do all this?

Wil was climbing up into the cockpit of the jump ship, eager to see what kind of changes would need to be made.

"Homestead," I began, "did you need permissions for this reconfiguration?"

"Requisition, distribution, and reallocation of resources all require authorization."

"So...who gave you the authorization for all this?"

"That information isn't available," said the homestead.

That must mean Richelle did it. Her ability to manipulate things remotely was...well, not as troublesome as when Telesis was doing it, but still troubling. I didn't want to be suspicious, and I trusted her thoroughly. Still.

Wil's torso emerged from the cockpit. "Can you hand me the wimble?" he said, pointing to a jumble of tools on a rolling cart next to the ladder leading to the cockpit.

"What's a wimble?" I asked, going to the tools.

Wil pointed to what looked like a dull black square box. As soon as I touched it, the box lit up from within and tiny hairs sprang out. They felt warm. A code of some kind raced across the face of the box. I went to carry it up the stairs.

"Just toss it." Wil was in his element. He had downloaded the specs he needed, he had tools to use and a task to perform. The fire of purposeful work was in his eye. I hoped, for his sake, there would be some danger involved. Wil liked a bit of danger.

He caught the wimble when I threw it up.

"How does it look in there?" I asked.

"We're going to have to strip this back to the fuselage. Most of this equipment will have to go. It's all built for short distance travel, not interstellar..." He continued talking, but he had dived back into the cockpit and I couldn't hear the rest of what he said. He was excited to begin.

When I turned toward the elevator bay, Vie was already halfway to the hangar.

"Tab, we need to talk," she said, stepping in.

A jolt of anxiety shot through me. I wasn't quite ready to talk.

"Is your subvocal to Richelle active?" she asked.

"No," I said. "Do you need her?"

Vie nodded and I relaxed. We weren't going to talk about what had happened between us. Or worse, about her and Wil.

"Hang on, I'll hail her."

As I pulled the skin back on my wristwatch and pressed the hail, Vie asked, "Would you know?"

"What do you mean?"

"How do you know when it's active?" Vie asked. "Wil and I get a request from the other, but then we have to enable our channel on each end. Is that how it works with you?"

"I get a buzz in my watch, then there's this enable switch," I said. "But I don't think she'd listen in, if that's what you mean."

"It might be possible though?" asked Vie.

"Richelle wouldn't do that," I said.

Vie crossed her arms and was about to respond, but the tac pad in the tool cart blinked on and Richelle was there. I'd never seen a tac pad work that way.

"Tab, Vie. What is it?" asked Richelle. I didn't want to be suspicious, but her tone was odd. And how had she known to show herself on the tool cart's tac pad?

"I've had a look at these filament things we saw," said Vie. "They're spreading all around the upper atmosphere, weaving together. It's like a net that's constructing itself."

"That doesn't sound good," I said.

"No," agreed Vie. "But Richelle, you've said there's nothing to worry about."

"I've seen all the information you've seen, Vie, and I'm certain these things are aimed outward if they're aimed at all."

"These things are deforming phase space in some of the interstices," Vie said.

"I expect that will continue, but I don't foresee it being a problem." Richelle was being unusually terse.

Vie was concerned, as much from Richelle's reaction as from the self-constructing net above us. "How can you say that?" she asked. "I've never seen anything like this."

"I don't even know what you're talking about," I added, "but it sounds dangerous to me, Richelle."

"What about navigation?" asked Vie. "If we can't contact the satellites, we can't get coordinates. Our ship's ability to locate itself would be… wiped out."

"That won't happen," Richelle said with confidence. "And I'll be with you until you're out of the Thalinraya system, so I can help."

Vie looked at me hard for a moment, then back to the small image of Richelle on the tool cart tac pad. "Richelle, I have to say this. I don't know where you're getting your information. I don't know how you have the access you have to the homestead or why you're monitoring everything we do. But given all that…I don't know how you expect us to trust you."

We looked at one another for long moments. Sounds of Wil at work inside the ship floated down to us, but all else was quiet.

Richelle wasn't going to volunteer an explanation.

"Richelle," I said, "You know I trust you, but the people at Telesis were keeping things from us. Now it seems like you're not telling us everything either."

"I'm sorry," said Richelle, her voice breaking a bit. "I can't tell you everything I know and I can't tell you why. I'm not deceiving you, but there are some limitations on what I can say."

Vie didn't know how to respond to that. I didn't either, but a terrible thought occurred. "Are you withholding something about my father?" I asked.

"Oh, Tabit." If she wasn't hurt by the question, she was doing a great job pretending to be. After a long silence she said, "Tab, I don't know anything about what happened to your father. I tried to get a reflected image but it doesn't work. I don't think there's anything else we can do." After another silence she said, "I'm sorry, Tab. I don't suspect we'll ever know what happened."

There it was. Someone had finally had the courage to say it.

"We could send one of you there in the jump ship," continued Richelle apologetically, "but I'm afraid it would take too long. I don't think it's safe to delay. I'm sorry, but I think you need to let him go."

Vie was frozen next to me, waiting to see how I would respond.

Richelle's tiny face in the tac pad looked up at me from among the tools on the cart. She knew there was another way. If anyone could have figured it out, Richelle could. Why wasn't she suggesting it? Did she not want me to know whether my father was alive or dead?

Or, did she think I'd be too afraid to do it? I *was* afraid, but that didn't mean I wasn't going to do it. Now more than ever.

"I'm telling you as much as I can," Richelle continued. "I can help Wil get the ship ready in six days. But we don't have time for—"

"I understand," I interrupted. "It's okay." I felt Vie's hand on my elbow. "It's okay," I said, looking her right in the eyes. "Really."

"I'm sorry, Tabit," said Richelle.

"We're all sorry," I said, turning back to the tac pad, "but we have other things to deal with. I'm curious…where are you?"

Richelle was surprised by the change of subject. "I can't tell you that."

Vie turned back to Richelle too. "Richelle, you've got to meet us halfway. How can we trust you?"

"Richelle shook her head sadly. "I know. I know, but I can't tell you that."

Vie's face hardened. Her eyes lifted from the tool cart and she said to me, "I think we need to reestablish contact with Telesis."

I expected Richelle to say something, but there was only silence.

"Do you think it's safe?" I asked.

"They can't take control of the homestead again until we've gotten rid of the V-12 infestation. You made sure of that. So yes, I think it's safe."

"Richelle was able to get in and do things without our authorization," I said. "No offense, Richelle."

"None taken. But my situation is different."

"Why?" I asked.

"I can't tell you that."

"Do you know how maddening that is?" said Vie. "You're making it so we can't trust you."

"I'm aware. And I agree; you *should* contact Telesis."

That took Vie by surprise. "You do?"

"Yes. You're right, they may know something."

"And you don't think it's dangerous to establish contact with them again?" I asked.

"No. Vie's right, the homestead isn't going to accept their authority until you've eliminated the danger here, and that's not going to happen."

"Okay, then let's head down to the FaRcom cel," said Vie, adding, "Wil should be included in this."

"I agree," volunteered Richelle. "You should all be involved in this. I have a request, however. And this may erode your trust in me even further, but I'd like you to avoid mentioning me."

"Why?"

"It's complicated and I can't tell you most of it. The outline is this: the Unicon and I had a falling out. You remember that I had been granted a lot of latitude on my estate to do things differently. I had an arrangement.

But after you left, that arrangement broke down and eventually I was forced to leave. I've gone into hiding."

"You're in hiding?" asked Vie.

"I am. And I'd prefer not to give them any clues about exactly where I am."

"But even if they knew we were in contact," I said, "it wouldn't help them. You could be anywhere."

"You may be right, but I'd rather not take any chances. If they were able to trace my communications with you, I fear they might be able to locate me."

"You think they'd arrest you?"

After a pause Richelle said, "No. I don't expect arrest is what they're after."

"You think they want to *kill* you?" I asked. "Why?"

"You know I have different ideas about how...different life forms should be treated. About what rights should be extended beyond just humans."

Vie met my eye again. Her life was a testament to this truth.

"I'm aware," Vie said. Whether she meant to echo Richelle's characteristic phrase, I couldn't tell.

"I acted on those ideas at my estate. They tolerated it for a time, but then..." She looked off to one side and was silent so long I was afraid she wasn't going to continue. Finally, she said, "They decided the special licenses I had arranged should be revoked. But they didn't tell me they had done this, they simply came. They destroyed the estate."

"What do you mean, 'destroyed'?"

"I mean exactly that. Every living thing there was incinerated."

"Everything?" asked Vie. "Every*one*?"

"Everyone." There was a world of emotion in her voice. Anger. Pain. Regret. "This was only a few years ago; most of the people you knew were already gone. But yes, everyone."

In my mind I saw ships racing over the estate, firing lasers, dropping bombs. Fire and smoke and desert spires collapsing. People and animals running, hiding, screaming. Dying.

Everyone. It was horrible.

Wil came into the door of the jump ship at the top of the ladder. "Vie!" he said brightly, but his face fell as he registered the mood. "What happened?"

Vie said, "We're heading down to the FaRcom cel to open a channel to Telesis."

Wil's mouth dropped open. "Huh?"

CHAPTER 24

"HOMESTEAD," I ORDERED, "open the FaRcom to the control center on Telesis."

Vie had already called up some gauges on the floating panels to measure computation levels in various systems. Richelle had recommended this. If Telesis tried to hack in through the FaRcom connect, these would alert us so we could shut the connection down.

Behind us, next to the iris to the hallway, was a nondescript tac pad. Moments earlier Richelle had been talking to us, using that as a com panel. Now she had blacked it out so it looked like a normal tac pad, but she was still there, ready to monitor the coming encounter. We were as safe as we knew how to be. We waited in silence while the homestead made the connection.

And then we were standing in the Telesis control room. The wrap-around panel of the FaRcom made it feel real. Six or seven people were gathered around a bank of holo desks and dedicated displays in front of us. Behind was a door onto a larger room that looked like the main operations center. Several people peered in through the doorway.

Kiku was standing at a long, shared holo desk facing us. Beside her were two men, one of whom had a garish metal implant arcing from just above his left eye to behind his left ear. I wondered what it was for. I'd never seen anything like it. The other man, either legitimately young or someone whose reju therapy had been more skillful than most, spoke first.

"Thank Him, you're safe. We thought we'd lost you. Are you safe?" His urgent but gentle concern was overdone.

"Who are you?" I asked, hoping to come across as confident.

"My name is LarsaMi Yrl." Vie touched my arm. Yrl. If it was true, it meant he was from my parents' Feremite community. The one to which I nominally belonged.

So he was probably *genuinely* young. His delicate earnestness made sense too—he was that kind of religious. Most Feremites were.

"You're from my father's house?" I asked.

"I am," he said, grateful I'd recognized him as a fellow Feremite. He smiled religiously and said, "My grandfather was in chapter with both your father and your mother." He evidently thought this would put me at ease.

"So you were the closest thing to family they could find?" said Wil bluntly. I nearly laughed, but Vie had caught my attention. She nodded to the floating panel on my right, which indicated there was a large amount of static in the FaRcom connection. It wasn't static, of course; they were trying to hack back into the homestead. It didn't look critical yet.

"I am an instructor at the ETS institute," explained LarsaMi, "and a specialist in Stage Four terraforming. I've been trying to help them understand what might be happening there."

"Great," I said, "that's what we're trying to figure out too."

Kiku leaned forward, "I am so glad you were able to fight off whatever that was. We were so, so worried."

"Were you?" challenged Wil. Vie gave him a weary look. He took a breath and leaned back.

"Our people were doing the best we could from here," said Kiku, "but you were right to take local control back. You and your homestead must have done very well."

"We're alive anyway," I said. Wil snorted.

"I'm not able to draw any data from their homestead," said a technician to Kiku.

"We want to get caught up with how things stand there," said LarsaMi. "Can you give us temporary control of your homestead so we can download what we need?"

Vie, Wil, and I exchanged looks. "No," I said. "When we gave you control last time you lied to us. Repeatedly. We're not giving you control until you've told us what's really going on."

"We don't know what's going on," said LarsaMi, "that's why we need access to your systems there."

"You know more than we do," I said. "I think you know what these invading things are."

"We told you," explained Kiku, "a stray terraforming seed was accidentally sent to your system. There's reason to believe—"

"Homestead," I said, "sever the connection to Telesis."

The panel around us wiped clean, leaving only the floating panels populated with displays of computation levels, which fell precipitately. The tac pad behind us flashed on and Richelle was there.

"You were right to cut that short," she said. "Well done. They've left some bread crumbs and TH bots in your system though. I'll take care of it. I'll be right back."

The tac pad went dark.

"Anything?" I asked Wil and Vie. We'd planned to compare notes about the people and the room on Telesis after our encounter.

"Only a few of their displays were visible," said Vie. "We recorded everything; I can magnify those later and see if there's anything revealing. Most of their panels are screened though."

We looked at Wil, who shook his head and said, "They're still lying to us."

"I don't understand why though," said Vie. "What do they have to gain? We could help them."

"We *would* help them if they were helping us," I added.

"What if we're in their way somehow?" asked Wil. "What if this thing is theirs and they need us out of the way."

"How would that work?" I asked. "We were sent here to do work *for them*. Our whole reason for being here is to do what they want us to do."

"I don't know," shrugged Wil.

"What if during our transit they changed their minds," reasoned Vie. "If...I don't know, if something in this system or this sector changed and they need this planet for something else."

"This planet is all about malibdi." Wil was emphatic; this was his territory. "There's no more important use for it. No! Way! Malibdi is too valuable."

"Could it be some kind of interior battle going on," I suggested. "A different company wanting to take over the planet. If it's worth so much, that might happen."

"The Unicon wouldn't let that happen," reasoned Vie. "It would disrupt trade everywhere."

"Could it be different factions within the corporation?" I asked.

"How would that work?" Wil said, parroting my objection to his earlier idea.

"I don't know," I said, doing a fairly good impression of Wil, who snorted a laugh in response. Vie smiled. There was a lot of tension, but snark still eased it a bit.

The tac pad blinked back to life. "I believe you've let them sweat enough," said Richelle. "You want to keep them off balance. Don't let them have too much time to regroup and make a plan."

Vie and Wil nodded. We repositioned ourselves and I said, "Homestead, reestablish the FaRcom to Telesis."

Richelle's panel went dark a moment before the wrap-around panel blinked to life.

"TabiTal," said LarsaMi urgently as soon as they were back with us. It didn't look like they'd changed anything, but there were more people crowded at the door in their control room, peering in. "Please don't sever the connection. They really are trying to help you here."

"Have you worked with them much?" I asked, letting anger into my voice.

"I…no, I'm…no. But they seem like good people," he said, looking around lamely. "I've been here for several days now and they really *are* trying to figure out how best to help you."

He was a tool. I turned away from him and addressed Kiku. "Kiku, I need you to answer this honestly. If I think you're lying I'm going to sever the connect again and we may not call back. Do you understand?"

She looked around uncertainly for a moment, then pushed her blond ponytail back over her shoulder and nodded. "I wish you trusted us, Tab. But alright."

"That man over to the left," interrupted Vie. She was pointing to a plainly dressed man who was standing to one side, leaning against an instrument panel. "I want him to answer our questions." I looked over at Vie. "She got permission from him," she explained.

Several of the other people in the control room looked over at the slim man nervously. Kiku was looking even more uncomfortable. "I will answer you truthfully," she said.

The man pushed away from the instrument panel and came forward, moving with ease and authority.

"My name is Reginew Ofree. I can answer your questions." There was strength in his flat voice.

"What is your position?" I asked.

"I'm the VP of Operations for your sector." He folded down his angled collar, revealing a string of interactive chevrons down his neck, including one from Telesis Corporation.

This guy had a high position in the corpse.

"We were told the satellite array around Thalinraya was not functioning properly," I said. "Was that true?"

Without hesitation or apology he said, "No."

"Then we were sent to T-12 for no reason!" Wil almost shouted. "We risked our lives for no reason!"

"Wil," I said, "let me do this."

"Tab," the man calling himself Reginew said, "it's time we talk. But you are going to ask me some questions that have classified answers. The people in the room with me here don't have the necessary clearances. Why don't I go to my office where we can get a secure connect. I need you to give me five minutes, then reestablish this same com. I'll have it routed over to my channel."

We hadn't expected this. Vie looked at me and raised her eyebrows.

"Okay," I said. "Homestead, sever the connect to Telesis."

"Have you heard of F-A-C-E...FACE?"

This was going in a direction I hadn't expected.

"Yes. It's for Free Autonomous Computational Entity, right?"

"That's right," Reginew said. He was sitting in a room that looked very much like the com cel in the homestead: interactive panels all around the walls, an interactive desk.

Vie said, "There's no evidence that such a thing exists. The ECF, FACE, all those are just rumors."

"No."

"I thought the FACE was just a boogeyman," said Wil, backing Vie up.

"Me too," I agreed. "I thought it was a Feremite thing, to scare kids away from technology."

"Well, it's real," said Reginew, leaning forward on his desk. His sharp elbows rested on data displays he had called up in case he needed them for his explanation. He had rolled his sleeves to his elbows, and we could see an elaborate holo tattoo on his left forearm. It was cycling through some kind of calculation. It might have been a medical tat, in which case, Reginew might be hundreds of years old. Those tats hadn't been used in ages.

"We think FACE has come to the Thalinraya system," he said. "We had no idea it was in that sector. We don't know how long it's been there, how it got there, or what it's doing there." He leaned back. "We don't know much."

"What is FACE, exactly?" I asked.

"We're not even sure about that." He smiled wearily. "Rather than you asking questions and me repeating 'I don't know', why don't I tell you what we *do* know."

"Okay."

"I assume things there are stabilized enough that listening to this for a few minutes won't put you in any jeopardy."

"No," I answered, glancing at the floating panels as I did so. There weren't any spikes in FaRcom activity. Telesis wasn't trying to hack in this time.

"Alright then. From what I know—and I have to tell you I don't know everything—there are military classifications I have no access to. But from what I know, FACE budded out of a university project. This was many years ago, when different universities were still pursuing AI technologies without much regulation. This was in the days of the Ambit."

"The gaming age?" I asked.

"It's sometimes referred to that way. Apart from military applications, a lot of the first designs were driven by entertainment. Human life spans hadn't yet been significantly extended, and most people put their efforts into applications that would realize profits during their lives. Their horizons were much smaller. But to continue: from the time of the earliest quantum computing there were prohibitions put in place on most AIs." He took a breath before continuing. "But so long as their systems were firewalled, airwalled, and completely isolated, universities could build experimental AIs outside the prohibitions. As with some of the scientific breakthroughs provided by early machine learning, they started producing effects we couldn't account for. We still can't."

He referred to something in his desk, then back to us.

"What happened?" Wil asked.

"Progress. We're not sure. Some of those early AIs either escaped their university systems or someone or some group decided to bypass the safeguards and release one or more into the early Ambit. Free-ranging AIs were already camouflaged in the Ambit when the Unicon took over. They had learned how to code themselves somehow, and they bypassed all the governors that had been placed on them. And these were digital creatures, free in ways we could never have imagined."

"But how can they…" I began, not quite knowing what I was asking. "These AIs were just code, so couldn't they…turn them off? I mean, you can search for code. Couldn't they just find them and erase them or something?"

"No. The digital world is their world, not ours."

"You made it," said Wil.

Reginew steepled his fingers and said, "Think of it this way. We live in the physical universe, and when we immerse in the dataverse we're like people who swim underwater. We need equipment—tanks so we can breathe, masks so we can see, fins so we can move around. But for fish… things underwater are easier. Because they're *optimized* for that environment. They're native to it. Well, AIs are even more a part of the dataverse. They're not optimized for it, they're made of the same stuff. It's not only where they live, it's *what they are*, which is why it was easy for them to remain hidden. Trying to find one was like trying to find…not a fish in the ocean, but rather *a fish-shaped bit of water* in the ocean."

He let that sink in, then continued. "When we started traveling to different sectors—and I mean in the physical universe—the AIs hitched a ride. At first they were like parasites, just living inside our computers. Like bacteria in our gut: not much harm and, who knows, maybe even helping in some way. When we knew of them at all, we never really found them to be a problem. They weren't malicious. They weren't doing anything, they were simply there.

"But think about terraforming technology. It requires a lot of autonomous decision-making and activity. The first ships we send to any new system have to be independent and self-sufficient. They must obtain their own fuel, extract resources for their own maintenance. They must respond to their environment and build new and better machines. Apparently one AI learned from this and managed to free itself. It built its own machines and set out on its own. We refer to it now as FACE.

"It's not clear when this happened, but it was certainly centuries ago. And where FACE went, how far it expanded, what it learned, what it wants now…we simply have no idea."

I glanced over at the tac pad where I knew Richelle was listening. How much of this did she know?

"They *are* boogeymen," said Wil.

"Of a sort, yes. More of a boogey*man*, if we understand the front correctly."

"What do you mean?" I asked.

"It seems to be a single AI."

"How would you know?"

"If more than one AI had been liberated, we would expect to see them coming into conflict with one another, not just us. We don't see that. This thing needs resources, but to get them it's fighting us, not other AIs. It's a single force, a unified and emancipated front."

"And this thing could have evolved," said Vie. "It could have created whole new technologies."

"That's one of the reasons we sent you to V-12. The satellites showed there was a great deal of activity there, but we had no idea what it was doing. It has ways of hiding EM activity that we've never encountered before."

"Why not tell us that?" I asked.

"Yes. Well. It wasn't my decision. But look, everything I've just told you is highly classified. The Unicon has an interest in trying to deal with this problem without causing a panic. As I said, many of the people you've dealt with up to this point aren't aware of what's really happening there. I believe they were acting in good faith."

"Not the most efficient way to handle things," observed Vie.

Reginew nearly smiled. "No, that's certainly true."

"But who really cares?" said Wil. "It's a kid and two syns on the outskirts of shunt all. Who'll find out anyway?"

"I can assure you, that was not our attitude. We are making every effort to figure out how to help you there."

"Why did you crash the gravion when we got to V-12?" Wil pressed. "Everything was fine until then. It's like you wanted them to come after us."

"Now that *was* my call, and I can explain." He leaned forward again, earnestly. "First, we didn't think FACE knew you were there, and we wanted to keep it that way for as long as we could. Our intel suggested it would sense the use of any powered flight or rocketry, including gravions, which is why we steered you away from those. That's why we told you the satellites were out of commission too. We didn't want you using those modes of transport. When you got close to V-12, however, things within the volcano changed significantly. Whether it was you or that probe you sent into the siphon we don't know, but something was causing a lot of new activity."

"What probe?" I asked.

"The one that entered the siphon at the impact site," said Reginew.

"My hog," said Wil defiantly. He wasn't apologizing.

"In any case," said Reginew, "I sent the gravion as a diversion."

"Great," said Wil sarcastically, "poke the hive. That'll help."

"That's how it turned out, but that's *not* what I intended. We don't know much about how FACE operates. You, in fact," he said, speaking directly to me, "have the honor of being the first person to come into physical contact with it."

"There are three of us," I said, correcting him.

"I'm sorry?"

"There are three people here."

"I see," he said. "Yes, of course. I apologize."

Wil grunted.

"From my perspective," he said, obviously trying to move on, "here's where things stand. I want first and foremost to keep you all safe, but I can't do anything for you so long as you have us shut out from your homestead. I need you to restore our access to the satellites and the outpost stations to—"

"Even if we believe your explanation, how do you expect us to trust you after all the lying you've done?"

"I understand it's difficult, and I apologize for how things have been done up to now. But look at it this way: what reason do I have to lie to you?

I've given you the information I have—*classified* information. All I want to do now is help you. There's one more—"

"Why?" I asked.

"Because we sent you there. We have a responsibility."

Wil summarized his opinion with an unimpressed burst of air. "Pfff!"

"And if you insist on being cynical about it, which I can understand, realize we also have a legal obligation to take 'reasonable and necessary precautions to ensure the safety of our employees.' With your father out of contact, you," he said, singling me out, "are our only remaining employee there. We are legally bound to do what we can to ensure your safety."

"Where is my father?"

"If I knew I would tell you. We don't have any more information than you have. Much less, now that you've locked us out."

"So the image Kiku showed us of the crash site was bogus?" I challenged.

"It was." He held out his hands. I found the gesture easier to believe when it came from the synths at the capsule. "I'm sorry. We were stalling for time and trying to keep you motivated. We don't know you; we don't know how quickly you might fall into despair. It was a bad call, but it really was done because we thought it would help keep you safe. There wasn't anything you could do for him anyway."

He was admitting to these lies because he had no alternative. He wasn't sincere, he was working us. The fact he was still using my father's situation for leverage enraged me.

It also made me certain that it was time for me to take action. I was going to find out what happened to my father.

"And you still don't have any idea where he might be?" I challenged.

"No. I'm sorry. We don't have any more information than you do. The satellites in Thalinraya's system won't be able to see that location for weeks, and we don't think you have that much time."

"What does that mean?" asked Vie. She hadn't spoken in a while, but now she leaned forward.

Reginew licked his lips before continuing. "We have detected an EM lattice being built around Thalinraya. We've—"

"What is that?" asked Vie quickly.

"We don't fully understand it," said Reginew, holding his hands out once again like Hig, "and I don't have the onboards to explain. It's some kind of…positron multiplier that…I can't explain. We don't know how it works, but we've seen it before, around other planets visited by FACE. And in the three other cases we've seen, after about eleven days, the planet becomes…undetectable."

"There were people on these planets?" I asked.

"Negative. You're the first."

"Are you saying," asked Vie, "that this lattice somehow cloaks the planet?"

"That's what we think, but we don't know. These are remote systems and we haven't been able to get any physical recon, so we can't be certain. What we do know is you've only got a few days to reconfigure your jump ship and get out of there. I can help you with that."

"But, let me guess: you need us to give you control of the homestead first," I said.

He exhaled, then continued in a weary tone. "Look, if there were some way I could get you to trust me, believe me, I'd do it."

"Get us in touch with Tab's fourth-gen grandmother, Richelle," said Vie, unexpectedly. "We trust her."

Why was she bringing Richelle up? She knew Richelle had asked us not to mention her.

Reginew was caught off guard. He held a breath for a moment, then said, "I wish I could, but…I can't do that."

There was something there. He was holding something back.

"Why not?" I asked.

He looked down before responding. "I'm sorry to tell you this. Your gen-four grandmother is dead."

There it was: proof he was lying again.

"Liar," said Wil bluntly.

"I know you were all close to her. If I could get her online to talk to you, I would."

"You would not," continued Wil in a rage. "You're the ones who destroyed her estate!"

Reginew started to respond but came up short. He cocked his head to one side like Thius and squinted at Wil. He seemed to be losing his composure for the first time, and he said, "How do you know about—"

But the panel froze. Reginew was immobilized, his face screwed up, transitioning from confusion to...something else.

Then the image pixelated and went dark.

CHAPTER 25

"THIS IS GOING TO BE A huge shock to your system," warned Richelle for the eighth time.

"Then let's make sure we program it right," I replied.

"There's no need to be angry with me."

"Well, there's no need to keep trying to convince me not to do this either. I'm doing it."

Vie and I were in the medic cel, which had been reconfigured for my procedures. It was much more crowded than when we'd come to fix Wil's leg. Surgical baths and other bulky equipment had rolled out from the walls and risen from the floor. There was more gear on the ceiling as well.

"The first bath is ready," said Vie, who was keeping herself busy and ignoring the tension in the room.

I was busy too, flushing out the coffin-like surgical baths. Richelle moved from one small panel to another, following me around the cel.

"Richelle, can you double check the chemical levels?" asked Vie.

"They're fine," said Richelle, appearing on a panel near Vie. "Tab, listen to me."

"I need to see for myself. You're not going to talk me out of it," I said, aiming a jet of spray to rinse out the third surgical bath. "I don't want to hear any more."

After our connection to Telesis had been cut, Vie had stayed in the FaRcom cel to try to figure out what had broken the connection. Wil and I couldn't be of any help, so Wil went back up to the jump ship to work on more of the retrofitting. I considered staying to talk to Vie, but she didn't seem too eager. And honestly, I needed to be alone to build up my courage.

I had my habitation cel migrate to the southern edge of the homestead and open an iris window so I could look down toward Glassfall Canyon. We were on Thalinraya because of my father. He and my mother were supposed to be Stage Five curators, but my father believed that the more we sacrificed, the closer we were to God, so he switched to Stage Four, which provided the longest tours, the most remote planets, the greatest isolation. Perfect.

We were here because of him. My mother was dead because of him.

So why did I feel obligated to figure out what had happened to him? Like I owed him that?

It was maddening. I wouldn't have felt any obligation to him at all if it hadn't been for those last weeks when we explored Thalinraya together. I almost wished we hadn't had that time and I hadn't grown...attached. It polluted my resentment with guilt.

I engaged a panel and pulled up an image of the third moon. He might be in some bivouac on the far side. In a few days he might look up to see our ship streaking away, leaving him alone here. How many days would it take for him to die after that? Knowing we had utterly abandoned him, how much longer would he endure?

We had no idea what had happened to him, and this would be true forever unless we somehow got up there. And there was only one way.

And only I could do it.

"I don't want to hear any more," I said, turning away from Richelle's image.

I had finished rinsing the third surgical bath; now I moved to the fourth. The panel next to it blinked on and Richelle appeared there. "If it really is the right thing to do," she reasoned, her already creased forehead furrowed further, "what's the harm in listening to me?"

I switched off the hose's nozzle and turned to face her. "Because, Richelle, you're my G4 gran and I love you and you're very persuasive. But this is something I want to do."

"You know your parents would never allow it," said Richelle. "They didn't even want you to have that watch. Augments and enhancements are forbidden by—"

"Are you really going to argue scripture here? You?" Her image was small in the surgery room panel, but I could see her turn her head away for a moment.

232

"This is dangerous," she said. "Hard vacuum augments are some of the most—"

I turned on the nozzle again and started flushing out the bath. "I know."

Richelle raised her voice to be heard over the spraying. "And irreversible, I'll remind you."

"I know! But I'm going up there. I'm not abandoning him without knowing."

Vie was scrolling through specifications and instructions on a panel on the opposite side of the cel. "The medical bots are ready for the second bath. Do I put those in now?" she asked.

"Wait on those," advised Richelle.

"There's no need to wait, put them in," I said angrily, shutting off the spray and facing Richelle's panel. "I'm doing this."

"I'm not telling her to wait because you might not do it," said Richelle, vexed now herself. "The bots are activated when they hit the solvent. If they're in too early, they may not have enough battery life to do what they need to do when *you* get in there. We would have to assemble more bots, which would delay—"

"Okay, okay."

"Tab," said Richelle, softening. "I will help you with this and I'll do everything I can to make sure it goes right, but you must understand my concern."

"Of course," I said, "but…I need to do this." When she didn't respond I added, "And Wil needs a few days to retrofit the jump ship. This'll keep me out of trouble while I wait."

Richelle rubbed her eyes with the heels of her hands.

"Can you get me the specs for the assemblers?" Vie asked Richelle, kindly pushing past my attempt at humor.

"I already sent them to the second sievel," said Richelle. "They're processing Tab's genome now for material integration algorithms."

"What're those?" I asked.

"Your body would normally reject augments like these. There's a lot that needs to get done. How much do you want to know?" Richelle was trying a new tactic now. "Do you want to know how your bones will be impregnated with beryllium mesh? How bedded 6 titanium will stitch with your reinforced, plasticized tendons? How your scapular pickups will be—"

"Okay."

"How your blood and skin cells will be impregnated with oxygen ticks so they can distill—"

"Okay, okay."

She paused and assessed me before saying, "It's going to be painful."

"You can't scare me off. I'm going to do it."

Richelle sat back on her bed, trying to think of another way to convince me not to do this. Her little image in the panel suddenly looked old and sad. The curtains in her room billowed inward with some breeze off the water. The shoreline outside the window looked fairly close.

Vie decided to make use of the pause in conversation to broach another subject. "Richelle, how could Telesis think you're dead?"

"They scorched the entire estate. There was nothing left. Everyone there died."

"But you weren't there?"

"I wasn't. Dumb luck."

From how she asked the questions, I could tell Vie had more than a casual interest in this. And as I thought about it, Richelle's response was a little odd. She didn't like to leave her estate and rarely did so.

"Where were you?" I asked.

"I took you all to the Ashala oasis once, 27.3 clicks south of the estate. Remember?"

I did. It looked like a couple of trees standing alone in the desert until you got near enough to see the canyon. It wasn't large, but it had some of the strangest trees I'd ever seen. We sat in the shade of a cliff wall all day, watching a constant stream of bees that rose up from the canyon and disappeared into the desert above. The bees were bright blue and yellow when they were low in the canyon, but as they rose their color changed to a mottled dun that would have made them impossible to see against the colors of the desert above.

"With the camo bees?" asked Vie. "By the herriot ranch?"

"That's the one. I was painting it. I've taken up painting. After you and Wil left I spent more and more time away from the estate."

Vie nodded and noted something on her instrument panel. "The D'fers are processed," she said.

"You're almost ready to start. If we do it as quickly as we safely can, you'll need about nineteen hours in solution. You'll need much more recovery time."

"Okay."

"Tab, you know—"

"I'm doing it, Richelle."

She finally accepted that I wasn't going to back down on this one.

"Let's get Wil in here. He's going to need to fetch some materials from the storage area."

I asked Vie to turn away before I got into the first medic bath. Vie smiled at my modesty, but Wil seemed relieved.

"Modesty is not going to be possible here," said Richelle. "Both Wil and Vie are going to need to help you during this."

"Why?"

"When they flush you between baths they'll need to—"

"Flush me? What are you talking about?"

Richelle expressed her disapproval by tucking in her chin. "You didn't expect to be conscious during this, did you?"

"Why not?" I asked.

"Oh, Tab!" She actually chuckled. "You have no idea. This isn't something you can be conscious through."

"Why not?"

"For one thing, you need to be intubated. Can you withstand that?"

"What is it?"

"The auto surgeon will grow tubes into your nose and down your throat. There will have to be one grown into your anus too. You'll be submersed completely, then—"

"Just do it!" I turned away from her panel.

After a disapproving moment she said, "The first step is to anesthetize you."

"No."

"Tab, you can't possibly—"

"No! Just let me get in there."

Wil and Vie stood awkwardly by. Neither wanted to get involved.

After a pause, Richelle said, "Alright. Here's what we'll do. We'll start without the anesthesia. I want you to put your hand on your stomach. As long as your hand stays there I'll let Vie withhold the anesthesia. But if your hand moves, that'll be our signal."

"Fine," I said. It didn't matter, I just wanted to get on with it.

I dropped my robe and climbed into the surgical bath. Vie moved to come closer but Wil stepped forward in front of her.

"I'll watch," he said.

It was like stepping into a water-filled coffin. The liquid was chilly. As I lowered myself in and the lid was shut I looked up to see the ceiling of the thing was covered with nozzles of different sorts. There were also levers and other little mechanical gizmos I chose not to look at too closely. A small window looked out; Wil was peering in at me. He clamped the lid shut.

As I placed a hand on my stomach I started to feel a tingling all over. The liquid surrounding my body, I remembered, wasn't water but some medical solution filled with nanobots. I wondered how aggressive the tingling was going to get.

It didn't matter; I could take it.

I gave Wil the thumbs up. He looked away, said something, then looked back in at me. Several things happened at once.

Two suction cups shot down at my face and worked themselves expertly under my eyelids and over my eyeballs, sliding cold folds all the way around the balls to the back of my sockets. The tubes that shot up my nose had a sandpapery texture; the ones in my ears were slick worms at first, but they suddenly flared out and tiny, hooked needles anchored themselves in place all up and down my ear canal. I won't mention the tube that came up from the bottom of the bath, but the one that forced my mouth open was like liquid plastic, flowing as it came in over my teeth and tongue and down my throat, hardening instantly as it advanced. I couldn't hear anything at this point, but I was fairly certain the tub's lid couldn't be muffling my screams.

Wil must have recognized the hand signal somewhere in my flailing spasms. I was grateful. The bursts of shattering light and splintering pain finally fractured into pieces and fell away into a chasm of blissful unconsciousness.

CHAPTER 26

WHEN THINKING RETURNED, I WAS LYING on a table in the medic cel, connected by several tubes to whirring and gurgling machines in the wall beside me.

"You awake?" Wil asked. It felt as though my brain were resting on a bed of needles. Wil's words pressed the brain down so it was pierced in many places.

"You awake?" he asked again. This time the question reverberated inside my skull, bouncing off the hollow interior until the echo of it resolved and I could pick out the individual words. After I had worked through them a few times I felt like I understood the question. Not in time. He asked again. "You're wincing. Are you awake?"

"No," I said. My own word reverberated too, but differently. Wil's words were a snare; mine was a kick drum.

"He's awake," Wil said in a volume that constituted violence.

There was movement, then Vie's whispering voice, "Are you in any pain?"

I appreciated the whispering, but even that was hard to take.

"Yes," I whispered, hoping they'd take the hint.

"Where?" asked Vie, close to my ear.

"Everywhere."

"We have to keep your eyes covered for eleven hours," said Wil at full volume.

"Okay," I whispered.

"Your eyes need to be protected from the radiation," explained Vie.

"Okay."

"She almost stopped it," said Wil.

"I did not."

"You did too," Wil said. Raising his voice so I'd know he was talking to me, he said, "You were screaming. It sounded pretty bad."

"Could you...speak...quietly? Please."

"Oh," said Wil in a lower voice. "Sure."

"Do you remember anything?" whispered Vie.

"No."

"You don't want to remember that," said Wil emphatically. "Trust me."

"Thanks."

"Do you want a pain processor?" whispered Vie.

"Yes."

She probably placed the mechanism gently in my hand, but it felt like she was breaking bones.

"Richelle says three or four taps is usually enough, some people need five for...

I lost track of what she was saying after the twelfth tap. This time unconsciousness came like a warm, dark wind. I was a leaf, happy to be swept away.

There was no light, but the pain had a kind of electric arc to it that was visible to my mind. Bolts of it shot out in all directions, sometimes bursting apart into fireworks that rained down little stinging cinders. *Flash*—a burning in my back and shoulders. *Bang*—stabbing pain in all my extremities. *Flash*—cramping, aching nausea.

"Are you awake?" Wil was there.

"No."

"Ha. Good one. Vie says you'll be able to..."

The pain processor was still in my hand. The warm wind was coming again, and I kept tapping until it had completely surrounded me.

"Are you awake?"

"No."

It still wasn't funny, but Wil gave a little charity laugh.

"Hey, where's the pain processor?" I asked, alarmed.

Vie spoke this time. "Richelle said not to let you have it until you'd done—"

"Give it to me!" Ugh. My own voice was clubbing the baby seal of my brain.

"Sorry Tab," said Vie, "we can't.

Wil tried to change the subject. "Want those things off your eyes?"

"Has it been eleven hours already?"

"More like thirty."

It felt like I'd been unconscious a few minutes at most.

"Okay."

"Lift your head," said Vie. Her voice was close.

I tilted my head up and she reached down to remove a band that was holding the pads over my eyes. A dull, fuzzy light blossomed and I suddenly realized my eyes were already open. I had thought they were closed.

"Ugh." I felt…wrong.

"What?" asked Wil.

"Oh…"

"What is it?" asked Vie gently.

I could feel something moving across my eyeballs. I reached to touch them.

"Don't touch them," said Vie.

It felt as though jelly was being pushed in and around my eyeballs. It wasn't painful, but it was so bizarre I instinctively reached up again.

"Don't touch them," she repeated.

"What is that?"

"Those are your nictators," said Wil, leaning in. "Those look good."

The fuzziness was resolving, but my eye sockets were getting more difficult to manage. It felt like there were animals of some sort crawling all in and around my eyes.

"What're nictors?" I asked.

"You went in for this procedure and you didn't even research what it was going to do to you?" chided Vie.

"Can you just tell me."

"Nictators," Wil said, gloating over the fact he knew something I didn't. "They're your visual enhancements. For ultraviolet, infrared, whatever."

"I thought I was just getting radiation protection." It was hard not to rub my eyes.

"That's there too," said Vie. "And your retinas were replaced."

"Feels weird."

"You get used to it," Wil said. "Give it two days and you won't remember how it felt before."

I'd forgotten that both Wil and Vie had undergone similar things when they were younger. Because he'd been intended for work in mines, Wil had night vision.

"How do they work?" I asked.

"What do you mean?"

"How do I get the enhancements to work?"

Wil raised his eyebrows in disbelief at my ignorance. Vie explained: "They have volitional control. You just have to want to do it and it'll be done."

"Look at us in thermal," suggested Wil.

I had heard of thermal images, but I'd never seen one. I wondered what it would look like. I wondered again, harder.

"It's not working," I said.

"You have to want to," said Vie.

"I do."

"Wow, you must have a weak will," joked Wil. "Want it harder."

"Have you ever seen an infrared image?" asked Vie.

"No. What's that got to do with it?"

Vie sighed. "Thermal imaging is a kind of infrared imaging. If you've never seen one before you'll need to be really deliberate about telling yourself to see it. The first few times it'll have to be a clear instruction."

"A clear instruction to myself?"

"Yes," she said patiently.

That seemed absurd. I said out loud: "I want to see a thermal image."

"Not 'I want,' " said Wil, as though the phrase were absurd. "Your onboards will think you're making a request of the homestead or something. You have to learn to instruct yourself through your onboards."

"That's weird."

"It'll feel normal after a few times," Vie reassured. "Give yourself an instruction."

I said aloud: "TabiTal Yrl, see in thermal imag—"

I startled. There was a tickle at the corners of my eyes and suddenly the colors in the room had completely changed. Almost everything was a dull gray and the light strips above were whited out blurs, but Wil and Vie looked like someone had painted them in glow-in-the-dark colors; they had turned into vibrant topographical maps of green and blue and red. Wil said something, but I couldn't pay attention because his opening and closing mouth was the strangest purple blur. I've never tried recreational processors or enhancements, but this was what I always imagined they'd be like.

"...other wavelengths. Is it working?"

"Oh yeah," I managed. "Unless you just tipped six paint cans on your head."

"I thought so," laughed Wil. "You've got a funny look on your face."

"I think you're ready to sit up," said Vie.

I turned to look at her and was suddenly aware that her thermal image was almost indecent.

"See normally," I said to myself. The normal lighting returned.

Wil reached over and pulled the sheet down. Thankfully I was wearing shorts, though how they got onto me was a question.

"Go ahead and sit up," Vie said.

I angled my arms to lift myself up and they felt...alien. Hollow. This part I had researched, but knowing what was going to happen was completely different from the experience of it. My bones had been infused with beryllium fiber mesh and hollowed out for all the computers and mechanics needed for vacuum stabilization and travel.

I reached back and felt the slight bulge of the hematopor at the base of my skull. This was the new unit that would clean and replace my blood cells now that I had no bone marrow. I felt further down my back and found the hard scapular attachment plates. These could be used for any number of things, but I would be using them for my solar sails.

I had done it. I was part machine.

As though my body wanted to remind me that I was still part human too, I suddenly became violently nauseous.

"Uh oh," I managed, "I think I might—"

Too late. My vomiting somehow short-circuited my visual augments, redeploying my infrared nictators. Wil recoiled from my stream in a surreal dance of kaleidoscopic color.

The next two days were spent in a makeshift gravity suspension chamber. I managed to keep use of the pain processor under control despite being sore all over, and I worked through a hurried battery of exercises to get fit for my flight. My entire body felt alien. I weighed quite a bit less than I had before, but I felt heavier. Muscular reinforcements were still growing and would continue to do so for about six weeks, but even those were made from composites that were lighter than my natural tissues. The sense of weight came, I think, from the odd new mechanics of my movement. It wasn't that I moved differently, it was just the movements themselves were made by new materials. Also, my weight had been redistributed. There was a lot of gear connected to my scapular attachment plates, which had mechanics that were elaborately connected to my arms and torso. It felt like I had a backpack stitched on.

But when Wil hooked on attachments—Vie was busy with other things and not as interested in the gear—there was an amazing transformation. I had always expected people with elaborate enhancements would feel like they had gear attached to them all the time, as though they had put on sporting equipment they simply never took off. This was different. Each device became a part of me as soon as it was attached. I can't explain it, but circuits had been grown into my brain and I intuitively knew how to work things. I practiced with extra mechanical arms, for example, and both Wil and I expected it would take hours for me to be able to do even simple tasks. But right away I was able to handle tools and operate controls with great dexterity. It was bizarre. I felt at once like a monster with these giant, articulated arms sprouting spider-like out of my back, but I was immediately able to use them like a well-trained athlete. Wil was looking through the observation window when I was trying the equipment in zero gravity, and he was as shocked by my agility as I was. We both got giddy, and I started doing silly maneuvers just because I could. Vie came in while I was doing four-handed cartwheels around the cel.

"You look like Hem," she said, disgusted.

The solar sails were the most difficult to master, but they had been constructed with five sets of jointed phalanges, so even these had an intuitive feel, like fingers. Their folding patterns were more elaborate than those of bats, but that's what I felt like when I was wearing them: a bat. I practiced with those for a while before trying them with the gear bag I'd have to tow.

"Lookin' like an expert," said Wil, as I exited the gravity suspension chamber after one of my last practice sessions. "You look like you were born with all that gear. Looks natural."

I smiled at the sentiment, but as he helped me take off the equipment I couldn't help wonder what my father would think. Would he be proud that I'd done this to help him, or would his stubborn faith force him to condemn me for having corrupted God's machine with the machines of man?

If he was alive, would he even let me help him?

"I've put together your flight path. You'll have it onboarded too, but I want to explain it."

Vie had put together a diagram in the Control cel. It showed Thalinraya and all six moons in their different orbits. They were frozen at 5:32 the following morning, the time we had set for my flight. Vie set the animation going and began narrating as a tiny figure launched off Thalinraya.

"Your propellant will get you out of the atmosphere and heading to the moon at 8.6 kilometers per second. At that rate you would reach the moon in about fourteen hours. Once we hit your sails with the laser propulsion we can quadruple your speed over the course of the hour you'll be in sleve. You'll be on this trajectory here," she pointed, "which we agreed on."

We'd had several conversations about the best way to make this trip. Because we didn't know what had happened, we had no idea whether landing there was worthwhile. Setting a course to land would have added days to the trip because it would have required a different trajectory, deceleration for the landing, carrying fuel for taking off again, and more. If my father was there and needed help I would certainly want to land, but doing it that way would take more time than we safely had on Thalinraya. Richelle said we had about six days before the filaments would be a problem, so getting there and back quickly was important.

I checked with Wil to be sure there wasn't anything I could do to help speed up the jump ship reconfiguration. He was elusive at first, but finally he reassured me I didn't have the onboards for the work anyway. He'd do it alone and it'd take four days. That left two days of wiggle room before we needed to abandon the planet.

"The FACE sites are in this region," Vie continued, pointing to a holo globe of the moon. "It's drilled in, but it doesn't seem to be doing anything on the surface at any of the sites. We'll keep them monitored as you fly by though, just in case. Here," she rotated the globe, "is the surface on that far side. Here's your father's landing site and here's where you'll be passing over. You'll have a clear view."

The problem with doing a quick flyby was that if my father *did* need help, a flyby wouldn't do him any good. So Vie designed a flyby trajectory that didn't go directly over my father's landing spot but close enough to allow me to see what had happened. The advantage of this trajectory was that the moon's gravity would sling me back to Thalinraya about seven hours after passing behind it. That would get me back in time for us to get in the jump ship and leave within the safe window. If, however, I saw something that made me want to land, when I came out on the far side of the moon Vie could hit my wings with the satellite lasers again to decelerate me and turn me back. It would take twenty or so hours to get me back to my father's projected landing site, but it would work. And if my father had already survived the many days he'd already been up there, another few hours likely wouldn't hurt.

It was a strategic compromise.

Of course, I couldn't help envisioning the worst-case scenario: flying by at seventeen kilometers per second, my father signaling he had three hours of air left, knowing I couldn't return in time to save him. This possibility was vanishingly remote, but it *was* possible.

"If you need to land, here's where we'll turn you back," Vie pointed. "If there's no need to land, you'll continue on this trajectory until here, when we'll start your deceleration for reentry."

CHAPTER 27

Wil assisted me to the gravion pad. Made for space, my Velksin suit was much less flexible in atmosphere and I appreciated his help. Richelle said she needed to be away for my launch in order to ensure that the growing filament lattice around Thalinraya would part for my exit and reentrance. How exactly she could do this, she didn't say. Vie was alone in the Control cel, monitoring everything.

When I was in place on the gravion pad, Wil retreated. It felt bizarre to stand at the center of the gravion pad alone, without a ship, propellant strapped to my back.

"Ready?" asked Vie subvocally. My tragus speakers were gone; I had normal subvocal augments now. It was oddly intimate, which I didn't mind with Vie. We seemed to have settled back into a comfortable friendship. I wasn't sure we'd ever speak about the kiss, and I was alright with that.

"I guess so," I said as I gave the thumbs up to Wil, who was standing at the side of the pad.

He was a better match for Vie anyway. Not because he was a synth, but because he was generally a better person than me. He was impulsive and a little hot-headed, but at least he knew what he thought about things. I was all mixed up. I wasn't even sure why I was out here getting ready to launch. Was it really a desire to get my father back, or was it the adventure of it? Or the chance to prove to everyone who had doubted—including me—that I was serious about getting augments?

A crackling from above drew my attention. Looking up, I saw the dark splitting of air as the orbital hooks pulled open a gravity trail. The coiling I'd experienced in the gravion now compressed my body. I had a sudden panic that the pressure would crush the suit, or rip its seams and make it unstable in space. The shimmering net of filament hung above too. Was I about to launch myself into some electronic fence that would shred me? What was I doing here?

These thoughts vanished the instant I was slung upward, like an arrow from a bow, sliding along the path of the gravity fissure. I lost vision from the acceleration and jerk in the first fifteen seconds, but I managed to maintain consciousness. When I could open my eyes again, the dark crease of the gravity trail extended up into the deepening purple-black of space. I was already through the troposphere, rocketing through the stratosphere.

Maybe I *had* lost consciousness for a bit.

"H-h-o-o-w-w d-d-i-i-d-d I-I g-g-e-e-t-t th-th-r-r-ou-ou-gh-gh th-th-e-e f-f-i-i-l-l-a-a-m-m-e-e-n-n-t-t-s-s?" I managed, despite the intense vibration.

"They parted," Vie said. "Don't talk now. Stay focused."

She didn't explain what I was meant to be focused on, since they were in charge of most of the mechanics of my travel. But speaking was difficult, so I left off.

Looking back, the curve of Thalinraya was already visible. It was beautiful—and alarming. To the north I could see V-12, covered now in a smooth, homogenizing black material that looked like obsidian. I wondered if it was the same cloth-like material we'd encountered at the impact site. Extending from the base of the volcano were muscular, octopus-like arms, except with giant round openings at irregular intervals, out of which poured devices. Due to distance and vibrating speed, I couldn't make them out, but they appeared to be massive. Tendrils sprouted from the top of the volcano and rose up into the lower atmosphere, spreading out to produce the filaments.

Things got darker as I entered the mesosphere and the planet below me began to appear more and more like a planet. I could see the terminator arc of the approaching night from one side of the planet to the other—the twilight zone. On the lit side, weather patterns and the outlines of continents were clear. So clear, I realized, some kind of onboard visual stabilization was beginning to work. I was still vibrating quite a bit, but my sight was unaffected. Somewhere within me were engines busily processing my visual field, countering the vibration to make it appear smooth and steady. I had been augmented in ways I didn't even understand.

That had always been true, I reflected. I had never known how my heart worked either, yet it had always beat away inside my ribcage, faster when I needed it to, slower when I needed rest, taking direction from brain centers I had never been in control of. Was this any different?

As the jerk fell off and then my acceleration slowed, I looked up again. The gravity path in front of me was fraying and the clear shield that kept me safe from atmospheric particles was wavering.

"You're almost to the GM waist," Vie said. "Get ready to unfold the propellant tails."

I crossed into the thermosphere and the vibrations decreased. The gravity path frayed more, its pull weakening proportionally. I unfurled the swallow-tail propellant extensions and waited.

"Nervous?" Wil was subvocal with me too. It was comforting.

"No," I said, wondering if I should be. But it was true: For some reason I wasn't nervous. I had changed so much over the past few days, and I had grown accustomed to trusting my enhancements. Yes, I was being flung into space with technologies I didn't understand, but how much could a single person ever really know? Not much. You have to trust, even your own unknowable body.

Which sounds like something my father might have said. Except he placed his trust in God, not science.

I had overheard Richelle talking to my father once. She asked him how he explained the lack of progress in religion. Everything else in our culture moves forward, she pointed out, but religion never does. Science brings us innovations that allow us to do more, go farther and faster, live more easily. Government extends our rights and creates more peace between planets and peoples. But religion rejects all this. "Truth," my father placidly replied, "cannot be changed or improved upon. Progress is an illusion."

Madness.

I came to the end of the gravity fissure about two thirds of the way through the thermosphere. As I came over the lip of the fissure at the end of the gravity trail, my acceleration ended. It felt as though my velocity would keep me going forever, but I knew I was already experiencing a slow deceleration. I needed to use the propellant to kick me out through the remainder of the thermosphere and exosphere.

"You need to—" began Wil.

"I got it," I said. The propellant was integrated through my scapula; as soon as I thought about engaging it, the swallowtails became rigid and the propellant started ionizing. Three seconds later I was shooting forward again, gaining speed at an even greater rate than when the gravion had launched me. There was nothing to stop me here on the lip of space, and the propellant got me past eight kilometers per second in no time.

I realized I hadn't even thought about my breathing. The oxygen generators in my hollowed-out bones must have kicked in with me unaware. The bubble over my face hadn't changed at all—it was comfortable and pressurized and full of what felt like fresh air. My fears about a torn suit were unfounded.

The propellant spent itself more quickly than I would have guessed; the swallowtail detached and drifted away from me. I looked back, expecting to see it fall quickly away, but it too was travelling at 14.1 kilometers per second now, in frictionless space. I followed its slowly rotating path and only then realized how far I'd already come from Thlinraya. I could see the entire planet, and it was already receding. It looked delicate. Vulnerable, but beautiful.

"You need to deploy your sails now," said Vie.

"My wings?" I asked, teasing. She hated when I was less than precise. But they felt more like wings than sails.

"If you must call them that, yes." I could hear the smile in her subvocal voice.

Without knowing how they had been folded in the first place, I unfolded the intricate oragimi of the wings until they spread seventeen meters out on either side. I had done this with smaller training wings in simulation, but I hadn't experienced the feeling of being at the center of something this large. I was a space moth.

"Ready?" asked Vie.

"Yeah."

Sixteen satellites orbiting Thalinraya aimed lasers at my wings. From all around the planet beams shot toward me, hitting my wings with micron precision. Which was good, since any strays would have incinerated me. It felt as if I was sending threads down around the planet, wrapping it in a net of red light. Really though, those beams were pushing me away with a terrible force. The acceleration was harder to feel in space, but the increase in speed was still perceptible in the changing attitude toward the planet below. After only sixty-four seconds of push I was travelling at twenty-seven kilometers per second. I had achieved the velocity and trajectory I needed to make the trip. Vie shut off the beams and I was drifting in space.

Well, *drifting* twenty-five times faster than a bullet.

"Everything okay?" Vie asked.

"Yeah." I was finding it hard to speak.

"What's it like?" Wil asked, enthusiastically.

There was no way to describe it. The vastness, the majesty of Thalinraya and its sun. The slow-motion spinning of the moons. It's a tiny word for such an immense thing, but I felt…awe.

"It feels peaceful. Quiet. Profound," I said. Then, self-conscious, I added, "Except for your voice."

"Ha ha," Wil said sarcastically over Vie's genuine laughter.

But it was true. It was profound. I had looked out the portholes in our ship when we'd awakened in the Thalinraya system, but I'd never been *in* space before. I could feel the lifeless cold just beyond my suit. Strangely, it didn't bother me. I trusted that the thin membrane separating me from the airless vacuum of space would do its job. I ought to have felt frightened—after all, my father had come to grief out here. But I didn't.

I suddenly wished Richelle were with me. Not physically, but on the subvocal channel. I wanted to share this.

"Vie," I said, "do you think when I got set up for hard vac like this there were cognitive changes?"

"I'm sure," she said. "You can't change a person's body without changing their brain. The changes to your musculature alone would require—"

"No, I know about all that. I mean emotional stuff."

"Why do you ask?" intervened Wil.

"Because I'm not afraid," I said. "I feel like I should be, but I'm not."

After a pause Vie said, "I didn't look at the specifics, but I would guess they did some things. Humans aren't made for…extremes like you're experiencing now. They probably put in some governors so you wouldn't freak out."

"Tell him what you learned about me," said Wil.

"Mining synthetics have strategic emotional valves that operate under different situations. Most of them are context-dependent, but they generally work to make the synthetic maximally functional in adverse conditions." Vie wasn't bothering to rephrase the information she had onboarded.

"I have no idea what that means," I said.

"It means," said Wil, "I only feel fear when it'd be *useful* to feel fear. They probably did that to you too."

It made sense that enhancements for the hard vacuum of space would require a whole host of inter-related procedures—from molecular augments all the way up to physical, mechanical, and even emotional alterations. When I'd asked to have the augments done I hadn't looked at all the particulars.

"So, am I an honorary synth now?" I asked. I was trying to keep it light, but I sensed they'd taken it seriously.

"Tab..." began Vie, but she trailed off.

"You're really not pretty enough to be a synth," interjected Wil, covering the sudden awkwardness.

The moon behind which my father had disappeared was floating in front of me now like a mushroom cap. The pock marks from several ECF landings were clearly visible, but there was no activity at the surface. Vie had said she would alert me if anything changed.

Also visible were the moon's distinctive striations in the southern hemisphere.

"What caused those lines in the southern hemisphere?" I asked.

"A comet barrage," said Vie. "There's a gang of about 6200 comets on a massively elliptical orbit around this star."

"Did you know that or did you just look it up?"

"I have it onboard," said Vie. "I accessed it, if that's what you mean."

The Velksin suit made it difficult to move too much—and I didn't want to shift my wings—so I tried to relax and enjoy the slow, stately grandeur of the planet's rotation below me, the moon's obedient circling, the indifferent stars beyond. There were three or four nebulae I could see. With my enhancements I could even zoom in and examine their wispy tendrils lit by ultraviolet or infrared light. I could compute the speed of receding galaxies to see how distant they were, the calculations automatically displayed by my onboards. I could call up a display of every parameter of my current mission—distance to my father's presumed landing site, speed of travel, rate of oxygen consumption.

Two lasers shot out from the ends of my wings, each aimed at some unseen object far in advance of the little ship that was me.

"What the heck was that?" I asked.

"I didn't think you'd want to do manual path clearance," answered Wil. "There was a point-four millimeter magnesium composite about 612 kilometers out. It was going to miss your left panel by about six meters, but best not to take chances."

"You never know when you might need to alter course," affirmed Vie.

"Wil," I asked, "did you know that thing was magnesium or did you access it?"

"Huh?"

"We're with you the whole way on this," said Vie. I know she was trying to be reassuring, but it had the opposite effect. Even out here, between planets, I wasn't alone. I didn't know how much of my experience they could access, but it was probably a lot. Undoubtedly they could see my heart rate, my temperature, electrostatic fluctuations in my skin. But could they see the visuals my eyes were producing? Did they know when I zoomed in on a nebula or traced the braided rings of the sixth moon? When I looked back at Thalinraya?

I wasn't sure why I cared, but I did. I wanted some of those things to be mine alone. An observed thought isn't really your own somehow.

I became acutely aware of my body in its Velksin suit—the joints, the places where my skin touched the lining, the overall pressure of the thing. In an odd way, my body felt like an appendage. I was separate from my body, looking at it from the outside. I wiggled my fingers and felt the resistance of the gloves, the separation of each finger from the next. They were like mechanical extensions, not me. Mine, but not me.

Hadn't my father always said this was so? That we are travelers, temporarily riding in these bodies but destined to leave them behind? In the past years I had grown to believe this was religious foolishness, but now I was experiencing something similar.

Was it the enhancements that were making me think this way? Was it because I had become altered, partly integrated with the computers I now carried in my very bones? Or was it just the natural philosophical pull of deep space?

I shut down all my monitors and began closing off my com channels.

"Tab, there's…what…what are you doing?" Vie asked.

"I've got a couple hours before I swing around the far side. I just want to drift for a while."

"No, you need to keep your systems up, Tab. What if—"

"He's okay," interrupted Wil.

In the silence that followed I was sure they'd opened a private channel to have a quick conversation. Vie wanted to keep as much communication open as possible. It was in her nature. Wil understood solitude. That was in his.

"We'll ping you in 2.13 hours if we haven't heard from you," said Wil. "Your course is perfect, everything looks great."

"Thanks," I said.

The com went off. I switched my visuals back to visible spectrum only. I turned off the diagnostics and recorders.

I was traveling many times faster than sound, but I relaxed. I was alone with my own thoughts. There would be no trace of the next few hours anywhere except in my own mind.

I couldn't say why, but that's what I wanted.

CHAPTER 28

"I'm so sorry," said Vie as she cut through the neck and down the shoulder of my suit.

We were in the hangar. I'd landed a few minutes earlier and Wil had set up a makeshift disassembly station. I held onto a hanging pully while he and Vie worked on either side with derotaxing scissors. Cutting the suit off was less complicated than growing it on, but it wasn't easy. Vie worried she was hurting me. Wil had already cut all the way down the arm to my wrist, casually casting bits of suit onto the floor of the hangar as he went.

"Forget it. How's the jump ship coming, Wil?" I asked as I glanced over at the vessel. The exterior was quite different now, with fins rather than wings and a new scaled material covering the forward portions. It was starting to look less like a jump ship and more like a rocket. The rolling ladder was pulled back from the hatch, which was taped shut.

"It's nearly ready. I wish there was a little more space for thrusters, just to push closer to the PLS boundary. The hull would take it and it'd save you about half the transit time. Can't do it though, the bernaculum takes up—*they*—the *three* bernaculua take a lot of space. Almost done though, so that's good. There's a bit more retrofitting on the engine, then it's good to go."

"Great. I'd love to see," I said.

"Oh, you can't." Wil laughed awkwardly. "Sorry, but there's adhesives curing and it's...toxic. For a while."

The snicking of their scissors on my suit was the only sound for a minute. I could tell Wil was curious to know more about my experience on the far side of the moon, but Vie had probably told him not to ask.

"You want to know what I saw back there?"

"It's okay," lied Wil. I had to smile.

"When I checked in with you before the transit behind the moon," I said, "we confirmed my flight path. That's the path I followed, nothing changed. I rotated my wings, fired my jomels, and rode the curve around the backside."

"They're sails, not wings," said Vie. She couldn't help herself.

"Let him tell it."

"After Thalinraya disappeared behind the moon and I lost contact with you two, it was pretty smooth sailing. I kept to the trajectory we'd planned. The parallel canyons came into view pretty quickly, so I had a good visual marker. A minute later the landing site was in view and there was just nothing there. I could see the triple crater on the highlands and there was nothing around it."

"No sign of anything?"

"I looked in infrared, I used lidar. Nothing. Nothing from FACE either. Just...nothing."

"On that side," said Vie. "FACE is on the surface on the side facing us."

"I did a sweep of the area thirty-six kilometers around the projected site," I continued. "There were no materials of jump-ship density. I swept for anything point-three meters across or larger. Even if the ship had completely broken up, something would have shown."

"He was there to do a gravity well. You don't think he could have—"

"There were no gravity anomalies either. I checked. He never landed...I'm sure of it."

"So we still don't know where he is," said Wil.

"All we know is he's not in this system," said Vie.

"How can you know that?" asked Wil.

"Because it would have shown up when I did my sweeps for asteroids and meteors that day the FACE ships arrived."

That seemed like a lifetime ago.

"So he just took off into space? Why would he do that?" asked Wil.

I'd been wondering about that all during my slow flight back to Thalinraya. I said, "All I can think is that he got the ship up to speed, something went wrong and he wasn't able to change his trajectory and...he went shooting off."

"That's not what happened." Vie said it reluctantly.

"What do you mean?"

"I looked. We know when he left, we know approximately how fast he spooled up, we know where he was going. If he lost control and just kept going, there's a pretty narrow arc where he could have ended up. I looked in that region and there's nothing there."

"He couldn't just vanish," said Wil.

"I don't know what happened," Vie responded.

"He wouldn't have decided to go somewhere else," I said. "Or just abandoned us."

"Don't be dumb," said Wil, as though I had suggested my father *would* have done those things.

"The homestead tracked his ship until it went behind that moon," said Vie. "He was definitely still bound for the landing site, he just never got there."

"Ready?" asked Wil, returning to the matter at hand. He had snipped down the last of my finger coverings.

"Go," I said.

He pulled on the glove, and the suit on his side pulled free from my hand and wrist with a sucking sound. The release of pressure was a relief, and the rest of the suit suddenly felt confining. Wil cut the suit down behind my shoulder and around the scapular pickups, peeling it down when it was free.

"Careful," warned Vie unnecessarily, as she pulled the fingers of my right glove off individually.

Wil went so much faster that he circled around behind me and helped take off my right side, his scissors working quickly and efficiently. When my entire torso and head were free I took Vie's scissors and told them I'd do the rest. I wasn't eager for Vie to see me naked again.

They left the hangar in separate elevator buds. Wil needed some materials for his work on the jump ship and took the new express elevator to the storage facility. Vie headed down to the commissary to get a quick something to eat before taking a rest. Wil had slept while I was returning from the moon, but she'd been vigilant during my entire flight. I could tell she was exhausted.

I had only just begun cutting the suit away from my hip when I heard my name. Richelle had appeared on a panel in the hangar wall. The bed in her room had been folded up into the wall and she sat at a modest desk next to the curtained window. Outside, the ocean was pushing waves against the shore. Richelle was wearing a brown hooded sweater, the hood pushed back.

I found myself wondering again where she was. Almost without thinking, I engaged my augments and calculated the angle of light outside her window. I mapped the angle onto a map of Thalinraya, saw where coasts intersected. Nothing fit.

She wasn't on Thalinraya. But how could she have parted the FACE filaments for my travel to and from the moon?

She must be at a facility with interstellar com. One that could manipulate FACE.

Where was she?

"Tab."

"Richelle," I said. "Where have you been?"

"I was attending to a number of things," she said cryptically. "I'm back now." She obviously didn't want to reveal anything about her location and, given our earlier conversation, I knew pursuing it would do no good.

"There was nothing," I said, moving on to the topic she must be contacting me about. "I didn't find anything out there."

"I know. I caught the last of your conversation with Vie and Wil."

"Do you have any idea what might have happened?"

"I'm sorry, I don't. But I need to talk to you about something else." She smiled without pleasure. "I've been doing an inventory of the satellites in the Thalinraya system. I had hoped to find more gravity clamps, but there are only about sixteen. The moons must have been usefully aligned from the outset of the terraforming."

"What are you looking for?"

"Do you know anything about europium?"

"No."

"Place your hand near the door pickup and I'll give you a download." She reached forward and manipulated something I couldn't see.

I put my hand near the tac pad and felt the data come into my head almost immediately. I had had a number of downloads during my hard vac surgeries, and I'd grown accustomed to using that data. But I hadn't taken in any since, and I wasn't expecting it to feel so…fleshy. There was a physical sense to it.

"Did you get it?"

I leaned back against a table, a little disoriented. "Yes."

"That's what I was looking for. As you can see, it's necessary for the bernacula. Only europium can go between +2 and +3 oxidation at the rate—"

"Hang on," I said, "I'm lost."

"You got the download?"

"I think so. I can feel it."

"Oh, that's right. You've not done this before."

"No."

"I'm sorry. Okay. Let's not try to integrate the download now, but you do need to open access to it."

"How do I do that?" I felt a sudden chill, with my Velksin suit cut away to my waist. I realized I was still holding onto the scissors. I placed them to one side and concentrated.

"It should be volitional," said Richelle. "Intend it."

I told my brain to open the onboarded information and…it was the oddest sensation. All at once I could see a responsive map to the new information troves, like highways leading to individual towns and cities. There were sixteen Unicon-legal and six recognized illegal uses for europium. I knew it with an intuitive feeling rather than a knowing; it was just a schematic list—names on a map in a town that I hadn't yet visited. I knew the shapes and names of the streets, but until I actually went through the town my knowing was…shallow.

"Can you see them?" asked Richelle.

"Yes. Sixteen legal uses."

"That's right. Do a deeper dive on the bernaculum entry."

This was much more disorienting. I had known bernacula had fluid baths in which a person was immersed, but I had never cared to know what the composition of those baths was. Now, instantly, I became aware of salinity levels, electrolytes, biobots, temperatures, drop-off levels, contingency schematics. I knew it all, and my knowledge wasn't deep, but I could see now how vital europium was to bernaculum function.

"Do you see?" asked Richelle.

"Yes. It feels weird."

"I know. Try to work past that for now. I need you to see that the europium is the only dopant that works with the DNA cleansing process. Nothing works without it."

"I can see that."

"Good. Well, that's our problem." Richelle leaned back, away from her desk. Her creased face looked more careworn than I remembered. "I've been trying to find europium in your vicinity and…there's not a lot."

"How much have we got?"

"You only have enough for one bernaculum. No more."

She pursed her lips and waited for my response.

Only one? No. That wouldn't work.

"We need three," I said.

"I know. There's nothing I can do. Even if we got all there is from the satellites, we'd still need about eighty more grams."

"How much do we have?"

"There were 180 grams cached in the homestead stores before you got here. You'll need 140 grams for your bernaculum."

I looked at my onboard parameters, did some quick calculations and said, "The time it'll take to get to Telesis will only require 122 grams."

"You need a safety margin. And even if you went with your minimum, Wil and Vie would each need eighty grams. You still wouldn't have enough even for one of them."

"Eighty? Why would they need less than me?"

"They're synthetics. The substitutions to their DNA don't require as much reuptake gasketing or cleansing. Their amino acids are… You have to trust me."

I didn't have that information in my onboards. "Why don't I have that data?"

"Nobody has that data, Tabit," said Richelle. "It's not legal to transport synthetics in bernacula. I did the calculations myself. And it doesn't matter—there isn't enough europium to sustain them in bern."

"If we have 180 grams, then we have enough for the two of them."

"Tab." She was using her "be serious" tone.

"What? Two times eighty is 160."

"I have always treated them as humans, but this is different. If only one of you can survive it has—"

"More than one *can* survive. Wil and Vie can both get out of here."

Richelle looked pained, but resolute. "I can't allow that, Tab."

"What does that mean, you can't 'allow' it?" I pushed away from the table against which I'd been leaning and came nearer to the panel. "We can save two people or one. Why is that even a question?"

"You are my gen-four grandson."

"What has that got to do with it?"

"Tab, be reasonable."

"I'm the one *being* reasonable."

"Not a single person on Telesis would—"

"Not a single person on Telesis considers them human! That's what made you different. Didn't you always tell me the differences between us were insignificant? That in some ways synthetics are *more* human than us? Well, I think that's right. So how can you say now I should... What *are* you saying?

"Tab."

"No. If there's only enough of this stuff to send me or them, it's them. No question." Feeling the nakedness of my torso suddenly, I looked around for something to put on, but there was nothing in the hangar. I pulled up the remaining portion of my suit and turned back to the panel.

Richelle seemed frozen for a moment. She could have been accessing some internal data, but it was almost as though the video feed seized up.

"I am aware of only one other place on Thalinraya that has enough europium," she said finally, "but I'm not certain I can protect you if you go there."

"Wait," I exclaimed, "there's more here?"

"It may not be accessible. There's a chance though."

"Where?"

"BLCI 1. It's a silo city. They'll have a prebuilt medical center there for the first settlers. There should be a stash of europium ready for reju therapies."

Basic Land-based City Initiators were prebuilt underground settlements known as silo cities. In the months before the first settlers arrived, the synthetics would wake and make their way from their capsules to the silo cities, which they would pull to the surface and get up and running

259

for the first colonists. By the time humans arrived, it should be a fully-functioning settlement.

"Give me a few minutes to see if I can arrange this."

"I'm not leaving by myself."

"Tab, I understand how you feel. I'll try to—"

"I will not go," I said simply. "Not alone."

Her blank look broke after a moment.

"I'm aware," she said with a chuckle.

CHAPTER 29

I FOUND VIE IN THE COMMONS CEL not long after extricating myself from my suit. She still looked exhausted, but this couldn't wait. I brought Richelle up on the display next to the game table and we explained the situation to Vie together. By that time, Richelle had done some research and found a way to get us to and from the silo city safely. Vie listened to the information about the europium without showing any emotion.

Vie and I went to tell Wil in person. He was working in the jump ship again, but he emerged quickly when he heard us and hurried down the ladder. He had stains and scorch marks on his work clothes, and he looked a little frazzled.

"You're being safe with the toxic fumes?" I asked, remembering how he'd had the ship's hatch closed off only an hour earlier.

Wil glanced up at the hatch. "Oh, yeah. It's still a little… I'm okay, but it's probably better if you keep clear." He wheeled the ladder away from the hatch, then turned to us. "What's up?"

We consulted with Richelle through the same panel I'd used earlier. Richelle had switched out of her hooded sweater, I noticed. I felt self-consciously suspicious, but I couldn't figure out why she was changing her clothes so frequently.

Wil kept looking back at the jump ship while we explained the situation. He'd been working on it a great deal, and he must have been frustrated by the idea that two of the three berns he was building might not work for lack of europium. But when Richelle described the procedure for entering the silo city and getting down to the medical facility where the europium could be found, Wil found his enthusiasm for the project. Wil loved adventure, and breaking into an underground silo city would be a good one.

"I can build a drill that'll get into that thing in no time," he said confidently. "And it'll be great to work on an opilion again. These things are..." He thumbed at the jump ship as he trailed off, then laughingly added, "No offense, little buddy."

Opilions were designed to be altered. They were modular and easy to reconfigure, not fixed for a single purpose like the jump ship. Wil was proud of his work on the ship, but the idea of going back to the easy adaptability of the opilion was appealing.

"We'd like to get over there tomorrow morning," said Vie. "Can you download the specs on Settlement One and get the opilion ready?"

"You got it," Wil said with enthusiasm.

We were back in the hammock chairs of the opilion before sunup the following morning. Richelle had told us not to fly. She was somehow disrupting the sensory apparatuses of FACE, but she couldn't hide us if we took to the air.

"That sounds a lot like what Telesis told us," I pointed out.

"They lied about their *reasons* for keeping you hidden," explained Richelle, "but that doesn't discredit their methods."

Vie was looking refreshed, having finally slept. Wil was glad to be driving the opilion again. We were all in fairly good moods.

The first leg of our journey took us through Glassfall Canyon. We had explored the canyon extensively prior to my father's disappearance, and we were familiar with its contours. Which made it all the more shocking when, coming down off the homestead's plateau, we encountered an impasse.

"Whoa," said Wil. "Look at this."

He had brought the opilion to a quick stop, so Vie and I were swinging in our hammocks when we looked up. In front of us, where our side canyon angled down to the main canyon, was a wall of broken crystals. Jagged shards clogged the entire valley, from one side to the other.

"What's wrong?" asked Richelle. She had been routed to a panel on Vie's side of the opilion's interior. When her image appeared it looked odd for some reason I couldn't identify. She was wearing a new, cream-colored shirt, which made her skin look a little darker, but that wasn't it. She was seated at the same desk beside the same window, the same curtains moved in the slight breeze, the shoreline just visible outside. The bed was still folded up against the wall.

I wished I could be closer to the panel. What was it?

"This is new," Wil explained. "These crystals weren't here before."

"Crystal extrusions are normal geology for this area," she said, while reaching to manipulate some device we couldn't see.

"Yeah, but—"

"Not like this." Vie finished Wil's thought. "We were here a few weeks ago and there was nothing like this."

High on a cliff to our right a mass of crystals let loose and fell. The new talus slope was so high, the crystals didn't have far to fall; they crashed down onto the heap below, slid down a few meters and stopped.

"How is it different?" asked Richelle.

"This whole side canyon here has gotten filled up with crystals in just a few weeks," said Wil. "I'm guessing it's a few million cubic meters of material. The composition is changing too. There's more orthoclase feldspar in the newer material. What?" he said defensively, in response to our looks. "You can tell by the colors."

He was right—the colors of the crystals had mostly been clear or tan before; now there were light yellows and greens and even a few violet mounds. More importantly, however, the mounds were huge, their slopes joining together in the middle of the canyon, making it impassable.

"Can you get through?" Richelle asked.

"I don't see how," I responded.

"Oh please!" said Wil, scoffing at my doubt. "Give me a second."

As he busied himself altering the opilion, Vie and I explained to Richelle how we had spent time in this part of Glassfall Canyon. We described the normal crystal falls and how this was a wholly different kind of thing than we'd seen before. As we spoke we kept hearing more falls, all around the canyon. There were a few muffled sounds from under the crystal field in front of us too.

Richelle excused herself to check on something when Wil turned and said, "Ready?" He had grown continuous track around the wheels and some odd-looking fenders in front.

"Are you sure this will work?" asked Vie.

Wil looked hurt and defiant at the same time.

"This thing could burrow through sand if we needed it to," he said, and without a further word he turned to the controls. We lurched forward, and in a moment we were climbing over the first of the crystal mounds. The tracks threw them violently behind us and crushed them beneath us, and for twenty or so seconds we made good progress. It must have been our initial momentum though, because we slowed and started sinking in the crystals. A moment later we stopped moving altogether. The track pushed the crystals back beneath us, but as soon as they moved, more fell down to fill in. The rotation of the tracks was simply digging us down.

"Stop," I said, unable to keep the alarm out of my voice. Wil did stop, but he looked determinedly forward.

"Hang on," he said, reversing the tracks. Crystals broke apart and shot forward, but the opilion only sank further. He stopped and swore. He tried moving the tracks slowly. We sank. He pulsed the tracks. We sank. I looked at Vie, who shook her head slightly to tell me not to say anything.

Wil grew oars and supplemented the slowly moving tracks with oaring. That worked a little, but we were still sinking more than we were moving forward. The crystals were so slick against one another, they worked like ball bearings. The opilion simply couldn't get purchase. After a few more strokes the oars disappeared. Our pod was almost completely submerged beneath the crystals. Lights came on outside the opilion, lighting up the crystals around us like a 360-degree kaleidoscope. We were stuck.

"What's going on? Where are you?" asked Richelle. She had just returned her attention to us.

"We're crossing the crystal field," said Wil.

Vie touched his shoulder, then said, "We're stuck, Richelle."

"Give me a minute," said Wil.

For thirty minutes he tried several more methods to get us through, the most promising of which was shooting a parachute ahead, deploying it and using it to pull us forward. Richelle suggested using grappling hooks and the sides of the canyon, but when she learned that this would require the use of explosive propellants, she told Wil not to do it.

"I really don't want to call attention to you," she explained.

They tried a few other methods, then I suggested we use air to jet above the crystals.

"I don't want you to use propellants," said Richelle.

"Wait," said Wil with renewed enthusiasm. "I could set up magnetic fans and lift us up that way."

Wil and Richelle discussed magnetic fields, and I could tell Richelle wasn't at all happy about resorting to this method. But we were stuck and nobody could think of any alternatives. It took Wil only three or four minutes to reconfigure the wheels, removing the tracks and rotating the wheels out to work like levitation discs. He had to monitor this transformation through schematic diagrams—the wheels themselves were covered, and all we saw was a sort of churning in the broken crystals. According to the schematics, however, the wheel rims now contained magnets, and as the other magnets migrated to the newly-grown fan blades, the blades began to turn. Crystals shattered.

"Easy," said Vie.

"I got it." Wil had a joystick control in his hand now. His thumb wheeled the fans up to a greater speed. The blades churned crystals, smashing and pulverizing them, but the weight of the crystals on the opilion kept us down. His thumb wheeled more. All of a sudden we burst upward, shedding crystals to all sides and rising into the air.

"Down!" shouted Richelle.

Wil thumbed the fan speed down and we fell back onto the sea of crystals with a crash. Vie's hammock swung into mine.

"Got it, got it." Wil wheeled up the fans again and we began to hover close above the crystals, which whirled beneath us, sliding and clinking in the wind.

"Stay low," said Richelle.

"Will do," said Wil, and we started forward.

We flew a meter or less above the crystals, down into the main canyon, which was...an ocean of crystals. We hovered our way across, climbed up a narrow, sculpted chasm on the far side, and finally onto the plains beyond. As soon as we were off the crystal debris Richelle urged us to go back to normal locomotion, and the opilion's wheels rotated and morphed back to their normal state.

For the next couple of hours we rode in silence, Wil stewing in sullen embarrassment at the controls, Vie concentrating on schematics of some sort, and me... Well, mostly I just watched the landscape roll by. The further we got from the canyon the taller the grasses got. The land began to undulate beneath us, rolling up into swales like ocean waves. It was plain land, but lovely.

I was curious about why Richelle was being so mysterious. She had said we should ping her when we arrived at the settlement, which must mean she was off doing something else again. But what? Where was she? I had the feeling she had fled far from Histon, and I wracked my memory for some mention of a place she might have gone. Panticaya? Would she have gone to a prison planet?

An alarm chirped from the front of the pod; the opilion slowed. Vie and I looked forward.

"We're there," Wil announced excitedly. The adventure at hand had finally lifted his mood.

Wil maneuvered the opilion between huge metal pillars, up and over a meter-high metal rail and into an open area beyond. The rail turned out to belong to a massive circular track, 100 meters in diameter. The metal pillars were two of the four legs of the Collins Extractor. I had onboarded a great deal about silo cities for this trip, so I knew what I was seeing.

These starter settlements were grown underground in vertical strips, with the streets and buildings grown as single units. These hung in vast cylindrical storage chambers—thus "silo cities"—that protected the settlement components from radiation and other local issues. When it was time, the synthetics from the workforce capsules would come and use the Collins Extractor to open the silo and pull out the streets and their attached buildings. Silo city plans always had a circular plaza at the center, with streets fanning out like the petals on a flower. The rail track of the extractor marked the edge of the plaza; the streets would fan out from there. Once extracted and laid out, the cities were immediately ready for use.

"How many streets does this silo have?" asked Vie.

"Five," I replied. Both Wil and I had onboarded all the information about the silo so that we would know where to find the medical facility with the europium.

I looked around at the tall grasses that stretched unbroken to the horizon in all directions. I tried to imagine the round plaza that would be the hub of the five half-kilometer streets which would extend outward. There would be a thriving community of people and synthetics, all busily doing whatever it was such people did—growing the city outward, living their lives.

Though probably not here. Not now. Thalinraya was being taken over by FACE, and we were preparing to abandon it. What would happen to this place, I wondered. Was it ruined? What would FACE do to the planet? Did it have little children computers it would raise into bigger, grown-up computers? The image came unbidden: little toddler computers skipping down the five spokes of the settlement, tossing balls back and forth. I laughed.

"What?" asked Wil. He had positioned the opilion at the center of the ring and was reconfiguring it to start drilling down.

"Nothing," I said.

Our hammocks cinched up as beneath our dangling feet the floor of the pod irised open. Below us was a circular patch of smoking ground. Wil had already begun the process of breaking into the silo.

The opilion had grown several anchoring braces, and the pod stood like an invading alien over a smoking circle of grass. Working a joystick in the cockpit and viewing the outside through his main panel, Wil manipulated a nozzle beneath the opilion. A jet of air blew the smoking, ashy material away and revealed the blue metal cover of the settlement. Five seams came together just at the center of the cleared area. It looked like a giant metal iris.

The easy thing would have been to open it with the Collins Extractor, but Richelle had asked us not to engage it. She worried it would attract the attention of FACE. So Wil used a laser to cut through one of the metal sections about two meters from their common joint. When that was done, a magnet swung down and clamped onto the now-detached section, which was lifted free. The legs of the opilion bowed during this process so that we dipped slightly until the heavy metal triangle was deposited to one side. I wondered what kind of metal it was.

We stared down into the dark triangular hole. Although we couldn't see anything, the knowledge that there was a half-kilometer freefall right below us was unsettling. Wil used an overhead handhold to pull his hammock around and held out a shuttlecock-shaped device, grinning.

"Recognize this?" he asked. Disappointed by our blank stares, he pulled one arm down. All of the arms were attached to one another with rubbery netting, so now the five arms fanned out to form a disc. "See!" Wil said, nodding, apparently at his own cleverness. Vie and I exchanged looks. We didn't see.

Exasperated, Wil explained: "It's a replica of a settlement. *This* settlement," he added. "I designed it—it's exact." He released the arm and the thing sprang back to its shuttlecock form. I could see now that the arms were indeed very much like the vertical streets of a silo city. And there were, in fact, little etchings of horizontal buildings along the arms.

"Let's light up the big silo city with a little silo city," Wil enthused. "This should take about 13.4 seconds," he said. He turned a dial and the feathery webbing of the device glowed orange. "Anyone want to time it?" Neither of us volunteered. Wil dropped the thing.

It fell into the inky black and receded. We watched in silence as it seemed to fall an impossible distance, growing smaller and fainter. I realized I was holding my breath. When it had become just an orange dot many seconds later—exactly 13.4 seconds, I'm certain—the skirting shot out to the sides and the thing drifted to the left, then settled. A second later an impossible amount of clear, white light blossomed in the dark. It was blinding. What had been an inky blackness was now almost too bright to look into. From our vantage we couldn't see much, but the cavernousness of the space below us was clear.

"Might have overdone it with the beta decay switching," said Wil, grinning.

"Whatever that means," said Vie with a roll of her eyes.

Two of the panels in the opilion came to life simultaneously. Richelle was displayed in both. She was wearing a different blouse with a floral pattern. Once again, it was a weird time to have changed clothes. There was something else too. Something about the image itself. The window or the curtains, the light from outside...

We gave her a status update and told her we were about to enter the silo.

"How does it look?" asked Richelle, who apparently couldn't see our perspective.

"Wil made it so we'll be rappelling into a light bulb," I said.

"Well...hurry." Richelle's voice wasn't reassuring.

"Why? Did something happen?"

"I believe FACE knows something is going on in that region. You're not in immediate danger, but you do need to get a move on. Wil, how long will this take?"

"Shouldn't be more than twenty or thirty minutes," he said, reaching behind and working some controls.

"Good. I'll be back." Her connection was gone.

"Where's she off to?" asked Wil.

"No knowing," I said.

"She's acting…oddly," observed Vie.

Suddenly it came to me—it was the water outside the window. The shoreline. It was reversed.

What did that mean? Even Richelle couldn't switch a shoreline around. Was it a screen then, not a window? Or…

Was it even real? Could the entire thing be a fake—the window, the room, the bed? That would be fairly easy to do. Which brought up our original suspicion about Richelle: could *she* be fake?

No. No, she knew too much.

"Let's do this," said Wil. He maneuvered a pair of spinnerets from the front to the bottom of the opilion pod and began extruding stranded plasma rope down into the hole.

I had to concentrate. I had to put Richelle out of my mind for the time being.

The iris below us closed off and our hammocks lowered and released us. Lockers at the rear of the pod sprang open and we geared up. Vie helped Wil with his harness. I was sure he could do it himself—better than I could—but he played up his difficulty with the straps and buckles.

"Need a hand?" offered Vie, seeing that I had noticed and trying to cover.

"I got it," I said.

When we were ready, we backed away from the lower iris and Wil opened it. There was a kind of funnel net below us that narrowed to a single strand when it went through the opening of the settlement. Wil produced some auto prusiks, which I hadn't seen since our time at Richelle's estate. That seemed an eternity ago, racing up and down the guy wires in the desert air, dangling from the auto prusiks as we slid back down, daring one another not to use the brakes until the last second.

"Didn't expect to be assembling these here," he said, "but I'm glad I had the specs for 'em."

"Wouldn't it be easier just to have the opilion lower us down?" Vie asked. Seeing the look on Wil's face, however, made her immediately add, "But these will be more fun."

"It's not just for fun, these are for easier movement," he said, clipping his to his belt. "They're faster and more autonomous than having the opilion winch us around."

"What's that for?" I asked, pointing to Wil's holster.

"Grappling gun. Like yours," he said, pointing to the utility belt I was wearing, "only bigger."

Way bigger, I thought.

"Let's go," Wil said, enthusiastically. He donned his helmet and leapt down into the rope funnel, working his way down to the knot at the triangular opening. He reached through the ropes, lifted the one extending down into the silo, and clipped on the prusik, which he'd already attached to his harness. He flipped on his headlamp, stepped out of the safety of the rope netting, and dropped into the settlement.

CHAPTER 30

THE PRUSIK CAUGHT WIL A FEW feet down, where he swung back and forth, in and out of our sight. "Come on," he called.

I climbed down through the iris and attached my prusik, but it took a moment for me to build up the courage to slip through the netting and ease my weight onto it. Wil had slid down five more meters and his weight dampened my swinging as I came onto the main line. As soon as I was through the triangular opening and hanging below it, I could look around the vast interior of the settlement. It was one of the more disorienting things I'd ever seen: an entire city turned on its side and folded together.

The streets of the settlement extended vertically down from where we were. Four of the five petals were folded in on themselves, the buildings pleating together like the fingers on two interlocking hands. It was a wonder of origami and engineering. The petals folded down the center of the streets so that the roofs of buildings on one side folded into the spaces between buildings on the opposite side. It was hard to tell from this angle what the buildings were, but I thought I could make out residential and commercial sections on different petals. A half-kilometer below us, where the streets met, was the plaza that would be the city center.

One of the petals wasn't folded. The broad expanse of its street was exposed to the interior of the cavern, and the buildings on either side were clearer to see. This section was devoted to more affluent homes. Mansions, really.

"Wow," said Vie, who was monitoring what Wil was seeing through a camera bud on his helmet.

"Yeah," said Wil. Then, lifting his face to where I dangled above him, he said, "I'm setting my prusik for a 185 meter drop. Set yours for 180, just in case."

"I thought the lab was only 155 meters down," I said.

"It is, but we need to swing over to it."

"Got it," I said, trying not to think about the drop we were about to perform or the pendulum swinging we would be doing after. Wil had planned this expedition; now I was wishing I had asked a few more questions.

"I'm reading only 300 meters of rope," warned Vie. "That means 200 meters of fall if you go all the way down and come off the bottom of the rope."

"The rope doesn't go all the way down?" I asked.

"Doesn't need to," said Wil, "your prusik has a break. See you down there," he added, then released his prusik and went into freefall. Instinctively, I grabbed onto the rope. He was laughing as he fell away from me, down toward the bright light at the plaza half a kilometer below. The rope bounced and whined as it flew through his open prusik, but when it reached 185 meters it clamped. The flex in the rope bunjeed Wil back to vertical, but it still looked more abrupt than I wanted.

I set my prusik to 180 meters, programming in a maximum velocity well shy of freefall. When I released mine, I sped down the rope in a more controlled way.

"Weenie!" shouted Wil up at me as I raced down toward him. I kept myself vertical by letting the rope slip through my gloved hands.

"I'm holding here at 175," shouted Wil.

No! He had said he was going to 185 and told me to go to 180. If he had stopped at 175 I was about to drop onto him. I fumbled at the prusik control, but it was moving around too much. I started spinning, flailing.

"Go down, go down!" I shouted. Vie said something I couldn't hear.

"Huh?" called Wil, looking up at me, oblivious. I raced down at him, out of control. My prusik read 170. 171. I looked down. He was grinning up at me, unaware of the danger. I closed in on him.

"Look out!" I screamed. But just as I was about to crash into him the prusik tightened around the rope and brought me to a stop. I bounced up and down, my feet scarcely a meter above Wil's head.

Wil was laughing. "When we get back you have to look at my video feed," he said. "You have to see your face!" I couldn't catch my breath. My prusik read 180 meters.

"What did you do?" I demanded.

"He set his to stop him at 182 meters," said Vie exasperatedly. "He's just messing with you."

"It was a joke," he said as he pulled out his grappling gun.

I couldn't help grinning as I cursed under my breath.

Wil aimed his gun and shot the large fusion plug at the medical building. As soon as it had struck the wall it began growing roots in all directions, presumably into the wall as well. He aimed higher for the second shot, and the second plug dragged a line after it, arcing out toward the wall. Attracted magnetically to its mate, the second plug swung down and sideways and snapped into place. A moment later a light on the grappling gun lit up, indicating that the two slugs had fused and the line was ready to use.

Wil clipped the gun to his harness and reeled us over to the entrance. By the time we reached the building, my adrenaline from the fall was finally dissipating.

The medical building was located on a petal that was folded perfectly down the center of its street, the buildings from either side fitting tightly together. There was little room to negotiate between. This was good, because once Wil had gotten us over to the buildings it was fairly simple to wedge ourselves between them and move along to the entrance we needed. Orienting ourselves, however, was nearly impossible. We were hanging from a rope next to buildings grown horizontally toward one another along vertical streets. Wherever I looked there was an unexpected roof or sideways column that made no spatial sense.

"It looks like that Escher immerse," commented Vie.

"Feels that way too," said Wil. "Why do they do it this way?"

"It's the most cost-effective way to get the whole settlement ready before the settlers arrive," I explained.

"But why not use plasma materials like they do with the homesteads?"

"Three reasons," I said, cross checking my onboard information as I spoke. "First, plasma materials are vastly more expensive to make, maintain, and use. Unless there's a compelling need for them, most corporations keep their use to a minimum. Second, the first settlers imprint best if they arrive to solid, consistent structures. That's why the buildings and streets are fixed like this. Third, psychological studies—"

"You know what you're doing?" interrupted Wil.

"What?"

"You're spewing information from your onboards."

"I am not!" I protested, realizing it was a lie even as the words came out of my mouth.

"Right," scoffed Wil, "you talk just like that. 'Plasma materials are vastly more expensive to make, maintain'—"

"Okay!" I said.

Wil snickered—an odd sound subvocally. He was right though. It was amazing how quickly the process of onboarding information had become second nature to me.

"Why is everything so colorless?" asked Vie subvocally. "Everything looks sort of…unfinished."

I was careful this time to use my own words. "The colonists are meant to personalize things. Like the synths do in the workforce capsules—same principle. They give it whatever style they want, expand in whatever direction they want. Build a city that's really theirs."

"You mean, have their synths build them a city," said Wil.

It was true, but I didn't need to say it.

We climbed along the windowed front of the blocky medical building, then up and over the corner to the entrance. The light Wil had dropped down to the plaza didn't reach in here. Heavy shadows angled over a pair of double doors hanging sideways in front of us. We stood on the side of the entry and switched on the headlamps built into our helmets. Vie's fingernail lights would have been useful.

I had a sudden vision of her as a little girl, exploring some dark cavern with her little fingers. In the reflected light, her face was dimly lit. It was a child's face, full of intense curiosity that was only just keeping the fear at bay. It was a lovely face, already full of intelligence and kindness and… My chest felt tight.

Wil put his grappling gun away and hooked our rope around an urn that was attached to the walkway right beside the entry. We disengaged our prusiks. No infrastructure would work until the petals had been extracted, so I pried open the doors with a magnetic lever. The upper door stayed put, hanging shut because of gravity. The lower door slid down into the wall, our floor. We ducked down and entered the building.

Some light bounced up through the windows, but for the most part we were dependent on our headlamps. While walking across the windows I was able to look down into the next building, which was from the opposite side of the street and upside-down to the interior of the building in which we were walking. Of course, we were walking on the building's vertical surface. On windows.

It was difficult to stay oriented.

The patterned floor of the building's foyer on our right was too porous to use the climbing suction cups Wil had brought, so he used his grappling gun and prusikked us up to a large welcoming desk. From there we were able to grapple and prusik our way over to a hall that led in the direction we were going. There was something unnerving about the angular dark, but we boosted the power to our headlamps and pressed on.

We walked along the walls and doors, leaping over side halls. There were decorative geometric patterns—almost a circuit board—spreading across the floor to the right, but the ceiling on the left was a blank plane. There were probably embedded light strips, but they weren't yet activated and we couldn't see them. It got me thinking, as we made our way, how the walls of a room always match, but the floor and ceiling never do. I wondered if underground mines felt disorienting like this. I was about to ask Wil when we came to the door to the storage area we were looking for. It was in the ceiling.

"That's it," said Vie.

"Oh, you think?" Wil responded jokingly. He was ahead of me, already underneath the door. Vie was obviously looking through his helmet cam.

Static burst in our subvocals.

"Vie!" Wil said, suddenly concerned.

Nothing. Then another burst of static.

"*You need to get out of there!*"

It was Richelle.

"What happened to Vie?"

"I'm here," Vie said. "What's going on?"

"They know you're there," said Richelle urgently. "They're coming. Get out, now!"

"We just got to—"

"Wil, get out of there!" I had never heard Richelle sound scared. From Wil's look, neither had he.

We turned and bolted. Our lights flew crazily around the hallway as we ran and leapt over the first side hall. I tripped on a door frame and stumbled, but Wil righted me as he came up behind. We ran on.

"What's going on, Richelle?" asked Vie. "I'm not seeing anything."

"I'm slowing them as much as I can. Tab and Wil, how long?"

"Two minutes to the rope," said Wil. I wondered how quickly we'd be able to prusik the more than 100 meters up to the opilion. "How bad is this, Richelle?" Wil was obviously in better shape than me; I was still recovering from my surgeries. "Are we going to need to go airborn?"

"If you can, do it."

"Vie, take the opilion to emergency config 3," ordered Wil. "It'll tell you the battery draw is too great, just override that."

"Got it."

We'd come back to the opening onto the foyer. Wil reached for his grappling gun, looking up for a place to shoot it.

"Jump it," I said. It was only four or five meters down to the reception desk. The side of the desk wasn't large, but it would certainly be strong enough. From there we could climb down the inside of the desk and drop down to the windows.

"Seriously?"

"What's happening?" said Vie. She must have turned her attention away from Wil's feed.

I stepped past him, judged the distance and leapt before I could think about it too much. The light from my headlamp wheeled around the foyer, air whistled past. My legs crumpled beneath me as I landed on the desk. I skidded forward, grabbing onto the sides to arrest my momentum.

"Nice!" shouted Wil.

I reached around and opened some drawers in the backside of the desk, using these openings to climb around and down to the recess for the receptionist chair. I stood on the wall of the cubby, leaning out to look back up to Wil.

"Go," I said.

Wil leaned back, then stepped out into space. He passed over me and landed with a crash on the side of the desk. He rolled onto his side, which made it impossible to stop his momentum. He skidded off the far side of the desk, slid flailing down the angled front and was freefalling again. I scrambled around and down, but he had already hit against the windows before I got to where I could see him lying on his side.

"Wil!"

"What's going on?" There was panic in Vie's voice.

"I'm good," Wil said, but his voice was strained. He pushed himself up onto his knees and looked up at me. "What are you waiting for?" he managed.

I dangled from the bottom of the desk and dropped. Wil was standing by the time I hit the windows. He gave me a silent gesture to indicate he was okay, but also not to say anything. We headed for the entrance.

"Richelle, there's…wait. Wait, are those…"

"What's going on?" asked Wil.

"Hoverships," said Vie.

"I sent them," said Richelle. "Tab, how long?"

"We're almost to the rope," Wil said, ducking under the door and sprinting over to the urn where the rope was fixed. "Who's up there?"

"Ships," said Vie. "And ground vehicles."

"They're synths," said Richelle. "Hurry."

"Synths?"

"Yes," confirmed Richelle.

Wil was attaching his prusik. "Where did synths come from?" His voice was still strained.

"They have opilions too," said Vie. "But…what are those?"

I swung my prusik around and attached myself to the rope below Wil.

"Vie, put up your defenses!" Richelle shouted.

"What? How?"

"Hit cliwa 32-0!" shouted Wil. "You on?" he asked me.

"Yeah."

Wil leapt off the edge, dragging me with him. We swung wide, crashing into the opposite building before careening back toward the windows of the medical facility. There was nothing to do but hold on as we smashed into the carbon glass. Our momentum spun us around and brought us back into the opposite building again. We crashed twice more before swinging free, penduluming out into the open space between the vertical petals of the settlement. The light Wil had dropped was dimming now; the vertical city was in a sort of twilight.

There was another burst of static, then an explosion.

"Richelle!" screamed Vie.

"What's happening?" Wil craned back to look up at the opening above us.

"They're attacking!" Vie cried.

"Stay where you are," said Richelle.

Wil had already engaged his prusik, which was drawing him slowly up the rope. I engaged mine. Several more explosions sounded in quick succession.

"The synths are attacking?" shouted Wil.

More explosions. Wil was straining to see what was happening above. He tore off his helmet in frustration. His wild red hair looked like flame in the light from my headlamp.

"No!"

"What's going on?"

"Stay where you are." Richelle said again. "Tab?"

"We're coming up the rope!" I shouted.

"They're killing them!" screamed Vie.

"Who?"

A much larger explosion. The vibrations from it came down the rope. Vie screamed again.

"Vie!" Wil was out of his mind.

"The excavator's coming down!" Vie was nearly crying. I'd never heard her voice so strained. "They're killing them all!"

"Stay where you are," ordered Richelle. She must have thought Vie was getting ready to bolt.

A row of semicircular hoods shot out at us from along the street of the one open petal. Crashes and small explosions sounded from the folded streets of all the other petals. Lights flickered everywhere.

"What are those?" shouted Wil.

"Streetlights," I said. They blinked on, hovering in a line above and below us, lighting the street to our side. Someone was tapping into the settlement systems. Were they trying to destroy it? Was it their way of attacking us?

An even larger crash sounded on the surface, followed by more explosions and what sounded like laser fire.

"Vie!"

"She's alright," said Richelle. "Hurry on."

"Wil, hurry! They're slaughtering them." There was more horror in Vie's voice than panic.

"Who?"

The rope jerked and now we were racing upward much faster. Vie or Richelle must have engaged the opilion's winch. More explosions sounded as we raced toward the triangular opening. In only a few seconds we were through.

It was a war zone.

The huge Collins extractor was on its side and in flames. Above it, a boxy aircraft was spiraling out of control, also on fire. On the ground were a dozen or so opilions, several already disabled and one looking like it had been blown to bits. Synthetics were running through the grasses, crouching at various places around the circular track of the extractor. Above them were gray drones of some kind. They shot down at the defenseless synths, tearing them to pieces. Bodies came apart suddenly, glistening organs tumbling out onto the ground. A kneeling synth was holding his own intestines; next to him, a smaller synth suddenly became a pink cloud. Whips of flaming oil lashed down, painting fiery arcs across whole groups, which scattered like mad fireflies. Those that paused to help or gawp in horror would suddenly stutter and jerk, then burst like blood-filled balloons. It was a nightmare come to life.

Red drones flashed past, shooting at the gray drones. I followed the flight of one to where it banked over a group of differently dressed synthetics. From a different workforce capsule? They too were running to avoid the gray drones, but they were getting cut down just as fast.

Two meters away the ground exploded, dirt and grass flying. A shoe cartwheeled past with a foot still inside of it.

"Come on!" Wil had already disengaged from the prusik. He was climbing up into the opilion pod.

A curtain of electricity swept down from the west, folded in on itself, darted down to the extractor track. Synths all around the circumference of the thing were flung back, unconscious or screaming and crying. Smoke rose from dozens of broken vehicles.

I climbed up into the rope funnel and took off my prusik. Wil yanked me up into the opilion and tossed me to one side as soon as I was free. The iris to the pod floor closed.

"Disengage the anchors, I'll lift us off."

Wil made his way past Vie to the cockpit. Vie, visibly shaken, was working instruments at a side panel. Wil squeezed her shoulder as he passed.

"Get in your harness," he said. Vie and I both clambered into our hammock harnesses as Wil limped forward, holding his side.

There were drones fighting other drones in the sky, synthetics on the ground being mowed down. From the higher vantage inside the opilion's pod the carnage was more striking. Grasses all around had been sprayed with blood, opilions and other vehicles were on fire. One synthetic, horribly ablaze, was running and spreading fire to grasses outside the extractor track. Steam rose from small craters where acid grenades had been dropped.

"Richelle," I shouted, "what is going on?"

"I'll tell you later. Just get out of there."

"Anchors are up," said Vie.

"Lock yourselves in. Here we go," said Wil. The legs of the opilion shot flames down at the earth and we lifted. But after only a few feet we jerked to a stop. It felt like we had risen into a ceiling, and I looked up, thinking there might be drones holding us down.

"What's happening?"

"I don't know." The jets fired angrily, but something was holding us.

"You didn't disengage the net," said Richelle. An explosion concussed us sideways. Wil swore. He worked the controls and the floor of the pod irised open again. Sound flooded back in, explosions and lasers and screaming. The rope funnel disengaged and fell, the weight of the rope pulling it down quickly through the triangular hole. It slid down but abruptly came to a stop, one cord reaching up to the underside of the opilion. I couldn't see what was holding it.

I started to remove my harness. "Stay there, I got it." Wil was already climbing back. He hadn't yet put himself in his harness, so he was quicker than me. He pushed past Vie and got down onto his belly to reach through the iris.

"Careful!" said Vie.

"Hurry!" said Richelle.

Wil spread his legs to brace himself and scooted forward to reach a little further. The cord came free, the rope funnel dropped and disappeared into the settlement.

Another explosion burst in the air above, shaking the opilion. Pieces of flaming metal rained down, whirling and spiraling as they did, pinging against the exterior of the opilion. One arced close under the opilion's belly, and Wil's head jerked sideways. From where I was I could see that the thing had spun through the side of his face, laying open his cheek from his mouth to his ear. Blood bubbled up and over his face. He reached to cover it and his braced legs slipped. He fell forward, out of the opilion and down toward the triangular opening. His arms and legs splayed, but he was turning over and couldn't orient himself. One leg hit the side of the opening, but his torso went through. Cartwheeling into the hole, he fell down and out of sight.

CHAPTER 31

VIE DISAPPEARED INTO THE HOMESTEAD before I had gotten down from the opilion. I followed her in and took an elevator to the habitation cel corridor, but her cel was irised shut. She obviously wanted some time alone. The iris to Wil's cel was also shut, perhaps forever.

Except...my father, as Principal One, had had override capabilities, even to private habitation cels. That's how he'd been able to force me to come with him on those first trips, when he was trying to train me to take Mom's place. Would that level of permission transfer to me now that he was gone?

"Homestead," I said, "open Wil's habitation cel." The iris immediately opened, the fins retracting into the vitreous. I felt instantly guilty. I was violating his privacy, whether or not he was gone. What did I hope to see, anyway?

Through the opening I saw some jump ship schematics on a panel next to his bed. On a larger panel in the sitting area were schematics for gravion insert rings. Next to them were other winged aircraft I had never seen before.

Wil had been bred to live and work underground, but his heart had always been in the sky. He lived to be airborne. I remembered his mad laughter when he launched that first opilion off the continental break, soaring out over the plains toward the Auger Station. His whoops of joy when riding in the gravion. I remembered how he had launched himself off the desert spire before I even knew his name.

Emotions welling up, I told the homestead to close his cel and made my way to the Control cel.

"Homestead, what's the status of the pale?"

"Secure, 92.3 percent charged. We've had 1,613 communication requests from 45.121, 907.488, and 607.411."

"Where's that?"

"The Telesis system. Given the intervals between com requests, ninety-two percent appear to be automated."

"Any com channels open?"

"You instructed me not to open any com channels. I will adhere to that directive until you supersede it with another."

"Thanks. Can you get a satellite view of the silo city BLCI 1?"

The main panel blossomed with a satellite image zooming in on the area we had recently fled. It was devastated. Smoke rose from fires on all sides. Broken vehicles were scattered around, some still on fire. It looked like dozens of drones had crashed or been shot down.

"Stop zooming in," I said. Bodies were everywhere, and none were moving. I didn't want to see them any closer.

Seeing it from this perspective reminded me of EllGray[3]. It wasn't the best immerse, but remember the beginning, Dayr? Starting in the clouds above a battlefield and sweeping slowly down as the dramatic music underscores the narrator's backstory. Once we got down to the field of battle, the narrator told us the names of the fallen knights, the houses indicated by their banners. Remember the king's mud-spattered head on the pike?

The carnage was at the beginning of the game to impress on the player how important things were. It raised the stakes of the game. But Dayr, the battlefield I was looking at now was real. And there was no point to it—it was just senseless slaughter. Worse than senseless, this massacre was our fault. ECF was clearly after *us*, not the synths. They were collateral damage. They were unarmed and unprepared and…mowed down.

Why?

On the display, a long, jagged line of fire was sweeping outward to the west of the killing field. A grassfire, blown by the wind. The burnt area behind it looked like the map of some dark continent. The wreck of the extractor was the largest thing visible. It was crumpled on the southeast side of the circular track. At the center of the circle was the scarred area I knew contained the triangular hole into which Wil had fallen. I half expected to see light from inside, but it was dark. In my mind I could still see the row of streetlights hanging vertically in the dark, shining across to buildings which would never be used. With all the explosions and chaos, the lights may have stopped functioning by now. The light Wil dropped would have gone out. Or, I imagined without wanting to, maybe his broken body was simply covering it. He'd be lit up like an x-ray, his broken bones visible through translucent skin.

I turned away from the display, then took a step back, startled to see Richelle on the opposite display.

"I'm sorry, I didn't mean to startle you." She was sitting rigidly on the edge of her bed, her hands clasped in her lap. "Tab. I am so sorry."

"What happened?"

"I tried to keep—"

"What were they doing there?" I demanded. I couldn't keep my voice steady.

"They were monitoring surface masses much more discretely than I—"

"No, I mean the synthetics. What were they doing there? How did they get there?"

Richelle took a breath. "I sent them. As soon as I knew you were going there I—"

"Why?"

"In case you were spotted. And you were, at the canyon."

"But why send *them*?"

"I thought they might be able to help. And as it turned out, they did. Because they came from three capsules, their movements drew the attention—"

"Three capsules? Three?"

"Three. Two made it to you, but—"

"You opened *three* capsules?"

"You knew that," she replied. "We opened all the capsules on the continent."

Three populations of synths had been slaughtered.

"When did you plan this?" There weren't three capsules close to that settlement.

Richelle leaned forward earnestly. "Tab, if I hadn't sent those synthetics out from their capsules when I did, FACE drones would have been on you much earlier and in much greater force. You never would have made it out of there. FACE drones would have had only one target. You."

"Did they know who was attacking them?"

"No. They were celebrating, Tabit." Richelle was getting defensive. "They were fulfilling their greatest ambitions in life, going to do the one thing they were designed to do. They were joyous. They were *singing*."

"And now they're dead!"

"Yes. They're dead." There was a rigidity to her face I hadn't seen before. "And in their last moments they were terrified. Some of them I'm sure were in pain. I'm sorry. There's nothing I can do about that. I did what I needed to do to save you."

"So you sacrificed all of them for us? Kill a thousand to save a couple?"

"They are synthetics, Tab."

The way she said "synthetics"—I had heard many people use that tone, but never Richelle. She had always railed against that bigotry. Had it always been an act?

"So it's okay to use them any way we want? Didn't you used to call that idea inhuman?"

"Tab, listen to me."

"Homestead, zero out all panels in the Control cel."

Richelle disappeared. I stared at her absence, not knowing what to think or feel.

I lay in my cel. The activated plasma of the featureless walls allowed them to morph quickly into many different configurations, but there was something about their very flexibility that made them…nauseatingly bland. They certainly didn't feel like home.

Richelle had tried to contact me a number of times, first subvocally and then through the homestead. After I had refused the connection six times, I instructed the homestead not to put any requests through to me. I'd had a few hours of quiet since then. I hadn't floated my cel up to the perimeter like I usually did. For some reason I didn't want to see the outdoors.

I thought a lot about Wil and our pointless trip to the settlement. There still was only enough europium for one of us. Wil's sacrifice hadn't even solved that dilemma.

I spent some time strategizing how to convince Vie to go instead of me. Finally, I slept.

During sleep, my mind probed my new memory augments. While awake I had avoided accessing the recordings from the silo city, but they were there. They pulled at my unconscious mind, and flashes rose up into my dreams. Fire. Explosions in the air. Wil's cartwheeling fall into the dark.

It wasn't restful. I was going to have to learn to manage those files better if I ever wanted peaceful sleep again.

I sat up, feeling my new body: eyes, scapular pickups, foot fihns on the outside, reinforced bones and brain on the inside. I didn't even know what most of it was.

The image came again: Wil falling in the dark, turning end over end, flailing out in pain and fear, knowing…

I rubbed my eyes until whorls of light and color erased the image. Wil wasn't bothered by it now anyway…he was dead. His pain was gone, as if it had never existed. When Vie and I were dead, his death wouldn't even cause anyone's heart to ache. Which would happen to me too. I'd die and get recycled for parts. Forgotten forever.

If Wil had a choice, he'd probably like how he died. The thought was comforting, though I couldn't say why it should be.

"Vie is requesting entry to your habitation cel," the homestead announced, interrupting my thoughts.

"Let her in," I said, grabbing a shirt and pulling it over my head.

The cel irised open and Vie was there. She'd been crying, but now she had a determined look on her face. She stood near the entrance, composing herself before speaking.

"Richelle contacted me." I had nothing to say to that, so I waited. "I didn't want to talk to her, so she sent a message. It's addressed to both of us. I think you should see it."

Vie stood there rigidly. She wasn't going to say anything further.

"Homestead, do I have a message from Richelle?"

"Affirmative."

"Play it."

Richelle's image appeared on the wall panel beside the entry to the bathroom. Once again she had changed her shirt. She now wore a darkly patterned scarf as well. I suddenly remembered the changed coastline out her window. The curtains weren't billowing, so I couldn't see it now. Was that intentional?

"Tab and Vie," Richelle finally began. Because it was a message and not a com, she looked vaguely forward, not at us directly. It made her seem older somehow. "I can't tell you how sorry I am about Wil. I wish I could go back and change my recommendation about how to get the europium you needed, but I can't. If it helps, I'm certain Wil would be proud that he died helping you two escape. He was..." Richelle looked down for a moment to gather herself, then resumed. "I loved him too. Now. I have some information you're going to want to have. I don't know if you trust me or if you'll even listen to this, but you can contact Telesis and...well, I don't know what they'll do. But I don't believe they have reason to lie anymore.

"When FACE spores came to ground on Thalinraya, you couldn't have known what they were. When Telesis got control of your systems, however, I'm certain they knew right away. FACE hadn't been active in this sector yet, so they were surprised, but they knew.

"They panicked. With you there alone and Tab's father missing, there really wasn't any way they could counter the incursion. Six spores came down, twelve strands launched, eleven made their way to resource centers. FACE was positioned to take the planet, and there was nothing Telesis could do about it.

"As you know, Thalinraya is the only source of malibdi in this sector, and it's rich with it, meaning FACE was about to take control of this entire sector. 146 star systems. Telesis couldn't allow that. So they sent you to the CA station—the Core Auger.

"They told you that you were programming the Station to produce energy to power up the satellites. As you know, that was a lie; the satellites were never without power. When you discovered you'd been lied to, you dismissed that trip to the Auger Station as merely a distraction. So did I. Had my curiosity been at the proper setting, I would have looked into it, but I was otherwise occupied. It wasn't until your observation of the crystal eruptions at Glassfall Canyon that I became suspicious something more significant might have been done. And it was. The sequence you initiated that day was a drilling program."

Richelle paused, smiled sadly and said, "Wil could explain this better than me. It's complicated, but the drilling you initiated, and that's continuing right now, is hollowing out a cavity next to Thalinraya's liquid metal core. There's a temporary dike that separates the liquid core from the cavity. In a few days—I would guess in about twelve days from now—the dike will be intentionally breached. The liquid core of the planet will shift suddenly. This will unbalance the planet and compromise its orbit so that… Thalinraya will be destroyed."

Richelle must have known that we'd need some time to take this in and she paused before continuing. Vie was stone-faced; she'd heard this already. Telesis had gotten us to destroy the planet we were on. It was the first thing they'd had us do.

Of course it was.

"It will take time," continued Richelle, "but there will be substantial and immediate effects. There will certainly be tectonic shifts. There will be earthquakes; volcanos will go off. This will start fires, tsunamis…I imagine the supervolcano on the southern continent will erupt; an ash cloud will envelop the planet. It will be…" She smiled sadly before finishing: "biblical."

Vie showed no emotion as she listened. Her eyes were dead.

"Whatever life survives will have at most a few years. The orbits of the moons around Thalinraya will also be disrupted. These things are hard to anticipate, but it's likely that the third and fourth moons will collide in the second year post-event. Given their composition, the resulting meteor bombardment will scour Thalinraya. Without the moons, the orbital perturbations will magnify one another until Thalinraya spins out of control. I've examined several million simulations and the most likely scenario is that it will plummet into the sun.

"Telesis had you do this because they couldn't allow FACE to gain control of the malibdi on Thalinraya. So they had you set in motion the destruction of the planet."

And we'd done it enthusiastically. Wil had tricked out the opilion—he'd been so excited to be able to drive. Vie had programmed the station. I had given authorization. We'd all been working to kill ourselves.

Vie stood with her arms folded, staring at Richelle. She wasn't holding emotion in—she was without emotion. It was scary to see her like that.

"FACE has learned this now," Richelle resumed. "It knows there is only a small amount of time to stop the sequence. The mechanics of what is happening are too far underground for it to intervene directly, so the only way to stop the sequence is to alter the program you initiated. To do that, they need to get into the homestead and decrypt the instructional sequence. Some of them hope to stop the drilling and reverse the process; others hope to simply shore up the dike to make it a permanent feature. Most of us believe it's a lost cause, but they have to try.

"I doubt it can get through the layered Vsevolod encryption even if they get access to the homestead, but they will try. There's really no other choice." Richelle took another breath and lifted her chin. The curtain at her window billowed in suddenly, revealing the coastline. It was no longer reversed.

Had I imagined it? When we were done listening to Richelle's message I'd go back and check my visuals.

"They're preparing another attack. This time they'll want to capture the homestead, not destroy it. It's a trickier problem. They're going to be delayed a few hours because they need to build new...machines. You should have about fifteen hours."

I drew in a breath and looked at Vie.

"The attack will fail," said Richelle simply.

Now Vie glanced at me, but there was no emotion or curiosity.

"I have access to their systems," continued Richelle, "and I can intervene when the time comes. But I can only do this once. It will delay them, but it will not stop them. It will take them a while to mount another offensive, but by that time I will not be able to help. At all. To help you during the first attack, I will need to reveal myself to them. After that I will need to leave. You will be on your own."

There was a finality to Richelle's pronouncement. It was almost a threat.

"Tab and Vie, I need both of you to hear me about this. Only one of you can make it off Thalinraya at this point. Tab, I know your opinion of me has suffered in the past forty-eight hours, but I hope you can remember that I have loved Vie even longer than you have. I broke laws to bring her to my estate. I reengineered her genome twice. Vie, you remember the times we spent together. You know I love you.

"But you only have resources to get one of you away from there. What is the best use of those resources? Consider what escape means for each of you. Tab, you are human, which confers on you certain rights in any world controlled by the Unicon. You may not like it, you may not agree with it, but it's simply true. If you were to arrive at any world, you would be taken care of. They would undoubtedly question you about your relationship with me, but most of the problems I've had arose after you left. There is every reason to believe you could go on with your life. But"—and here Richelle leaned forward—"what about Vie?"

Richelle gave us a moment to think it through ourselves before continuing.

"If an interstellar ship arrived with an illegally augmented synthetic, what do you expect would happen? Most likely she would be terminated immediately. If they were able to connect her to me…I'm afraid her death would only come after interrogation and memory extraction. I am no longer welcome in the Unicon, and anything that might lead them to me would be very interesting to them. If they knew of our relationship and felt Vie was somehow withholding information from them—which she could do, given the augments I've given her—they would torture her to find out where I am."

Vie didn't react. She looked indifferently at Richelle's image. I wanted Richelle to look over at Vie, to engage her directly. But this was a recording, not a live com.

"I'm sorry, Vie. Tab's status as a human protects him. It isn't fair, it isn't just, but it is *true*. If you were to leave Thalinraya, both of your lives would be wasted.

"Tab, I know you hate this situation. I do too. But it isn't of our making, and the best we can do, the best anyone can do, is to make the most of the situation they're in. Putting Vie on the jump ship would be a waste. It wouldn't help her, and it would kill you.

"Please. Both of you. Listen to me. You need to put Tab on that jump ship as quickly as you can. I've arranged a targeted breach in the EM net that FACE is constructing around the planet. It's automatically signaled by your jump ship reaching 10,000 meters, and it will work even after I'm gone. It's the last thing I can do for you.

"I love you both. I loved Wil, and I'm sorry we lost him. I'm sorry you're in this situation and I know it's hard." Richelle reached up and rubbed away an invisible tear. "Vie, I love you. I can't save you. I'm sorry. I hope you understand. Tab, I love you too. This is the hardest thing I've ever asked of you. Of anyone. And I know it feels like I'm telling you to be selfish. I'm not. It's the only sensible thing. Please. Get yourself on that ship and get off this planet before it's too late."

Richelle exhaled and looked to one side, as though consulting a panel. She reached up and touched an earring—a gesture I'd seen her make a thousand times when she was preparing to say something difficult.

"I have some things I need to arrange. I won't be contacting you again. I wish I could be there with you. Only to...to wrap my arms around you one last time. I love you. Goodbye."

CHAPTER 32

"It's never going to be fair," said Vie. The sky behind her was a twilight wash of unnamed colors. "Fair has nothing to do with it."

We'd taken an elevator up to talk outside. I had hoped to walk down to the breakfields, but the conversation we'd begun in the elevator became too intense. When the iris had opened we barely stepped out, and now we were standing outside the main entrance. The view across the breakfields toward Glassfall Canyon was spectacular. It was the sort of view, and the sort of sunset, Vie and I would normally love to share together. But this wasn't the time. Vie was being stubborn, and I had to convince her I could be stubborn too.

"Think about it," I said. "I have had so much more freedom in my life than you have. I have—"

"Freedom?" she mocked. "Are you serious? Your parents were Feremites! I have augmentations you couldn't dream about, and I've had them since before I could walk. You never had *any* before you had your hardvac surgeries. And I've been just as many places as you have. I've done just as many things. Tab, we had *different* childhoods, that's all. Don't paint me like a victim. I'm not Wil, and I'm not convinced our lives are any worse than yours. I *liked* my orphanate."

"Vie, come on."

"You have no idea, Tab. It wasn't like your upbringing, so you assume it must have been awful. It wasn't. Honestly, there were times at Richelle's when I wanted to go back."

"You were being raised to be a worker."

"So were you! Hello! Did you have a choice about where you went, what you studied, what you were going to do with your life? No. I was programed in vitro to be a communications synth. So what? I was also programmed to *like* it. And I did. I *liked* learning about it, I *liked* onboarding packets that made me good at it, I *liked* living with other synths who were studying the same thing and who also liked it. I had friends who understood me. We got to spend lots and lots of time together. It wasn't so bad. And I was a lot less lonely than you were."

"But I was born a human."

I regretted saying it immediately. Vie rolled her eyes and looked out at the colors of the sunset before responding. She tried to calm herself, but when she turned back it was clear she'd failed.

"Alright, TabiTal Yrl, you're human. What difference does that make?"

"Like Richelle said, it means I've always had rights. You haven't."

"What rights did I want that I didn't have? No, really, tell me. How was I deprived?" She was angry. "I'm not Wil, Tab. I don't wish I was anything more than I am. All of us are out here in the back of nowhere because of things beyond our control. None of us chose to be here. Wil is dead. I can't leave. But it doesn't help either of us to waste the chance you have. That cheats all of us. Wil too!"

I hated her cold logic. I said, "This is what you do: You make things sound reasonable, but really you're only trying to win the argument."

"Sending me will *do...no...good*! Richelle is right. They wouldn't just let me skip off the ship and start a new life."

"I'm sure there's someplace we could send you."

"Where?"

"I don't know. Maybe back to your orphanate if you liked it there."

She shot me an incredulous, derisive look. "Don't be a pog."

I felt heat behind my eyes. "You know this isn't fair," I pleaded.

"Alright, consider this then." Vie sensed my emotion and used a calmer tone now. "I was the one who reprogrammed the Auger. What would happen if FACE managed to capture the ship as it leaves?"

"Richelle said she had arr—"

"What if she's wrong? What if they capture the ship and I'm in it? You know what happens then? They don't need the homestead, they only need to tap my memory and reconstruct what I did. They'd be able to untangle the code I onboarded, decrypt what they need and stop the process Telesis started."

"That's not true."

"Yes it is! I was the one who interfaced with the homestead to reprogram the Auger Station. They can get what they need *through me*."

"You don't remember how it worked."

"I don't need to! All they have to do is sift through my archive." She pointed at her own head. "It's all archived in there. One of those things we synths come pre-packaged with. A safety mechanism. It's in there, whether I want it to be there or not."

This was probably true; synthetics had onboard memory caching. Police departments used it regularly to see what kinds of crimes had happened in their presence. Even if they weren't involved, their memories were often used in court.

"So I can't send you because they might capture you and get your information?" I said.

"Yeah, among other reasons."

"But they could capture you here if you stay."

"Not if they can't capture the homestead."

"But what if they do?"

"If I'm here, they can't."

"What does that mean? That you'll...what, you'll blow you and the homestead up?"

"One of us will have to do it." She was serious. "Tab, think it through. If you were here and they were about to capture the homestead, what would *you* do? You're about to die anyway; do you want them to get Thalinraya?"

"Why should I care?" I asked.

"Come on. You'd rather let FACE win this planet, get the resources, steal the sector? You'd take the computer's side against humanity? You wouldn't." Vie's eyes flared with determination.

"I don't know."

"You wouldn't! You'd do the same thing I'd do—torch the place."

I wasn't so sure. Telesis had lied to us, again and again. We were nothing to them.

The evening wind was picking up and the sound of thumpers came through the dome. They sounded close. I was glad a few at least had survived the attack on the homestead. Three moons were cresting the escarpment.

294

"It's better this way," said Vie, more calmly than before. "I have no future in either case. You do. So if anything good is going to come out of this…it's got to be you who leaves."

Vie spent a few hours onboarding what she needed to continue Wil's work on the jump ship. Her augments were much more comprehensive and dynamic than mine, and she'd been using them much longer, so it made sense for her to be the one to finish what he'd started. It still felt odd. I was trying to think of a way to get Vie off the planet instead of me, but realistically…what chance did she have leaving here alone? None really. It wasn't fair, but it was true.

Suddenly Vie was standing in the iris to the commons cel, crying with abandon.

"What's wrong?" I asked, rushing over, thinking she'd been hurt.

"Come and see…see the ship," she managed, then turned and left.

I followed her up to the hangar. The changes Wil had made to the jump ship were even more obvious now. The fins had complicated ridges, the nose was blunted, several of the windows had been covered. It looked much more rocket-like.

Vie waited for me at the top of the ladder, then stepped aside to allow me to enter first. With foreboding, I stepped past her into the now-unfamiliar ship. The seats and flooring had been removed. The area to my left was a tangle of odd new equipment. Looking right, I realized why. The interior of the craft had been reconfigured for weightlessness; all the equipment was oriented toward the center of the fuselage rather than the ground. This meant that some of the panels were upside down to my gravity-bound eye.

Vie came in behind me, carefully stepping over gears and instrument panels. She didn't say anything, but I followed her gaze aft to where the first bernaculum had been added. It looked out of place, like a large metal coffin that didn't quite fit. Rising up the walls around it was all the support equipment that would keep the bern's occupant in homeostasis through the years of transit: blocks of gourminid gel, pumps, sensors of various kinds. Behind the bern were newly installed engines. The normal engines of a jump ship would never be able to bring it to interstellar speeds, so Wil must have been…

Wait.

"Where are the other berns?" I asked.

"There aren't any." Vie looked at me, waiting for me to process this fact. It took a few seconds, but when she saw the realization in my face she nodded. "There were sixteen schematics in his files," she said, "all with different configurations. He did his research and looked at a lot of different possibilities. All of them fitted the ship out with only *one* bernaculum. He knew."

"How?"

"Materials lists are with the schematics," Vie explained. "He was good with materials. He would have known there wasn't enough europium for all of us. He chose this design before Richelle told us about the settlement." Her voice cracked. "He knew we couldn't all make it, so he'd already reworked the aft compartments to accommodate larger engines. So you could make the transit faster."

My mind raced. Why hadn't he told us? Why had he gone to the silo city at all, if this was his plan? If we'd gotten the europium, would he have changed the ship again, added more berns? Would there have been time?

Vie was crying softly again.

"He could have been setting it up for you," I said. "He loved you."

After a long moment, Vie looked away. "It was for you."

"You can't know that."

"Yes, I can." She looked back at me, a flash of anger in her eyes. "If he'd intended it for me he wouldn't have bothered to load all the europium in the cyclers. Synths don't need as much. It takes a lot of energy to keep europium warm enough for use out there. If the bern was for me, he would have saved the space and energy. And so you know, he had a schematic worked out that *would* have done that. He considered it." She took a breath before finishing the thought. "But he rejected it. He chose this one. He wanted you to go."

It was hard to believe. Wil was a man of the moment, not one to look ahead. Yet here he had foreseen something that neither Vie nor I had. And he'd kept it hidden.

Which meant he had known he was going to die. And Vie too.

Vie was lowering herself out of the drop ship. I climbed down the ladder after her.

"If you needed any more convincing, I hope that does it. You always wanted us to vote on things. Well, there's Wil's vote," she said, pointing to the ship. "So it's two to one. You're leaving."

CHAPTER 33

THE ATTACK CAME SOON AFTER DAWN.

The homestead informed us that the initial attack was underground, so we experienced it from the Control cel, watching schematics on the various boards. The main panel displayed a 3D rendering of the underground area of the pale, the homestead barely visible at the top, sitting above the much larger underground storage complex. There were all sorts of icons and numbers and markings that made no sense to me, but the overall situation was pretty clear. A ring of red-colored objects was closing in on the pale, which was protected by a plasma sphere that appeared silvery-white. What I had always thought was an aboveground dome was actually a sphere that extended below ground to protect the homestead and resource storage areas from underground threats as well.

There were several dozen glowing blue icons around the periphery of the pale. They suddenly pulsed. I was about to ask Vie what they were, but I remembered my onboards and accessed them instead. I immediately became aware that these were sentinids, automated alarms that monitored storage tanks for leaks. They were supposed to be aimed in, but now they were aimed out and generating EM pulses of some sort. The blue pulses had become arcs, the arcs had joined to create a circle of blue that expanded outward toward the incoming red objects.

I asked the homestead if something had been done to the sentinids.

"The polarities of the T-6061 Sentinids were reversed thirty-two minutes ago."

"Who did that?"

"The order is not tagged."

"What does that mean?"

"The order is not tagged."

"Did it come from Telesis?" I asked.

"The order is not tagged."

"It had to be Richelle," I said. "She's the only one who would know how to do that."

"But do what?" asked Vie. "What's going on?"

We didn't know, and all the homestead knew was that external EM fronts were about to meet EM fronts that the sentinids had generated. The solid blue circle expanded inexorably outward toward the ragged red scarves that were advancing toward the pale. It looked like an old-world video game.

"Homestead, what's going to happen here?" asked Vie.

"Can you provide a timeframe?" asked the homestead, frustratingly. But before Vie could clarify her question the first of the red lines hit the solid blue one. Instinctively, I winced.

Nothing happened. The lines merged, then the red bit passed through to the other side and continued on its way. Three more red bits merged with the blue line. They too passed through.

"It's not doing anything," I said. The relentless closing in of the red scarves seemed more ominous than ever. Hundreds more were passing through the blue line now.

"What was it supposed to do?" I asked Vie.

"I have no idea," she replied.

"Homestead, is there anything we can do to stop those things? Do we have any underground defenses?"

"The anomalies are already inside the obsidianized dikes and approaching the dome defense."

We were at the center of the schematic, and the red scarves were converging on us from all sides. Panic was about to set in, but then the most advanced red scarves began to arc away from the pale.

"They're changing direction."

More of them turned. It looked like a flock of birds that had decided, in their uncanny way, to change direction simultaneously. Those outside the blue circle continued inward, but those red bits that were inside the circle were all turning away.

It was a chimerical military ballet. The blue circle seemed to be giving the red scarves new orders. We watched as they gathered in a circle, exactly the size of the pale, two kilometers to the northeast. They joined together in a loop, fused into a glowing ring, then grew threads across the interior. This was a smaller version of what FACE was doing to the entire planet.

Vie ran some diagnostics on a side panel. "It's an EM field. A really powerful one. It would have allowed them to prevent us from communicating with Telesis."

"And Richelle said they needed to capture the homestead, not destroy it," I said. "That makes sense."

"A level-seven meteor shower is commencing," said the homestead.

A meteor shower? I looked at Vie.

"It can't be," she said. "I checked when we were looking for your father. You were there."

It was something from FACE.

"Orbital hooks are being engaged," announced the homestead.

"What? On whose authority?" I asked.

"There's been a breach. I can trace it if you like."

A low thrumming raced around the homestead. It was reconfiguring.

"No, just shut them off."

"I am currently unable to do that. Meteor impact in six seconds."

"Where?"

"Here."

"Get down!" Vie shouted. We both dove to the floor. I only hoped the homestead could withstand the bombardment. I couldn't remember how big a level-7 meteor bombardment was, but the scale only went to 9.

There was a whining sound. We cringed.

Nothing happened.

Vie brushed her hair aside and looked up at the monitors.

"What's going on?" I asked. "Where are the meteors?"

"Two hundred and sixteen meteors were arrested by orbital hook intervention. They are currently hovering in a helical array over the pale."

"What are they doing?"

"Hovering is a condition of suspension or buoyancy approximating weightlessness, characteristic—"

"Are they doing anything else?" Vie asked angrily.

"Negative."

Vie looked concern at me. "Whatever they're doing might not be registering."

"The jump ship," I said, already starting toward the door.

Vie was right behind me. We raced into an elevator bud and rose quickly to the surface. As we did, Vie handed me a maser. I'd forgotten we had assembled them earlier. I took mine, hoping that Vie felt as self-conscious about it as I did. I'd only ever done anything like this in an immerse with you, Dayr. Doing it for real felt more like pretend than the immersion did.

The elevator opened in the work area beside the jump ship in the hangar. When it irised open our weapons were already raised, but there was nothing. The jump ship was fine; the hangar was unchanged. Cautiously, we stepped to the hangar's huge open door and peered up. Hovering in a complex pattern over the entire area were what appeared to be soccer-ball sized silver balls, shimmering in a way that suggested liquid or plasma. They didn't appear to be doing anything, but the fact that they weren't being shot down was alarming.

"Shouldn't the defenses be taking those out?" I whispered to Vie.

"Yeah," she whispered back. "I don't know what's going on."

There was a small tac pad next to the door. I engaged it and whispered, "Homestead, why aren't those hovering things being attacked?"

The homestead sounded tinny in the tac pad. "They're being held in place by our gravity hooks. The defense systems take that as authorization for their presence."

Vie shrugged. She didn't know how this was being done either. Those things looked menacing though.

"Can we force an engagement?" I whispered toward the tac pad.

"We can attempt to engage," said the homestead.

"What does that mean?"

"They are oscillating between potential states faster than I am able to record. It may be they are impervious to attack."

I looked at Vie, whose mouth had come open.

"What's wrong? What does that mean?"

"I think it means," she whispered, even quieter now, "those aren't objects. They're wickets."

"Wickets?"

301

"Dimensional stents."

The only time I had encountered that phrase was when Richelle described the portals on her estate.

"Like CLD gläss?"

"Yeah, but these aren't necessarily recursive and may not be bent back to locations in our dimension. They could go…anywhere."

Suddenly they were more ominous than ever.

"Should we shoot them down?" I asked Vie.

"I have no idea," she said. She looked up again and added, "They don't exactly look…friendly. And considering where they came from…"

"Homestead," I said, "shoot those things down."

Lasers erupted from all around us, the air crackled and hummed. Richelle told us the homestead had grown defensive installations, but the reality of them was shocking. There were so many, and they came from so many different angles. There were steady beams of light, pulses, shots. The air shimmered in lines from lasers outside the visible spectrum. They all rose up at the silver balls and…disappeared. The balls didn't react with the lasers at all, they just swallowed them.

After a few seconds the lasers stopped and some kind of explosive projectiles were launched. About a dozen converged on a single orb. Like the lasers, the rockets disappeared into it and were simply gone.

"It's not going to work," said Vie.

"The objects are unreactive," said the homestead. "Although their oscillations do shift as they take on physical matter."

"Oh, shifting oscillations. That's helpful," I said.

"Uh oh," said Vie.

Sprouting from the orbs were fine white filaments, like thin beards hanging down. At first it looked like they were blowing in the breeze, but as they lengthened it became clear they were waving about independently. They reminded me of sea anemones, but these were creepily ominous.

"Do you feel that?" asked Vie.

I did. The air was filling with static. The filaments lengthened and whipped around like flagella, as though they hoped to swim the orbs away. The longer ones flayed out to the sides in a way that was clearly coordinated.

"They're trying to join together," said Vie.

"Oxygen levels are dropping," announced the homestead.

"What? Where?"

"Within the pale."

These things were going to starve us of oxygen.

"What about inside the homestead?"

"I am currently sealing the interior. Oxygen levels will be maintained at appropriate levels."

"We have to get back inside," Vie said, turning.

"Wait." I grabbed her arm to stop her, then pointed. "What's happening there?"

Several of the filaments had reached far enough to connect to those from neighboring orbs. These were winding around one another, creating thicker ropes. Not only were these ropes turning black, they were also producing black tendrils that were reaching down to the ground. These had the same liquid look as the orbs, but they looked more actively dangerous, like arms reaching down for something to throttle.

"We need to get down!"

An explosion concussed us to the ground. The filaments, ropes and black tendrils separated from the orbs and fell from the sky, all of them fizzling into nothing as they fell. Grey, thorny husks fell from the orbs, which lost their shapes. They were like silver eggs someone had cracked all at once. The shells fell, the liquid interiors wobbled in the sky for a moment, then they all shot toward one another like magnets. They met in the sky over the geometric center of the pale and disappeared in a dark explosion. Where most explosions release light, this one shot flames of darkness in all directions. I was reminded of the gravion paths the orbital hooks pulled apart, only these shot haphazardly, every which way. Then the shards of darkness recoiled back to the center. As they drew back, they seemed to draw on everything around them. Vie and I were lifted a meter off the ground and pulled out of the hangar toward the recoiling darkness before it annihilated itself, at which point we dropped back onto the earth.

We scrambled to our feet. All was still.

"Are you alright?" I asked.

"Yeah. You?"

"I'm okay."

There was a burnt smell in the air. Other than that, there was nothing. Nothing hung in the sky, nothing had fallen to the ground. It was as though we'd imagined it all.

"The anomalies are gone," said the homestead, its tinny voice coming from inside the hangar.

I looked at Vie and began laughing. When I heard how crazy my own laugh sounded, I laughed harder.

CHAPTER 34

"ARE YOU READY?"

"Ready or not."

I had onboarded the FaRcom protocols, so I knew that there were still three distinct vulnerabilities. But we'd taken precautions and set up monitors. If Telesis tried to get control of the connect, we'd have plenty of time to shut it down.

I looked across the Control cel to where Vie was placing a chair on a table to partially conceal a panel. We'd done this with three of the seven panels we were about to activate. We'd also brought in random items and scattered them around the cel: a pillow and some of my father's clothes, two of Thius's artificial sticks, tools from the hangar, food packs. When I'd brought in a few rocks to scatter across a table and onto the floor, a mischievous expression had blossomed on Vie's face and she'd disappeared for about an hour. Now there was also a small tortoise, happily munching away at a tray of vits under a holo desk.

We were building visual chaos. It was one of our tactics to keep Telesis off guard. We were also shunting the FaRcom signal here to the Control cel and parting it out to the various panels in the cel. Vie figured out how Richelle had done it, but Vie was reversing two of the feeds to further confuse them. When we contacted Telesis they would see us in pieces, in a different location filled with objects that would make no sense. Finally, we'd also identified several blind spots where they wouldn't be able to see anything. I'd placed green food trays in those locations as visual markers.

If all went well, they wouldn't know if we were surviving an apocalypse or just going insane.

Vie pulled out her maser and set it in a visible place on a chair, then said, "Let's do it."

"Homestead," I said, "open the FaRcom to Telesis."

The main panel fragmented into polygons of color, then the Telesis control center appeared. A man I had never seen was seated at a panel set. He looked up, surprised.

"TabiTal. TabiTal?"

"That's me," I said. Looking around I could see pieces of the Telesis control center in the different panels around the room. The panels on the left side of the room showed a flashing yellow light. Our connection had probably set off an alarm there.

The poor com operator was fiddling with data in his holo table, trying to figure out what was wrong.

"There's something wrong with your signal," he said. Through the side panels I could see other operators beginning to come to his area.

"There is a Nguyen-coded warble on this com channel," said the homestead calmly. "It appears to be threaded to spike through protocols."

"If you attempt to take control of this communication," I warned, "or anything in our system, I will cut this line and not call back."

"Don't do that. Don't—just a second." He manipulated more data, then glanced worriedly at several people coming up behind him.

"Your signal is..." he floundered. "Hold on, let me clean this up." He was panicking.

"I'm cutting this channel," I said. "I'll open a new one in an hour. Make sure it's clean and someone with authority can talk to me. I have questions. Homestead, sever the connect to Telesis."

The panels went dark.

"That didn't take long," observed Vie, trying to sound glib. She didn't do it as well as Wil.

"I didn't think that guy was worth talking to," I said.

"No," Vie laughed, "that guy was not in charge."

"Affirmative," said the homestead, though what it was affirming wasn't clear.

We had an hour until we contacted Telesis, so Vie busied herself with data gathering and I made my way back to the fun cel I'd set up to work on the satellites. I was repositioning them to get better information about ECF activity.

Using my augments was becoming second nature now. When I went to the second moon I hadn't really understood how the augments integrated themselves and used different body systems. I thought I was smelling things, but it was the augments testing whether my olfaction could be harnessed as an interface. The augments did this with all my systems, introducing information in ways that I could hardly perceive at first, scaffolding out my intuition. Before I knew it, I was responding to index maps in my peripheral vision, thermal cues in my fingers. These went off when my onboards held potentially useful information. A lot happened beneath the level of consciousness.

It still felt new, but many of my augments were integrated at this point. I was actually looking forward to repositioning the satellites. All of the calculations were done in the background, so my experience of the task was almost purely kinesthetic. Instead of pouring over tables and charts, plotting trajectories and adjusting rotations, my new augments allowed me to just feel it.

As I hooked into the systems of the HPA Multi-Functional cel, I smiled at the thought that our nickname was finally true: it was a fun cel. My Vendi nictators slid into place and I was a spiky satellite in orbit. Information sachets migrated to their needed addresses and it took a minute to sense my shape and mass, my solar panels, my antennae. But when I could finally feel my bulky body, it felt…free. I shifted my weight, spinning and turning like an aerialist, adjusting my view of the planet below in order to see what I wanted. I shuffled through available filters, zoomed in or panned out as I liked, adjusted my solar panels for maximum energy. My size and shape were intuitive; I was dancing, weightless, above the planet. I could feel the gravity ripples from the circling moons, the gentle solar wind, the loving pull of the planet.

When my dance was done and I was positioned to gather the information I wanted, I left that satellite and inhabited another. And then another. It was more enjoyable than any immerse I'd ever done.

I was fairly sure Wil and Vie had no enhancements like this. They would have mentioned it.

The iris to the fun cel opened and Vie was there. When I retracted my nictators and disengaged my interface, I saw that she looked serious.

"Can I talk to you?"

"Sure."

She looked around the fun cel. "Mind if we do it outside? I could use some air."

I thought we were going to the hangar, but when the iris opened Vie turned left and brought me right around into the express elevator that had been built for quick access to the storage area.

"You want to go down?" I asked.

"No," she said. "Homestead, take us to a crow's nest."

The iris closed and we began rising up toward the dome. I wasn't aware elevators could do this. As it rose above the confines of the homestead, the walls of the elevator bud became clear, like a glass bubble. I looked down and saw the plasma of the homestead coiling around below the elevator, building a stalk that pushed us higher and higher.

"The dome is about to be prised," announced the homestead.

A moment later we had pushed through the dome into the desert air above. The top of the elevator cel peeled down to waist level, and we were standing in a half-egg-shaped enclosure above the dome in the open air. We were forty meters above the ground, but there was a faint, charred smell on the breeze. Looking down, I could see the pockmarked and scorched earth from the previous battle. Looking out…

To the west, the sun was piercing the clouds with rays of yellow velvet. Vie was on that side, and she looked like some kind of religious figure with the sunset behind her. To the south there were fogs rising from several of the arms of Glassfall Canyon. Thalinraya never felt so otherworldly.

"This is amazing," I said, lamely.

"I onboarded a lot of new specs," said Vie. "I didn't know about this feature either."

We spent a few moments looking, breathing. Then Vie leaned against the rim of the elevator on her side and faced me. "We have something else we need to discuss."

I wasn't sure I wanted to hear what was coming next, but I said, "Okay."

"You're going to leave. I don't want to talk about that anymore," she said, lifting her hand before I could speak, then letting it fall kindly on my arm. "We're done with that discussion. But. I am going to stay, and FACE is going to come back. When it does, the homestead is going to be overwhelmed. Without Richelle's help we would have been overwhelmed last time. So..."

"So where are you going to go?" I said, anticipating her question.

"No! That's..." My question had taken her by surprise. "I can't go anywhere. FACE might capture the homestead. It might be able to stop what we started at the Auger Station."

"So what?"

"*So what*? Tab, I—"

"Richelle helped us because she didn't want us to die," I said quickly. I'd anticipated this, but I wasn't sure my arguments were ready. "That doesn't mean she wanted us to stop FACE. I don't think she cared about FACE. Or Thalinraya."

Vie squinted doubt at me. "You can't be serious."

"She didn't tell us to destroy the homestead. She could have, in her last message. She didn't."

Vie leaned back against the rim of the elevator. "She didn't have to say it, it's too obvious. She would never have wanted FACE to take over. Come on."

"Vie..." I wasn't sure how to make this appeal. "If FACE saves the planet...you could have *years* left." She started to object, so I pressed on. "Think of all the places to explore, all the animals—all the settlements you could turn out! All the synth capsules you could open. Think about meeting all those people. Hig! Finding out what cultures they developed in transit here. You could have a long life, with friends and—"

"Great," said Vie, smiling. "I get to wake up whole cultures to tell them their entire reason for being is gone. 'Welcome to the world! I'm sorry there's no real reason for you to be here.' " She was beautiful, even in her sarcasm. "Tab, you're being ridiculous."

"No, you are. Do you want to die?"

"Of course not, but...I appreciate what you're doing. But Tab, it wouldn't work."

"You don't know that," I urged.

"Let's say we let FACE stop the process and save the planet. Do you really think it'll let me open the rest of the workforce capsules and start a civilization here?" She was smiling at least. "It sees all humans and synthetics as a threat. It wouldn't let me just live out my days, if that's your idea." She looked away. "And I wouldn't want that anyway."

"Vie."

"It's true. And Tab…" She let out a breath and turned back to me, smiling again. How could she be so calm about this? "It's not even much of a sacrifice, really. I've had a great life. Much more than was intended for me. Richelle allowed me to follow a unique path, and I'm grateful."

"Vie," I pleaded, "why do you care who has this stupid planet? What has the Unicon ever done for you?"

"The Unicon is not my enemy. And if I have to take sides and help people or…whatever FACE is. Computation. If I have to take sides, I'd rather be on the side of people." I tried to formulate a rebuttal, but nothing came. Vie smiled again. "And in a way this makes me part of something larger. The bits of foam on the edge of the wave, right?" Seeing that I didn't understand, she continued: "EzeLia? 'We may be destroyed when we arrive upon the beach, but what a ride we will have had. And we don't want to be ourselves forever.' "

"What's that from?"

Vie burst out laughing. "Really?"

"What?"

Her smile was so genuine my heart ached. "EzeLia, Book Two, Chapter Two, Sura Eleven," she said. "You have plenty of storage now, you know."

"Okay, okay."

She was laughing. "A Feremite ought to have his own Bibles on board."

"They're not *my* Bibles!" I protested, but I was smiling now too.

Wil, I remembered, had also onboarded the Feremite Bible. Both of my friends had done this, though neither had any interest in religion.

Something in that thought made my throat tighten.

"Anyway," Vie said finally, "I've enjoyed…this is going to sound funny, but I've enjoyed dreaming. Synths don't usually get to dream, you know."

"I know," I said.

"Well," she said carefully, "I don't want to be…less than courageous, but if I could, I think I'd prefer to go in my sleep. I could set the soporifics in my cel to a deep dream state so I'm just…dreaming when it happens."

There it was. She was talking about her own death. My throat was so constricted I couldn't breathe.

Sensing my discomfort, Vie went on. "I researched it, and there are actually protocols for having the homestead destroy itself. It'll need your biometrics for authorization, so you'll need to set the timer before you leave."

In other words, Vie couldn't really kill herself. She needed my help.

We looked at one another. The breeze had picked up. Stars were starting to prick the wash of light.

I couldn't speak. I nodded.

"Thanks," Vie said, her own voice tight.

Wisps of fog were still roiling over Glassfall Canyon. I wondered what vast energies were being expended deep inside the planet that emerged here as these softly shifting vapors. There was something profound in the delicate tendrils. The brutal energy of boiling magmas far below emerged here as these ephemeral mists, reaching up into the night and dissipating as they did so.

Clouds scudded by, obscuring the distant moons. It was beautiful.

And soon, it would all be gone. As would we. My onboards alerted me to a poetry cache. Some background engine had cross referenced my emotions and my live visuals with Vie's bible quote and come up with a verse.

Was it prompting me?

I spoke the lines out loud:

"We are as clouds that veil the midnight moon;
How restlessly they speed, and gleam, and quiver,
Streaking the darkness radiantly! yet soon,
Night closes round, and they are lost for ever."

"That's lovely," said Vie, looking up toward the clouds.

The verse was tagged "Percy Bysshe Shelley." The naming convention was odd—probably some ancient artist collective. I saw there was a large file I could expand to learn more, but I decided not to. I didn't want information, I just wanted to be with Vie and experience this melancholy beauty.

I reached over and held her hand.

CHAPTER 35

"Homestead, open the FaRcom to Telesis."

Two hours had passed; hopefully they were sweating. Vie had given me the nod and I had turned back to the main panel. The tortoise was slowly chewing something green and stringy. Part of a food tray, as it turned out.

The main panel flashed a screen of different colored panes, like a close up of a stained glass window, then there were three people facing us. Reginew, who we had dealt with before, was flanked by a man on his right and a woman on his left. The woman sported copper metallic lipstick and eyebrows, which only emphasized the imprecision of her reju therapy. The man was plain in every way apart from his old-world bowtie.

"Thank God you're back," said Reginew earnestly.

"You don't believe in God," I couldn't help snarkily replying.

"Tab," he continued, ignoring my comment, "if you've been talking to your gen-four grandmother, Richelle, you need to know she's a construct. She's not real."

"How do you know?" I challenged.

"Because she's dead. If someone claiming to be Richelle has contacted you, it's either someone pretending to be her or it's a construct."

"What's a construct?" asked Vie. Looking past her, I could see several Telesis technicians looking in through the side panels. Apparently they still hadn't figured out how we were fragmenting the signal. Or, probably, where we were.

"A slaved-code character built around a real person's personality algorithms," explained Reginew. Turning to me, he added, "It's a technique used in gaming all the time, and it's not hard to do, TabiTal. Have you been talking to her?"

"That's impossible, right?"

"I am trying to help you."

I looked at one of the green food trays on my right and raised two fingers, as though signaling someone. "I've got this," I said.

Turning back to Reginew I could see it had worked. His lips pursed slightly and his eyes darted to one side. He was getting subvocals. They were wondering who else was here with us. They probably thought it was Wil.

"I need to know your status," he said.

"I don't think you do," I responded. The people around him were becoming more uncomfortable, some fidgeting, others freezing in place. "Here's how this works: lie to us and we'll cut this connect forever." I paused to let that sink in, then asked: "What did you have us do at the CA Station?"

That *really* got the other two shifting around. They were wondering how much we knew. I held a hand out to the green food tray, pretending to stop someone from intervening, and said: "Let me rephrase that. I know what you had us do at the CA Station. I want to hear you say it. I want to hear you tell me the truth, and if you don't, I swear I will sever this connect for the last time."

I heard the strength in my own voice and realized I wasn't bluffing. I wasn't sure what he wanted from us, but I knew what we wanted from him, and it wasn't worth listening to more lies.

"It's complicated," he finally said.

"The mechanics are complicated, the outcome isn't," said Vie. "Tell us what you had me do there. What was the code I gave to that drilling station?"

The woman spoke. "I designed that code. It compromises the core of your planet in order to spin it off its axis." Her voice was soft, at odds with her severe, coppery makeup.

"And you did that because you knew FACE was here," I said. Looking at Reginew I added, "Didn't you?"

"From what you seem to have learned on your own," continued the woman, "you must know that we only did what we had to do. I'm sorry."

She almost sounded sincere.

"Why didn't you tell us?"

"We were going to," said Reginew, "but you cut us off."

"That's a lie," said Vie with sudden intensity. "You were never going to tell us. You were going to let us die." Vie slammed her hand down on the holo table. "You *wanted* us to die."

"That's not true." It was the woman again.

"Then why did you send us to V-12? You knew we were going to get attacked."

"You *forced* the attack," I added. "You purposely crashed the gravion right when we got there."

"We didn't know that would happen," Reginew cut in angrily. "As I told you, I—"

Vie stepped forward. "Wil is dead because of your lies!" She was crying. "If we hadn't regained control of the homestead, we'd be dead too. Admit it!"

The woman looked past Reginew at the man with the bowtie and nodded. He cleared his throat and shook his head in an odd way. Did he have some kind of tick? Then, in a nasal voice, he said, "We have almost no information about the capabilities of this particular enemy. The situation demanded that we place the resources of that planet beyond its reach. Once that was accomplished, the only possible benefit we could get from that planet was information. What are its technologies, capabilities, processes? What are its aims? We deemed it appropriate to use this opportunity to gather intelligence. It wasn't aware you were there. We tried to use that fact while we had the upper hand."

"You were using us."

"In a matter of speaking, yes," he conceded. "But our goal here—and this is not an exaggeration—is to protect humanity. This is an intelligence bent on our destruction."

"How do you know that?" I asked.

The copper-lipped woman answered. "A year before you left, the sixteen moons off Voffrich were lost. Do you remember that?"

I vaguely remembered this. Three of the largest terraformed colonies in a distant sector had been lost in a freak comet barrage. "That was FACE?"

"It was. And we've lost seventeen more planets since then," fumed Reginew.

"Only two fully inhabited," said the bowtie in his squeaky nasal voice. Reginew shot him a frustrated look.

"FACE came from people," protested Vie.

"All kids rebel against their parents eventually," said Reginew.

"He's telling the truth," said the woman. "We really had no choice. We had to get as much information from there as possible."

"But why not tell us?"

I flinched at a sudden crash on my left. Vie had thrown her maser at a side panel, where a woman was peering in at us.

"Back off!" Vie growled at the woman. Several people backed away from different panels around the room.

"Why didn't you tell us?" I repeated.

"Would you have helped us, TabiTal?" asked Reginew. It was a challenge. "You were worried about your father, and between finding him and saving yourselves, would you really have agreed to go probe that thing? I don't think so. You were a scared kid. You still are."

"General," said Bowtie to Reginew.

So, Reginew was a general.

"TabiTal," he said in his nasal squeak, "I'm with the Unicon." Now we were getting somewhere. We had government, we had military, and we had...Telesis corpse? What was the woman's position, I wondered. "I apologize for how this has been handled. And before we make any more requests, I'd like to know what you want here."

Vie cocked her head.

"What do you mean?" I asked, stalling while I tried to figure out the next move.

"You've contacted us again. Why?"

"Because we wanted to know what you know about FACE. To see if you could help us. But since you don't really know anything, there's no point, is there?"

"What did you want to know?" he asked. When we didn't respond right away, he added: "Were you suspicious about Richelle?"

"What do you mean?"

"Has she tried to contact you?"

Vie nodded to me, then glanced at the other green food try on her side.

"We've been in constant contact with her ever since we locked you out," I said.

"I knew there was a construct there," said Reginew to the woman, angrily. Turning back to us he added, "It's a construct, kid. She's dead."

"You *think* you killed her," I said, "she told us. But she wasn't on the estate."

Reginew looked exasperation at both of the others, then said to us, "She was!"

"No," said Vie, calm now. She turned away from Reginew and addressed the other two. "Either his information is bad, or he's lying to you."

I smiled inwardly. She was good at this. I wondered if her earlier anger had been as spontaneous as it seemed.

"Whoever or whatever made that construct is probably controlling this syn too!" Reginew was railing at me, his face even redder. "You're being used, kid!"

"You can't hack a person," I said.

"The hell you can't! Kid, do you know how deep FACE has infiltrated our systems?"

"Reginew!" The little man's nasal voice was weak and foolish sounding, which made it all the more impressive that Reginew immediately backed down.

"Tab," the woman said calmingly, "we have reason to believe FACE is capable of creating constructs."

"For my gen-four grandmother?" I said. "FACE just happened to have her construct ready to go?"

"We don't know what it's capable of," she said. "But we have reason to believe it's been collecting data on…a great many human beings."

Vie was concentrating hard on what this woman was saying. I wanted to dismiss it as outrageous, but… Could it be possible? Reginew had said FACE had infiltrated their systems. Could they have infiltrated Richelle's estate on Histon?

"And consider this," said the woman, leaning forward on her elbows now so that her face was lit from the data displays in her table. "How else could she have contacted you? You're in an isolated location out there. How could your real gen-four grandmother contact you there?"

That was true. I'd assumed that somehow Richelle had been able to bypass the normal channels and create her own FaRcom. But what if it was true that there were no off-world connections. That would mean…

No. She couldn't be just a construct, she had defended us from FACE, working with new and changing data. No construct could do that. She knew everything about our histories together, much more than a simple construct would have known. She had the same mannerisms, the same attitude, the same tone of voice. She was giving us advice, helping us.

Vie grabbed my arm, her face suddenly blank. "What if she apotheosized," she subvocalized urgently.

If nobody had been watching us I might have laughed. Richelle? I'd heard her joke about people who uploaded versions of themselves, believing life in digits could be the same as real life. Richelle had told me about the "hollow men," and she'd laughed about it. But it was possible. It even made a kind of sense. She knew where we were going, she'd helped us get ready, she'd…

She could have uploaded into the ship before we launched, then forced her way into the homestead when we got here. If anyone could have broken into the homestead it would have been her. And if she'd done that…she could have actually been here with us the whole time. The homestead had more than enough processing power to harbor her. That's how she knew so much about what was happening here. That's how she could have maintained contact with us so well. She'd been here the whole time!

Except… She'd been on her estate when they thought they killed her, and that was years after we left. She couldn't have been in transit with us if she was still back there. No, she couldn't have come with us.

"…Have known." Bowtie had just made some point I had missed.

"You don't know Richelle," countered Vie.

"I don't care who she is, she died in the desert on Histon," said Reginew. "And even if she managed to apotheosize and make herself into a bundle of algorithms, there's no way she could have gotten it to Thalinraya."

Another thought was forming. It had the texture of something true, but I wasn't sure I liked it. If Richelle had really been on the estate on Histon when they attacked it, how could she have gotten here?

I thought back to that first time my watch clicked. It had been just as FACE ships arrived. She knew so much about it. How it was going to attack, how to manipulate it and defeat it, at least temporarily.

I wasn't sure what FACE was or whether it was even possible, but Richelle had done so many crazy things in the past. And if the Unicon was coming after her...

"Why did you attack Richelle's estate?" I asked, breaking into an exchange between the woman and Vie.

Reginew's face went blank. The other two grew still as well. There must have been subvocal conversations zipping all around.

"We're about to die, you might as well tell us." Vie couldn't have known why I was asking, but she was backing me up.

Reginew leaned in. "Your gen-four grandmother thought she was above the law. She was doing all kinds of experiments down there." He turned nastily to Vie. "*You* should know that."

"She had special authorizations—" I began, but Reginew cut me off.

"They were revoked! But she kept on!"

Reginew was giving their game away. Whatever Richelle had done, both Telesis and the Unicon hadn't liked it. What could Richelle have done to make the whole government angry with her? She'd finally pushed some boundary too far, but which one?

I had a sudden vision of her in the moonlight atop a desert spire. The creases in her face, the twinkle in her eye.

These people had nothing for us. We knew more about FACE than they did. They weren't going to tell us anything about Richelle. Whatever Vie was going to face after I left, they couldn't help. That was the only reason we'd used the FaRcom again, to see if there was anything more to be done for Vie.

I turned to her, feeling calm but sad too. Certain. "They're not going to help, Vie."

"No," she replied simply. "I know."

"We can help you transform the jump ship to make it ready for interstellar travel," said the woman.

"How helpful," I said.

I was about to sever the connect when the homestead interrupted, announcing in a flat voice, "A Ty3 Rover from workforce capsule IS2 is entering the pale."

Everything froze.

"What?" I managed.

"TabiTal, give us control," ordered Reginew. There were rapid movements in many of the other panels around the room. People in the Telesis control center were rushing to different displays. "Give us an override, kid! We can secure your perimeter."

We'd already secured it.

"Homestead, the perimeter is secure, correct?" I asked.

"Correct," intoned the homestead.

Vie had gone to a holo table and was calling up a visual.

"TabiTal," Reginew shouted, "you need help!" There were other people on Telesis shouting orders to one another.

"A Nguyen-coded warble has been attached to the FaRcom channel," said the homestead.

I barely registered it. How could the homestead let a rover enter the pale? It was completely against defense protocols.

"Can you see anything?" I asked Vie.

"It's a single rover. It's coming across the breakfields from Glassfall."

"You are about to be attacked!" urged Reginew. "You need our help!"

"Homestead," I said, "why are you allowing that vehicle into the pale?"

"You authorized full access to both Wil and Vie," replied the homestead.

The air left the cel.

Wait. Did that mean...

"Wil?" I managed. "Is Wil in that rover?"

"Affirmative," said the neutral voice.

"Wil?" echoed Vie with disbelief.

"Affirmative."

It couldn't be.

"Is he alive?" I asked.

"Wil is at the controls of the Ty3 Rover."

Vie let out a guttural noise as she turned and raced through the com cel's iris.

"Homestead, sever the connect to Telesis," I shouted. There was a whirl of motion right before all the panels in the room went blank.

I grabbed Vie's maser from the table as I ran after her. Her elevator was already irising shut, so I leapt into the neighboring elevator bud and told it to take me to the front entrance. It sped through the vitreous in the other elevator's wake. I could see Vie's vague outline, moving like a caged animal in the bud ahead of me. It was the longest ride I'd ever endured. When my elevator finally arced to one side to park next to Vie's, I was more keyed up than I'd ever been. I leapt out, the maser held ready.

Vie was past the entrance, running down into the darkness of the scrub and cactus field that led toward Glassfall Canyon. Without thinking, I switched to night vision and the landscape before me was suddenly glowing green. In the middle of the field was a squat vehicle on tracks. It jerked to a stop and an old-school door opened on one side. The engine cut out. Vie slowed and stopped about ten meters in front of the vehicle. There was something suddenly ominous about the tank-like machine. I couldn't see any weapons on the front, but nothing was emerging either. The door stood open.

Then there was movement on the side, behind the door. Legs. Someone was using the door as a shield. I raised the maser. I knew Vie couldn't see as well as me in the dark—Wil and I had visual augments, but she didn't. I was about to yell to her to get down when the door slowly got pushed back toward the vehicle.

Vie raised her hand and pointed at the figure there. A dim beam of light shot out from her finger. I'd forgotten about her fingernail lights. It wasn't bright, but it was enough.

Wil was standing there, holding onto the door for support. Most of his face was covered in a blood-stained cloth, but it was definitely him.

Vie burst into a run again. Wil staggered forward too. His clothes were ragged and one arm hung useless at his side. He stopped a few meters from the vehicle and swayed.

"Careful!" I shouted, running myself now.

Vie came toward him so fast he winced, but she halted just shy of him. They assessed one another silently for a moment as I jogged up and switched to normal vision. There was enough reflected light from the moons and stars that we could see one another at close quarters. Wil's shirtfront was a carapace of dried blood. His face above the makeshift bandage was streaked and filthy, his hair matted. Vie was looking at him, but partly turned away too. She was crying.

Wil brushed something off his forehead with his wrist—two fingers were bent awkwardly. His other arm was limp at his side. He looked over at me, back at Vie. "Are you guys okay?" he asked in a papery voice.

Vie stepped forward and wrapped her arms around him. He grimaced, then wrapped his good arm around her.

"Iss okay," he rasped, patting Vie awkwardly. "This iss the story uh the little synth who could."

CHAPTER 36

IT LOOKS LIKE THINGS ARE PROGRESSING faster here than Richelle and I expected, Dayr. The earthquakes have gotten worse. There's a bulge in the eastern ocean and the continental rift has spread enough that the flooding of the interior has… Well, there's a lot of chaos here.

At least the night sky is entertaining. The moons have begun wobbling in their orbits, which has caused the ice volcanism on the second moon to go into high gear. It's spewing liquid like a burst water balloon, and because it has no atmosphere the stuff drifts away from it, trailing after the moon in an intricate twisting pattern. It looks like a slow-moving firework.

I don't expect I have much time left. I need to finish this up and get it to you.

Vie spent a lot of time looking after Wil once we got him back. She was overly solicitous and monopolized his nursing so much, I was hard pressed to talk to him at all. She even had him shut off his subvocals most of the time, saying he needed to rest. I was eager to learn how he had escaped, but it was two full days after his miraculous reappearance before I got the chance.

Vie had been programming his surgical baths in the medic cel, and she told me not to bother him. He managed to subvocalize he'd like to see me though, and I sneaked in after she had gone. I knew he'd been enjoying her attention, but I was glad he missed me too.

He was lying on a bed with his arm extended into a surgical bath where, suspended in the fluid, it looked like a medical illustration. Bones were still exposed; bots were threading veins and nerves out into the solution prior to weaving them back into place.

Wil felt nothing.

"It wasn't that big a deal," he said after I'd sat down on the edge of the bed next to him and grimaced at his wreck of an arm. "I was clumsy. I was trying to free the opilion—you saw. I lost my balance. I tried to stop my fall, but I couldn't."

"You got shot in the face," I reminded him. Luckily, the spinning shrapnel hit him just in front of his jaw. It cut through his entire cheek and part of his tongue, and he lost two teeth, but had it been even an inch higher it would have torn off his jaw and probably killed him.

"How's it look?" he asked, reaching up with his good hand to feel the long surgical ribbon that was still in place. He was going to have a great scar.

"Looks good," I said.

"Well," he said. "Anyway. As I was going through the hole, I calculated I had about ten seconds before impact. About 9.5 seconds to terminal velocity, then another half a second until I reached the city center."

"You thought that?" I asked.

"Yeah. Why?" he asked.

"I don't know. It's not what I would have thought."

"Well, my height was going to be a function of gravity and the time elapsed from—"

"No, I meant I would have been panicking, not thinking. At all."

"Oh," he said. "Well. Anyway," he continued, "my leg hit the side of the hole, so I was spinning when I went through. The first thing I did was arch my back and spread my arms and legs to shuttlecock myself to stabilize my descent."

"Like you were skydiving?"

"Exactly. Remember when I drove the motorcycle off the geodetic elevator platform on Histon?"

"Yeah," I said, remembering how he'd raced off the edge and pushed away from the falling cycle, tumbling first but then arching his back. "You had that flying suit thing."

"Yeah," he scratched under his chin with his free hand, smiling at the memory. "That was amazing. I wish I'd had one of those in the silo. Anyway, I figured stabilizing would only take three or four seconds, so I'd still have more than six seconds to do what I needed to do."

"You were making these calculations while you fell?"

"Yeah."

"Synths are different from people."

He grinned. "You're just realizing that?"

The veins and nerves swayed in the surgical vat like sea grasses in a tide. It was mesmerizing.

"As I came stable, facing down, the hovering streetlights were racing by. I thought I might be able to use them to track my progress, but they were sort of swimming around. Some of 'em weren't even aimed over at the street anymore."

"The administrative street is the open petal."

"Anyway," he said, uninterested in my details. "I spotted some buildings below me. I thought I could hit one with the grappling hook, so I pulled the gun out."

"You were just going to shoot the hook at something?"

"What choice did I have? I thought I could hook onto something and hopefully swing into the crevice between the sides of the petal."

"You did that?" I asked.

"Let me finish," he said, frustrated that I wasn't allowing him to build up steam with his story. "Anyway, I'm falling, I pull out the grappling gun and extend my right arm like this." He demonstrated with his left, as his right was currently dismantled.

"Did the wind make it hard to move your hand?" I asked.

"There was pressure, but no."

"Were you worried about dropping the gun?"

"No."

"But you're seeing the central plaza coming up at you this whole time?"

"It wasn't coming at me, I was heading down toward it. I pulled out the gun and aimed for the corner of a building on one of the folded petals."

"And you could aim with all that wind?"

"Do you want to hear this or not?"

I burst out laughing. "Okay, go," I said.

"I was still shuttlecocked out as I aimed to my right." He was gesturing as much as he could, lying there. "So, I was like this, and I didn't see the hovering streetlight below me. I crashed into it. Argh! I could feel my arm break."

A little alarm reminded Wil not to move his arm too much. Muscles and tendons in his arm were pulled away from the bones. Some of the bots doing the work were large enough to be seen swimming in the solution. The largest were building skin out along the periphery of the bath.

"Anyway, I was spinning again worse than before. The floating lights were spinning around, the buildings were turning over and under me, I was completely disoriented. I had no time to right my fall. Even if I was able to grapple onto something, I'd need to do it in the next three seconds or the pendulum from my swing would take me into the city center anyway. So I just pushed my right arm out again and shot."

"Without aiming?"

"Yeah. And it hit a hovering streetlight about a meter away from me."

"No way!"

"I know!" My enthusiasm was making him more animated. "I couldn't have hit it if I'd tried. But it was so close it fused right away, probably partly from the impact. So, I pulled the trigger again and the rope attached immediately. But because it was so close, and right on my fall line, it was like a dead drop, which could have broken me in half if it'd been solid. But the light was hovering, so when the rope came taught my weight pulled the light down. It dipped, but then whatever orients those things realized it wasn't where it was supposed to be, so it arrested my fall and tried to get back to its hover location. I have no idea how those things are powered, but they—"

"Gravity magnets," I said. I was getting used to accessing information from my onboards as conversations went along.

"Oh," he said, nodding, but obviously uninterested. "Anyway, it pulled me back up until it was hovering where it thought it was supposed to be. And so there I was, dangling from a hovering streetlight about a hundred meters from the bottom."

"With a broken arm."

"With a broken arm, yeah. And blood pouring out of my mouth."

"What did you do?"

"For a minute I just hung there, trying to assess the situation. I could hear the battle going on up above. I saw the opilion leave."

"We didn't know—" I began, but Wil cut me off.

"Not you too. Look, *anyone* would have left. Don't worry about it, okay?"

"Okay," I said. Some purple liquid swirled into Wil's surgical vat. We were distracted by it for a moment, but then Wil continued.

"Anyway, I was hanging there and there wasn't any reason to hurry back to the surface. You were gone and—"

"Sorry."

"Shut up! You were gone and it sounded pretty chaotic up there. So I got out my medical kit and took two taminoid tabs, then wrapped up my face and my arm as best I could and just waited."

"You did that while you were hanging there?"

"I had two taminoid tabs." When he saw my blank expression, he added, "They're military grade—it's in your onboards, look it up. Anyway, after a few hours things quieted down up above and I decided it was time to try to get out. I'd had time to work out a plan. I prussicked up to the streetlight and tied directly onto that. I detached the grappler, reloaded it, and shot at the next streetlight above me. It took me a couple of shots 'cause I was shooting lefty at that point, but I finally got it."

"Oh, so you—"

"Yeah. I prussicked up to that one, tied in, shot at the next one."

"That's brilliant!"

He was pleased at the compliment. He smiled and said, "More desperate than brilliant. What else could I have done?"

"Uh…fallen! Panicked or passed out or dropped the gun or…done something stupid like I would have done."

"Anyway. I was able to climb up from one streetlight to the next to the next. Toward the top they were closer together for some reason, so I started skipping a few."

"When the settlement unfolds to the surface, the top part is the outskirts of town, so they design more lights there."

"Oh." Wil wasn't interested. "Well, I finally grappled up and through the hole."

"With one arm!"

"The prussics do the lifting, I just rode them up. When I got up it was devastation all around. There were downed drones and copters and crawlers and all sorts of exploded machines everywhere. Smoke was rising. I started hiking toward the homestead and after a while I started coming across the bodies."

He paused for a minute and looked at his healing arm. I'd seen a little of what he must have seen, but that carnage up close must have been horrible.

"FACE, whatever else it is, is thorough," he continued grimly. "Nobody was alive. There were a lot of people that had obviously been torn apart in this...chaotic way, but I kept coming across this one injury. It was a burn at the person's temple. After I saw it a few times I started seeing it everywhere, sometimes on bodies that had no other markings. It was execution."

"Why would they kill everybody?"

"To be thorough," he said, angry and disgusted. "There's no reason, it's just...a computer kind of a thing to do. Better to leave no possible problems. I mean, why not? It's all just ones and zeros, right?"

There was nothing to say to that.

"I was making my way through this massacre when I found a little tractor kind of a thing. It was loaded with provisions—they must have thought they were going to the actual settlement. The provisions had been blown off the back, the three synths in the cab were dead, but it looked like it might still work. So I pulled the bodies out, started it up and...it was slow, but here I am.

"Oh," he added suddenly, "and get this: the tracks on that thing were slow, but they were perfect for getting across Glassfall. I was right, we just needed a lighter vehicle."

I didn't remember him saying that, but I let it go.

A day later his arm was reconstructed, though he said it still ached. He had a *lot* of aches, for which Vie gave him a great deal of welcome attention. He went back to his habitation cel, but Vie was usually there with him, bringing him food, rubbing his shoulders, keeping him company. I caught him smiling guiltily when she was rubbing his leg the next morning. "It was a compound fracture," explained Vie. I thought about suggesting he go back to the medic cel and use the automated physical therapy there. If he really was in pain...

But I was happy for them. I was a little surprised that I didn't feel jealous, but I didn't. They were enjoying one another, and what else did they have?

What did any of us have anymore?

The following day, when I finally worked up the courage to have the hard conversation we needed to have, I couldn't find them. I'd been avoiding subvocalizing with either of them—I could tell they were enjoying their privacy. After searching all the fun cels, the commons, and their habitation cels, the homestead finally told me they were in a crow's nest. I took an elevator up to the field and saw the thick stalk of plasma reaching up through the dome, which was still in place. It was day, and through the dome I could see their indistinct forms, leaning together and looking out toward the east. Wil seemed to have his arm around Vie.

I sat on the field and waited. The homestead had done a good job cleaning and restoring this area. Outside the dome there was a lot of scorched earth, but inside it was clean and tidy again. The assembly station to my left even had bicycles hanging ready again, as though someone might want to go for a spin through the cratered battlefield outside the pale, just for fun.

I smiled. The mindlessness with which the homestead restored things was...comforting, in a way. I looked across the field and imagined Thius tearing off after a stick.

Looking up through the dome at Wil and Vie, I thought back to when we were all children, when Wil's recklessness wasn't a good match for Vie's sense of responsibility. His humor didn't match her seriousness; his sense of adventure clashed with her need for stability. Yet now, each seemed perfectly positioned to admire the best parts of the other. It seemed so natural for them to be a couple.

Which made it all the more tragic that they'd only realized it now, so close to the end. The two of them were going to die on this planet while I rocketed back to Telesis. And I was going to have to set the homestead for auto destruct.

If that's what they wanted. We hadn't talked about it—that's why I was waiting for them. We needed to decide on the timing. Vie had said she wanted to set her soporifics for deep dream sleep. Would she still want that? Would Wil? Dreaming is a solitary thing, and they might want to be together at the end.

I looked toward the hangar. Whatever Vie and Wil decided to do, I was going to climb aboard that ship, crawl into the single bernaculum and have them send me on my way, leaving them to die. I wasn't sure I could do it. And, I reflected again, I might not even want to do it. Where, after all, was I going to go?

My parents and Richelle were gone, and the only other close contact I had was you, Dayr. And no offense, but coming to live on a prison planet wasn't attractive. So where would I go? Back to Telesis? Even if they let me live, what would I do? Go live in the burnt-out ruin of Richelle's estate? Since I had already undergone the hard-vac augments, there was really no reason not to have the reju therapy, which meant I could extend my life as long as I wanted. But what for? I had no idea what I wanted to do.

I looked up at Wil and Vie in the crow's nest above the dome and realized just how selfish my thoughts were. Their situation was infinitely worse than my own. For them, the problem wasn't that there was no place they *wanted* to go, it was that there was no place they *could* go. I had options, but they were outlaw synths. Even if we had two berns, which we didn't; even if we had enough europium, which we didn't...

I sat up straight. A thought had suddenly formed, but as soon as I recognized it, it shot up like a firework and exploded.

No, it was...impossible.

No.

But then the sparkling trails of the spent firework began to solidify, and I realized my augments must have been working on this in my subconscious mind. These scintillating trails weren't fading, they led to solutions. For Wil, for Vie. For me.

This could work.

CHAPTER 37

TWO MINUTES LATER I WAS IN an elevator heading down to a fun cel to see if my plan could work. I had the homestead call up bernaculum statistics from our trip here, comparing my bern composition with those needed for Vie and Wil. I referenced interstellar maps, compared interstellar navigation systems, did projections and forecasts, researched navigation law. I onboarded jump ship schematics and checked the engineering and mechanics with the homestead. I didn't want to talk to Wil and Vie until I was sure.

I went up to the hangar where the jump ship was kept to see what Wil had done, not only to the ship but also to the bern. I measured, checked, rechecked. All the numbers worked out. The reengineering wouldn't even be that difficult.

I made my way back down to the Control cel. On the way there I strategized how I was going to contact her. If I was right, she wasn't dead. She wasn't gone either. I ought to be able to contact her.

I had been trying to understand FACE, but I was hung up by thinking of it as one thing. Since Richelle had gone, however, a new idea had come to me. Hadn't she referred to FACE as *they* rather than *it*? Not consistently, but I thought I could remember her talking about it more like it was a community. What if it was more like a group, composed of individuals that tried to work together but didn't always succeed? Free Autonomous Computational Entit*ies*, plural. If it were like that, a person who had apotheosized might be able to join it. Or *break* into it. If anyone could do that, Richelle could.

Of course, joining and breaking in were two entirely different things, and not knowing which it was presented problems. If FACE was made up of individuals, Richelle was obviously working against what most of them wanted. That might make them angry, in which case I really didn't want to give her away.

I arrived in the Control cel with a plan. I knew it wasn't perfect, but time was pressing.

"Homestead, I want to use the communications satellites to blanket Thalinraya with a message."

"What is the target of the communication?"

"The whole planet. I don't want to target anywhere in particular, I want to…like old radio did. Send out a signal that goes everywhere. We can do that, right?"

"Affirmative. What is the message?"

" 'Gav's needle is on Thalinraya. The entrance is barred but we want to go up. Open the door.' "

"I don't understand."

"You're not supposed to. When can that be sent?"

"Immediately, as soon as I know where in the spectrum to send it."

"Start with twenty hertz and move your way up by a factor of five every minute until you hear the response key."

"What will constitute the key to the response?"

"It will start with 'Boots694, Forest13.' "

" 'Boots694, Forest13.' Understood," intoned the homestead. "Shall I send the message?"

"Yes," I said. "If you get a signal of any kind that starts with that, contact me wherever I am. Use my subvocals if you need to."

I turned toward the elevator, but before I could make a move toward its round iris, the homestead spoke. "I have received the response key and a request to open a channel of communication."

I froze.

What?

No.

I turned back. I couldn't believe it.

"The specific key?" I asked. "You received a response beginning Boots694, Forest13?"

"Correct," said the flat, indifferent voice. "But the response has not come from Thalinraya."

Not from Thalinraya? Impossible. "Where is it from?"

"The third moon."

The third… I looked to the main panel. "Show me where the signal originated."

The familiar map of the moon appeared, the crater where my father ought to have been was in the lower right. The signal originated in a subsurface station on the plain on the near side of the moon. This was the FACE installation Vie had pointed out earlier. I'd flown right over that area.

"That station is not one of ours, is it?"

"It is not."

"How long has it been there?"

"I do not have specific data on that. Fewer than 103 days."

What did this mean? Had FACE attacked my father? Had my father joined them?

No. I needed to think clearly, not wildly. FACE had an outpost on that moon. Were they in communication with the outposts on Thalinraya? And how could they possibly have the code there? Unless it was Richelle. But why would she be on that moon?

"Were there other responses to the message?" I asked.

"Negative."

"So there was no…no indication they were trying to break the code?"

"Negative."

"Could anyone have overheard the key when I said it to you just now?" I asked.

"Negative."

"And there's no com channels open?"

"Negative."

"To anywhere?"

"There is no communication coming into or exiting from this installation. The only communication we've received in the past twenty minutes is the key response you requested."

There was no other explanation.

"Open the channel." Who was going to be there? Richelle? My father? An algorithm representing FACE?

There was a crackle, then a droning buzz.

"Tab?"

"Richelle?"

There were no visuals. The panel reverted to a swirl of colors and abstract shapes that registered our voices by switching colors and shapes each time we spoke.

"Oh Tabit, you're alright! I wasn't sure I'd stopped the advance in time." There was a swirling, metallic sound to her voice, but it definitely sounded like her.

"Richelle, I need to verify your identity."

"I'm aware."

I smiled. That phrase was almost enough, but I needed to be certain. "The Unicon people said you were dead."

"That's not to task. You said you were going to verify my identity."

"Okay. What is the story behind the key you just sent?"

"That is the password Gav used to keep you and Wil out of the orbital elevator. Boots694 was his first pet, a crested desert parrot. Forest13 was a moon parrot. But if I was someone else and I had that code, chances are I'd know the story too. It's hardly an effective way to verify who I am."

"You're correcting me. Why?"

"Because I know you can do better."

A sense of relief washed through me. "And I just did," I replied. "You're my gen-four grandmother, but you could never stop being my teacher too."

A swirling, metallic laugh preceded her response. "I see. Yes. Well done."

"How did you get my message so quickly?" I asked.

"I suspect you already know that."

"You're in FACE."

"I am."

"You apotheosized?"

"I did. I had to." The metallic swirl of her voice seemed more prominent suddenly.

"And now you're on the third moon."

"That's not exactly correct," said Richelle. "Distributed is, I think, the word that comes closest to capturing it. My compression is least restrictive in the third moon installation."

Whatever existence she had, I realized, was probably beyond my comprehension. She was distributed? Partially compressed? My mind couldn't grasp it.

"I hadn't expected to hear from you until you were back at Telesis," she said in a swirl of color.

"I'm not going," I replied bluntly.

"What?!" The algorithms producing her vocal expression were quite good. The incredulity and outrage in her voice were perfectly rendered. "Tab, you must."

"No, listen. Things have changed."

Richelle was surprised and relieved when I explained about Wil's escape and return. Then I told her about how I planned to reconfigure the bern. Before I could finish, she interrupted.

"Tab, I understand your feelings and it's all very noble, but you have to consider yourself here. Not in a selfish way, but putting your needs into the equation."

"I've done that."

"No, you haven't. Sacrificing your life for—"

"I'm not."

"Not what?"

"Sacrificing myself. I don't plan on dying."

After an uncomfortable space, she said, "I don't understand."

She was lying. If she was, at this point, pure computation, she could have run millions of simulations and assessed trillions of options before even asking me the question. She had to know there was only one way out.

Maybe she just wanted to hear me say it.

"I thought I would do what you did."

There was an even longer silence. I wondered how much an apotheosized person could actually feel. The silence suggested she was feeling something, but it might just be calculated to create an emotional effect in me.

"I'm not sure that's a good idea," she finally said.

"You did it."

"I did. But it's still…"

"I've decided."

"It doesn't solve the problem of Wil and Vie, Tab," objected Richelle. The abstract colors and shapes registering her voice were more subdued now. "Even if they could escape somewhere, there's nowhere for them to go."

"I thought about that too. I have a solution."

I explained to Richelle my idea. She objected at first, but after a few minutes she weakened. I'm not sure whether it was my reasoning or my stubbornness that finally convinced her, but in the end, she agreed to help. With *both* of my plans. So I was able to present the ideas to Wil and Vie with Richelle's endorsement.

That was three days ago. Now the first of the two plans was ready. But who should get naked first?

It was a tricky question. I'd put a lot of thought into it, but I still wasn't eager to actually bring it up.

"Vie, you almost ready?" I asked through the iris to her habitation cel.

"Yes."

"I'll check that Wil's ready." I headed down the habitation hall and turned left, down the hotplate hall and past the fun cels. Wil was in the medic cel getting his hair cut. I figured Wil would have to get naked first. It wasn't a politeness thing, though there was that too.

The medic iris opened and Wil stepped out. He was wearing a plain white robe and an anxious expression. His hair was shorter and spikier than ever.

"Your hair looks surprised," I said, hoping to ease the tension.

"This is not what I told it to do." He was clearly disappointed.

"It looks fine," I said.

He scoffed at my reassurance and pushed past me. I followed him past the fun cels, back into the habitation hall. I wanted to catch up to him before he got to Vie's cel to talk to him about getting naked, but as soon as we were around the corner we could see Vie coming out of her cel. She was wearing a yellow robe, tied close around her slim form. And she was bald.

"What did you do?" said Wil, hurrying forward.

Vie smiled shyly, then thrust her chin out. "You don't like it?"

"No, I just..." Wil didn't know what to say.

I did. She had never looked better.

"You look more like you than ever," I said. "Amazing. Beautiful."

She blushed, then looked at Wil and said, "Did you record that?"

"I just wasn't expecting it," he protested, blushing in turn.

"I felt like this was a new beginning, so I thought I'd...try something different."

Wil stared at her with undisguised admiration. After a long moment of awkwardness, she took his hand. "Here we go," she said.

"I guess so," he replied.

We crowded into an elevator bud and took it up to the hangar together. We didn't say anything during the short trip, nor did we say anything beyond what was necessary as we climbed into the jump ship and checked all the systems. Everything was in order.

We couldn't put it off any longer. I knew this was harder for them than me, so I opened the lid of the bern and turned to them. But Wil spoke before I had a chance to.

"I'll get in first." He undid his robe and let it fall. Just like that. Vie looked the other way while he stepped into the bern.

The viscous fluid rolled up around his legs. "I'd forgotten how it tingles," he said. He squatted and laid himself on his side. I moved to the head of the bern and held his mask ready. He glanced over at Vie, then back at me.

"Thanks," was all he said. He took the mask and fitted it over his face, lowered his head down into the fluid and rolled as close as he could to the far side, making room.

"He's set."

Vie stepped closer to me and glanced down into the bern. When she looked at me again her eyes were glistening.

"Tab, I..." She put her arms around me. I could feel her uneven breathing.

"I'll see you again," I said. "It'll be a while, but...I'll be in touch."

"I hope so."

"Count on it. I may even be waiting for you when you get there."

"I hope so," she said again, her voice breaking.

"And I'll work on Richelle to get the re-embodying research going."

I lowered my arms but Vie kept hers in place. Awkwardly, I hugged her again.

"Have we ever hugged before?" I asked.

Her laugh broke the tension. "Shut up," she said, and she stepped back.

I looked the other way as she took off her robe and stepped into the bern. After a moment she said, "I'm ready."

I fitted the mask onto her face and she lowered her head beneath the liquid, turning onto her side to fit beside Wil.

There was something innocent about the way they were laying there, spooned together. I thought I would feel embarrassed, but...it seemed natural.

I touched Wil's shoulder, gave him a squeeze in farewell. He raised a wet hand out of the solution and gave a thumbs up. I touched Vie's shoulder. She reached up and squeezed my hand with her own. When she lowered her hand again she slipped it between Wil's arm and his body, causing him to startle comically. When he realized what the sensation was, he grasped her hand and pulled it around, holding it to his chest. As he did so I could have sworn her fingernails glowed dimly.

"This is the story of a new beginning," I whispered.

And that was the last I saw of them. I lowered and locked the lid, flooded the bern chamber, then started the machine that would put them to sleep for years. It was strange to think my body would be gone in a matter of a week or so, while these bodies would be traveling past star systems for years to come. It would be a little more than three months to them, but it would be thirty-two years, to those of us in the standard frame. So, more than a decade after my body had turned to dust—had been ionized in the star after Thalinraya had taken its fiery plunge—these bodies would still be racing through space, Vie embracing Wil the entire time.

I closed the hatch, descended the stairs, and had the homestead roll the jump ship to the gravion pad. From the hangar's control I said a silent farewell. After checking all the systems and coordinates three times, I launched it.

Because of the FACE filaments, I couldn't use the orbital hooks, which meant this was an old school launch, with fire and boiling smoke and a roaring that nearly deafened me. But the altered jump ship worked perfectly, streaking up and away in a flawless arc. The ship shrank quickly, and the filaments parted for it, just as Richelle had said they would. Once the ship was through, the strands closed back together and all I could see was the flames of the engine behind the ship. Moments later even that had dwindled to the barest idea of flames. And then they were gone.

Had they needed to launch themselves they would have lost months of travel time, but because they were in suspension and already in bern, the ship was able to gain speed at a much greater rate. Not that it mattered. They had years of travel ahead of them. Not so many as they would have had if Telesis had been their destination, Dayr. Your planet, Panticaya, is much closer. But thirty-two years in transit is still a long time.

Please be good to them. They're the best people I've ever known.

CHAPTER 38

RICHELLE CONTACTED ME A FEW HOURS after Wil and Vie had left. She was sympathetic, but she also wanted me to get started with some augmentations I would need for my apotheosis. Simultaneous uploading of different functions is essential, and I didn't have enough outbound bandwidth yet. So I needed to get some quick surgeries. She set up an oscillating channel from the homestead to the third moon in order to oversee the process herself.

The next day the planet started coming apart.

The initial shocks rippled through the homestead. I was just waking up when I felt a judder followed by a rolling motion. The homestead informed me that an earthquake was under way, and I hurried to the Control cel. Visuals from the satellites showed volcanoes going off all over the eastern hemisphere. Two in the western hemisphere were spitting a little, but in the east it looked like Armageddon. In an hour the visual spectrum showed nothing but roiling ash clouds, but other spectra showed that fires had broken out in many places across the eastern side of the northern continent. The southern continent was aflame from end to end, except on its western coast where a tsunami had leveled forests and washed over hundreds of kilometers of deltas and bayous. And the earthquakes continued.

Richelle contacted me and let me know the dike in Thalinraya's core had been breached. Neither of us knew if it had been breached as planned or if this constituted something going wrong, but it didn't matter. The planet was unraveling; there was no going back now.

Most elements of FACE had anticipated more time before Thalinraya's core would be compromised. Now there was nothing they could do to stop the planet from being destroyed, which, Richelle informed me, also meant they had no interest in me or the homestead. There would be no more attacks. After everything that had happened, they were giving up. I was finally safe.

On a dying planet.

Richelle appeared on the main panel, standing on one of the spires at her estate on Histon. Earlier I had asked her not to render herself. If she was only computation at this point, I didn't want her to pretend she still had a body. It seemed like a lie somehow. She pointed out that her voice was only a rendering too, but that for psychological reasons I might want to allow her to have a visual rendering as well. She mentioned that even FACE used parallel communication channels.

I agreed to let her have her visual, though I found the spire scene a little contrived, especially because her rendering engines gave her new clothes every time they displayed her. I'd mentioned this to her, but she'd been unable to fix the glitch. Now she was in a flowy, patterned gown she never would have worn in life.

"What will FACE do now?" I asked. "Will they try to leave?"

"Oh Tab, you really don't understand the Computational Front, do you?"

"Don't I?"

"What would be the point of them leaving?" she asked.

"To save themselves," I replied.

"The things they build here, the machines they use—those are not them. They're physical extensions only."

"Like copies?"

"The concept of copying is not so straightforward as you suppose."

"Is there more than one copy of you?"

"Ah," she said, sounding pleased that I had thought to ask this. "No. Not quite. I have extensions in several systems, though time and space don't always allow me to know the status of those. I haven't copied myself, and once I did there wouldn't really be two of me anyway. They'd diverge quickly. In principle, yes, there's no reason a personality nexus couldn't duplicate. But what you call FACE has placed certain prohibitions in place, and most of us abide by those."

"This is all very strange."

"Once you've apotheosized you'll look back and think the same thing about how your life to this point has been. In many ways, shedding your body is the most freeing thing you can do."

"In many ways, but not all?"

"No. Not all. A body has certain sensibilities which aren't transferable."

"But it's worth it?"

"I made great improvements in the process before I did it myself, and we've made further advances since that time."

"But neither of us really had a choice."

"No."

I wondered what it would feel like. Would it be like death? I remembered back to when we arrived at Thalinraya. My mother's body under the sheet in her bern. If her religion was right, she'd undergone something like apotheosis. I hoped it was true.

"Tabit," said Richelle, cutting into my thoughts.

"Hmm? Sorry."

"There's something I need to tell you," she said. "I've sent a probe to search the far side of the moon here. The moon your father traveled to." Something inside me recoiled. I waited for her to continue. "There's a deep canyon on that side. I found his ship there. It had crashed. From what I could see, he would have died instantly."

I was filled with a sudden anger. None of this would have happened if he hadn't dragged us to this forsaken rock. "I don't care," I said.

"Don't care?" said Richelle. "I don't understand."

"We're only here because of him," I began. "My mother is dead because of him."

"Tabit, no. What are you saying?"

"We could have had a post on a populated planet, a Stage Five planet. That's what my mom wanted. But he had to do something with more sacrifice, something to get him closer to his God. So—"

"Stop," said Richelle, angry herself now. "You don't know what you're saying."

"I'm saying you were right not to trust him. He was a selfish, stupid—"

"Stop. Stop," said Richelle again. She pointed a finger at me. "Stop!"

I folded my arms and leaned back. "Are you going to defend him? You?"

"I'm going to tell you something you need to know." When she was sure I wasn't going to interrupt she continued. "You're wrong about your father."

"He switched them to Stage Four, that's why we're here," I said.

"I'm still speaking. Now, do you remember when you began coming to my estate?" I pursed my lips and waited for her to continue. "Do you know why you were allowed?"

"My *father* didn't want to let me come. Mom had to convince him."

"You couldn't be more wrong. Having you come to live at my estate was your father's idea."

"It was not!"

"It was."

"Why would he do that? He hated you!" It was a cruel thing to say, but it was true.

"He loved your mother," said Richelle. "They were on a fast course for their Stage Five certification, but...she wasn't strong. She needed to focus."

"What do you mean, 'She wasn't strong'?"

Richelle took a breath. "Your mother had an old-world disease called cancer. If you're not familiar with it, take a moment and access your onboards for uterine cancer."

I did. It was a horrific disease. There had been preventatives and cures for centuries, but they were technological solutions. A person had to be willing to use them.

What a fiasco.

"Because she was a Feremite, she wouldn't take in any bots or go to any surgeons," explained Richelle. "She agreed to a few modest, non-technological therapies, but she knew she had only a few years to live. Ten at most. It wasn't enough time to complete the training for Stage Five terraforming." Richelle let that sink in. "She and your father decided together to switch their course of study. Your mother wanted desperately to have a *useful* life. She was a Feremite. Helping to establish a whole new world—seeing it, breathing the air, helping to colonize it with His children—that was her dream. For the greater glory of the God that was killing her." Richelle couldn't keep the bitterness out of her voice. "Stage Four training is much simpler, so the course could be completed more quickly. It was their hope she could complete the training and get to a new world before the disease took her. Your father was disappointed, both because Stage Five is much more interesting work and because he knew the expense involved in switching courses. But he agreed to make the switch. For your mother."

The switch to Stage Four was for my *mother*? We were here for *her*?

If this was true, everything I'd thought I knew about my parents was wrong. Why hadn't they told me?

"Your father didn't like me," said Richelle, "but he agreed to let you come to my estate so your mother could try to fulfil her dream. It was a sacrifice. An act of love."

He'd been so cold and distant after my mother's death. But then he'd been...kind. In those days before he'd gone to the moon we had grown closer than we'd ever been. I'd seen sides of him I had never known existed—curiosity, playfulness, intelligence. Were those things finally surfacing because the pressure and pain had finally been lifted?

"Your father had many faults," said Richelle. "He was an arrogant, close-minded, religious bigot. But he wasn't selfish. He loved your mother. That's why he brought you all to Thalinraya. It was for her."

Over the next few days, FACE turned their attention to building ships to take away as much surface malibdi as they could. It wouldn't be much, but they could at least cut their losses.

It was during this time that I started putting all this down for you, Dayr. Richelle suggested you might want to know about Wil and Vie before they arrived. If you and your mother were going to harbor them, she reasoned, you were at least owed an explanation. They're not normal synths, after all.

So I sat down in a fun cel and started remembering as much as I could, from the time the first FACE ships came to ground. It's been my main occupation as Thalinraya has come apart.

Everything about Thalinraya has been changing—its center of mass, its magnetic fields, its orbit. Annoyingly, this meant the satellites needed constant adjustment, and apart from getting this to you, I spent most of my time doing that rather than helping Richelle make the arrangements necessary for my apotheosis. When it was ready, three days after Wil and

Vie had left, I went into the surgeries essentially blind, trusting that what Richelle had planned for me was going to be what I needed.

It proved to be worse than the hard-vac surgeries. It was quicker, but the pain was more intense. The fact there was nobody else there made it worse too. Richelle tried to comfort me, but her voice wasn't nearly as calming as the touch of Vie's fingertips on my temples.

When I thought of Vie, there was a deep ache. It felt like the sort of thing that would never go away. Maybe I had loved her after all.

I admitted as much when I was lying in the Medic cel recovering from the surgeries. Richelle was in a small panel next to my bed, trying to comfort me. I was in pain, unguarded and emotional, and I confided in Richelle, telling her about the feelings I had had for Vie. I told her how it was embarrassing, to have fallen in love with a synth.

"Tabit," she said, shocked by my feelings. "Loving Vie was probably the most human thing you ever did." It was such an odd thing to say. Vie hadn't even been human.

"What do you mean by that?" I asked.

"You opened yourself to Wil and Vie, remember? You wanted to feel for them, to undo your inoculations. And you did."

Undo inoculations? I had no idea what that meant. I did remember that when I'd first met Wil and Vie, my feelings for them had been confused. I'd talked about it with Richelle and she'd helped me. She'd...

"What was that pill you gave me?"

Richelle looked inward for a moment, then said, "That's a long story."

I looked around the Medic cel. "All I've got is time," I said.

Richelle smiled, then adjusted her posture before speaking. I wondered what algorithm was at work in this gesture. Was she feeling something during that space of time, or was the computer-that-was-her intending *me* to feel something?

"Synths were first invented to take over work done by robots," she explained. "This was back when market forces were still unregulated. Humans realized a lot of work could be mechanized, and they created robots to do most of it. But after time, companies found that humans preferred to have certain tasks done by other humans. Not because it was more efficient, but because it gave them a sense of superiority. Humans have an instinct toward domination; we like to have inferiors. So, the market responded. Corporations invented synthetics, and they quickly replaced robots in many areas.

"But humans have another instinct: empathy. Unfortunately, the first synths provoked this emotion in some humans. Most. It made it…not so pleasant to exercise power over them. This was a problem for the corporations. It was harder to sell products that caused unpleasant sensations in their customers. They needed a way to interrupt people's empathy so that they could sell more synths.

"This was at a time when human infants received inoculations immediately upon their birth. There were protections from various diseases, but there were also neural bots that scaffolded the growing brain so that later augments and enhancements would function properly. It was all relatively benign, but the corporations petitioned the Unicon to have more bots added to the inoculations. The new bots would block empathic channels toward synths so that people could enjoy using them without triggering any sense of…disgust or guilt or shame.

"The Unicon, of course, agreed. For hundreds of years now, humans have been inoculated against feeling any humanity toward synths. They can enjoy treating them as inferior without ever feeling the empathy that might get in the way of that…pleasing sensation of dominating another."

This was uglier than I'd ever imagined. People had been manipulated away from feeling anything for synths by corporations? The whole thing was driven by commerce?

"I reversed the inoculation in you, as you'll remember," she continued. It had been such a small pill. "That reverse engineering allowed you to experience empathy for them. Given who you and Vie are, it naturally led to affection."

"Because synths are so human-like," I finished.

Richelle laughed. "No, TabiTal. Because they *are* human. The Unicon can fool people into thinking they're not, but you and I know differently."

I lay there staring at the machinery on the ceiling of the medic cel, thinking how strange people were. In the days before technology, people had made slaves of one another. Now, after so much progress… Well, what progress?

"Synth genes are grown from specific human stem lines, right?" I asked.

"Yes. One of the amino acids was substituted by a synthetic replacement. It didn't really change anything, but it did allow business interests to say, 'These are no longer human.' "

"You don't think it makes a difference?"

"I think, as the first Bible says, 'A recipe for bread produces bread, whatever the color of the ink.' "

It was frustrating that the computational Richelle not only still talked in riddles, but the riddles were from the Feremite Bible.

"Let me ask you," she continued, "how 'natural' does a person have to be to be a person? You've got augments now. Your body is significantly different from the one you were born with. Are you still human?"

"Of course," I said.

"I agree. But you are far more changed from a 'natural' human now than either Wil or Vie. Any way you hope to calculate it—by genetic material, weight, mass, cognition—you're less human than they are.

"Soon you will leave your body behind. Will the Unicon be justified in hunting you down? They'll try. And they'll say they're justified because you're no longer 'human.' Should that be enough? In relinquishing your body, will you also relinquish your right to be free and alive?"

My brain hurt, whether from the augment surgery or from Richelle's philosophy, I couldn't tell.

"You know Wil's theory?" I said, hoping to deflect her to another topic. "He thought you'd brought Vie and him to your estate so I could have playmates."

She looked horrified. "He did not!"

"When he was little," I clarified. "Not later." Seeing her look I added, "They both loved you."

Richelle looked off to what would have been the Histon skyline if it had been real. "And I loved them," she said wistfully. "All of them."

I assumed she meant all the synths on her estate. I thought back on Wit and Ein and the others I had known. She had created a place where synths could be much more than they were elsewhere. Where they could be fully human.

"Do you know why they destroyed my estate?" she asked, not looking at me.

I sat up a little in the medic bed, sensing this was important to Richelle.

"No."

"Vie and Wil are not like other synths," she said.

"None of the synths on your estate were like other synths," I responded.

"No. But Vie and Wil were special. Synths are, by design and by law, sterile. Did you know? It's part of the augmentation they receive when they have their glasses ceremony. They're not born sterile, they're *made* sterile. By law."

But Richelle had taken Vie and Wil from their orphanates as children. They hadn't gone through the glasses ceremony.

"Vie and Wil were the first synths I managed to help avoid that fate. I wasn't sure whether it would work. As far as I knew, synths had never been allowed to mature naturally. But they both turned out normally. As their genes would have them.

"They were my proof of concept."

"What were you intending?" I was horrified at the thought, but I had to know. "Were you going to mate them?"

Richelle threw her head back and laughed. "Heavens no! No, no, no." She could barely contain herself. "No, I only wanted to know that it would work. That synthetic people could actually grow and mature normally. I needed one male and one female to be sure, but I never intended they should... No. The whole point was to make them free."

"So they could come here?"

"No, I never intended them to leave my estate. I would have preferred to keep them with me. But," she said, turning serious again, "one cannot open the cage and then demand the birds stay inside. They wanted to go with you. That was their choice, and they were free to make it.

"After they had gone, I had gathered enough information from working with them to implement my plan. I contacted the Unicon and convinced them to allow me to do research on prepubescent synths. I told the Unicon I had plans to improve certain mental and physical characteristics, but it required earlier intervention. I had credentials and clout, and they agreed to let me work with younger synths."

"You brought more child synths to your estate?" I asked.

"I did." She was having difficulty going on. I dreaded it, but I had to know.

"Were they like Vie and Wil?" I asked. "You didn't…they didn't have their glasses ceremonies?"

"Correct."

"How many?"

"Six hundred," she said, her voice breaking. "There were six classes of one hundred each, aged ten to fifteen."

Six hundred synth children! I didn't want to ask, but I had to. "And they were all killed?"

"All. Incinerated."

"Why?"

"Because synths are not humans," she said, finally looking at me again, "and they have no rights. But they're supposed to be sterile. So, because these beautiful children had not undergone their prescribed surgeries, they were butchered. Somehow they found out what I was doing on my estate, and they came and…"

I had seen hundreds of synths slaughtered outside the silo city. It was horrific. How much more horrific if they had all been children.

Wil had been enraged by the cold, calculated executions of FACE. He'd thought their methods were a result of their computational nature. But people, as it turned out, were just as capable of inhuman slaughter.

"Why," I asked carefully, "did you want all those synth children?"

Richelle's image was silently weeping now. She turned a tear-streaked face to me, but her voice was strong. "Can you not guess?"

"No."

"Have you heard of the synth revolts?" she asked.

"Yes." I said, remembering the revolts had happened nearly a thousand years earlier, but not much else. "I don't have anything onboard about them," I admitted.

"No, you wouldn't. Most of that information is classified. But did you know that they were successful?"

"I thought…they'd all been killed. No?"

"They all died, yes. But thousands of them were never killed," said Richelle with odd satisfaction. "No, the main group of them were never defeated. They fought bravely for two years. They won their freedom and three small worlds on which to live. And the three worlds they inhabited knew peace for seventy-two years. Seventy-two *free* years. Until they all died. Because, you see…they were sterile."

Richelle wrapped the wide sleeve of her blouse around her hand and wiped her cheeks. "People will continue to breed synths, sterilize them, and raise them as slaves until they are stopped. It doesn't matter that synths are as human as you or I. More human than most people who pride themselves on being so." She let the sleeve fall, sat a little taller, and looked a challenge at me. "Do you understand now?" she said. Her jaw was set. "For a revolution to really take hold, you need more than one generation of revolutionaries."

The following day, as I was recovering from my surgeries, there were constant earthquakes, each more intense than the last. A great chasm had opened on the southern coast of the northern continent, connecting an unnamed inland sea to the ocean. The entire sea had drained 60 percent in a matter of hours, and the release of the weight had caused the continent to bulge alarmingly. The rest of the sea was draining more slowly, but the homestead predicted a super eruption there in twenty six hours.

When I took an elevator bud to the entry and looked out, I found the devastation almost unbearable. Intellectually, I knew this was one world of many millions in our galaxy, and I hadn't even been here that long. Still, seeing it become a wasteland like this was difficult. I imagined the forests I'd seen, all now either on fire or under water. The flocks of flying lizards we'd flown over when Wil drove the opilion off the continental shelf would be dead now. Everywhere animals were dying or hiding from the ash, the water, the magma, the fire. Vie's beloved tortoises, too slow to get away. And even the ones who weren't dead yet, the ones who held out the hope they could save themselves or their babies, wait it out, figure out a way to stay warm, find something to eat, a place where they could breathe. They were all doomed.

What might this world have become?

Yesterday, I remembered there were still synth capsules on the southern continent and one on an outlying island that hadn't yet been awakened. Thousands of people still in suspension, not knowing they would never wake up. The thought of them sent me to the Control cel, where I hailed Richelle. I told her I wanted to wake the remaining workforce synths.

"Why?" she asked.

"Because they're going to die in their sleep otherwise."

She waited for me to continue. When she realized this was my full argument, she said, "And?"

"Well…they deserve to wake up." How could she not see this?

"Wouldn't it be more kind to let them die in their sleep?"

"No!" The thought was appalling. "They deserve to know what's happening to them."

"How will that benefit them?"

"It…people should know…what's happening. Have a chance to say goodbye to one another. It's their right! We can't just let them die."

"Tab, you can wake the remaining capsules, but you should think it through first."

"Think what through? A person has a right to know how their life is ending."

"Some people who live in great physical or emotional pain choose to end that pain by giving themselves enhancements until they die," she said with annoying calm. "Toward the end, they sometimes imagine they are someone else or in some other condition or place. In a case like that, should we remove their enhancements to remind them they are dying and in great pain? Is that our responsibility? Our right?"

"That's not what's happening here."

"No. Here the situation is more clear-cut. These synthetics will be waking to a world they have every expectation will be a veritable Eden—a bright new world filled with beauty and purposeful work. Instead, they will be waking to a world that is descending into chaos, and getting worse. They will be frustrated because they will not be able to fulfill the functions for which they were designed. In their few waking hours they will witness the destruction of the environment, the despair and deaths of their friends, and then they will themselves die, most likely in great pain."

I opened my mouth to reply, but nothing came.

In the end I decided not to wake them. The carnage we had seen above the settlement entrance swayed me. I knew they were unlikely to suffer any direct violence like that, but burning or drowning or choking on ash—were these any better?

I still don't know if it was the right decision.

Things have gotten worse. The super-volcano went off and the ash is raining constantly. I can see steaming geysers and spouts of flames down in Glassfall Canyon. The smoke isn't as heavy as it has been, but the thumpers are all gone, burned or suffocated in their burrows. Mostly I stay in the homestead now and breathe the filtered air.

The earthquakes have gotten worse. Some of the longer waves seem to hit the homestead in a way that makes the plasma want to liquify. Not good.

The moons are swinging in their orbits, which has sent Thalinraya's tides into chaos. Richelle says it's a positive feedback loop that'll get worse and worse until it tears the mantle apart.

A few minutes ago she appeared on the panel in my habitation cel.

"It's time," she said.

I knew she was right.

I'm heading down to the Medic cel now.

It's been a comfort writing this to you, Dayr. It's given me a sense of purpose these last days. I hope it'll help you understand Wil and Vie. And if I am able to get in touch with you, I hope it'll help you understand my situation too.

I'm in the Medic cel now. Richelle is watching from her wall panel, standing on the pretend spire at her pretend estate on Histon.

"It feels real, Tab. You'll see."

I guess I will.

I'm hooked up to the equipment, which is shunted along the hotplate directly into the FaRcom, which has been redirected to the third moon installation. I'll be off Thalinraya faster than if I were in a ship.

My heart is hammering like mad in my chest. Maybe it knows I'm about to betray it.

"I've opened the com links, the shunts are open and functioning. You're ready."

I don't feel ready, Dayr. But I probably never will.

"You're ready. Press the button."

Richelle's getting kind of pushy.

Another quake is rocking the homestead. If a quake hits while this is happening, could it...mess it up?

"It will only take about fourteen seconds."

Fourteen seconds. Enough to upload my entire personality. All the memories of everything I've ever done, every place I've ever been, every person I've ever known. All their details. The way my mother comforted me when boys at school had been mean. Vie's jawline. The sound of the crystals falling in Glassfall Canyon. The rainbows in the jets of spray from the atmospheric scrubbers.

Fourteen seconds for all of it.

"The processing afterward will take about three minutes, if it makes you feel better. Really Tab, you're ready. Press the button."

Richelle set it up so that when I press the button it'll send this transmission to you too, Dayr. She thought it would be comforting if I could talk to you right up to the end.

"Is it comforting?"

I can't tell. I'm afraid.

"It'll be over in a moment. Tab, you're ready. Press the button."

Suddenly I want to say goodbye to something. Homestead?

"I'm here."

I want to thank you for everything.

"Your gratitude is acknowledged."

I'm talking to a computation engine. Ugh.

I'm about to kill myself and I feel embarrassed. That makes no sense.

I wish Thius was here to say goodbye to. It would be sad to leave him, but...

"Your cortical mapping is working perfectly. Everything is ready. Relax."

What will it feel like?

"Like waking from a dream."

I find that hard to believe. But I don't need to believe, I only need to do it.

Dayr, please take care of Vie and...

I said that.

I wish I could be sure I'd told you everything. It's all mixed up all of a sudden.

"That's normal. You're under tremendous stress. It will be over when you press the button."

Why did my father go to the third moon?

"You need to calm down, Tab. Press the button."

Why did my mother die? Why did Telesis push all those liars at us?

The trip to Auger Station was amazing. Vie was so beautiful. The wind came in the opilion's irises and whipped all around. And then that pack of snakes...

I can still feel the damp mist behind the underground waterfall.

Falling down the rope in the silo city.

Hig's booming laugh.

"You're starting to hallucinate. Press the button, Tab."

Growing up, my life was so much plainer than other kids' lives. They had augments, did immersions all the time.

I've made up for my dull childhood now. I've crammed events for a whole life into the few weeks here.

I didn't want to come here at all. If these last weeks have been my life's one adventure...I didn't choose any of it.

I'm choosing this next adventure, I guess.

It's time to leave. The planet. The life. Everything.

"It's going to be okay, Tab. All you have to do is press the button."

You say it's like sleep. Mom used to tell me to think of something good just before sleep.

Hmm.

We're rocketing off the continental cleft and Wil has grown wings for the opilion. My stomach is fluttering as the opilion's fall turns into a glide. Ha! Vie's terrified scream turns to delight. Wil's laughter is open and free and joyous.

We're friends and we're together, thrilling to a new experience.

If I can only take one thing, that's what I'm taking.

Here goes.

TERMINAL DISPATCH

AFTER ABOUT THIRTY SECONDS I OPENED my eyes. There had been a buzzing and a warmth, but something must have gone wrong. I checked the equipment.

"Richelle, something's not working," I said.

The homestead's flat voice responded: "The communication channel to the station on the third moon is no longer operational."

"We lost communication?" I asked.

"The connection was terminated."

"Can you get it back?"

"Likely."

"Do it."

While waiting, I tilted the head gear to one side and checked the equipment. It looked okay. What could have gone wrong?

"The connection to the third moon is open," the homestead said, indifferently.

"Richelle?"

"Affirmative." It wasn't her normal greeting, but it was her voice.

"Something went wrong."

"No. Everything worked perfectly." She wasn't displaying her image.

"Well…obviously it didn't."

"Why do you say that?"

"I'm talking to you. I'm still right here!"

"Yes."

"So…it obviously didn't work."

"It worked flawlessly. Your cortical mapping is being compressed and your social, emotional, behavioral, and other algorithms are being processed and balanced. It will take several minutes." Her voice had a clinical quality, like that of the homestead.

"But why am I still here?"

"Where did you expect to be?"

"I thought I would apotheosize."

"You did."

A terrible realization shot through me.

"That doesn't…that doesn't kill you?" I asked.

"Why should it?"

"So I'm here, but I'm…I'm there too?"

"In a sense. We refer to what you call 'you' as your offal."

"Awful?"

"Offal. Discard. When you engaged in the process, you agreed to make your computational nexus your primary locus. I can't contact you right now because you're still being processed."

How could I have failed to consider this? It made perfect sense, but I'd never thought about it. I'd been in a hurry to get the augments, then, when I was recovering, the whole planet was blowing up and I…just never looked into it.

I had made a computational *copy* of me. Well…but that was the *primary* me now. There was still this meat me, but this was just…offal.

"Who do you consider you are talking to now?" I asked.

"Your primary personality is computational. A useful metaphor for your physical body might be the shed skin of a snake after the snake has moved on."

"That…doesn't do it for me." There was silence. "Richelle?"

"I have other things to attend to," she said.

She was being colder toward me than she ever had.

"Wait, you don't even…you don't think I'm me?"

"You do not have 'me' status, no. You were a substrate for the personality construct that was TabiTal Yrl, but now you are merely residue."

I didn't know what to say to that. It was too much to take in. My other me would probably be able to process this in a nanosecond, but it was taking meat me more time.

"You're telling me the copy we made…that's *me* now? I'm not me anymore?"

"Consider: whatever discomfort you feel—pain or confusion or doubt—will dissolve in a matter of hours or days, when Thalinraya comes apart. The original you that apotheosized will persist much longer. Which would you have me attend to?"

I didn't have an answer to that either. It was true—the meat me was more ephemeral than the digital me at this point.

"We are as clouds that veil the midnight moon..."

It wasn't comforting.

I sensed Richelle was about to terminate the connect, and I didn't want her to.

"What...what am I supposed to do now?"

"Whatever you like. Thalinraya is terminal; nothing you do there will matter. The time left to you is entirely your own."

I could hear the com link disconnect.

"Homestead? Is the connect to the third moon terminated?"

"Affirmative," said the homestead.

I took off the equipment and returned to my habitation cel.

That was a few minutes ago. Now I'm sitting here recording this word squirt of these unexpected last minutes. The account of my very short life as nobody.

I honestly don't even know what to do. I guess I'm just...waiting for the end.

What do you do when you're alone at the end of the world? When nothing you do will ever mean anything to anyone else?

I sent you my word squirt a half-hour ago now, Dayr. Hopefully you'll get this and open it as well.

Not that it matters. I've done what I intended to do, and I don't really have an identity any more. I don't have anything to say to you even, except just...that life is stranger than you expect.

I wonder how the computational me would think of this me. "Oh, I got a message from that body that used to be me? How cute."

If you talk to the computational me, tell me I said hello. Oh—and can you tell me to work on planning ahead a little more. I don't know if my computational self will have the same failings I have as a live person, but I really could have done better with the planning.

The homestead's parabolic antenna is acting weird. After I'm done here, I'll climb up there to check that it's working enough to send this. Then I'll...I don't know. Take a walk. Probably down to Glassfall Canyon. There was a wind that cleared the ash from the air for a while. Hopefully I'll be able to see what's going on down there. Before it's all gone.

Dayr, you're going to meet Wil and Vie. I'm jealous. You'll like them, I'm sure. When you meet them, please tell them I loved them. I don't know if my computational self will say things like that, but they should know.

ABOUT THE AUTHOR

Author photo by Hannah Nichols

DAWSON NICHOLS works at the Institute for Learning and Brain Sciences at the University of Washington, but he lives in creative writing. His stage works, such as *Virtual Solitaire* and *Escher's Hands*, have won awards at dozens of international theatre festivals. His podcast, *The Fourth Ambit*, is available on most platforms.